Luminarium

ALSO BY ALEX SHAKAR

The Savage Girl
City in Love (stories)

luminarium

· A NOVEL ·

ALEX SHAKAR

SOHO

Chapter icons by Ivonne Karamoy.

All rights reserved.
Published in the United States by
Soho Press, Inc.
853 Broadway
New York, NY 10003

Library of Congress Cataloging-in-Publication Data

Shakar, Alex, 1968–
Luminarium / Alex Shakar.
p. cm.
ISBN 978-1-56947-975-9
eISBN 978-1-56947-976-6
1. Twin brothers—Fiction. 2. Virtual reality—Fiction. 3.
Coma—Patients—Fiction. 4. New York (N.Y.)—Fiction. I. Title.
PS3619.H35L86 2011
813'.6—dc22
2011013331

Printed in the United States of America

10 9 8 7 6 5 4 3 2 1

For Olivia, the Shakars,
and all my other guiding lights.

Lead me from the unreal to the real.

—Bṛhadāraṇyaka Upanishad

luminarium

1.

august 2006

S	M	T	W	T	F	S
30	31	1	2	3	4	5
6	7	8	9	10	11	12
13						

Picture yourself stepping into a small, cuboid room. In the center squats an old recliner, upholstered in black vinyl. To the chair's back is affixed a jointed metal arm, possibly on loan from a desk lamp. At the end of the arm, where the bulb and shade would have gone, hangs instead a sparkly gold motorcycle helmet, a vintage, visorless number with a chin strap.

"It's safer than it looks," the woman standing beside you says, with an edge of humor. Her eyes and hair verge on black, her skin on white. Her voice has a hoarseness you might associate with loud bars and lack of sleep, but other things about her—from her black skirt and blouse to her low, neatly fastened ponytail—suggest alarm clocks and early-morning jogs. Her name is Mira, short on the *i*. Mira Egghart.

Safe isn't the first word that comes to mind. A dozen or so symmetrical holes have been bored into the helmet's shell, and from each of these holes protrudes a small metal cylinder, and from the top of each cylinder sprouts blue and red wires, forming a kind of venous net over the hemisphere. That first word might be *demented*. Or *menacing*. The thing has the look of some backroom torture apparatus, slapped together from junk on hand with the aid of a covert operative's field manual.

"Have a seat," says Mira Egghart.

Maybe you're thinking better of it. This could be your last opportunity to blurt apologies and flee. But just suppose that things haven't been going well for you lately. Assume, for the sake of argument, that in fact things have been going very, very badly. I hesitate to say how badly. Let's say you founded a company that has more or less been stolen from you, and now you're just about broke. Broke and alone. Having split with your fiancé months before. And that these circumstances barely even register because someone very close to you has been losing a battle with cancer. Or has slipped into a coma. Perhaps this person is your business partner. Your best friend. Your brother. Your identical twin. Let's go for broke and say all of it, all the above, and that the thought of being back out on the busy midday sidewalk—among all those people with places to go and lives to lead—is enough to make you want to sit for a spell. Allow for the possibility, too, that—God help you—you're already a little bit into this Mira Egghart.

Presto. You're Fred Brounian.

Or who he was then.

Fred Brounian sank lower in the chair than he'd anticipated. The springs were worn. A tear in the vinyl ran along the inner wall of one of the arms, bleeding yellow foam. He was facing the door, and next to it, a rectangular window set into the wall, which he only then noticed. Behind the glass lay another room, smaller still than this one, just deep enough to fit two office chairs at what must have been a shallow, shelf-like desk supporting the two flatscreen monitors whose backs he could see. As he watched, a tall, thin, sixtyish man with a gray Roman haircut floated into view, like a walleye in an aquarium. The man eyed Fred impassively over the straight edges of a pair of half-frame reading glasses slightly wider than his head. Then the man, too, lowered himself into a chair, sinking behind the monitor and out of view.

"We'll be watching over you the whole time," Mira Egghart explained. She crossed to the other side of the recliner, taking a plastic jar from a steel serving trolley. "I'm going to stick some electrodes to you. They're just to record brain waves and vitals. I'll have to apply a little gel for conductivity."

She confronted him with a glistening dollop on her fingertip, and proceeded to rub cool spots of the stuff onto his temples and the center of his forehead. Silvery rings adorned at least three of her fingers, moving too fast and close for him to get a good look. After gelling each point, she reached down to the table for a poker-chip-sized white pad and stuck it on. Her eyes avoided his as she worked, darting instead around the various features of his cranium.

"Undo the top two buttons of your shirt, please."

She counted down the ribs from his clavicle with a sticky fingertip, dabbed more gel, and painted a tiny, wet spiral over his heart. Her hair smelled like freshly opened apples and something ineffable—*dry ice*, he thought—one of those dizzying alchemies of hair product research. From the degree to which she was leaning over him (he counseled himself not to look down her blouse), and the slight squint in her eyes, he thought she must be nearsighted. The wrinkles at the corners suggested she was around his age, mid-thirties. Her nose, though not indelicate, had a slight finlike curve to it, which taken in combination with those dark, peering eyes, gave her the slightly comical look of an inquisitive bird. He wondered how many condemned men, as they were being strapped into electric chairs, had spent their last moments checking out the ladies seated among the witnesses.

She reached up and pressed the helmet onto his head.

"The session will last twenty minutes. All you have to do is sit back and relax. Let's get you reclined. The lever's on the right."

He did as told, window swinging away, ceiling swinging into view. Directly above, in the firmament of perforated tiles, a poster of a spiral galaxy had been taped. Mira Egghart's upside-down head, like a wayward planetoid, floated into view.

"You probably won't want to, but if you feel you need to stop, just say the word—the helmet has a mic attached. Or if you can't speak, just wave. Please don't handle the helmet yourself."

If I can't speak . . .

She left the room, switching off the light. The instant she did so the air grew swampy and his skin prickled. These days, Fred didn't like the dark, nor any hint of confinement. He could turn his head only slightly in the helmet, but by keeping his eyes trained down his face, he was able to see Mira now standing in the control room. She leaned forward over the desk, reaching up toward the top of the window, her blouse taut against her breasts and lifting to reveal a glittering stud in her navel as her fingers clasped the pull of a black shade. She brought it down in one quick motion, after which, just above the window, a dim red bulb went on.

As best he could with his head immobilized, Fred looked around the room:

Steel trolley.
Jar of gel.
Red bulb.
Blacked-out window.
Galaxy wheeling above.

Subject: Help, Avatara
From: George Brounian

He was at his usual booth in the cafeteria of the old Tisch Hospital building, worlds away from the NYU Medical Center's ultramodern lobby and newer additions. It was lunchtime, the stink of gravy unwholesome in these antiseptic conditions. If the place were really working the way it should, he always thought, those microbial mashed-potato mounds, along with everyone scooping them into their mouths, would have been sprayed with disinfectant and swept down some chute with a biohazard sign on the door.

As talismans against being thus expunged, the doctors and nurses had their lab coats and scrubs and ID badges. Long-term visitors had to improvise their defenses. At the table to his left, the woman with eyes permanently blasted from crying had her stainless-steel knitting needles and chain-link fences of pink and fuchsia yarn. The old guy in the three-piece suit (the same one every day, with what looked like a chocolate pudding stain on the vest) had his table-wide gauntlet of stock listings (in search of the magic buy or sell that would pay his wife's hospital bills, Fred imagined). Fred himself, whenever he claimed a booth down here, would swing open the barricades of his briefcase lid and laptop screen with the authoritative air of a doctor sweeping the curtains around a sigmoidoscopy patient. He, too, had his daily examinations to perform—his tentative probes up the asshole of the cosmos, trying to figure out what this unrelenting shitstorm showered down on him and his fellow hapless sentients was all about, and whether there might be any effective way to treat it.

On the day in question, six months to the day since George had been wheeled through the ER doors, and three months, more or less, since a team of IT workers had mercifully stuck a wireless router to the cafeteria wall (visitors couldn't websurf up in the wards), Fred had been reading an online article by an MIT professor who claimed that the universe was a giant quantum-mechanical computer, computing every possible occurrence in parallel, spawning exponentially expanding infinitudes of alternate realities at every moment—this particular reality being only one decoherent history in this unfathomably vast multiverse of the possible. He'd managed to find the hypothesis somewhat consoling, as it seemed to imply that he had other twin brothers out there, an infinite number of George Brounians, a portion of whom, by sheer statistical necessity, wouldn't be at this moment lying wrapped in tubes and wires like some fly bound in spider silk, waiting to be eaten. He'd been half entertaining the idea of leaning over to impart this happy news to the knitting woman, when it struck him that there would also be an infinite number of people whose parallel lives were more or less the same, and an identical number whose lives were somehow worse. Picture an infinite number of Fred Brounians, sitting in an infinite number of hospital cafeterias, pawing an infinite number of five-day beards, contemplating an infinite number of Fred Brounians, when in comes an email from their comatose twin.

The body of the message was blank. The subject heading meant little to him. Avatars—computer ones—were a regular part of their business. There was also a mystical connotation, he was pretty sure, some kind of god or apparition or something. Some of the less socially equipped programmers in the office had been following an animated series called "Avatar" on Nickelodeon. No other references immediately came to mind. As for that final *a*, Fred didn't know what it signified, though it rounded out the word rather nicely. As for his brother's name in the sender heading, it might not have fazed him—after all, the message must have been a server glitch, or a bit of viral marketing malware—were it not for the word "help." There were all too many reasons George could need help at any given moment. One poorly propped pillow and his air passage could be cut off. A little vomit or even postnasal drip could asphyxiate him or slide down and infect his already damaged lungs. Dozens of things needed to be done for him every day, and any lapse of attention could result in his death. Not that Fred believed there could be any connection between this email and a medical emergency. But there he was, dazedly heading for the elevators.

He found George much the way he'd left him an hour ago, lips in that leftward droop, head tilted to the same side.

He touched George's shoulder. Spread open one of his eyes. Which tracked nothing.

"Dude. You've got something to say to me, say it to my face. Hey."

He tickled him. He knew the spot, of course, side of the ribs, a little to the front. The slightest of flinches. Not even.

"Something happened?" asked a nurse, poised for a miracle.

He told her George had sent him an email. She thought this was funny.

He stayed with his brother for a while, doing the usual, massaging George's hands and feet to aid blood flow, smoothing the sheets to prevent wrinkles from chafing his skin and giving him lesions, holding up one end of a one-ended conversation, asking him what the deal was, joking that next time he should have the courtesy to write more than a subject line. Fred tried to keep it light around George, when he could. He wanted the world to seem like a place his brother might care to revisit.

He was helping the nurse logroll George into a sling scale for the daily weight check, when, with a jolt, he realized he'd left his laptop downstairs. If it was gone, there'd be no affording another. He darted into the hall, slalomed around gurneys, jumped down flights of stairs, reaching the cafeteria just in time to see someone making off with it, with his whole briefcase—a woman in a dark blouse and slacks and pulled-back hair, heading for the exit. He was charging at her, about to call out, when he got a line of sight on his table, and saw his own briefcase and laptop just as he'd left them.

The woman, meanwhile, set down that other briefcase on a booth wall, popped open its gold clasps, and extracted, with silver-ringed fingers, a sheet of sky-blue paper and a roll of tape. He wondered—briefly, nonsensically, he was tired—if the briefcase might be George's, if the woman might know him. Women never carried these big, boxy kinds, and George, too, owned one of them; George had bought Fred and himself a matching pair, their monogrammed initials the only difference, ten years ago, when they'd started their company. The style had been outdated even then, but that was the point—George had hoped the old-school captain-of-industry look would help them feel more

CEOish. Returning to his table, Fred continued watching the woman. She approached the bulletin board slowly, yet once there, attacked with swift rips and fingerstrokes of the tape, then stepped back to regard her handiwork, a little wide-eyed—proud, if still overwhelmed by the enormity of what she'd done. Then she blinked, and spun, one hand shutting the briefcase, the other pulling it after her out the door.

The old man licked his finger, and, with such slowness as might stop time itself, turned a page of newsprint.

The knitting needles click-click-clicked.

After staring at the mysterious email a while, peering into the empty pane where the message should have been, Fred looked up *avatara* on a couple of reference sites. A Sanskrit word, literally meaning "descent," referring to incarnations of Hindu gods. Or, more generally, the descent of the divine into the form of an individual. The avataras were innumerable, legend went. Whenever there was imbalance, injustice, or discord, they would appear to set things right.

The coincidence of the email's arrival on this half-year anniversary made him wonder if it was a prank of some kind. Probably not. Who could have been ghoulish enough to send it? Whoever it was might have known George, though. *Avatara* was the kind of word he would have loved using, though Fred had never heard him use this one specifically. George had been into such stuff—mudras and bandhas, siddhis and miracles, an inner world he could care about, Fred imagined, precisely because it was in no way existent, in no way subject to any law or whim other than George's own. Not that George ever found any answers that really worked for him, or did so for long. Perhaps because his twin tended toward idealism, Fred had become more specialized in doubt. It didn't exactly translate into practicality as often as he would have liked; yet until recently, he'd prided himself on not being the type to sit around thinking about God's great plan for him, or even to sit around researching the possibility that the universe was a giant quantum-mechanical computer. Or to nearly tackle some woman for carrying George's briefcase (still calling it that—*George's briefcase*—in his mind). Or to daydream about avataras—*what would they look like?*—descending to hospital cafeterias from the pure blue sky.

He'd been gazing off at that square of blue paper for several minutes. At last he walked to the bulletin board. His first reaction was to laugh, silently. Not so much a laugh as an imagined laugh. His own, or George's. They had the same laugh, and these days, even in the simulations in his head, it wasn't always easy to tell them apart. Sometimes the solution was for the laugh to replicate and divide, so that it was both of them, virtual George and virtual Fred, sharing a laugh at this so-called study.

Do you feel . . .

Your life is without purpose?

Your days are without meaning?

There's something about existence you're *just not getting?*

Are you . . .

Agnostic??

Scientific study

George's laugh was delighted at what seemed to be a developing theme of the day. Fred's own was just grimly amused. The word *agnostic* made him suspicious. Some kind of Scientology pitch, probably. *But no,* his Inner George was saying, *look at that.*

The smaller print at the bottom: *Department of Neural Science, New York University.* Followed by a Web address. The pedigree made Fred curious. He returned to his laptop and typed in the URL. A page appeared, dense with text:

Among the healthful psychological qualities associated with individuals who describe themselves as having experienced a "spiritual awakening" are:

- A sense of well-being and connectedness in the world.
- A sense of "being in the moment."
- A sense of union with a "higher" force.
- A sense of calm detachment from everyday difficulties.
- A decrease in negative emotions such as anger and fear.
- An increase in positive emotions such as compassion and love.

By reproducing the "peak" experiences commonly associated with spiritual awakening, this study hopes to help participants change their long-term cognitive patterns, leading to enhanced self-efficacy and quality of life. It should be stressed that these sessions will not involve religious indoctrination of any kind.

The treatment, the site went on to state, involved visualization exercises as well as subjecting the brain to mild but complex electromagnetic impulses, the effects of which were not thought to be harmful or permanent. Possible short-term side effects included nausea, dizziness, and disorientation. No known long-term side effects, but as with any new area of research, risks could not be ruled out. Those selected would be paid fifty dollars for each of four weekly hour-long appointments, and some follow-up interviews over the ensuing months. At the bottom of the page were links to articles about other studies: one finding that church attendees had stronger immune systems, while those without a spiritual practice suffered the stress equivalent of forty years of smoking; another concluding that people of faith exercised more.

I'm not really thinking about this, am I?

I believe you are, Freddo.

He closed the browser window, determined not to be. But staring into the blue light of his screen, he began reconstructing the woman's face. And that doppelganger briefcase sailing out of the room. *Fifty bucks for an hour's work,* he thought. He was here at the hospital all the time anyway. *If the study were here, too . . .*

Even with these reflections, he'd never have returned to that website were it not for those other reasons, harder to explain, even to himself: Because if George were the one sitting here, he—George—would have done it in a heartbeat. And because a sizeable part of Fred wished it *were* George here instead of him, felt it should have been. And because, clicking on the link and filling out the questionnaire, Fred was able to feel what George would have felt—a peculiar, tense electricity in his chest and limbs, as though the study's purported electromagnetic signals were already coursing up through the keyboard. Like the onset of panic but without the nausea. Like the opening hole of despair but more like hunger. A sensation so long unfelt he couldn't straightaway place it as hope.

Ten minutes had passed, and if there was one thing Fred was now sure of, it was that this fright wig of a helmet didn't do a damned thing. It felt just like any other helmet—padded, close, and hot. He couldn't feel anything resembling a current, couldn't hear anything but, possibly, the slightest hum, coming from somewhere behind the chair. From beyond the room came other faint noises: footfall on the floor above; a distant siren's wail, trailing off so gradually it seemed never to fully end. The shade was still down, the observation window black. What was the use of having an observation window, if all they did was drop a shade over it when the experiment began?

The *experiment*.

That word had never been used, of course. "Study" had so much more reassuring a resonance, to the studied and studiers alike. But what was it they were really studying here? The whole deal must be a sham of some kind, he decided, one of those power-of-suggestion-type experiments, an elaborate sugar pill administered to see whether the patient might be suggestible enough to effect his own spiritual transformation. He berated himself for not trusting his instincts and bolting the moment he'd seen the suite's tiny reception area, little more than a widened hallway beyond a door off the elevator bank, into which a coat rack and a couple of classroom chairs and a metal desk had been crammed. The desk had nothing on it—not even a phone—and no one had been sitting behind it. But he hadn't been able to face the obvious. Sure. The quirkily hot science nerd chick with the vaguely erotic gel rubdown, the bespectacled wizard in the control room, the seven-page questionnaire and three-page liability waiver—all verisimilitude enhancers, avenues of suggestion-delivery. This gaudy piece of junk on his head—nothing but a stage prop. Fifteen minutes now, it must be, and nothing. Who knew, maybe they didn't even expect him to imagine any experience here; maybe they were testing something else altogether, like how long a person might submit to sitting here like some mental defective in a Burger King crown, waiting for his divine purpose to be revealed.

How dare they.

How dare they take advantage of desperate, unhappy people like this. He was a second away from ripping the piece of crap off his head, leaping out the chair.

Then what?

How about picking up the trolley and driving it through the goddamned window?

Then what?

Where to then? The coma ward? The office of his ex-company? His parents' apartment?

The lava cooled in the pit of his chest. Expanding his lungs around that congealed lump seemed more effort than it was worth. What was the point? So sad it was funny, even, imagining he could shuffle in here slope-shouldered, head under a cloud, and stride back out transfigured, head poking above said cloud, bathed in epiphany. Funny/sad/maddening. The combination was exhausting, and before he knew it he was drowsy, drifting off, half in pain, half in pleasure, to a sound in the room he hadn't noticed before: a faint and, now that he was attuned to it, almost painfully high-pitched tone. Sometimes, lying in bed late at night, he'd hear small, insistent noises like this burrowing into his ear. This tone, though, wasn't a single note but an interval, possibly a major seventh. There was a smell in the air, too, like wet earth and ozone, and the sound was broadening and flattening out, sounding first like applause. Then like escaping steam.

Then like a shearing of machine parts—a hot little saw burning from the front to the back of his skull.

And here he goes, seeping out into the room.

No difference between his sweating palms and the sweating vinyl of the chair. Between the compacted springs within the chair and the tensing and relaxing of his muscles.

The helmet pulsating within him like a second scalp. The charge of its net of wires his own hair tousling in a breeze. The chair beneath him an internal pressure, the frame and stuffing the weight of his own bones and innards. Air and time alike circulating within him. The high electric whine: within him. Like a voice. Like a pulse. Like a single, continuous thought, a focused point of attention expanding, carrying him outward in all directions. The galaxy approaching, as if he might contain it all, every last thing everywhere, but for the fear, rising up like an arm to pull him back.

Maybe he moans, or maybe it's the electric sound, sliding down again to a low hum and ratcheting like the sealing of a vault, as, with a nauseating snap, the world presses in:

Hot vinyl crawling beneath his palms.

Helmet crimping his skull.

Reddened galaxy glaring down at him—blindly—like the muscled socket of an eye.

"So," Mira said. "How did it feel in there?"

She sat nearby in an office chair, a notebook computer balanced on her stockinged knees. Fred was noticing, in the light from the standing lamp beside him, the faint outlines of contact lenses in those dark eyes of hers.

She was examining him as well.

"Fred?"

"Yes. It felt . . ." He laughed. He shook his head.

"Why did you just laugh?"

"It's just hard to find the words. I'm feeling a little . . ."

"Disoriented?"

"Spacey, yeah."

"That will go away soon."

He felt along his collarbones, the walls of his chest. "It felt like a jailbreak."

"Oh? How so?"

As he attempted to describe the sensations he'd felt—the expansion, the freedom, the envelopment of the chair and the air around him—she began to type without breaking eye contact. Her typing was beyond fast, more words, he was pretty sure, than he was managing to speak. She seemed at once excited and intent on hiding her excitement behind a veneer of objective inscrutability. It was hard to stay focused on what he was saying. The soft clatter of keys made him hyperaware of being a test subject. Yet, too, in a tactile kind of way, there was something delightful about the sound. He could almost feel the little concave buttons springing beneath his own fingertips, the electrical impulses zapping through the circuitboard and the nerves of her arms.

Almost, but not quite. Not like he might have been able to under the helmet. To the contrary, there was a subtle pressure he was now sensing, exerted by all that wasn't him—Mira, the keytaps, the four walls of her tiny office, the second recliner of the day she'd sat him down in (older-looking than the last, though in better repair), a cloth-covered artifact from about the same era as that gold helmet, its course fabric woven from several shades of unnatural blue.

She kept typing after he'd finished. Adding her own commentary, maybe. As she did so, she bridged the awkward silence with a drawn-out nod. There was a hardness to the set of her features he hadn't noticed in the low light of the helmet room.

"So if it was like a jailbreak," she said when the typing stopped, "what would you say was the jail?"

There wasn't a simple answer to this. The bars had been neither within nor without. He hadn't even known they'd been there until they were down. He felt a need, a cell-deep hunger, to try the session again, see if he could go farther, contain the whole room, contain other people completely. What would that feel like? How much could he hold? How big could he get?

"What happened to me in there, anyway?" His question tumbled out with a sudden force, almost accusing.

"What do you feel happened to you?"

"But what *really* happened to me?" To the extent he'd been able to imagine what would happen here at all, he'd anticipated some kind of drugged-out, blissful high. What he'd just experienced seemed of another order.

"You'd like to know the technical aspects of the process?"

"Right," he said. "Yes."

She looked pleased, like he'd just bested a maze and won a piece of cheese.

"That's good. Because I intend to explain it to you. It's very important, for our purposes here, that you understand it. But let's talk about what brought you here first. Is that all right?"

She didn't wait for an answer, just started clicking around on her computer, calling up the relevant data. Now that his disorientation was on the wane, he was starting to decide that, actually, he didn't much like this woman, didn't much care for her condescension, her impeccable posture, the overall feeling she gave him that he was sitting slouched in a petri dish, looking up through a tube of microscope lenses into her giant, peeled eye. A few minutes ago, when he'd grabbed her forearm to steady himself upon getting up from the helmet chair, her eyes had popped like his hand was electrified, like he was some experimental slime monster that had breached the containment barriers. Or maybe his grip had just been too strong. As they ticked across what he assumed was his file on her screen, he noticed her contact lenses again. And still that squint. He contemplated telling her she needed a new prescription. It wasn't a particularly confidence-instilling detail.

"From the application it sounds like it's a pretty hard time for you right now." She nodded again, giving him permission to be having a pretty hard time right now. "Can you tell me a little more about George? Is he still in a coma?"

"As of this morning," he said, steeling himself.

"You wrote that he had lymphoma, and then lapsed into the coma. So the one caused the other?"

In the gunmetal bookcase on the wall opposite him, at the corner of a shelf with some stereo equipment and a stack of recordable CDs, a snow globe caught his eye, one of the few decorations in the room, a New York skyline of maybe twenty years ago submerged in brackish water.

"They said the cancer cells probably produced a hormone that caused his sodium levels to drop too low. Apparently it's not uncommon. The coma resulted from that."

"Are they still trying to treat the cancer?"

The room closed around him like a fist.

"They can't. Or won't, so long as he doesn't wake up. He went through chemo and radiation when he was first diagnosed. Then it spread to his lungs. Then they told him he only had two or three months to live and he gave up treatment. That was seven months ago. The last six of which, he's been in the coma."

He knew what was coming next. He was resenting her before she even asked.

"Was there ever a discussion about just"—her voice was quieter now—"stopping treatment?"

"Early on, they didn't want to put him on life support. My parents probably would have caved. But I insisted. After a couple weeks, he didn't need the life support anymore. He's been on his own power ever since."

He said it like a boast, like he felt no guilt whatsoever about what he'd committed to putting everyone, including George, through. On Fred's first and last visit to a therapist a couple months back, when he'd made the mistake of relating these details in a less self-assured manner, the woman had assumed he was remorseful about his decision, and proceeded to offer her cloying reassurances that it was a mistake any loving relative could make. Mira's reaction was in its own way worse: a look of sympathy stopping just short of approval. Before she could say anything, he went on:

"The doctors don't know why he hasn't died. They see no point in doing more tests, but the cancer must be in remission, seeing as he's still . . . around."

She closed her eyes, opened them. "Don't take this the wrong way, Fred, I'm merely asking. This isn't *quite* my area of expertise." The way she deployed that *quite* emphasized that in fact it was, broadly speaking, within her expertise. "But six months is a long time to be in a coma. Are there any signs of brain activity?"

"Some. Especially in the brain stem. People have come back from that. Not often, I know. But it's happened."

He couldn't blame her, this time, for busying herself with half a minute's typing. He looked around the little office some more. His guess was she hadn't been here long. A few large textbooks—neuroethology, neurotheology (he wondered briefly if one of these was a typo, and if so, which), neuropsychology—on the bookshelf. Van Gogh's starry night above her bulky metal desk.

"Does George have a wife, children?" she asked, before looking up.

"No children. He got divorced two years ago."

"Before the lymphoma was diagnosed?"

Fred nodded.

"And you?" Mira checked her screen. "You broke off a wedding engagement recently?"

The same terrain, along just about the same route, had been traversed with the therapist. Was Mira Egghart a therapist? Or was she simply here to observe?

"We split up a few months ago."

With the therapist, he'd gone on to describe breaking up with his fiancé as the second biggest mistake of his life. He didn't bother elaborating this time. Mira was giving him another of her discerning looks, or maybe he was just imagining it. The parallel between George's love life and his own was a sore spot.

"After George got sick?"

"Yes. That probably played a part."

"Are you seeing anyone now?"

He entertained the idea of turning her question into a joke, or a proposition, but then—imagining her hearing the same jokes from every bestubbled emotional charity case from every hospital cafeteria across the city—thought better of it. He shook his head.

"I suppose you don't have much energy for dating at this point," she said.

He gave her points for the wry tone, the warmth in her eyes.

"Being broke and living with my parents doesn't help much either," he said.

Looking down at her typing fingers, she almost smiled, with him or at him, he couldn't say.

"So let's talk about your parents for a second. Are they religious?"

"My mother's started doing Reiki. It's a . . . Japanese . . . energy . . . healing kind of thing."

"Yes, I've heard of it. Have you ever tried doing it?"

"No. Not for her lack of offering."

"So why haven't you?"

"I don't know if I should be encouraging her."

Mira didn't betray a judgment, about his mother or about him. "Did you grow up with any religious training or spiritual practices?"

"None."

"Any kind of transformative life experiences you'd classify as spiritual?"

"You mean like visions?"

"Like anything."

"I've never seen the Virgin in my cornflakes, if that's what you're asking."

The answer seemed to satisfy her. "Last subject, occupation. You wrote that you and George started a company together. Some kind of computer company, was it?"

"Software design and consulting."

"And you wrote that you lost it? I'm afraid I know even less about business than I do about computers. How does one lose a company?"

The biggest mistake. He grinned miserably, glanced at the ceiling.

Go ahead. Inner George. *I didn't patent it.*

"It's like losing a sock," Fred said. "Only more lawyers are involved."

She didn't smile, not even out of politeness. Instead, to his surprise, her face went sad.

"George's joke?" she asked.

Stunned, he blinked. "How'd you know?"

"I'm psychic."

They stared at each other.

Finally, she smiled.

"That was a joke, too, Fred."

And then it was happening again—the expansion—happening right here: he and Mira afloat in the same balloon, one organism with two bodies, two goofy grins. Merging with a La-Z-Boy had not come close to preparing him for this. It was like he'd known her forever, or twice that long. Like everything he'd ever felt a lack of was here, right in front of him.

Yet almost before he'd realized it was happening, it was gone, gone so fast he might have concluded it had never happened at all, but for the confusion and the longing in its wake. The atmospheric pressure in the room had suddenly doubled, and gravity had done the same, pressing him into the chair. He wanted to tell her about the experience. He wanted it back. It seemed impossible to him that she hadn't felt it too. But she was already closing her laptop, moving on.

"Thank you for being so patient, Fred. Now that you've answered my questions, I'll try to answer yours."

She turned her head to one side, and pointed at the upper back portion of her skull. Her eyeball swiveled to the corner to regard him as she spoke.

"The parietal lobes are located about here in the brain. Their main job is to orient you in space. In order to do this, they've got to know where you end and everything else begins." She faced him again. "It may sound like an easy job, but it's not. To do it, the lobes require a constant supply of impulses from the senses. What monks can sometimes do through meditation, and what we've done here through the application of electromagnetic signals, is to block that stream of sense data from entering the region. The lobes continue looking for the self-boundaries, but with no information coming in, they can't find them. And so you perceive a porous, expanded, possibly even a limitless sense of self."

She watched him, gauging his reaction.

"Does that answer your question?"

Was there mockery in the words? He couldn't quite tell. There was a flatness to her tone. But her look was dead serious.

He smirked, the way he couldn't help doing when he was embarrassed. He felt like a child. He wanted to throw a tantrum. An absurd reaction, he knew. He'd walked into a laboratory and had his head stuck in a helmet full of solenoids. What kind of explanation had he been expecting?

Maybe just not so precise an explanation. Maybe he'd been expecting her to say that they didn't know how it worked, just that it did. Thus leaving at least a shred of the mystery in place.

"So what's the point of giving me this experience at all? What could it possibly mean to me, now that you've explained that it's a trick?"

Jerked around as he felt, he was even now trying to will back that illusory connection with her.

"We're not out to trick you, Fred," she said softly. "Quite the opposite. We need you to know how everything works here."

"And why is that?"

She sat forward an inch.

"Because we believe that the emotional power of the experiences and their rational explanations will counterbalance each other. And that over time, you'll learn to weave both into a larger tapestry."

With his fingertips, he explored the bunched threads of the chair arm, searching for an opening, a way to envelop them. Her tapestry image was beguiling—clearly, she'd prepared it in advance. Turning it over in his mind, though, he found the flip side not so picturesque.

"So you're saying that I'll end up tricking myself? And you're so confident I'll weave myself this rosy fantasy tapestry that you don't even mind telling me in advance?"

Her voice rose, if slightly, for the first time in the interview, and there was a new fierceness in her look. "It's not fantasy we're hoping you'll find. Not at all. It's a more informed kind of faith." He got the feeling she almost thought better of it, but then, with a breathy self-defiance, she added, "I think of it as a faith without ignorance."

For a while, neither of them spoke. He looked off, toward the bookshelf, into that miniature kitschy skyline, pickled in its brine.

"Would you like to continue, Fred?" she asked, her tone even again.

His eyes wandered to the black briefcase on her desk. His own was in the hall closet. She hadn't so much as glanced at it while showing him where he should stow his things upon arriving for his sessions.

What say you, George?

No answer. Inner George was as torn as he was.

Lest his voice crack, he didn't speak, simply nodded, at which point Mira Egghart got up, placed her computer next to the briefcase, and came over and switched off the lamp. A moment later, she appeared crouched at his feet, having just plugged a nightlight in the shape of a fat little star into the wall.

"Before you leave," she said, the little star setting her knees and face aglow, "I'm going to give you a visualization exercise, a little story with some images. Just lean back in the chair, make yourself comfortable, and close your eyes."

"Is this hypnosis?" He'd let the woman magnetize his brain with barely a second thought, yet this new prospect made him unaccountably wary.

"There's a lot of stigma attached to that word." She stood, the light now playing on the nylon gloss of her legs. "How deeply you allow yourself to be affected by the story is entirely up to you. I'm going to record the visualization on a CD as I tell it to you now, and I'd like you to play it for yourself every night this week before you go to sleep. In a week, at your next appointment, I'll make you another."

She picked up a knitted blanket from the end table, and after he leaned back, she floated it over him.

"Are you comfortable?" she asked.

In the dim light, her pale complexion glowed eerily, her eyes stared dark and fathomless.

"What if I fall asleep?" he asked, with an anxious tremor.

"Worse fates have been endured," she replied.

Fred stepped out of the Psychology and Neural Science Building onto Washington Place, in the city of New York, on a mid-August Monday in the year of 2006, to the sight of a cloud on a digital taxi ad and a plume of exhaust as it pulled from the curb. The oneness was gone, but that phrase of Mira's—"a faith without ignorance"—remained lodged like a splinter in his brain. His first thought was that it was simply a contradiction in terms, like a night without darkness, a sky without air. But wasn't a foothold of reason in that sheer cliff of faith precisely what he himself had been trying to obtain through all his recent readings in science? Just last night, for example, beneath the thirty-year-old, faded glow-in-the-dark star stickers of his childhood bedroom, fleeing his nightmares via his laptop screen, through a chain of hyperlinks to the outer reaches of cyberspace, he'd been reading about the anthropic cosmological principle, how the universe was so finely tuned for life as to arouse suspicion: how, if there had been four extended dimensions instead of three, planets would have flown right into their suns; how, if the cosmic expansion rate were one part in a million billion less, the universe would have remained a sweltering 3,000° Celsius and collapsed back in on itself billions of years ago; how the chance of such cosmological constants having emerged at random was something on the order of every member of his high school class winning the lottery and getting struck by lightning in alphabetical order. If some greater force and purpose were at work in all this, he wondered, then why all the subterfuge? Why all the arbitrariness of quantum fluctuation and genetic mutation? Why the absurdity of brains that could simulate some sense of that greater life only when they misfired? What good was a truth that could be perceived only through delusion? How would one ever really know what the truth was, in such a system? How would one ever know from one moment to the next the right thing to do, the right way to go?

Which way? He stopped at the corner of Broadway, a woozy enervation setting in.

It had rained earlier, ozone mixing with exhaust and perfume and the smell of baking garbage, and a vengeful sun was now reclaiming the terrain, as were the pedestrians, veering around him with high-end shopping bags and candy-colored cell phones. The study, as it had turned out, was on the main NYU campus, twenty-seven blocks south and four avenues east of the Medical Center, but by the time he'd found this out, he was already sold on the idea of enrolling. He'd told himself that the study's proximity to his Tribeca office would rob him of excuses and force him to start putting in more appearances. The terms of the sale of the company to Armation had guaranteed him a salary as an independent contractor for six months. These six months were almost up, and as he hadn't been occupying his seat there much during this period (or for the six months preceding), he wasn't as certain that his contract would be extended as he would have liked. If the axe did fall, George's skinflint health plan having been drained and abandoned long ago, Fred might have nothing to pay the next hospital bill with but the fifty bucks a week from the helmet study; that and a similarly double-digit payout working the occasional birthday party magic show, which their father, through various displays of frailty and unspoken need, had dragooned Fred into. Fred's parents didn't know how dire the straits were—he'd been keeping this from them, their own retirement savings being modest at best—and he wasn't about to ask their younger brother Sam to kick in, as Sam had been against George's life support early on (cold-bloodedly, Fred had decided) and totally uninvolved in his care ever since.

He should go south, to the office. There was a teleconference with the Orlando team. He'd missed the last one. It hadn't looked good.

Though it wasn't for another three hours. He could drop in on George, just for a while.

Standing here all day's always an option, Inner George chided, mirthful and bright.

He headed north, up Broadway, a well-trod route between the office and hospital, as he had more time these days than money for train fare. Eyeing his frayed, fuzzy, checkered shoes (George's, actually—a joke purchase his brother had made in the Czech Republic on a meandering post-divorce vision quest), Fred began to feel the summer air gusting around the loose threads, to feel the dry heat of the sidewalk as if he were barefoot. Then he felt, it seemed, what the sidewalk felt, the pressure of soles, the tectonic thrum of a passing bus.

It lasted a second or two, after which he couldn't make it happen it again, not with the sidewalk, anyway; yet walking by Grace Church on the corner of 10th and glancing as he often did at the ornate wooden doors, for an instant he thought he was experiencing their weary bulk, their frozen bodybuilder strain, their indifference to the streets around them careening through time. Hard to tell. That timeless pull may just have been the usual flexion of memory. Back to 1988, a night in his and George's last month of high school when they'd wound up here after wandering all over town.

George had gotten into Caltech that day with a scholarship offer. Fred's own future was less certain. While George had excelled in school, Fred's accomplishments were mostly in the park outside the school: he could play a mean game of Hacky Sack, an even meaner game of hearts, and any number of variations on the 1-4-5 chord progression. It had always been something of a mystery to Fred how all those differences between the two of them had sprouted from the common root. They'd started out the same, identical bodies, identical brains. As infants, they sucked each other's thumbs. As pubescents, fantasizing about an older girl they liked, they masturbated each other's newfound erections. They completed each other's sentences, had a trick where if they happened to say the same thing at the same moment, they'd stop, grin, then continue their thoughts, saying the exact same thing again, and again, and again. They could go on for minutes on end like this. They'd follow each other into convenience stores, the second one coming in a minute behind, making all the same moves, picking up the same items, putting them back, striking the same pose for the security monitor, buying the same kind of chocolate bar, just to rattle the guy behind the counter.

Their divergence seemed to begin from nothing, or almost nothing. Fred had gotten a little scar on his chin from falling in the tub, and George would point at it and call him a mutated scarhead. George had chipped a front tooth, and Fred would tell him it made him look like the village idiot. When they were really angry at each other, they'd punish each other by putting themselves in danger—Fred sitting with his feet dangling over the edge of the roof, relishing George's anguish; George stealing away from home, Fred back in their bedroom sobbing so uncontrollably he hyperventilated and blacked out. Afterward, they'd compare notes, hungry for each other's experiences—George creeping to the roof edge while Fred held him for safety.

Their experimentations with difference continued in the virtual realities of the day, specializing in different Dungeons & Dragons characters, different videogames—George's mage to Fred's fighter, George's Centipede to Fred's Missile Command. The research inched forward with the accumulation of more or less arbitrary identifiers—the colors of their sneakers, lists of favorite baseball players. At some point, a threshold they weren't fully aware of crossing, they stopped having to make the differences up. They acquired their own friends, and girlfriends. George's crowd was more studious; Fred's more streetwise. They picked up their own musical tastes and political views (generally speaking, Fred had the former, George the latter, but they argued about them nevertheless). And now, nearing graduation, here they were, with their very own separate futures about to sweep them three thousand miles apart. They found themselves a little stricken at the prospect, a little amazed they'd let the experiment get so far out of hand.

They hadn't planned on staying out all night. They'd only wanted some pizza. But George wanted to go to the Original Ray's, because why bother with any place but the very source, and Fred kept lobbying for the Famous Ray's, because they must have been the famous one for a reason, so they ended up just wandering around with empty stomachs, their conversation moving from their possible pizzas to their possible futures, and how those futures might again one day converge. Perhaps because it was an interest they'd shared longer than most, they got to talking about the computer games they'd programmed on a series of rudimentary home systems, ones that came in kits and had to be soldered together, ones with tape decks as storage media and barely enough memory to make a starfield, much less fill it with blocky, antennae-scissoring aliens. They talked about the growing sophistication of personal computers, and of computer games, and how these things had been growing up right alongside them.

"It would be great to make serious games," George said, just before dawn. They were lying on the church steps, staring up into the pointy stone arch of the entrance.

The term "serious games," now used to denote games with real-world applications, didn't exist at the time. It sounded like just one more of George's late-night impossible yearnings.

"What's that supposed to mean?" Fred asked, though instantly he was pretty sure he knew exactly what George meant by it, could already hear in his mind's ear the ad-libbed soliloquy he was sure was on its way. Games that would change perceptions, soften hearts, expand minds. Escapist fantasies that would somehow also feed and clothe the multitudes. Fred was already plotting out the argument they'd have. For a while now, much the way Fred's far more adjusted fellow park-loiterers were experimenting with increasingly hard drugs, Fred was journeying ever more deeply into the gray-clothed, asymmetrical-haircutted, tattered-Camus-paperback-toting realms of angst. He distrusted games and seriousness in just about equal measure. He waited for George to define his fanciful term aloud so he, Fred, could set about picking it to pieces.

But after some silent thought, George's reply was as serene as Fred's had been cross.

"I don't know yet."

He'd stopped there, in front of the church, trying to will the oneness, but the city was the city and he was him, which might have gone on depressing him if it weren't for the small old woman who passed by, her hair a silver thicket of bobby-pinned whorls, pulling him in like a riptide.

He trailed her. He could barely help it. With each hobbled step she took, her brittle skeleton reverberated in the roots of his teeth. Heedless youth tripped past her in both directions, looking everywhere but ahead of them through their giant, insectile sunglasses. That pin-curled head would turn to track them, and no sooner had Fred glimpsed a hint of her blue eyeshadow than he felt his own head turning as well, to see what she saw, *how* she saw—the bared and tattooed skin, the flesh-tunnel earrings, the omnipresent earbuds and dangling wires—the alienness of it all, flashing around them like some scrambled dream.

They went a block, and another. He felt the drag and clomp of her big, beige trenchcoat and shapeless white sneakers. His own shoulder sank under the strap of her no-frills canvas bag, the kind given out by magazines and book-of-the-month clubs. It was like shadowing his own old age, but it wasn't frightening, was actually a comfort, having those perfect, packed pin curls clearing his path. They were like a shared secret, a secret weapon, a hive of wormholes that could suck in the universe, chew through time and all its indignities. The two of them against the world, he thought, as they crossed 13th, closing in on Union Square, the two of them against the pylons and the scaffolding and the phoneless phone booths and the fourteen-theater multiplex and the Virgin Megastore and the dozen or so kids—bubble-lipped, stiff-haired, lavishly bepimpled—loitering outside it, a couple of them smoking, a couple others snapping gum. The kids' eyes settled first on Pincurls, then on the strange man taking mincing steps five feet behind her. He didn't care, pretended not to notice them, pretended, as he sensed she was doing, that they weren't even here, that the Virgin Megastore had never been dreamt of, much less built. The two of them against it all, he thought, as she turned right on 14th, to reveal, to his sudden horror, that she was beyond heavily made up. A razor slash of dark lipstick. A spatulate cheekbone caked with rouge. Bright blue mascara around a wide, shocked, and wrathful eye.

She looked like a deranged clown-whore. What was more, the connection was gone. It must have been the shock.

He kept following her, feeling rudderless. He tried to merge with other people, more attractive people, to no avail. Meanwhile, Pincurls turned north at Fourth Avenue, to stare—or glare, it seemed to him—with those boiled and refrozen eyes of hers at the red-bricked, pyramid-topped Zeckendorf Towers complex.

The place was his lost Eden. It boasted a swimming pool, a gymnasium, a video library, yoga classes, roof decks, and also (at least as he remembered it in the last and, to his mind, greatest years of the second millennium) happened to be crammed with fashion models—in short, it was either revolting or deeply alluring, depending on the state of one's finances, physique, and possibly, to a lesser extent, political convictions.

In the late '90s, by no means rich but for the first time in his life possessed of any money to speak of, he'd discovered himself allured. This was after George had returned from Silicon Valley, flush with connections, a meeting with angel investors all lined up; practically all George and Sam and he had needed to do was print up business cards, and the three of them were slipping into the tech boom dream. Fred rented two apartments consecutively at the Zeckendorf—the first alone, the second and larger one with Melanie, his girlfriend at the time and soon-to-be fiancé. To this day, she was living large there, riding the new boom now, the war boom, with her cable news job. The building was along his usual office-to-hospital route, but even when it was out of his way, he sometimes walked by. His chances of spotting Mel coming in or out were next to none—she'd be at work, surely. The last time she'd agreed to see him for coffee, she'd held his hand and told him they needed to get on with their lives, and it would be better for both of them if they didn't have contact. Then he'd walked her to her door. Then he'd asked to come in, and she'd said no. Then they'd had sex in a stairwell. Then she'd told him not to call her again. He hadn't. But he couldn't stop orbiting the place.

Back at sidewalk level, he spotted Pincurls sliding through the automatic doors of the supermarket on the ground floor of the complex. *No way*, he thought. No way he'd follow her. He'd wasted enough time already. He needed to get to the hospital, or to forget about the hospital, go straight to the office, prepare for that teleconference—it would help his cause to impress them all today. But watching that haircloud float off beyond the glass doors, he couldn't let it go.

She was headed for the pharmacy aisle. The hope that he'd run into Mel / the fear that she'd be with the new boyfriend he'd heard about—both intensified. Passing the frozen foods aisle, with a gut-lifting inevitability he turned to look, and there she was, frozen with shock at the sight of him.

"Fred?" she said, after a year or so.

It took him a bewildering amount of time to process the fact that it wasn't Mel at all. It was Jill, George's ex. Both had wavy blond hair, but the resemblance ended there. Jill was taller and slimmer; even her face was taller and slimmer—her cheekbones higher, her nose thinly fluted. The two looked nothing alike, actually. Maybe he'd been too busy noticing other things: The diamond sparkling from the second to last of those fingers curled, at the level of her loins, around the handle of the red shopping basket. Her rounded belly bulging the ribbed cotton fabric of a shirt dotted with little printed butterflies.

He nodded, witnessed her involuntary little frown. He was Fred, not George. She'd known it, but knowing didn't stop the wanting. Even Fred had this reaction sometimes, looking in the mirror. They braced themselves for a conversation.

"Do you still live around here?" she asked.

"No. Do you live around here now?" he asked.

"No. Lamaze class." A weak smile. "Just picking up a snack before hopping on the train."

They stared mutely at the contents of her basket: A pint of ice cream. A jar of salsa. Fred's stomach gaped despite him—lunch wasn't in his current budget; anyhow, since his brother's diagnosis, he'd been living in terror of chemical additives, which put most of the foods he liked off limits.

"I don't mix them together . . . yet," she said. "I do eat the salsa straight out of the jar."

"Right. Congratulations, on the . . ." He pointed in the general direction of her belly.

"Thanks."

He'd known about that. And her engagement. Knowing it hadn't prepared him for the proof.

"Boy or girl?"

"Boy."

"Ah. My condolences, then."

Inner George fed him the line. He was all too aware of an ingratiating impulse to reenact George for her.

"Yes," she said, relaxing a little into a broad theatricality of her own. "Another man in the world. What can you do?"

"Well, there are always operations for that kind of thing."

Her smile decayed.

"I meant—I meant a sex change," he said, but the joke had already gone sour, and even the emendation sounded bad. There was an edge in his voice he couldn't quite control.

"Oh. Of course," she said, on guard.

They stood there. He reminded himself that George had barely allowed her to see him after the diagnosis, that they'd already been divorced by then. That it wasn't necessarily unreasonable of her to think she was allowed to stand here with a diamond and a fetus and a basket of snacks.

"So how is he?" she asked.

"He's . . . no changes recently."

She was saying that Fred's mother was keeping her posted by email. She was apologizing for not visiting George, saying she worried what the shock would do, trailing off, that diamond-ringed hand resting on her belly. He was staring at it, her belly, feeling he was afloat, curled up snug inside it. It was happening again. He yanked his gaze to the floor.

"Better get going," he heard himself say. He didn't mean *she'd* better get going. But he himself didn't move.

"I'm sorry, Fred. I didn't mean—"

"No. I know." He smiled. He was leagues beneath her, standing at the bottom of an ocean, rocks in his pockets, air all but gone. "Jill."

"Yes?"

"Do you remember George ever using the word 'avatara'?"

"Avatara?"

He nodded.

"You mean those . . . computer thingies?"

"Never mind. Stupid, just a . . . . Bye."

He approximated a cheery wave and was in motion again, in his confusion still taking those tiny old-lady steps off toward the pharmacy aisle. Reaching it, he ducked in, and there was the old lady herself, that glistening hair puff bobbing like a buoy on a sunlit surface, that canvas bag of hers swinging into view as she turned toward the shelves:

MODERN BRIDE

Absurdly, he sensed a kind of mockery in the words. He was still staring at the bag when she slipped an item inside—an eyelash curler, he was pretty sure, sealed in paperboard and plastic. All at once, her face transformed, those horror-show eyes closing up from the bottoms into serene half-moons, that lipstick curving into an absent, kindly smile. She looked like she'd just shot up. Like she herself had just taken a spin in Mira Egghart's chair. She'd expanded, absorbed those curlers—one less alienated thing in the world. She glanced his way and he pretended to peruse the toothbrushes. Without haste, she turned back the way she was going.

He followed, mimicking her motions, ambling and scanning, until he reached the personal grooming items, a mandala of files and clippers, brushes and barrettes. The eyelash curlers rocked on their metal rod. Just to the right of them, a column of tweezers rocked ever so slightly, too. For a moment he stood there, hypnotized by the frontmost blister pack, the tweezers like a silver wishbone rocking and glinting in the light.

He grabbed it and stuffed it in the pocket of his jeans.

At first he thought maybe Pincurls had spotted him, but he couldn't catch her eyes, and her expression seemed unchanged, still willfully carefree, as she made her way—a little more fluidly than he'd seen her move before—down another aisle and back toward the entrance. He followed, and, glancing up into a convex mirror near the ceiling, to his surprise and amusement, found his own expression now much the same as hers: the same faraway smile and crescent eyes. And more, he was expanding, billowing like a sail. The two of them were one again, two views of the same sun-dappled, arcadian vista. As one, gliding past Jill in a checkout line, the sight of her as painless as if he were on novocaine. As one, slipping through the automatic door to greet the city heat and light and bustle, all those people with places to go and things to do and good for them, more power to them. As one, having their arms clasped by a hefty, sweating, yet somehow balletically graceful man in a blue security jacket—at which point Pincurls looked at Fred, her expression having transformed once more, lipstick hooked like a scythe.

The birthday party was in Upper Montclair, New Jersey, at a big, white colonial-style house with a circular driveway. Muggy enough outside to stagger the gnats, so Fred and his father were performing in the recreation room, an expansive sunken area with glass doors leading to the patio, a large backyard, and some woods beyond. Five- and six-year-olds, about twenty of them, sat on the carpet, their faces bugged with wonder, suspense, even fear, as Vartan, eyes ablaze, pretended to dump one trick pitcher of water after the next into the giant cone of newspaper Fred held as though with increasing distress at the burden's steadily growing weight. Vartan paused after each pitcher, watching to see if Fred would collapse under the strain, while, on his knees, bent backward under the supposed weight, Fred groped behind his back, trying to reach his magic wand on the carpet. He motioned with his eyes back and forth between the wand and the birthday girl, who sat in a pink dress and plastic-gemmed tiara in the front row. The act was mostly in dumbshow, to the tune of deranged slide whistles, which at this point—the cassette tape long since baked by its eighties boombox—sounded closer to whalesong.

With the helpful urging of her mother, Fred finally made the girl understand that she should go pick up the wand. She approached tentatively, eyes like marbles, cheeks pulling a smile from the grip of her infolded lips. When she had it in hand, he whispered in her ear to wave it. Probably taking her cue from some videogame or other, she zestfully knocked his top hat off with it instead, then bonked him on the head with its heavy wooden star-tip. Thus renewing the ache that had begun yesterday, when the cop, busy signaling to his partner to go gently with the old lady, had let Fred's head bang against the doorframe while shoving him into the back of the squad car.

Close enough. Fred snapped open the newspaper, now magically emptied, and stood with the birthday girl to take a triumphant bow, while Vartan seethed convincingly, stamping around, then picking up a cone of his own, only to have it burst and spill water down the front of his tux.

Their act was all about filial conflict. The characters they played, father and son magicians, started out in a state of magnanimous cooperation, but soon became embroiled in an all-out war of one-upmanship. The tricks were all more or less standard variety, only progressively bigger. From the ever larger cones of newspaper, they proceeded to bigger and bigger interlocking metal rings; then to a series of increasingly capacious top-hats they popped open from collapsed discs, pulling out ever larger white-tuxedoed and top-hatted stuffed animals. Long ago, this top-hat number had built up to Vartan's production of a large stuffed panda, and then to Fred's whisking out a carbon copy of himself—white tuxedo and all. The moment never failed to stun—they'd always kept George well hidden until then. He and George had never switched off. They'd always done it this way, George popping out, Fred the one to pull him. George had loved being the magic itself; Fred had loved being the power that made it happen.

The best thing about that moment for them, better than the kids' delirious shouting, better even than the parents' astonishment, was their own dad's reaction: Vartan had never failed to look dumbstruck by the sight of them. He'd never done it quite the same way, either: one day he'd step up and prod and pinch them, frisking for the illusion; another, he'd stand there, his eyes unseeing, like he was going to faint. His gestures had never been broad or overblown, and though he'd often achieved a comic effect, he'd never struggled to get there. Vartan was a professional actor—at that time, a struggling one, the magic shows a fallback as paying parts had become scarce. Young as they'd been, Fred and George had been fully cognizant of the fact that what was for them an opportunity to shine was for their father a goading reminder of his failure to shine any brighter; but in that moment when Vartan reacted however he did, they felt themselves and the laughing children to be audience enough for him, as good as any Broadway house.

Today's substitute sequence—in which Fred conjured the panda, and Vartan found nothing to retaliate with but an espresso-sized top hat containing a white-tuxed gummy bear—evoked a different feeling. Vartan stared at that bit of clotted jelly in his fingers as if the last dregs of enchantment had been drained from the world.

For their grand finale, Fred and his father made the birthday girl disappear. After Fred made Vartan's wallet vanish and Vartan did likewise to Fred's shoes, Fred pulled the cloth off the table they'd been using, revealing it to be a giant box with a door in the side. He guided the excited princess inside, knelt, and slipped her a stuffed toucan he'd pulled from a hat a while back. She didn't look afraid—in fact, her little face shone with so much unadulterated glee he wanted to crawl into the box and vanish along with her. But just in case, he whispered that the toucan's name was Maurice, that he was a magician in training, and that he sometimes got scared of the dark. Fred then gave her a little flashlight to turn on in case Maurice got scared.

The girl clutched the bird, the flashlight, her eyes gemmy and hopeful, and suddenly, for the first time since yesterday, it was happening again. Fred was her. His mind bright and empty as a rising bubble in the sunlight. The world itself one big ball of magic. Everything good in it his.

He shut the door, feeling like he was locking up his own beating heart, and rose unsteadily to his feet. He was in no way a little birthday girl, he admonished himself. No, he was a hulking manchild in a white tuxedo, hewing the air with a spray-painted stick. As if this made the slightest bit more sense.

The box was mounted on ball bearings, and he began to spin it, running around it as he did, remembering what it was that had so saddened him as a thirteen-year-old that he'd felt he couldn't go on doing these shows: a sudden conviction, inarticulable at the time, that childhood—even in its best, most lucky and ideal form—was a merciless hoax, endlessly renewed, adults fattening up children's unsustainably giant egos so that later in life they could all suffer together, having those bloated bags repeatedly punctured and drained by one another and themselves. It was a view he pretty much held to this day, that this little birthday girl in the box and all her little friends would go on believing they were all princesses and Jedi Knights until their early to mid-thirties. At which point, out of a mixture of self-loathing, misplaced obligation, and poorly understood vicarious yearnings, they in turn would find themselves renewing the cycle, ballooning the selfhoods of the young. As he was doing now.

He stopped and opened the door, gazing, along with the children in the audience, at the empty false compartment. The little girl was gone, the oneness vanished with her, like the air subsequent to a punch in the gut. He hadn't wanted it in the first place; no matter, he could barely stand the loss of it. He almost forgot to take his bows (this was his moment of triumph, after all), almost just stood there pawing at the ruffled front of his tux shirt as Vartan pantomimed to the audience his worry that his brash young assistant had gone too far, *too far*, this time.

Then Fred was spinning the box again, the white/green/pink of the walls/yard/shouting little faces flying through the space opposite him where a ten-year-old, white-tuxedoed George should have been, grinning and spinning from the other side. Again, Fred stopped to open the door. Still no girl, the room ticking and juddering around the empty box. In their childhood shows, he and George had exchanged twin embarrassed, nail-biting faces at this point, which had always gotten laughs; but now, what with the turning room and thickening air, Fred's distress must have seemed too real. The audience fell silent, and even the girl's mother, a woman with a bump of a nose and wavy locks who for no especially good reason reminded him of Mel, stopped smiling and clutched her upper arms.

Vartan stepped up to Fred, pointing at him, then at himself, then at the box. Vartan's mustache and the stubble around it was almost as white as his thinning hair, which in turn was almost as white as his tux and cape and shiny plastic shoes. Maybe it was the sunlight, but Vartan's skin, too, looked paler than Fred had remembered it, so that his eyes, brown and deep-set in their ashen moats, seemed to be the only spots of color on him, which made them look all the more haunted and luminous as they checked Fred's own. Fred could see the question there, not the question of whether he would join forces with Vartan to combine their magical skills, but the other one, and Fred nodded, signaling both yes to the invitation and yes he was all right. They ran, they spun the box, the room whirling behind Vartan, his hair tousled in the wind. He was still giving Fred that sad, interrogative look, the same one he'd given him upon picking him up from the police station the night before.

They waved their wands, touched them together, and broke away just before the fuse Vartan had surreptitiously lit reached its destination at the top of the box. There came a flash of light, a smell of sulfur—Vartan insisted on using flash powder, even indoors—and the door dropped open. From the shouts of little voices, Fred surmised that they'd successfully rematerialized the girl, though he was having difficulty verifying it with his eyes—he hadn't moved quickly enough, hadn't looked away from the flash in time, and it had taken away large patches at the center of his vision. He edged toward the front of the box, blinking. He could vaguely make out Vartan's stooping form grabbing hold of a diminutive, pink-sleeved forearm, to the children's continued cheers. But aside from that shred of pink and a sparkle of tiara, he couldn't see the little girl herself, which made it almost feel like they'd failed to bring her back. Glimpsing the penumbral whiteness of Vartan bending at the waist, Fred too took his bow. Strange shapes and geometrical patterns appeared in the cloud-shaped afterimage of the flash—weaves of tiny radiating circles and stars—clapping children dimly visible beyond.

Vartan and Fred ate their slices of chocolate cake from little paper plates, acknowledged the gratitude of the bump-nosed mother, took their check from the husband—who, from his chrome-framed glasses and look of slight apology for his own wealth, Fred took, rightly or wrongly, to be a dot-com success story—then, in the boggy heat, loaded up the magic van and climbed in. Looking flushed, not even bothering to pull out of the driveway, Vartan fired up a bowl. He kept his head angled toward Fred as he smoked but otherwise showed little caution. It was late afternoon, and the suburban street was peaceful. A Mercedes SUV slowed as it passed; Fred doubted the driver could see what Vartan was up to, but in this neighborhood the mere sight of a dented old Astro van might merit a cell phone call to the police.

"You OK?" Fred asked.

His father exhaled steadily through his nostrils. "Sure. That was fun," he said, sounding convinced of it.

They sat there another minute, the feeble air-conditioning doing its best to cool them. Vartan took another hit. Fred slid his laptop from his briefcase, woke it up, and searched for an unencrypted wireless signal. A strong one popped up immediately. So much for the dot-com worker theory.

"What about you?" Vartan said. "You OK?"

"Me? Yeah, I'm OK."

His father went on peering at him as if through a fog. Fred himself was still blinking from the flash bomb, his brain still iridescing like a soap bubble from having merged with the birthday girl's bright little world of ignorance and possibility.

"You overdid it with that kid," Vartan said. "Spinning her so many times. You looked like someone was chasing you."

"I lost count. Got a little dizzy."

Vartan's stare was less anxious than abstractly contemplative. "Are you doing drugs?"

"Drugs?"

"Stealing to support a habit?"

"No, Dad."

He wished he hadn't had to call his father from the 13th Precinct house yesterday, but his credit card was maxed and the fifty-dollar station house bond had been forty more than he'd had on him.

"The tweezers weren't for a roach clip? Or some other . . . paraphernalia?"

"No, Dad."

Vartan had asked him why tweezers on the drive home from the station last night as well, and not wanting to go into the whole issue of having donated his brain to science, Fred had told him he'd had a splinter and simply forgotten to pay. The explanation didn't seem to have sufficed.

"Maybe you were just exploring new career options," Vartan said.

"Right. Starting at the ground floor. I'll work my way up. Shampoo. Razor blades." Fred opened his email, to check if Sam or any of the Armation people had replied to an apology he'd sent earlier for missing the teleconference. He'd opted not to mention the arrest, citing only an unspecified emergency he hoped they would read as George-related.

"Sure," Vartan said. "Those are pricey."

"Antioxidants. Gingko biloba."

"Not much of a health plan."

"Condoms. Feminine hygiene products."

Vartan scratched his pale head. "Do you need to pluck your hair? Is it some kind of sex thing?"

"No, Dad. It's no kind of sex thing. Can we get the fuck out of here?"

Vartan pocketed the pipe and pulled out. A similar farce had ensued in the station, when the cops refused to believe that the old lady and Fred didn't know each other, and she'd started shouting that he was some kind of pervert, following her around the supermarket. The fact that he was refusing to look at anyone for fear of merging with them wasn't helping matters. In a droll sort of way, as they mashed his fingers to a scanner and propped him against a wall for a digital mugshot, the cops peppered him with questions about his unnatural interests in personal grooming items and elderly women.

"Were you ever gonna talk to her? Ask her out on a date?" said one cop.

"Nah. He's the shy type," said another.

"But he had those tweezers to remember their lovely outing."

Then Fred looked up and, to his dismay, began merging with the wary-eyed picture of himself on the monitor. Then he asked to use the bathroom and started merging with the seatless, crusted-shit-bespattered metal toilet, as the cop peering through the window behind him, assuming Fred was too bashful to piss under observation, apologized:

"Just regulations. You'd be amazed how many guys try to kill themselves in there."

The elaborate system of food-and-drink shelving between the front seats swayed as his father, going too slow, braked and steered them onto Route 3. Vartan had bought the van a couple months ago from a friend for a few hundred dollars, and since that time had transformed it, as was his habit, into a secondhand second home on wheels, equipping it with, among other upgrades, beaded seat covers, a paper towel holder on the back of the driver's seat, an extra-long rearview mirror, matching trash receptacles on the insides of the doors. He'd installed high-decibel buzzers in the turn signals to keep himself from leaving them on by accident, and a radar sensor from a kit, which let him know his proximity to cars behind him while parallel parking. He'd even replicated a jokey Christmas gift George had perpetrated on a previous car, replacing the horn buttons on the steering wheel with two keys from an old computer keyboard, an F and a U, to allow Vartan's thumbs a more evocative honking experience.

"All right," Vartan said, drumrolling his fingers on the wheel. "So you wanted tweezers. People want worse things in life."

The truth was Fred didn't know why he'd taken the tweezers. The little implement had seemed somehow magical, the sword in the stone, destined only for him—probably just another merging effect coming on. Anyway, he certainly hadn't needed an eyelash curler.

"I saw Jill there," he muttered. "I wasn't thinking straight."

"Jill . . ." Vartan blinked. "How'd she look?"

Fred searched for the least descriptive word that would apply. "Fine," he said, and realized that one said it all.

Vartan sniffed, worked his pinky in his ear, then reached for the radio and turned on WINS. The newscaster was saying something about doctors separating conjoined twins in Utah, and Vartan's hand froze over the button, no doubt reminded, as was Fred, of the time he and George had gone trick-or-treating as conjoined twins one Halloween. Vartan had been working on a B horror flick that fall, and the makeup artist had done Fred and George up to look like they were joined at the head. They'd staggered around the small New England town where the film was based, collecting candy and watching people try to puzzle out where exactly the costume ended and reality began. The funny thing was how easy it had been for the two of them to walk leaned into each other like that. So natural that, for a while after they'd pulled free of the flesh-toned, suctioning goop, it was hard to walk upright on their own.

Having forgotten all about the computer in his lap, Fred now noticed that a message had come in when they were still in range of the wireless signal:

Subject: Help, Avatara!
From: George Brounian

Again, no text other than the subject line. The same subject line.

Or was it?

Fred checked his saved messages. The exclamation point was new.

"Can we stop by the hospital?" Fred asked, half in panic, half in ridiculous hope, the image of George sitting up in bed and chuckling to himself as he thumbed the email into a doctor's borrowed BlackBerry flashing to mind.

"Hey. Kiddo. You were there all morning."

Vartan had been there too, for an hour or so before the show.

"Maybe just to check in." Email or no, the nurses never swabbed the inside of George's mouth enough. Just thinking about how dry it got made Fred's tongue stick to his throat.

"I was going to drop you at the office," Vartan coaxed, "remember? Besides, your mother's there. Her cult's coming later. George'll have all the company he can deal with."

Fred had forgotten. Once a week, Holly and her Reiki group met in the ward to give George a healing. Unclipping his bowtie and tossing it in a cupholder, Vartan went on complaining about how she was going off the deep end, and Fred went on staring at that email, at that exclamation point. It could still be some new strain of spam or malware, he supposed. But two different messages. There seemed more intention in it now—more malice. Who could cook this up? One of those moral midgets at the parent company?

Vartan, meanwhile, was giving Fred notes: how he should explore the moment when the egg materialized in his mouth, how George used to have this thing where he just stood there with his mouth puckered, looking around; how he was over-milking the moment when he cracked the egg in Vartan's top hat, how George used to make it look almost unconscious, like his attention was completely somewhere else.

Prior to a few weeks ago when they'd started up again, it had been twenty-three years since Fred had last done the act with Vartan—with him and George. George had conceived of it three years before that, in 1980, the year Pac-Man appeared in the pizza parlor, the Empire struck back, and President Carter lost to an old actor with shellacked hair and a big-shouldered suit. Fred and George were ten, and Vartan's acting career was at a frightening low, all the more unsettling after a relative high just a couple years before, when he'd landed a small but memorable part as an Italian-American priest who quits the priesthood. Thanks to that movie, which would go on to become a classic, Vartan had become a recognizable figure in their Brooklyn neighborhood, and by association, Fred and George had experienced a certain local celebrity too. They'd been used to the extra attention that came with being twins, but this was a whole new level: bullies transformed themselves into protectors; teachers offered the two of them better parts in the school plays (on the assumption, presumably, that their genetic thespian birthright needed nurturing); and when their dad showed up to watch, he'd be mobbed for autographs.

Now their dad was spending most of his days at home, in his undershirt, repairing appliances, retiling the bathroom, waiting for his agent to call. Things were tense. The movie royalties were drying up, and the only other money coming in was from his mom's sporadic part-time cashier and secretarial jobs, which, having been a professional ballerina as a teenager before eloping with Vartan, she was too miserable doing to ever hold for long. Vartan would come home from his failed auditions and, after looking around like a cornered wolf, would start shouting about the mess the little apartment was always in. He and Holly would fight. He would storm out of the apartment. She would disappear into their bedroom.

One such night, to distract Sam from the tears pooling in his eyes, George started stringing magic tricks into a story. He'd always taken it upon himself to be Sam's protector—as children, he and Sam were nearly as close, in their own way, as he and Fred were. Sam trailed George around the apartment and the neighborhood, and George not only put up with it but encouraged it, happy to have a young disciple (whereas Fred and Sam were as likely as not to push each other aside). At first, it was George and Fred who were the dueling magicians, one-upping each other for Sam's viewing pleasure. Then George's ambitions evolved, and he had the three of them preparing a show for Mom and Dad, with George and Fred in the leads and Sam as their harried apprentice. George's plan came off as well as they'd hoped: a few nights later, there were Vartan and Holly, together on the couch, arguments on hold, cheering them on. Fred thought this would be the end of it, but then George pulled Vartan into the act, gave him a few directions, and their father started hamming it up with them, improvising a whole new routine. Then George was talking costumes with Mom. The goal, now, was a performance for Sam's upcoming seventh birthday party. And no sooner had this been accomplished than George was spreading the word at school, and Sam's friends were asking their parents if the Brounians could perform at their parties too.

By the time George and Fred pitched the act to their parents as a business enterprise, requests were already trickling in. Fred had already designed the phone book ads and reorganized the skits and come up with a list of new tricks and props they'd need for a bigger and better show. Vartan refused to even talk about it at first, but broke as he was, he couldn't hold out for long. He took to disguising his appearance, with a fake nose larger still than his own and a drooping, glue-on goatee, to combat the indignity of being recognized by the children's parents as the guy from the movie.

By no means was this a happy time for their dad, but with the empty hours filled by the construction of tricks and the driving and the performances themselves, Vartan began shouting somewhat less. He and Holly started reconciling. Within a year, he was finding roles again, playing more Italians (though he was Armenian)—from minor mob henchman to a man who reminisces over his mama's cooking, then holds up a jar of spaghetti sauce and exalts, "That's Italian!" Holly, meanwhile, quit her last part-time job to begin what, aside from raising the three of them, Fred sometimes thought of as her life's true work: her inner odyssey of personal discovery.

By 1983, the moonwalk was something people did on tile floors, the Jedi was returning, Star Wars was a dream of national defense, and Vartan was finally spending more time emoting in front of cameras than in front of five-year-olds. The tuxes were left on their hangers for longer and longer stretches, and this was a relief not just for Vartan, but for Fred as well. While Fred had enjoyed the attention, and the birthday cake, the act was mainly a reminder of an era he wanted to forget. Shaking fake treasure from his top hat as George caught it in his and Dad stared with simulated envy, Fred would think ahead to how Vartan would remain in the van after getting home, to smoke cigarettes and stare out the windshield; to how up in the kitchen they'd find Mom in one of her homemade house-dresses, paused for who knew how long in the midst of folding laundry, gazing out the back window. Fred would look into the spectating kids' unformed little faces, and feel like he was peddling a lie. About, if nothing else, what his family was, all the magic it didn't actually have.

George, Fred knew, felt differently. He was hatching ever bigger plans for the act: a theater piece, a TV special. Wearing his little white top hat, he started pitching these ideas to Vartan one night in the living room, dancing around, playing all the parts, and after a couple minutes, Vartan glanced up from his script.

"I'm trying to focus." He whip-snapped the pages. "Go play some-where else."

For a while after that, George tried to cajole Fred into continuing the act on their own. Up on the rooftop, the venue for most of their serious discussions, Fred finally spoke his mind on the subject.

"Magic is bullshit," he said. "People need to just get real."

For a moment, though George was nowhere near the roof's edge, from his expression, it looked as if he were falling, falling away into the distant, sun-drenched rooftops.

Then his face hardened. "Getting real is the bullshit," he declared. He considered further. "*You're* the bullshit."

"Any auditions lately?" Fred asked, as a matter of principle.

Vartan fiddled with the volume. War in Lebanon. Sunny and cooler tomorrow. High of eighty-four.

"Nah, it's hell out there," he replied, as a matter of form. He made a little flutter of his fingers, signifying the dissipation of his career into thin air. "I should've gotten a nose job. Should've changed my name when I had the chance."

It had been a very long time since Fred had heard Vartan bemoan his ethnic-ness (upon which he'd arguably built his early career); he was doing it now, no doubt, merely to elaborate the fiction that he was actively, or even passively, looking for work. In recent years, ethnic and nonethnic being somewhat less distinguishable or relevant in the gray-haired Vartan, he had been getting more parts than ever, playing non-ethnicity-specific cops and judges, lawyers and businessmen, innocent bystanders, relatives of the accused, and assorted well-meaning lunatics and senile people. He'd started rehearsals for a long-dreamed-of project, an off-Broadway production of *The Tempest* in which he was to play Prospero, when George was diagnosed.

"Changed it to what?" Fred asked, for the hell of it.

"Something American. Martin Brown. That would've been good."

When the three of them were children, their father had often told George that he was named after George Washington, Sam that he was named after Uncle Sam, and Fred that he was named after Fred of the couple Fred and Ethel on *I Love Lucy*, this having been the single most American person Vartan could think of. Many a night, Fred had lain awake wondering how his life might have turned out had he not been saddled with the name of that dull-witted, bald old man.

A modified pickup truck full of scrap metal cut them off, jammed the brakes, and to salt the wound, sent a cigarette gyring out the window to burst into sparks on the windshield in front of Vartan's eyes. The Vartan of old would have gone apeshit. The current one's anger was nowhere, dropped down some deep hole. Barely a *sonofabitch* and a few disorganized blinks. His thumbs, at the F and U keys, rather than pressing, merely caressed.

"So what'll you do, now that you're being let go?" Vartan asked.

Fred didn't move. Though every cell in his body flinched.

"Sam told you that?" he managed.

"Earlier today." Vartan rubbed the back of his head. "I didn't want to rattle you before the gig."

They sat through a longish auto insurance commercial. A longish vocabulary-improvement-tape commercial came on.

"You should go talk to him," Vartan added, laying a hand on the padded shoulder of Fred's jacket. "Maybe he can help you figure out how to get back on board."

"What makes you think he'd do that?"

"He's your brother. Why wouldn't he?"

"Because he's Sam."

"He's surviving. You could learn something from him."

"You think I'm going to crawl back to the people who stole our company and beg for a job?"

"Eat your shit, Fred. Live to eat your shit another day."

The scrap truck sped into the left lane. In the Escalade ahead of it, a cartoon Batman leapt into action on a flatscreen TV. A pudgy kid watching it in the backseat huffed on an inhaler.

"Anyway," Fred said, "they're moving the office down to Orlando before long."

Vartan smoothed his mustache with a thumb and forefinger. "Later this month."

"*This month?*"

"When's the last time you went in to work? Go talk to Sam."

"Why would I do that? Even if I could get my job back, I'm not about to leave George alone in that hospital bed."

Vartan thought. "Could you find a job here?"

Fred thought. "Given time."

Vartan glanced over. "Would you?"

They listened to George Bush talking up the liquid bomb plot, the news of which had just broken last Friday. Followed by a story about the singer Boy George reporting for his court-ordered community service, sweeping Manhattan streets for the Department of Sanitation. Fred fought down the urge to bring up going to the hospital again.

"If I did go to Florida," he said, "you couldn't go on doing these magic shows."

A kind of laugh escaped Vartan, a short exhalation through his nose. "Sam says there's plenty of acting work down in Florida for your company."

"My company."

"For their military simulations. Playing Afghan warlords. Iraqi sectarian leaders. Suicide bombers." He sucked his teeth. But a moment later: "Don't suppose they pay union wages."

"Not on your life."

Vartan nodded. He hadn't been remotely serious, anyway. After George's illness had begun last year, Vartan had dropped out of *The Tempest* and the production had fallen apart; and soon after George fell into the coma, their father was back in his undershirt, making cards float out of a deck. Then he was sitting around the Edison Hotel diner, idly disappearing coins and creamers, when an actor friend asked him to do a nephew's birthday party. Then Vartan was asking Fred how this or that sequence went. Next, they were rehearsing in the living room, both in their undershirts, making milkshakes in each other's top hats, shredding each other's newspapers and reconstituting their own. When Vartan had finally made it clear that he really was planning to revive the act, it was with an assurance that Fred didn't need to join him, that he could just do a version of it on his own, but Fred had been dubious. Even hauling the equipment in and out of the van was probably too much for his father to handle alone.

A story about Governor George Pataki came on. Something about consolation or compensation, but it was too many Georges and Fred had already turned it off.

"Sam says—"

"Tell me, Dad, what else does Sam say?"

The eyebrow hoist. The thumb shrug. "He says we should all move down there. Before New York blows up."

"Right."

Vartan's mustache spread. "All cities are doomed, he says."

"Right."

As they neared the Lincoln Tunnel entrance, the Manhattan skyline came into view. Palled by haze, it seemed to take on a shaky transparency, like a slide-show image from some never-to-be-repeated holiday vacation, the projector a relic, the vacationers themselves dead and gone.

Picture it, George instructs, in a noisy East Village bar, over pints at a dark booth with a sticky table. Their own world. On the Internet.

Fred and Sam try. It's the summer of 1997.

"You mean, like, with graphics?" Sam says.

Not just a world, a utopia, any number of them, George is saying. He makes a magician's hand-sweep over the beers, a faded friendship bracelet sliding on his forearm. He's just in from California, radiates sun and sea spray, his skin burnished, his hair a shade lighter than Fred's, even a bit wavy. Players could strike out on their own or form larger groups, he's saying, and everything in one's borders would be customizable—flora and fauna, tech levels, forms of government, the very laws of physics. Sam rubs his smudged pint glass with a Handi Wipe. Fred turns his cigarette on the ashtray rim, sharpening the ember.

A purer existence, George goes on. The avatars wouldn't get hungry or thirsty, wouldn't freeze or get heatstroke, couldn't be injured or killed. Postmaterial life, he proclaims with a smile. George himself could exemplify "Postmaterial life" right now, Fred thinks, with his yoga, macrobiotic food, loose linen shirt, crazy-bright future. George sits back in the wooden booth, hands behind his head, lounging as if on some beach chair, oblivious to the smoke, the college mob, the Jersey girls at the bar eyeing him—not Fred, not even glancing back and forth between them, Fred observes, torn in the usual way between envy and amazed pride. Weird how Fred's always been the slacker, at least from the world's point of view, but somehow George has always been the freer one. Chasing his goals with the grace and absolute devotion of a dog leaping at Frisbees. Whereas Fred, wanting to get real but never quite figuring out what real is, has been so leery of every rainbow he can barely follow them a step. From high school, he floundered from part-time programming gigs to community college stints, interspersed with desperate, footloose jaunts across the country. For the last three years, thanks more to the rising tide of dot-commism than his résumé, he's been treading water in a low-level position overseeing tweaks to an algorithm designed to predict profitable tech stocks—a dull job, and he suspects the product is working so far only because the NASDAQ is only going up. Sam is in roughly the same occupational hamster wheel as Fred is, slogging away as a system administrator for a stripling city government website; he may be a harder worker than Fred is, but he's intense and exudes stress and hasn't risen far.

As for George, after rocketing out of college near the top of his class, he's done well for himself out West, if maybe not quite so well as the family expected. He was highly paid for his programming and design work at three different game companies, but didn't stay at any of them long enough to get vested, never finding a project he felt was worthwhile. Anyway, the era is throwing off twentysomething billionaires like sparks from a forge; it's too much for George to sit at a desk working on someone else's dream. Because here, finally, is his own. And just think how evolutionary it could be, he's saying, how the avatars' immaterial nature could rub off on players over time, temper their baser desires, coax their mindsets up the pyramid steps of Maslow's hierarchy of needs, from physiological and safety needs all the way up to beauty, truth, self-actualization.

As if pulled by the same string, Sam lifts his glass to his lips as Fred lifts his cigarette. To be sure, George's vision is starry-eyed. Yet in the nineties, at least for those residing in the valleys and alleys of silicon under the expanding bubble of the boom, it isn't all that hard to imagine that even the real world is headed this way, that science and peace and the increase of wealth and trade are all ineluctably leading humanity to a not-too-distant future in which every basic human need will be met. In techie circles, bodily immortality itself isn't thought to be out of the question, even in their own lifetimes. There's talk of minds uploaded to storage banks, spare bodies hanging like so many suits in a closet. No shortage of resources, no enslavement to the dictates of the body, violence itself a vestigial act without meaning or consequence. Along what new lines will such a culture organize itself? This question, George is saying, is what will make their virtual world at once a recreational activity and something else, an edutainment, a training ground for the next inevitable phase of human evolution, for the postmaterial lives they'll soon be living for real.

"Urth." George spells out the word, raises his glass. "Say it with me."

Fred and Sam exchange a glance, the enormity of what George is offering them—rescue from their stalled little lives—beginning to break through their furtive reserve. In a minute, Fred will be saying it with him, and Sam will too. Before much longer, they'll be saying it again in a boardroom full of suits and a staggering view of, among the thousands of other buildings sprawled below, the little brown box that will soon house their sunny, lofty office. And, poof, George and Fred will be co-CEOs, Sam a CTO. And Fred will find himself giving in to life, blossoming in a way he'd given up hoping was possible. The dreaded pursuit of success, he'll find, is only a problem for those still clamoring at the gates. For those who've made it in, who are exactly where they want to be, there's no war, no work—just magic.

But that future is still a few seconds off. For now, he lets George squirm—pint glass hovering in the air, smile getting nervous at the edges—and savors the obvious: George needs him, too.

When Fred finally relents and raises his glass, George cuts him off:

"You're not going to smoke in the office, are you?"

As it will happen, he'll kick cigarettes within weeks. Though his response for now: what will seem in memory a never-ending smoke plume, blown in his twin brother's face.

Sam was right where Fred had last seen him a week ago: crosslegged in his Aeron chair, back hunched, head jutted, headset in place, black T-shirt rolled at the cuffs and tucked neatly into his black jeans. Close-cropped hair, patchy shadow of a beard. The unvarying nature of Sam's appearance wasn't a matter of personal inattention, but of decisiveness—the whole fashion question, in his view, had been settled—and, as well, probably, a deep need for constancy. He ordered identical backups of those black jeans and black T-shirts online and sent them out to be laundered on a rotating basis. He electrically trimmed his hair down to three-eighths of an inch every few weeks, and his beard to one-eighth every morning. Several times a day, of late, to renew his energy, he'd drop to the floor and do twenty pushups, with the result that sinewy muscle squadrons had begun taking up positions on the ridgelines of his otherwise skinny arms and chest. For someone who sat in a chair twelve or more hours a day, he probably wasn't in the worst possible shape. Though Fred wouldn't have called it health, exactly. Sam's eyes were too deeply ringed.

He was leaned into his dual-screen display as Fred approached, the left one crammed with microscopic lines of code, the right a window into the Urth environment—what appeared to be the hostage-extraction scenario. Sam's avatar, dressed in desert fatigues and holding an M-16A2 rifle with a grenade-launcher attachment, stood against a wall to one side of a gateway leading out of a barren, moonlit courtyard. Another soldier, identifiable from his girth and sparse blond beard as their lead programmer Jesse's avatar, stood to the other side, firing out into the street with a mammoth M-60E3, the jackhammer report of which rattled from Sam's headset. Out of ingrained habit, Sam joggled the mouse more or less continually, swiveling the view back and forth and up and down through the courtyard, a fuzzy, green circle of night-vision visibility sliding over the broken windows, kicked-in doors, and a narrow alley between two low buildings where a third soldier stood facing the other way. Watching the lifelike kick of the guns, the near-photorealistic chinks and eruptions from the bullet-riddled walls, Fred felt what he did every time he came in here: a dizzy mixture of liberation and oppression, adventure and drear constriction.

"*Holomelancholia,*" he remembered George pronouncing late in the office one night. "The inevitable disappointment of virtual worlds." Pleased at his invention, he'd allowed himself a rueful smile. "Mark my words. It'll be in the *DSM* by 2021."

"Fred," Sam stated, by way of greeting. It spooked the newer employees, this ability of his to tell who was behind him without having to turn and check. The trick lay in the reflectivity of the aluminum head of his desk lamp, which he used as a kind of rearview mirror. "I'm *trying* to cover you," he growled almost subvocally into his headset mic.

Fred heard Jesse curse from across the room as Little Jesse fell backward in the courtyard. Where the bridge of his nose had been was now a flattened well, out of which green-lit blood seeped over his face and onto the ground.

"What the hell . . ." A wave of unreality lifted Fred in his shoes. He couldn't double-check what he thought he'd seen because Sam kept shifting the view around.

"Where's it coming from?" Sam hissed into the mic, hunching closer to the screen.

"Was Jesse's nose blown off?" Fred asked.

Sam joggled and clicked, too busy to answer. Interspersed with the popping gunfire, a pleading voice which might have been their lead animator Conrad's emanated from Sam's earpiece. Little Sam turned into the gateway and fired off a grenade into a second-story window across the street. Then came a flash, a thunderclap, a hail of stone and smoke. As Little Sam backed into the courtyard, the canned sounds of a woman screaming and a child crying.

"That wasn't the one you said?" Sam called out. Bullets began chipping away the wall around him. He swiveled. The soldier by the alley was down. Something moved back into the darkness. Another explosion, this one making the whole screen flash, and then convert to black and white, the indicator-of-death feature they'd cribbed from

Dungeons & Dragons Online. Little Sam was down, blackened, missing an arm. Definitely. Missing an arm. Blood oozing from the stump. For a while, neither Fred nor Sam could take their eyes off Little Sam, whose soot-caked face bore Sam's own sunken cheeks, prominent nose, vacantly staring eyes.

"Yeah," Sam said, eyeing Fred in the lamp hood. "Whole new level of avatar deformability. It's like a real game now."

Fred nodded, that underwater feeling coming on.

"Still a ways to go," Sam went on, with minimal affect. "They want full, persistent human physiology now. Cumulative trauma, wounds that can slow you down, cripple and kill you over days. Hunger and thirst shriveling you up like a prune. Smallpox hives, neurotoxin tremors. Radiation. That's the big one. Sores on the skin. Hair and teeth falling out . . ."

On some level, Fred thought, Sam must have known the effect this singsong list was having on him. The increasingly deformable avatars had been getting steadily harder for Fred to stomach, a development he blamed less on the improving technology than on witnessing George's increasingly deformable body over the last year—rashes and burns, sutures and scars, IV punctures, bloody gobs coughed into wads of tissues or pumped out of him through silicone tubes. At Sam's mention of hair falling out, what flashed to mind was that first shock of going to George's apartment and finding his head shaved smooth. George had begun losing his hair and so had decided to get it over with. Fred had stood with him before the bathroom mirror, marveling over the transformation. The proportions seemed off, less cranium up there than either of them had expected. Fred was spooked by the alienness of it, one more step in an ongoing metamorphosis of which the physiological changes were only a part. Yet the physical exposure seemed to bring George back to Fred a little, too. Since the trouble with the company had begun, Fred had felt George gradually walling him out of his life; but in that moment, his brother surprised him, taking his arm and guiding his hand up to feel the dome. Fred was surprised how silken and warm a bald head turned out to be. "Gives me a whole new insight into skinheads," George remarked, the two of them still facing the mirror. "They try to look so hard and tough with those bald heads." He grinned. "But they must be feeling so bare-ass naked."

Still staring down at Little Sam's corpse, Sam rubbed his eyes with a thumb and forefinger. "Looks decent so far, huh?"

Decent, said Inner George, with dark emphasis.

"Decent," Fred repeated, unable to help himself.

"Real. I mean real." Sam's mouse hand darted and clicked the window shut. An angry gesture, though its main effect was to reveal his incongruously placid desktop wallpaper: palm trees on a beach, with ocean and sky beyond.

"Sounds like . . . work," Fred said, a half-hearted attempt to repair the damage. But he'd worded it too ambiguously, and Sam decided to hear another slight.

"Work, yes. That's what we tend to do here." Sam brought his non-mouse hand down protectively over his stomach. He had irritable bowel syndrome, and made no effort to hide the fact from those whose presence exacerbated it.

"Right. I guess I wouldn't know too much about that. I just loaf around in the hospital these days. Oh," Fred held up a finger, "almost forgot. George says hi, by the way."

Sam's reflected, melted-together eyes in the lamp hood had looked up to meet Fred's as he'd raised his finger, and Fred now had to watch them liquefy, and slink back off to gaze at the palm trees. He couldn't quite bring himself to apologize.

"I hear I got canned," he said instead.

Sam brought up another window on his monitor, this one containing a tactical overhead view of the Empire State Building surrounded by a flat, gray street map. He moved the terrain north, east, south, west, causing the building to churn in a slow circle.

"Word came this morning, Fred. You didn't give them much choice."

It figured, Fred thought, Sam would take their side in this. "What choice did *I* have? It's been one emergency after another."

"Right. Dad told me about your crime spree."

Now it was Fred's turn to smart.

"And your magic shows. You still smell like flash powder, by the way."

Vartan had won out, dropping Fred off here directly, Fred changing out of the tux in the back of the van. He now regretted not stopping in the hall bathroom to wash up.

Sam opened another Urth window—a side view of the skyscraper. The level of realism didn't yet approach that of the Iraq sims, but the building was recognizable. The structure was right, the windows all correctly placed.

"So now it's off to the mother ship, eh?" Fred said, after a moment.

Sam took his time to scan the statement for explosive compounds.

"Off to the mother ship," he allowed. "It's going to be a busy three weeks. We've got a deadline to meet and can't even stop working while we pack."

"So they won't even let you stay here, huh?"

"What makes you think we'd want to stay here?" He swung his head around at his dim little alcove, the still dimmer back area with all the other workstations, and by implication, the city beyond.

It shouldn't have, but the conviction in Sam's voice surprised and stung Fred. He thought of that single day six months back when Sam had come to the hospital. How he'd stood at the back of the room by the door while Fred and their parents had hovered over George, talking to him, holding his hands. Sam had remained for a few minutes, a half-hour at most, then, mumbling that he had to go, turned and slid away. Later, he'd explained himself by saying there wasn't anything he could do there, and that someone needed to be minding the business. Which Fred couldn't fully argue with; but then Sam had never returned, and the last time Vartan and Holly had gotten to see him was when they themselves had stopped by the office a couple months ago to say hello. Fred had the distinct impression Sam was counting the days, biding his time until he could put a thousand miles between himself and the rest of them. Sam's recent advice to their dad about all of them moving down there, Fred viewed as nothing more than a halfhearted sop to his guilt. The absolute least he could do.

"I don't know," Fred said. "Maybe I just have trouble picturing you in Bermuda shorts."

"I'll get some black ones."

They risked a look at each other, despite themselves, almost smiling. And suddenly it was happening again. The expansion. Enveloping the air between them, an unbounded region, more naked than skin. The distance from Sam was dropping away, and mentally Fred pulled back, wheeling some inner arms like he was about to fall from a plane. He didn't want Sam to be a part of him. He'd sooner have gone out and trailed the next batty old woman on the street. A flicker of fear appeared in Sam's eyes, perhaps mirroring Fred's own. Sam turned away, fixing once more on the palm trees on his screen.

"It's time to bug out of New York," he said. "Cities are fucked, long term. We're all agreed on that."

By way of punctuation, he clicked an onscreen button and the Empire State Building began to collapse. At first it seemed to be happening in that all-too-familiar way, a few stories three-quarters of the way up pancaking together like an inchworm gathering itself up for a step. From there, though, the movement took an alien turn: the upper part of the building toppling off at an angle, shearing the lower as it fell, causing entire floors just below the split to slip from their girders and columns like overstewed meat from the bone; then the upper segment exploding on the ground, the mangled stalk still standing in a pile of wreckage.

"Looks weird, huh?" Sam said. "Empire State Building's joints are riveted, not just seated, and its columns and beams are fireproofed with brick and cement. Twin Towers just used sheetrock. But the downside to the older construction is it's way heavier, so when it destabilizes, look out. See, watch."

Like a chopped tree, the remaining structure leaned and then came walloping down over the debris.

Fred felt his throat constricting to the diameter of a coffee stirrer. He fought down the shameful urge to flee the office for the open air.

"It's all real physics," Sam was saying. "Real structural data. The Army Corps of Engineers helped us plug it all in."

Real physics was the trademark of the Urth environment, what had early on separated it from all others. Their company hadn't settled for mere effects in the early days; they'd wanted a completely realistic array of action and reaction—real gravity, acceleration, wind factors, impact warpage, ricochet trajectories. Real physics had been something of an obsession for them, as they had quickly determined that making the experience of Urth more and more real was precisely what made it feel more and more magical. Arguably, it was more verisimilitude than their prototype Urth—an anime-style world of pastoral communes, treehouse villages, and underwater bubble towns among coral reefs—had really needed; and the quest had played a part in fatally delaying their never-to-be commercial launch. Yet subsequently, that same real physics code was the very property that made them valuable to Armation, back in the golden dawn of the war on terror.

Possibly fearing that the conflicts in Afghanistan and Iraq might somehow fail to go on forever, Armation had agreed to an inspiration of Sam's (without raising his salary or granting him a new title) and was now courting a potential client—the City of New York. Just as the U.S. military was using Urth to train soldiers for a new kind of war, the hope was that American cities would begin using it to train emergency workers, and civilians, too, for a new kind of peace. The idea, Fred had to admit, made all too much sense. The cost of doing live emergency response-training exercises in urban areas was pretty much prohibitive, even with the new Homeland Security funds. But Urth would allow hundreds of firefighters, cops, city officials, agents from the various federal agencies, as well as civilian volunteers to log on all at once from any computer anywhere and play out scenarios over and over, perfecting their response strategies without disrupting city life. The demo project under development, the main thing Sam and the others here had been cranking away at over the last few months, was a 9/11-style attack on the Empire State Building. If the city officials liked it and signed on as paying customers, the next phase would be to simulate, over a ten-by-ten-square-block radius, the aftermath of a small nuclear bomb.

"What do you think?" Sam asked. The question sounded deliberate, like he was asking about more than the spire. Most of the time, Fred got the feeling the mere sight of him caused Sam pain, like he was standing on Sam's bowels with every step. But then there were these other moments, when Sam seemed to want his opinion, his approval. Sam was proud of this project, proud for many reasons, but mainly—he'd found various ways of saying it in their none-too-frequent conversations over the last few months—proud there was no moral downside to this new direction, that the training was only for the saving of life, not the taking of it. He probably thought it was closer to what George would have wanted the company to be doing. Fred had his doubts, but either way, Sam was more in the right than ever, and had this been a year ago, Sam and he both would have been spinning it this way to George. Fred was certainly aware of no rational basis for the creeping anger and repugnance he felt at the sight of that virtual rubble.

"Hell of an achievement," he offered. Not without a garnish of sarcasm, but from his near whisper—the result of his airway trying to seal itself off—only the respect came through, so that his words trundled through Sam's mental bomb-detecting equipment without setting off an alarm.

"*Real* physics," Sam repeated, with another probing stare. "Actual engineering models, from the building's actual plans. You wouldn't believe how much work went into that."

"I believe it, Sam," Fred muttered. "So long."

He turned to make the trek to his long-neglected desk. To clear it out.

"Do you want your job back, Fred?"

Fred stopped. Sam had blurted out the question, a headlong leap into chilly water. Maybe he already regretted it. There had been a time, shortly after they'd just started up, when George had wanted, to Fred's surprise, to let Sam go, and Fred had to talk him out of it. He and George had fallen into their respective roles—George as the generator of big, woolly ideas, Fred as the shaper of those ideas into executable designs—with preternatural ease. Sam, on the other hand, though he was working diligently, obsessively, even, on the minutiae of the server-side code, was mulish and easily discouraged, coiled in so many knots it was a strain just to be around him. From his corner, at unpredictable intervals, would come grunts and curses, knocking everyone else out of their grooves and setting the air on edge. The slightest change they wanted implemented would send Sam into a brief frenzy, and Fred would have to sit with him until he came around to the fact that each new demand wasn't impossible. Sam had improved over time, but the fluid condition of the project, the ever-evolving design and ever-shifting delegation of tasks, continued to bring out the worst of his anxiety. Life in their office was perhaps, for Sam, a kind of extended flashback to the chaos and uncertainty of their hand-to-mouth, bohemian childhood. It wasn't until the partnership with Armation, with their feudal hierarchies and deadlines etched in stone, that Sam really began to thrive. Fred wondered if Sam had that much pull over there now, had ingratiated himself with the overlords to that considerable extent, and if so, to what extent he, Fred, should be feeling grateful for this.

"Can I get it back?" he asked.

"I sent out some feelers. There's definitely damage that needs to be controlled. But there's also sympathy out there. I think we could get you a meeting."

Sam waited.

Fred waited.

Which way?

Maybe the millionth time he'd asked Inner George this question over the last few months. Dad and Sam must have talked this possibility over. On the van ride, Vartan had kept assuring Fred that George wouldn't be alone, that their mother and he would be there every day, that no one knew how much longer this would go on, that Fred could still fly in on weekends. Perhaps—it wasn't impossible—he might even be able to work out some kind of part-time arrangement and be here more. And maybe, too (though his guilt shut him down as soon as the notion arose), if he had to live down there part-time, if he couldn't just get up and walk over to the hospital whenever he wanted, it might force him to start living his life again, at least a little.

He tried to imagine it, moving down there, leaving George in that guardrailed bed, going back to work with his other brother and his coworkers and friends on building the world they'd all sunk their lives into, for the men who'd stolen it from them. He couldn't imagine it. But he couldn't imagine the alternatives, either. His imagination simply hit a wall.

"Our first big playtest for the Empire State Building is next week," Sam went on. "Half the Military-Entertainment Complex will be there, taking the tour. It would help to show up to that, put on your best face, smooth things over. Meanwhile, you could get back up to speed here."

Fred couldn't make himself say yes. George was inside him, somewhere, freezing his muscles.

How else will I pay your bills?

I don't know, said Inner George. *Sell a kidney or two?*

Fred gave the slightest of nods. Sam responded with the same, his features tense from the negotiation. Fred couldn't tell whether Sam was pleased or disturbed by the result. He seemed both.

"Sam," said Fred, "do you remember George ever using the word 'avatara'?"

Fred gauged the blankness of Sam's stare. Fairly blank.

"Like 'avatar' with an 'a'?" Sam asked.

"Never mind."

Sam's eyes slicked again. "He didn't speak, did he?"

"No," Fred said softly. "He didn't speak."

Sam blinked a few times, mouth set in a line, then turned to his screen and clicked the buttons, a first to right the skyscraper, a second to bring it tumbling back down.

The last time Fred had managed to drag himself in here to the office, he'd been unable to bring himself to log onto Urth and contemplate the latest transformations. Instead, he'd spent the afternoon reading an article on the Web about self-organized complexity, how Chemical As and Chemical Bs would naturally, on occasion, combine to produce Chemical ABs and Chemical BAs; how Chemical A and Chemical AB would then combine into AAB and ABA, and AAB would split into B and AA, leading in turn to Chemicals AAAA, BBBB, ABAB, BBAABBBABABABBBBA; how one in a billion of these chemical combinations would be the perfect catalyst for combining A and AB, or for breaking up ABA into B and AA, and once catalyzed, these exchanges would become not merely occasional and haphazard but rapid and continuous, and a whole system of catalyzed exchanges would form; and how when such an exchange system got to be a certain size, it would, through natural and inevitable processes, split into two, in effect replicating itself, life thus emerging complex and whole from no divine spark, from nothing but its own senseless propensity to do so.

When he and George had first heard the term "Military-Entertainment Complex" at a sparsely attended game convention in early 2002, they'd chuckled, assuming it was a joke. But, like so many complex systems in this ever-complexifying world, the MEC was so well suited to its evolutionary niche that, improbable as it seemed, it was likely inevitable. The combination of a ready pool of Disney Imagineers, Pixar animators, and Electronic Arts programmers on the one hand, and a profusion of military bases on the other, made Orlando a natural location for a new industry of military simulations to take root. And like the formation of life itself from a soup of inert components, the new Los Alamos in the war on terror was forming not gradually and in piecemeal fashion but in a flash—whole, vigorous, and self-catalyzing. Almost overnight, a community of coders and engineers accustomed to crafting amusement park rides and transforming rodents, insects, monsters, and vehicles into lovable computer-animated characters were finding themselves charged with the mission of saving the free world.

Fred and his brothers' online utopian dreamworld, at the time, was seeming more a dream plain and simple by the day. A week before 9/11, they'd had all the financial backing they needed. A week after, they'd had none. In the following weeks, they'd trudged through the barricaded streets and acrid air to their office in a kind of shellshocked delirium, waiting for it all to go away—the filter masks, the fire truck convoys, the teary, camera-toting tourists—waiting for their old lives to return, seething at anyone (at everyone) who couldn't stop talking about the event, dissecting it, rehashing it, replaying it, reliving it with what seemed to them a barely concealed euphoria.

He and George, and to some degree Sam as well, had put up their own money to pay the overhead, the reduced salaries of Jesse and Conrad, and what severance packages they could cobble together for the others. After four months of this, Urth was close to bankrupt, and their personal bank accounts weren't far behind. Then those rumors of the military-simulation gold rush going on down in Florida started trickling in. Fred came up with the idea of pitching their world engine as a platform for distributed troop training and mission rehearsal. Sam was instantly for it. George was dubious, to say the least. Get him drunk in a bar and he'd go on about the militarization of society, the forty thousand companies already on the Pentagon payroll. But Fred convinced him, and George allowed himself to be convinced, that before long they could get back to their original vision, pursuing both projects in parallel, if need be. The three of them went to Barneys and purchased fancy blazers and matching slacks, which they hoped together would read as suits, and which they planned on returning if it didn't work out. They flew down to Orlando, and just about went door-to-door through the University of Central Florida's research park, where most of the contractors were based. Before the week was done, they'd gotten an offer.

Armation was an outfit fast becoming another Lockheed Martin, with every available finger in a different government pie, and, what with one war going and another rumored, was growing so quickly that at the initial meeting the VP in charge of strategic partnerships—a man named Lipton with a thin upper lip and the kind of horn-rimmed glasses that might have been worn by a boy scout troop leader circa the Nixon administration—seemed to have trouble enumerating all their current projects. Instead, he showed off a few baubles in the executive lobby. There was a backup space helmet designed for the Apollo 1 mission, which, as Lipton reminded them, caught fire on the pad, killing the crew; but there was nothing wrong with the helmets themselves, he assured them, and these were Armation's very first government contract. There was a picture of Dan Gretta, the CEO, his leathery squint and white teeth wedged between those of Jeb and George W. Bush. Next, Lipton passed around a wallet-sized picture of himself from the early seventies, decked out in a half-unbuttoned polyester shirt, shaggy hair, and enormous mutton chops. The former display was probably intended to convey the extent of Armation's influence; the latter seemed an ingratiating maneuver, coming as it did in the course of a rambling narrative about how the three of them reminded the man of himself in the bad old days, though they'd come to the meeting cropped and clean-shaven, in their returnable faux suits. Then came the hard sell, as Lipton confirmed, in so many words, what they'd been hearing elsewhere, namely, that in this world of military contract work, there were Primes and there were Subs. The prime contractors, generally the larger companies like Armation, were the gatekeepers, the only ones with access to the handful of military procurement officials, who they somehow managed to guard like prize Holsteins, so that all other firms seeking suck from the gigantic teats of the U.S. Armed Forces had to take it from the Primes by the glass. Security clearance badges, it would later become apparent, were brokered like invites to the Oscars, and it was regularly put into contracts that the Sub was expressly forbidden from ever contacting the Client directly, thus ensuring the Prime's continued dominance.

In retrospect, it seemed pretty obvious to Fred they were being conned, and that he should have retained two or three lawyers to spec the contract instead of just the one; yet even if he'd had a clearer idea how things worked down there, Armation's offer might have seemed like their only move. (And for quite a while, particularly during the first two relatively rosy years of their partnership, he was able to go on fancying himself quite the young entrepreneurial mastermind for making it happen.) The wording in the contract on the ownership of the software code was ambiguous, something he'd mistakenly believed could only work in their favor. He'd thought it would mean that Armation would become ever more reliant on them, when in fact it meant, for all practical purposes, that they were ever more at the larger company's mercy. The old code that was exclusively Urth's—or so the latest VP they came to know in that grim, final, fourth year of the partnership, a bellicose, lobster-skinned man named Gibbon from acquisitions told them—could be duplicated or otherwise replaced within a few costly but not prohibitively so months, and the new code wouldn't be shared, as had been verbally agreed to once upon a time, but would be exclusively Armation's, leaving the Brounians out in the cold with nothing but their old prototype, now years out of date and already beaten to market by Second Life and a slew of other commercial virtual worlds. By the time they thought to worry about being eaten, they were already sliding down their partner's gullet.

The phone rang, magnetizing Sam's hand to the receiver, the receiver to his ear, his other hand yanking down his headset just in time to avoid a collision. From the number of times he said hello, Fred could tell it was yet another conference call, probably a couple Armation guys and at least one HomSec liaison, judging from Sam's hyper-clipped tone and jargonizing. Occasionally when talking alone with him, Fred could still hear traces of the sweet side of the former Sam—vacillating, self-doubting, occasionally grimly humorous; but around the Armation execs and their military- and security-minded clients, Sam was fully one of them, manifesting that paradoxical martial ideal to which they all aspired: the commanding servant, the magisterial cog. He went on in this tone, punching out polite but firm requests for fire and smoke data, sounding more as if he were speaking from an underground bunker in an undisclosed location than from a fifth-floor Tribeca office.

Indeed, the office itself had taken on an increasingly bunker-like feel over the years. It used to have five large windows, but when their backing dried up, and before the Armation money came in, they'd been forced to cut a deal with the landlord, who'd proceeded to wall four of the windows off to create an expanded office space for the hedge fund down the hall—which was rolling in cash and wanted nothing but the cream, win-dowed offices with downtown views to inspire their hedging—leaving Urth, Inc. one small window alcove and a large, dim back area. The remaining window's sunny exposure had eased the pain somewhat, at least until a few months ago when Sam, whose desk happened to be in front of it, had declared the light was making it harder to see movements on his screen and covered the view with posterboard.

Through the meager desk-lamp pools, Fred made his way over to his desk. The newly gore-enhanced battle test was over, though everyone's eyeballs were still abuzz with adrenaline as they murmured into their headsets, conducting their post-game analysis, from which would be compiled lists of debugging and upgrading assignments for the Florida team, so that at the next scheduled runthrough the whole process might be repeated. At one end of the red plush couch (its upholstery a holdover from more carefree days) a blanket and pillow lay in a heap—evidence that someone, probably Sam, had spent the night. Fred nodded to Conrad (who acknowledged him fleetingly with his eyes while saying something into his voice-over IP headset), and Jesse (who, with his glasses filled with monitor light, gave the impression of not seeing him), and a few of the younger, reed-thin versions of Sam, headset-wearing and fuzzily facial-haired (who nodded back warily). They all no doubt knew Fred had gotten the axe. His very presence here was probably making waves of weirdness, guilt, and discomfort for all. He told himself he didn't care, that like some vengeful ghost, he'd go on haunting the office, and with a little luck, all their dreams as well.

Inward bluster notwithstanding, he stopped trying to make eye contact and more or less tiptoed across the room, nearly bumping into a new workstation, the little office's tenth, that had been plunked down in his weeklong absence, along with a twentysomething kid with a mop of curly hair and a face too pink and fresh for the surroundings. Fred wondered if all of them, even this new recruit he vaguely remembered signing off on, had consented without so much as a grumble to be packed up and shipped off to Orlando along with the hardware.

To make room for the new kid, George's former desk, long since pressed back into service, had continued its glacial migration from his old corner toward the art department; and Fred's six-foot-long, six-foot-high blue vintage 1993 Cray Y-MP supercomputer had been pushed, by some almost unthinkable group effort which had left a trail of gouge-lines across the hardwood floor, four feet farther into his own workspace. There were only about twenty inches of air now between the Cray and his desk, requiring Fred to climb over the arm of his chair and then slide himself at various counterintuitive angles down to a seated position. As a jokey birthday gift for Fred, for little more than shipping costs, George had bought the Cray off eBay, where he'd found it being auctioned by a fashion-trend-forecasting firm that had finally gone belly-up in the summer of '00. He'd kept hinting to Fred at the size of the gift, leading him to think it was a car, or even a boat. When it had arrived, in parts, in a series of wooden crates wheeled off the freight elevator, George had stuck a ribbon onto the nearest one, patted Fred on the shoulder, wished him luck, and gone home to celebrate his own birthday with his wife. It had taken Fred and George a week of late nights to assemble it. To at least attempt to simulate typical mainframe clean- and cold-room conditions, they'd duct-taped a pleated air filter over its intake vent, then duct-taped a floor fan to the filter. Once they'd done all this, however, they couldn't find any real use for the thing. They'd programmed it to speak in tongues through a voice synthesizer at an office party once; otherwise, it had just sat here, unplugged and collecting dust. Sam wanted it gone, but Fred couldn't bring himself to part with it, for sentimental reasons, though, too, the thing now seemed to be his last remaining business asset. Its new location, he understood, was a not-so-subtle escalation of Sam's ultimatum to use it or lose it.

At least the blue metal wall at his back afforded him a bit more privacy, made it easier for him to pretend he was hard at work, preparing to shuck and jive for his job. He laid his arms on his desk, his head on his arms, and tried to engage in a kind of self-help exercise, or maybe just outright fantasy, he'd invented for himself, in which he took on the hazy, barely imaginable persona of some future self well out of all these problems—a self for whom everything had, somehow, worked out happily—and regaled some equally vague group of future listeners with the story of his travails. They could be friends, acquaintances, even total strangers, these future listeners, at a party or a bar or any other likely place. *And there I was*, his calmly smiling future self would say, *so panicked about this Florida thing, so exhausted from those sleepless nights, so fried from all that helmet nonsense . . .*

And that was as far as he got before his mind started browning out and he was seeing the old woman's hair whorls starting to spin, feeling himself and all of Broadway starting to warp and whip around her, seeing the spinning box with the little birthday girl inside, seeing the girl through the walls in the flashlight's glow, her eyes like discs, the toucan cradled in her pink-sleeved arm. Then it was himself in there, or somewhere, without a flashlight, spinning in the dark.

A ping from his computer pulled him awake. He looked at the screen, his head still on his arms.

A message in his inbox. From the semi-secret industry listserv:

Subject: NUKIN' ODDS
From: MECSERV

Fellow MEC-AAns:

See link below for current NUKETHREAT odds. FRESH INTEL from CIA OPERATIVE EXCALIBUR'S TURKMENI SOURCES has handicappers upgrading NYC, what with the upcoming 5th anniversary (and that's wood, a coffin . . . er . . . *box* full of dreams, for all you thoughtful gift-givers!) to FRONTRUNNER STATUS at 3:2!

D.C., L.A., Chicago, 2nd, 3rd, 4th, respectively.

Want a longshot? Try your luck with KANSAS CITY—35:1!

Be Ye Fruitful & Multiply in the

```
        *formidable*

              *forgettable*

*untar-get-able*

        *stealthurb*
of MEC-AA!

CORPORAL PUNISHMENT
```

Excalibur. All the CIA operatives went by fantasy names like this. Dragonfire, Captain America, Pegasus, Beowulf. Yet one more piece of corroborating evidence, if any more were required, that the whole national defense complex—from the remaining Bush-Cheney Vulcans for the historical moment still suction-padded to their posts, all the way down to Corporal Punishment grinning from some Orlando cubicle or basement rec room in the surrounding Military-Entertainment Complex Accommodation Area—couldn't get a date in high school.

He hit Delete. Bringing the previous message into view:

Subject: Help, Avatara!
From: Ceorge Brounian

Idly, head still on his arm, he began mousing and clicking over the empty message pane, the closest he could get to feeling the space with his fingertips. Something appeared:

It looked like someone giving him the finger. That or redacted text. He sat up and kept playing with the mouse. The bars disappeared, smaller rectangles blinking in and out. He was highlighting words, words that seemed written in invisible ink.

He opened the text-color panel. Sure enough, the text was white. He switched it to black:

```
Cut off last time. Must kp messgs short.
Lookng fr a more stable & secure channel.
Time measrd in kalpas hre (4.32B yrs.) fr crissakes.
Who knows when we mght spk agin . . .
```

He read over it a few times, mystified. He brought up the first message and performed the same procedure:

```
Cloudbanks cloudwalled. Aethernet unhackable.
This limbo is dull dull dull.
```

Shock gave way to something darker. If nothing else was clear to him, he at least knew now that it was a prank, aimed at him, with full knowledge of George's condition. What else could that dull limbo be but a reference to George's coma? In which case, what? Was this some kind of campaign to guilt him into euthanizing his twin?

And again, who could be behind it?

Anyone, he realized. Any one of the hundreds of programmers he knew.

He climbed on his chair and snuck a look over the top of the supercomputer around the office, trying to catch someone sneaking a look his way. Nobody was. The post-combat discussion was over, and the dozen employees had all gone back to work, leaned into their screens.

Sitting back down, Fred arranged the two messages side by side, looking from one to the other. He hit Reply to the second, typed what/ who the fuck? and hit Send. He waited a minute, another. Nothing came back.

Who knows when we mght spk agin?

For the first time, he noticed the date and time stamp in the upper right corners of the messages:

Sent: Tue 8/22/2006 5:00 PM

The two stamps were identical, as though they'd both gone out at the same minute. And the time they indicated was neither ten days ago nor two hours ago, but six days, twenty-three hours, and fifty-five minutes in the future.

A light is on, and Fred's lids are cracked just enough to foggily make out blond hair, the swell of a breast beneath the sheet: Melanie, her head and shoulders propped on pillows against the headboard, reading one of those ad-thick, perfume-scented magazines of hers. He can't move, his body still asleep. Arms pinned beneath his weight. Nose buried in the pillow—he can barely breathe, is barely breathing, might suffocate. If he could only move a finger, then maybe the finger could move the hand, the hand the arm, and he could get this pillow away from his nose. Marshalling his will, he thinks he's succeeding, that his hand is moving, only to realize he's been dreaming the progress. If the dream pulls him under he might never get back, might fade to black and never even know. He focuses on breathing; if he can keep breathing louder, maybe he can gain control of his vocal cords and make a noise that she'll hear and then wake him. It's exhausting, but finally he's doing it, moans the words *wake me up, wake me up*—he's sure he does, he can feel them vibrating in his throat—but she ignores him. She won't wake him. Why won't she wake him?

From sheer bodily strain, tearing himself awake.

No Mel, just a vaguely Mel-shaped rumple of blanket.

No perfumed magazine, just, on the nightstand under the lamp, a decades-old LED clock radio and his mother's decades-old, used-bookstore copy of *The Power of Positive Thinking*.

No headboard on this fold-out futon replacement for the bunk bed he and George had shared.

No Zeckendorf Tower, or dream version thereof (everything in it, he now recalled, Mel's breast included, had seemed slightly aglow). Just his childhood bedroom, if he could even call it that, the space having been long since converted first to a guest room where no guests ever stayed, and over the last year into a kind of new-age showroom. A massage table lay folded up against the brick wall. A boom box and a small stack of ambient music CDs occupied the top of the dresser. To the closet door were affixed charts of chakras, meridian lines, calligraphic Reiki symbols with their various functions listed beneath—the Cho Ku Rei, to generate Reiki power; the Sei He Ki, to treat emotional pain; the Hon Sha Ze Shô Nen, for healing from long distances; and the Dai Kô Myo, the great illuminating light. The corner shelf by the bed had become a shrine to jade Buddhas, polished stones, a photo of George smiling in a gown and rakishly tilted mortarboard, his arm around the shoulders of Fred in his cracked and tattered motorcycle jacket. On the other shelves, his and George's old books mingled with personal-growth literature, tomes on shiatsu massage, channeling, reflexology.

Fred's own belongings—what few he'd kept from the Zeckendorf—were now stowed, along with George's, in cardboard boxes in the walk-in closet that had formerly doubled as Sam's bedroom. Fred had allowed three dresser drawers to be cleared out on his behalf, but otherwise had insisted no special accommodations be made for him, less out of con- sideration for his parents than for his own sanity; he wanted no signs of this arrangement being anything but temporary.

Out in the living room, he could hear the TV, one of those opinion- ating blowhard shows Mel was now producing. He glanced again at the clock. Just after eleven. Still the whole night to get through. His dreams, which these last few months had been all about being locked in some- place or otherwise going nowhere (running lost through endless corri- dors, lying pinned by phantom weights), were always the most disturbing and paralyzing here in this bedroom. Rather than come home from the office, he wished he'd just gone to the hospital for the night—some- times he could snatch a little paralysis-free sleep in the lobby's chairs; though recently, the security guards had begun giving him the homeless treatment, rousing him whenever he closed his eyes. And anyhow, with the Reiki group over there, he'd have only felt guilty, fouling their auric fields with his gloomster vibes.

For a seamlessly grafted segment of the dream, he now recalled, she hadn't even been Mel, but Jill. It was bad enough dreaming of his own romantic failures. Now he was dreaming of George's too.

Grabbing his laptop off the floor, for the dozenth time tonight he checked his email. Still nothing. What did those time stamps mean? Was something going to happen next Tuesday at five? What could happen? Should have confronted Sam. Seen if he knew anything, or had any ideas who might be behind it. But Fred had been stopped by anger—at Sam; at the sender, whoever it was; at the fact that he, Fred, was thinking about these asinine messages at all.

He vowed to ignore them, and cast around for something else to occupy him. He needed to make a résumé. His programming skills were obsolesced—computer languages changed by the year, by the month even—but maybe he could find something in project management here in the city and not have to move to Florida. Management positions were increasingly scarce, though; the market was choked with thirtysomething de facto managers and their defunct coding skills. And the salaries on offer would no doubt be considerably lower, and he was strapped as it was to pay George's bills. And even if he could pull himself together enough to come off well in an interview, he doubted many would want the baggage that hiring an ex-CEO refugee from a hostile takeover with a brother in the hospital would bring. He knew *he* wouldn't have hired himself.

His briefcase sat open on the floor, and in it lay the CD that Mira Egghart had made of her visualization exercise, on which she'd written "Week One" in surprisingly playful, loopy purple letters. He was pretty sure he wasn't going back for any more sessions, pretty sure he'd had enough of merging with old women and birthday girls. Knowing his luck, if he kept it up he'd probably merge with a dog and get arrested for crapping on the sidewalk, merge with a window washer and wipe his way off a ledge. He should probably count his blessings the old loon had only shoplifted and hadn't held up a liquor store. And that he hadn't mangled the little girl's fingers when he'd slammed the door of the box, or made her sick by over-spinning it, hellbent on outrunning the impossible, unspeakable joy she'd opened up in him.

As for merging with one's experimenter, he was more than pretty sure that this was the worst idea of all. Every time that vertiginous moment in her office, when Mira Egghart had seemed closer to him than his own skin, replayed itself in his mind, he had to force himself to remember that it wasn't real, that it was just a helmet-induced brain glitch. He reminded himself of her endless typing, her clinically scrubbed nods. And the way she'd dropped that bombshell of a scientific explanation and then asked—mockingly, he was almost sure of it now—if that had answered his question. And that mythical tapestry of reason and faith she'd spoken of. Could such a thing ever be? Could he even know for sure this was what the study was actually about?

No, he told himself. He'd be an idiot to go back.

Even so, he couldn't see much harm in continuing to listen to her CD. He found it calming. He didn't know why, exactly. Indeed, the little story she told—of a whole city coming unmoored and floating off—made him uneasy if he thought too hard about it afterward, though her half-hoarse, half-whispery voice close in his ear softened the edges. And any new stratagem to help get him through these nights was welcome.

But he didn't want to listen to it until his parents were asleep, the chances of disruption minimized, which wouldn't be for a while now.

Instead, he let his eyes fall shut again, risking paralysis for the chance of finding that old bed, of waking up in it to a sun over a skyline, and Mel's golden hair and skin and radiant heat like the sun itself rolling atop him. Though this time, all that came to mind when he tried to picture that swell of a breast were the faint freckles he'd never quite seen before, late one night toward the end, limelighted by the pulse of a charging laptop on the nightstand as she lay waiting for him in the dark. He'd reached across the bed, his hand cupping the mass, cushiony at the surface, cottage-cheesy beneath. Then, with the pads of three fingers, beginning to lightly prod counterclockwise, as the pamphlet in the oncology waiting room recommended, in a narrowing spiral around the nipple . . .

Her voice rippling with dread: "Are you giving me a—"

. . . before darting off like a jellyfish in the murk.

A soft knock at the door.

"Fred? Can I check my email?"

He sat up, leaning his back against the wall. "Sure, Mom."

She peeked in, the reading glasses she'd been using more lately low on her nose. "I'm not waking you, am I?"

"No worries there."

Taking a seat at the computer table, she regarded him with a quiet, searching wonder, as if he were some famous work of art she'd been hearing about all her life but had never until now seen. She gave him that look a lot, these days. Maybe it came from gazing at George's sleeping, unrevealing face, day after day.

"Vart said the show went well," she offered.

"He said that?"

She glanced at the ceiling. "His actual words were, 'Everyone survived.'"

"Now that I'm a convicted felon, I suppose that's a concern."

"I didn't realize shoplifting was a felony these days."

"It's a class-A misdemeanor."

The maximum punishment, Fred was startled to learn in his online research, was a year in prison. Which would certainly solve his housing situation. The most likely outcome, though, was something called an "adjournment in contemplation of dismissal," which meant that if he could steer clear of criminal activity for six months, the charges would be dropped.

"And I guess I'm not convicted yet," he went on, "if you want to get technical. But 'alleged misdemeanorer' doesn't got the same ring to it, you know?"

"Oh, it sounds a lot better to me."

She'd looked worried, though not overly so, when Vartan had brought him home from the police station the night before. Her smile was sorrowful, but there was a trust in it too, a faith in him, which, like her faith in everything else lately, seemed to him quite possibly unmerited.

"There's probably a reason it happened you can't see yet," she said. "Maybe you'll need those tweezers for something down the road."

Briefly, he envisioned himself killing a terrorist, a very cooperative one, with a well-aimed tweezer-slam to the eyeball. He didn't bother informing her they hadn't even let him keep the lousy thing.

"So how'd the, um . . . session go?" he asked, while they were on the subject of her magical thinking.

"It went well," she said softly, "really well."

He waited for some indication of what this meant. Had there been any change? Had George moved or something? Cracked an eyelid?

"Oh yeah?" Fred prompted, the enthusiasm too thin, the challenge beneath too plain. He could read the pained calculation in her eyes, and was sure she could read it in his—he readying himself, out of a sense of duty to her, to stand in her path; she, out of a sense of duty to George, and to that strange new path itself, stepping swiftly around Fred.

Her smile broadened. "Oh, and on the subway ride home, *Guy* told us all about his trip to South Africa. He was studying with a *sangoma*, a Zulu shaman. They initiated him by bathing him in the blood of a goat." With her head tilted up to keep the glasses on her nose, the reading lenses now magnified her eyes. Her face shone with a kind of creeped-out amazement. "*Guy* actually drank the blood, too, and did this ritual dance, and went into a trance. Then he was possessed by a Zulu ancestor."

Fred had to admire her deftness in changing the subject. *Guy*—pronounced by Holly, and presumably by *Guy* himself, the French way—lived on the next block, with his wife, Dot. Dot was a graphic designer, Fred thought he remembered his mom telling him; as for *Guy*, Fred didn't recall her mentioning an occupation other than the energy work. Fred had once run into him and Holly on the sidewalk. *Guy* looked to be around his age, wore a ponytail, might have been an inch or two taller than him, or maybe just had better posture. If *Guy* had any trace of a French accent, Fred hadn't been able to detect it.

"Is that so," he said. He wondered if she was thinking what he was thinking, namely that if it were George sitting here with her instead of him, George would have been keen to hear about *Guy's* adventures. Were it Fred now in that coma, she and George could have stood over him in that hospital room doing their mumbo jumbo together, along with this goat-blood-quaffing Frenchman, whose name she uttered with the kind of unself-conscious enthusiasm, Fred couldn't help but feel, that a mother might exhibit for a son.

"They were hiding a wooden idol, and *Guy* had to find it," she said. "The ancestor made him speak in tongues and do flips. Then he ran into a hut and found the idol. He said he went right to it!"

"That's . . . one hell of a tourist attraction."

"In the graduation ceremony, he had to wear its gallbladder in his hair." She laughed. "He showed it to us. The sacrificed goat's gallbladder. He still has it."

"He should have it taxidermied. Mount it over the mantel."

"He's going to have it made into a necklace."

"Even better."

Her look joined in the humor, almost complicit in the absurdity, except Fred got the distinct feeling that there was a larger absurdity she was seeing, an absurdity he himself was a part of.

He held up *The Power of Positive Thinking*, hoping to get a few points for trying. "So how is this book, anyway?"

"It's really good. I thought you'd been reading it. You've had it out on the table there for two weeks."

"No. Not yet." He'd taken that particular one down from the shelf on the day he'd applied for the helmet study, in the hope that just having it in plain view would inspire him. It hadn't occurred to him to actually read it—he'd assumed the title said it all. That gambit not quite having worked, he picked up a sliced-open, apple-sized stone with a sparkling black interior that had been sitting on the alarm clock. "This is a nice one."

"It's from a vortex."

"A vortex?"

"There are a bunch of them around Sedona, Arizona. They say the energy there is so powerful it twists the juniper trees. They say you can feel it swirling up out of the ground."

"Sure." He turned the stone over, hunting for a price tag. "Why wouldn't they?"

Her smile forgave him. Even so, she looked suddenly tired.

"You probably need to sleep," she said. "I won't be too long."

She turned toward the computer, waiting in silence for it to wake up. The happy glow had faded from her face, replaced by the monitor's pallid illumination. The miracle worker was gone and she was just his mother again, a small sixty-two-year-old woman with expressive eyes and faintly trembling fingers—an as yet mild case of a medical condition called essential tremor—hovering over the keys. He clutched the vortex rock, wanting to bash his skull open with it, out of guilt, out of anger, out of guilt about the anger. Why should he begrudge her any equanimity she could lay hold of under the circumstances? Yet it baffled him how she could spend an evening with George and come home looking like she'd been to a spa, like it was he who was healing her. For a couple weeks after George had broken the news to her just over a year ago, they'd worried she might not even survive the shock. Her tremors had grown so severe she could barely bring a fork to her mouth, could only drink through a straw. Her mind couldn't track a conversation for more than a minute, and then she'd need to go lie down. At that point, the Reiki had just been one more hobby among others—journaling, dance classes, guitar lessons—her perennial, never-quite-fruitful attempt to find her purpose on Earth. But with George's illness to motivate her, she soon went back and immersed herself in the training as never before, becoming what they called a Reiki master. And then one day, her eyes closed, her faith-healing hands held out over George, she'd had a vision, a mental image so real she'd taken it for prophecy, of George opening his eyes, right there in his hospital bed, and smiling at her.

Somehow, probably through the nurses, word of George's continued survival had spread, and she now had patients all over the hospital asking for her help. She spent part of her time there these days making the rounds, beaming her energies to all and sundry. What did they feel, or imagine they felt, all those desperate people? Fred clenched the vortex rock tighter still. When it began to hurt, he released his grip and gazed at the indentations it had formed in his palm.

"How do you turn this thing on, anyway?"

Holly stopped typing and looked. He gave the rock a shake.

"It's on already," she said.

"What does it feel like, this energy stuff?"

She considered. "It's different at different times. And different people feel it in different ways."

"So how do you know it's the same thing you're all talking about? How do you know it's real at all?"

His voice had risen. He regretted this, as well as the accusation in his tone. But she didn't seem to mind.

"Yeah. Sometimes we all sit around and ask ourselves if we're crazy." She thought, then added quietly, "But it is real. The more you do it, the more you know it." Once more, she fixed on him that searching, appraising gaze. "You should come next week. We could give you an attunement, and you could see for yourself."

An attunement. The term sounded comfortingly technical, as if they might simply replace a couple misfiring spark plugs and set him running good as new. He thought of Mira's question, so value-neutral, nonjudg-mental—why *hadn't* he tried it?

"George's energy was so strong tonight," his mother said, a near whisper. "All of us felt it."

"You did?"

She nodded. "Above his crown chakra, especially. And his throat chakra, too. I felt like he was getting ready."

Part of Fred wanted to fall into her arms and cry. Part of him wanted to scream and shake her until she snapped out of it.

"Getting ready?" he asked.

"To come back to his body." She smiled, her weary face luminous. "And *speak*."

Five

    ... Just relax. Nothing to do now. Nothing to worry about. Nothing even to think about. For these next few minutes, just be free, as free and relaxed as you know you can be. As I count down from five to one, you may notice a feeling of deepening relaxation with each number, and with every word I say. And at the count of

four

                    without trying to change it, just focus on the gentle motion of your breath, flowing in and out. With four, you may notice your breath becoming slow and relaxed, and the rest of you also becoming slow and relaxed. Just imagine your breath seeping into every cell of your body as you breathe in, and seeping out as you breathe out: your whole body relaxing with every breath. So that when

    three

             comes, when three is here, and it is here, you may have already become aware of how heavy your arms and legs have gotten. A heavy, drowsy, comfortable feeling in your arms and legs, so that the more you focus on your arms, your legs, the more relaxed they are, and it's getting to the point where you can't even lift them, they're so heavy now. Go ahead and see for yourself how heavy they are. It's funny, isn't it, how easy it is to relax? And you can just let go now, even deeper, at the count of

    two

          and notice this warm, drowsy heaviness spreading through you. Outward from your heart in rippling, relaxing waves. Rippling through the muscles of your back and abdomen, through your internal organs. Down through your hips and legs and feet and out through your toes. Out through your shoulders and arms and hands and fingertips. And up, in a great, warm wave, through your neck. Maybe you're already thinking about how it will feel when it washes up into your head. Go ahead and let it, feel it ripple over your face, relaxing every little muscle—around your mouth, around your eyes, all the muscles of your scalp. Now let it seep deep into your brain. . . .

one

So deeply relaxed. Your mind too heavy for words. Let the words disappear. Only pictures, now. I want you to picture the city, late at night. No cars, no people, no noise. Just you, out on a quiet street. It could be any street you want, Broadway, or any one of the avenues, whatever you like. It's just you there, you and a chair, a comfortable recliner, in the middle of the sidewalk. You're comfortable and reclined, and looking up, you can see the buildings like tall cliffs reaching into the night sky, the long, dark canyon of them stretching in both directions.

There, look. A little white balloon, rising past the windows and up into the blackness.

And there, a sheet of newsprint rising up, caught in a breeze.

And one of those outdated, pink "While You Were Out" memos slips floating out an open window.

And it's not just the breeze, is it? Because here come other things drifting out the windows. Here come chairs, and desks, and copiers, and bulletin boards, all as weightless as that first helium balloon. Here come phones and keyboards and monitors, twirling slowly by the wires that join them all together. Here come pens and pencils, and the windowpanes too, the millions of them, rising into a long, sparkling cloud, like a second Milky Way. Here come the filing cabinets floating out, and drawers from the cabinets, and papers from the drawers. There goes a city bus, its wheels still slowly turning as it passes through the cloud of papers. The whole city is rising, dancing free in the sky, and the freer it is, the more peaceful you can feel. Out come the bricks, now, joining the dance, streams of them pouring steadily upward. And the shelves from the stores. And the items from the shelves—jackets and sneakers, vitamins and magazines—falling away from you, falling slowly up.

Maybe you're wondering: where are they going, all those pieces of the city?

Just think of it as a break, for now, a vacation. Just let all those things take their well-deserved rest, let them float and twinkle and rise. Just picture their freedom, from here in your chair, watching your city up in the air . . .

august 2006

S	M	T	W	T	F	S
30	31	1	2	3	4	5
6	7	8	9	10	11	12
13	14	15	16	17	18	19
20						

The red bulb.

The control room window, black shade drawn.

The black perforations in the white ceiling tiles, a night sky in reverse.

The glossy galaxy, masking-taped to the tiles, creased from former folds. Must have come in a magazine.

No expansion. Maybe it wouldn't happen today. He should probably be relieved if it didn't, Fred told himself, but he knew he'd be disappointed. The spontaneous outbreaks of oneness had for the most part ended with the birthday girl, a day after the last session. For a day or two after that, he thought he sensed an episode coming on again a few times, but none did, and when they didn't, he began to miss them. He wandered around the hospital, through the coma ward and its sleepers minded by nurses and machines, through the various other wards, getting out wherever the elevator doors happened to open, through Radiology, Endoscopy, Rehabilitative Services, trying to join with them, merge all those disparate pieces of suffering with his own, fit them all together like a puzzle to see what the whole picture meant or was any good for. And he sat by George, of course, trying to expand and contain him, but here the effort felt fruitless in a different way: expansion wasn't the right tool. George was already a part of him. But a no-longer-knowable part. Fred felt like the neurology patient he saw surrounded by doctors and residents the other day, a guy who could only sense one half of his body, the other hanging limp.

Fred wandered through Neurology more than once, the possibility of running into Mira in the back of his mind. He wanted to meet her on level ground, as it were, not as a test subject looking helplessly up at her from this or that recliner. He wanted to challenge her about this "faith without ignorance." From her conviction, it had seemed like something personal, something she herself had come to possess. He wanted to know how, how she'd managed it, with all that scientific reason so evidently crammed into her brain.

And he wouldn't have minded chewing her out about his arrest.

And seeing if he could make her smile again, too, just to reassure himself that the moment of impossible connection he'd felt with her after the last smile had been nothing more than a neuronal misfire.

But he hadn't run into her, nor had he really expected to; he was pretty sure both she and the other guy, the older man behind the glass, were academics, with no reason to be in the hospital other than to post the occasional flyer and stock their experiments with desperate fish like him.

For all his and Mira's imagined conversating, in any event, when she'd sat him down in the chair ten minutes ago, they'd barely managed hellos.

"How are you?" she'd asked, in a clipped sort of way, unbuttoning his shirt.

"OK," he'd said, not knowing whether the question was clinical or friendly or just the usual formality. "How are you?"

She hadn't answered for a moment, maybe considering how such a question from a test subject such as he should be dealt with. It was a hot day for a long-sleeved blouse. He could smell the not unpleasant scent of her sweat, jasmined with deodorant.

"OK," she'd finally hazarded, swirling gel over his heart.

She'd pasted him with electrodes, pressed on the helmet. He'd idly watched the sway of her skirt as she left, then looked over to find the man behind the window giving him a stern look over his reading glasses.

Ten minutes. Maybe twelve. Still no expansion. Maybe a lightheadedness, nothing more. He wondered if his desire for it was getting in the way, if it would only come when not watched for.

He tried to let his mind roam farther afield. He thought about those emails again, for the thousandth time in the last few days. Tomorrow was Tuesday the 22nd, the date on the messages. Would anything happen at 5:00 PM tomorrow, and if so, what? Another message? Or something else? In his efforts to figure out what avataras might have to do with George, with either of them, he'd done some more research over the weekend. Among the prominent avataras in Hindu mythology, one—or rather, two—piqued his interest: a pair of identical twin avataras, Nara and Narayana. According to one site, Nara stood for the human, Narayana for the divine. Other sites told the story of Nara and Narayana doing battle with a power-seeking demigod named Sahasra Kavacha, so named because he was born protected by a thousand *kavachas*, or coats of armor. In order for just a single one of those coats to be broken, the attacker would have to fight him for a thousand years, and the moment it shattered, the attacker would die. The attacker's only means of cheating death was to do penance for a thousand years. Since Nara and Narayana were twins—one-in-two—they were uniquely qualified to perform both of these feats at once. Nara attacked while Narayana prayed, and when, after a millennium, Nara broke a kavacha and died, Narayana's long penance earned him the boon of getting Nara's life back, whereupon Narayana would take his turn attacking and Nara would take his penancing, the two of them spelling each other down through the millennia. According to one site, they succeeded in killing Sahasra Kavacha; according to another, Sahasra Kavacha fled with his last coat of armor intact but a new era was ushered in regardless. There was a general concurrence that the kavachas, the coats of armor, symbolized layers of delusion.

Was any of this a reference to him and George? They'd always rejected the idea of twins being one-in-two, deriding those who would tell one of them something and expect the other to know it later, or befriend one of them and talk to the other in a familiar tone. In plenty of circumstances, they reacted in opposite ways. On a spontaneous dead-of-winter camping trip, upon finding a steep mountain trail covered with ice, George had insisted on clambering up it on all fours, while Fred had driven to the next level and waited for hours, wondering all the while if he'd be better off waiting at the bottom for George to slip and tumble back down. In similar fashion, a few years later, while Fred had gone up to the office roof to watch the smoking towers with an old Walkman radio and an all-but-useless cell phone (and while Sam, fearing looting riots, sarin gas, and all-out war, was busy making repeated trips from the office to the local deli in a filter mask, buying up all the canned goods they'd sell him), George, unbeknownst to him and Sam, was marching from his Battery Park apartment straight into the coming cataclysm.

Over the ensuing years, a programmer's joke began circulating around the office, renewed with each stunt of his—anything from a snide comment at an Armation exec's expense to an all-night New Year's bender ending in a swan dive from a first-story window ledge into the hood of a parked car—that George did shit like this because he knew he had a backup copy. The joke succeeded in tweaking both of them in different ways—George because it explained away his flair for living, Fred because it explained away his living at all—but at bottom it annoyed them for the same reason jokes like this always did, reprising that old one-in-two fallacy. They weren't the same person. This was obviously true. But when George became ill, when even then he kept up that distance from Fred he'd been cultivating since the deal with Armation had begun to sour, the other side of that truth waylaid Fred—that they weren't entirely two different people either. As they sat side by side waiting for George's CT scan, Fred joggling his left foot, George his right, about to determine whether or not the chemo and radiation were working, Fred understood his individuality to be no more than a variety of hologram, one still in a stereoscopic image of which George was the other. Fred was Fred because George was George. In no other light did Fred's own existence make sense. Inclining his head toward George's, that long afternoon, Fred muttered that at least if the treatments hadn't worked George would have a backup copy. It was a joke, a playful mockery, meant to lighten things up; but Fred also hoped it might reconnect them, might signal the extent to which he shared George's plight at the same time he was eluding it.

"It's like you'll be living on," Fred offered, doing his used-car-salesman impression, a smarmy smile, a brushstroke of fingers in the sterile air.

George matched his gesture with the opposite hand. Fred knew without looking that George was matching his smile as well.

"It's like you'll be dead," George replied, every bit as brightly.

Mind drifting now, drowsy from weeks of nights of half sleep. Still trying to will the walls of himself to open up, to expand and contain the bulb, tiles, shelves, poster, to be all things, space itself. Straining to keep his eyes open, no longer quite sure what it is they're taking in.

There's a pattern to the stars in the galaxy poster, not just one swirl but thousands, an intricate weave, swirls within swirls in all directions. It's so clear to him now he can barely believe no one's spotted it before. He'll publish his findings to the world, to personal acclaim, universal joy, the end of all wars. George was right, after all. Things aren't what they seem. This can't possibly be anything but proof of divine order.

Then Fred's awake again, or so it seems. Only, the poster has grown, the stars so close he's almost flush up against the paper.

He's afraid: fear comes in ripples, emanating from his center. He can feel nothing but these ripples, he realizes, neither the chair beneath him nor the helmet on his head, nor his head itself.

He can turn, and despite his fear, he does so, slowly in space, to see the room below:

The steel cart.

The reclined black chair.

The reclined body in the chair. Checkered shoes splayed. Eyes shut.

For a second he thinks it's George, never having seen himself from the outside. But there he is. That crazy gold helmet on his head.

A change in the light draws his attention to the control room window. Mira raises the shade, painting herself and the oldish, sleek-haired man into existence with a single, upward stroke. They're standing side by side, bathed in pale-blue monitor light, peering through the glass. For a confused interval, Fred's still above them, but then, as though a stopper has been plucked from a drain, he's plunged back down, stuffed into too many sensations at once. A dry tongue, a drier mouth. A pulsating scalp, too hot, too tight. Eyeballs sliding beneath a warmish gauze of some kind . . .

. . . *eyelids.*

He can't seem to open them any more than the millimeter they already are, though this is enough for him to make out Mira and the man again, gazing down at him, their expressions slack, their eyes misted and lost in the sight of him, like a mother and father awed by the mystery of their sleeping infant. As they watch him, the man puts his arm around Mira, cups her narrow shoulder in his hand.

She lifted off the helmet. Then gave him a closer look.

"Everything OK?"

He thought about answering her. He couldn't quite remember how to do so, through what medium or biophysical process. Then he heard someone very close to him murmur an assent. The voice was his own, or a rough approximation. He swallowed painfully around the dryness in his throat.

"Do you feel like you can get up?" she asked.

Again, he contemplated the mechanics. He began lifting his arms and legs, but recoiled at the feel of all those muscles slithering around his skeleton, electric eels in a coral bed.

"Do you need a while to get your bearings?"

Her voice was perhaps even a little more hoarse than last week. It didn't rise, though the concern in her eyes made him aware of the fear that must have been in his own. He felt that fear directly now, feeding back on itself, folding into panic. Trapped in this snakebed of a body. The air only accessible through narrow tubes of skin. For his sake more than hers—to convince himself that, unlike in his nightmares, he could at least move this fleshly carapace—he nodded.

"Just relax. I'll come back in a few minutes."

Her hand hovered, tentative, over his shoulder. For a second, she rested two fingertips there. Then turned and left.

No one here but a body in a chair.

Fred in a body.

A nauseated one, flinching from its own feel. The only spot of comfort was the lingering impression of her fingertips through the fabric of his shirt, a reminder of the good side of having skin. He cultivated that square-inch patch, tilled and tended it into a full-body embrace. Imagined her sitting down sideways on his lap. Wedging her arms between him and the chair. Pressing her palms to his back. Her breasts to his ribcage. Her cheek to the side of his neck. He started to feel normal. The fear subsided.

He tried to get up again, successfully this time, locating his feet and rising to balance above them. Walking wasn't hard: a regular oscillation, which, once begun, took care of itself. In the hallway, he found the control room door open and the Roman-haired guy in his seat, taking Fred's measure over the flat horizons of his glasses. The man's look was neither amiable nor disdainful, just penetrating. The brown of his eyes, from this closer perspective, looked as if it had seeped slightly, like a dye, into the surrounding whites. For a moment, Fred thought the guy was going to say something, but then those dyed eyes wandered back to his computer.

Continuing down the hall, Fred found Mira in her office, sitting in profile, an elbow on her desk, those same two fingers propping her head at the temple, stretching the skin at the edge of her eyebrow. Her eyes were closed.

"Made it on my own," he announced.

She started, nearly knocked her takeout coffee onto her laptop. He lowered himself into the blue recliner, and she put the computer on her lap and swiveled to face him. Her game face on now. Focus. Professional-grade compassion.

"So, how did it go?" she asked.

"It was . . . different from last time," he said, locked more on the act of speaking than what he was saying.

She waited.

"I went completely out of my body this time." The fact only really sunk in then. "Jesus. I had an out-of-body experience."

Her lips twitched, almost imperceptibly. Then she caught herself, modulating into a calm nod. "Please describe it for me. Tell me in as much detail as you can."

She was eager at the news, it seemed, but not quite surprised. He was about to ask why when the obvious struck.

"You did something new to me. Didn't you?"

"We can discuss that. But first, why don't you tell me about it?"

He stared at her. "I was up at the top of the room. I saw myself down there."

She typed. Nodded. Typed some more.

"How . . ." he burst out. "How could you possibly make that happen?"

"If you could, Fred"—she sounded impatient—"I'd like you to—"

"Please. Just tell me."

She was clearly flustered. He could see he was disrupting her protocol. After a moment, though, she seemed to decide it wasn't worth the fight. She closed her laptop, leaving it balanced on her thighs.

"All right. There's a small region of your brain called the angular gyrus. Right about here."

She turned to display the side of her head and pointed just behind the upper part of her ear, where her hair flowed around and down toward a dark metal barrette.

"Like the parietal lobes, which I told you about last week, the angular gyrus also plays a role in helping you perceive your own body. If you remember, the parietal lobes may help mark the borders of where we end and the outer world begins. But the angular gyrus appears to be what allows us to perceive our bodies as our own in the first place."

She'd gotten over her momentary annoyance, her face animated now. It struck him that the times she lectured him about the science—angling her head this way and that, moving her hands around like semaphore flags, unleashing torrents of jargon—were, oddly enough, the times she seemed to him at her most natural and unguarded.

"The fact that our bodies are ours seems pretty obvious to us," she went on, spreading her hands, "but it's actually a pretty complex operation, neurologically speaking, requiring a lot of sensory-data analysis and mental mapping. When the angular gyrus misfires, we still have a sense that there's a body present, but we don't feel like it's ours anymore. It just doesn't feel like any part of us. The result can be a free-floating sensation, or even a sensation of being outside of our own bodies."

"OK. But . . ." He shook his head. "*I saw my own face.*"

"Yes, it's strange." She took a moment to nod in sympathy. "And even if there is a neurological explanation—"

"Which is?"

She hesitated. Then relented, sparing him the psychobabble. "Your brain spends a lot of its energy building models of the world around you. To do this, it relies in part on the data from your senses and in part on your imagination to fill in the blanks. You can tell the difference between me speaking to you now and a daydream because your brain has evolved another function that acts as a reality flag, which it plants in whichever of the competing scenes at the moment is most vividly sensed. You have more data coming in from this room than from your daydream, and so your brain decides that the room is the thing that's real at this moment."

As she said this, bracketing the air around her face with her hands, he had one of those eerie moments of doubt, wondering if he weren't in fact dreaming all of this—up in the air, down here in the chair, no difference.

"The way this function seems to work is that *something* always has to be real," she was saying. "So when there's a lack of sensory data to determine the reality of the moment, the imagination is called on more to fill in the blanks. When you dream, and you're cut off from most of your sensory data, your imagination goes into overdrive, and since they're the only game in town, your brain marks those imaginings as real. You could sense your body and face, but since your angular gyrus was jammed, so to speak, you felt they didn't belong to you. Since the room was dark, and the feelings were unfamiliar, your imagination did its best to construct a coherent model of reality."

She sat back.

"It's a lot to take in, I know," she said.

"I saw you, too. Down there," he said.

"Did you?" She cocked her head, interested in a study-related sort of way. Re-opened her laptop. The typing again.

"You and that other guy, behind the glass, watching me."

The typing ceased. Something changed in her look. He could see her trying to hide it.

"Did he put his arm around you?" Fred asked. He mimicked the motion, putting an arm out, cupping the air. "Like this?"

Her eyes, probably his too, went a bit round.

She narrowed hers. "Let's take this more slowly, from beginning to end. Tell me everything you saw."

"I don't know. There isn't much more. Most of the time I was just sitting in the chair, daydreaming. Then I was up there. You raised the shade. He put his arm around you. A split second later, I was back down . . . back inside . . . seeing you from that angle."

She smiled faintly, blinked for an extended moment, self-reproachful.

"OK," he surmised, already bitter. "So you're thinking that my eyes really opened when you raised the shade. And it just took a few seconds for my brain to figure it out."

"Fred," she said softly. "Why does it matter so much to you what I'm thinking?" Her look probed. "What are you thinking?"

It sounded like doubletalk. At the same time, it was a fair question. What *was* he thinking? There was nothing the experience could have been but some kind of hallucination. He knew that, didn't he? They'd induced it with an electromagnet, for God's sake, just like last week. Yet even more than last week, he was crestfallen. The freedom, the sense of release, had been even greater this time. All he wanted was to be up on that helmet room ceiling again, unbounded as the air itself, watching from on high as Mira's stockinged legs appeared behind the rising shade, one arm rising with the cord, the other supporting her as she leaned forward over the narrow, cluttered desk. . . .

The white Formica desk . . .

Bathed in the monitor light . . .

"Whose sketch pad was it?"

Mira looked at him askance.

"On the white desk, in the control room," he went on. "The desk I couldn't possibly have seen from chair level. Do you draw, Mira?"

"It's a hobby of . . . Craig's," she said slowly. "Sometimes he sketches things."

"With those flat drawing pencils, right?"

A current shot between them. She swallowed before she spoke.

"What was on the sketchpad, Fred?"

"*What was on it?*"

She looked like she might be holding her breath.

He tried to remember. "I don't know." He shut his eyes. "All I see . . ." He peeked at her. "It was blank. Wasn't it?"

She looked away.

"I'm sorry, Fred," she said tersely. "I didn't mean to give you the feeling I was testing you."

But she had been testing him. And he'd failed.

"But how could I—the sketchpad *was* there."

She still wasn't looking at him, embarrassed, it seemed to him, at her own disappointment.

"You're thinking I could have seen it on the desk at some other time," he said. "Like on my way past the control room from the hallway. Or through the window before I sat down in the chair."

"Yes," she admitted. "That's more or less what I'm thinking. Or part of what I'm thinking."

He tried to recall the minutes preceding the session. He'd followed her down that hallway, noticed a run in her stocking at the back of her left knee. They'd passed the control room door, which was open, wasn't it? Yes, it probably was. Had he seen the sketchbook then? Maybe he had. And he'd stood there afterward in the hall exchanging that look with the man, Craig. The desk had certainly been in view then. Though the sketchbook had been closed by then, hadn't it? But wait, had it been there at all by then? Already, Fred understood it would be impossible to know if the out-of-body experience had been real, that in all probability it hadn't, and that even in the utterly unlikely event that it had, it might as well not have been, for all the good it would do him now.

She leaned forward. "I know this is difficult. But try to put aside the question of whether you were up there in some objective, provable way. Just close your eyes, and tell me how it felt."

He clenched his fists. It seemed a pointless exercise. But there was a strange urgency in her tone, and in her look, and anyway, a part of him longed to sink back into the memory. He let his eyes close, tried to coax the corded muscles in his chest into admitting a full breath. He floated in the dark.

"Like . . . nothing at all," he said. "That one ripple of fear, then nothing."

"I see a smile, I think," she said. "So it was a good nothing?"

"No. Not good."

"No?"

"The best nothing imaginable."

He opened his eyes. She was smiling, too.

Her expression changed, became tinged with concern.

"Now you seem sad," she said. "Why?"

No oneness. Though her smile had been lovely, had made her face so surprisingly soft. He leaned his head back on the chair.

"Coming back down didn't feel so hot," he said.

"What did it feel like?"

His flesh recoiled anew. He wondered how he could communicate it. "Like I'd been squashed." He held out an upturned palm, then brought his other palm down on it with a hard slap. "Splattered like a bug."

Her face changed again, her eyes going unfocused. A reaction beyond empathetic pain. She looked a bit like she was going to be sick.

"Everything all right?" he asked.

She glanced off, blinking.

"Excuse me," she said.

He'd upset her, he thought. "I didn't mean to sound pissed off about it."

"No. You didn't do anything." She cleared a few fallen strands of hair from her face. "Just let me catch up on my note-taking." Eyes retreating, she began to type.

He regretted his ingratitude, suspicion, frustration. She must really want her lunatic contraption to do some good, he decided.

"Late night last night?" he asked.

She looked up. "How did you know?"

"I'm psychic."

A duel of raised eyebrows ensued.

He pointed at the to-go cup on her desk. "That much caffeine this late in the day usually signifies a late night." Inner George counseled him against mentioning the increased hoarseness of her voice, and the slight, glossy shadows under her eyes.

"Who needs sleep, right?" he added, instead. More or less a personal mantra for him these days.

"I get mine in the day, mostly," she said.

"A day sleeper? That I wouldn't have guessed."

She opened her mouth as if to reply, then, with a droll look, checked herself. "Let's keep this focused on you, shall we? Last week, we didn't get to talk about the sleeplessness and nightmares you mentioned on the forms. Has the visualization CD helped you get to sleep at all?"

"A little." It hadn't at all. But it made being awake somewhat more bearable.

"I'm glad. And your dreams?"

Last night, in the hour or two of sleep he'd gotten, he'd dreamt he'd been sealed in the wall of his and George's childhood bedroom. Worse than sealed—merged in it, molecules hopelessly scrambled. He'd been practicing a new magic trick of some kind, an attempt to pass through walls, it must have been. On the wall's other side, from the living room, he could hear Holly and Vartan talking and walking around in there, wondering where he'd gotten to. He related all this to her, not going into the suffocation, the straining, panic, remorse.

"Sounds awful," she said, nevertheless.

"I have a lot of dreams where I can't move."

"Sleep paralysis."

"There's a name for that?"

She nodded.

"Then sometimes I think I've managed to tear myself awake, but it's only into some other dream."

"False awakenings," she said.

"You know a lot about bad dreams."

For a moment, she just looked at him without saying anything.

"Not just bad ones."

She returned to her typing. He closed his eyes and tried to will himself up out of his body. One more impossible desire for the collection.

"Mira," he said, his eyes still closed.

"Yes, Fred?" he heard her say.

"If you keep peeling away the ignorance, do you really believe there'll be any faith to be found underneath?"

He looked, and found her eyes keen on his own.

"I do," she said. "And if you can find it, it will help you learn to be alone. And to feel that you're never alone."

Inwardly, he scrutinized her words, turning them this way and that—*alone, feeling never alone*. Was she talking about a kind of insight, or yet more self-delusion?

She set the laptop on her desk. Then she stood, switched off the lamp beside him, and seconds later appeared in the nightlight below.

"You're lucky, you know," she said.

"Lucky?" His throat ached with constriction. "Why?"

She draped the blanket over him, confiding with a whisper:

"Many of our subjects can't even get off the ground."

Whether or not Fred had actually left his body, he was now more conscious of being encased in it all the same. His lungs and bowels felt like over-squeezed sponges. His head felt clamped in an invisible vise. A faint, electric irritation lingered in his nerve endings. The act of shuffling his feet along the sidewalk, making all those muscles clutch and loosen over and over, while not technically difficult, was more work than it should have been, as though the city had been rolled up, shipped, and unfurled onto the surface of some larger, higher-gravity planet while he'd been under the helmet, imagining he was hovering above it. He kept replaying those split seconds of derangement, hoping for some scrap of proof he might have missed. That galaxy poster had seemed so close he thought he could recall the texture of the paper, like seeing into the subatomic foment of space itself. But he could have imagined this. What about seeing himself in the chair? He couldn't quite recover the details. The attempt itself might have been changing them. Perhaps there had been something a little off about the shading of his face— almost computer-animated, as if he'd been looking down from a tactical view at an avatar of himself. Though that seemingly unreal cast could just have been the dim red light, in which case, it *could* have been real. Or at least realistic.

If not real.

He'd never really believed those accounts he'd read, in the early days of George's coma, of patients who'd awoken to recollect having floated above their bodies, witnessing the operating rooms, the doctors at work, the family members sitting around the bed. He'd never really believed his own daydreams, over the last few months, of George being up there, either. Of George trailing wherever Fred went, like a balloon on a string.

Sharing it all, sights and sounds and mental impressions. As close as they'd been in the best of times—closer, even, now that George was always on call, wafting overhead, free as the summer day.

Sorry you're not real, he told Inner George.

The least of my problems, Inner George assured him.

Feeling drained and needing to sit down, and having time to kill before the magic show he'd have to do with Vartan later in the afternoon, he wandered east to Washington Square Park and found a free section of bench amid the lunching office escapees, summer school students, and sweating but determinedly leather-clad tourists. Sunny and breezy, a merciful eighty-two degrees. Crowds around the defunct fountain, cheering at a street performance. Vendors under the Arch, turnstiling in cash and out pretzels. For a couple years after 9/11, the Arch had been off-limits, caged by a chain-link fence, merely awaiting restoration; though at the time, one had gotten the feeling it was to protect it from terrorists, or perhaps to prevent the Arch itself (what with its Frenchified airs) from committing some treasonous act. But the Arch, a couple years ago now, had gotten its facelift and was looking as young and fresh as the swarming youth around it, and this change had brought Fred a twinge of disappointment. He supposed he preferred dwelling on signs of the city's rot and crumbling infrastructure to acknowledging its renewal, all the ways in which it was actually succeeding in getting younger and hipper and richer right in step with its residents. This latter phenomenon could make him feel doubly cheated out of his former life, make him feel like the attack had been merely a ruse, a mock fainting spell, to win the city sympathy and an allure of vulnerability, to make living here seem not just a luxury but an act of heroism, too, so that all those newly heroical investment bankers and hedge fund managers and trustafarians, and anyone else who had it all could now *really* have it all—the doormen and wraparound terraces and gourmet delis *and* the moral superiority. And who knew, maybe it really could all keep right on perpetuating itself, a city of ever more concentrated riches and hipness and sexiness and youth. Maybe it could all get so bone-meltingly gorgeous that every visiting fanatic with a suitcase bomb would go weak-kneed and start worshiping the bronze bull, that the very rising oceans would peel back in awe. Or maybe, at any rate, it could last to witness its own perfect completion, every last arch and parapet in place, like some afternoon sandcastle, just in time for the end.

Leaf shadows rippling on the paving stones.

A sun-bleached *Daily News* cover page flapping in the breeze:

3½ TEARY STARS
FOR 'WTC'

... and a picture of Nicolas Cage in a fire helmet.

Across the path, a throwback Rastafarian perching on the back of a bench called out to Fred like some mutant human-songbird hybrid.

"Smoke," he chirp-rasped. "Smoke, smoke."

According to *The Power of Positive Thinking*, which Fred had finally read over the weekend, people could realize their desires through a triune process of "picturizing," "prayerizing," and "actualizing," terms every bit as reassuringly technical-sounding as the attunement he'd agreed—in a fit of open-mindedness, filial guilt, desperation, and rash curiosity following his mother's announcement that George's "power" was growing—to receive at the next Reiki meeting. To picturize was to create an image in one's mind of the intended outcome, to see it as clearly and vividly as possible. Overnight in the armchair in his parents' living room, unwilling to return to his bedroom after that dream of being trapped in the wall, he'd spent a sleepless interval trying to overwhelm his entrenchments of doubt with a barrage of arguably not absolutely impossible futures, among them one in which he and George and Sam found themselves standing on a Florida golf course with Lipton and Gibbon, and, sure, why not, the CEO, Dan Gretta, too. Fred had never met the man but he knew what he looked like from that picture in the lobby, so it hadn't been hard to picture him, one arm out around George's shoulders, another around Fred's, his teeth lighting up at some joke George had just made, something about a congressman they'd just bought, perhaps.

A woman in platform sandals walked by, pushing one of those double-wide urban assault strollers Fred had been seeing everywhere.

Down the benches, a guy in thick glasses opened the *Post*, the cover showing the purported killer of a child beauty queen sitting in a first-class cabin:

SNAKE
ON A
PLANE

"Sense, sense," proclaimed the Rasta.

Fred lowered his eyes to the checkered shoes splayed before him, and picturized that when he looked up, he'd see Mira coming down the path, lunch bag in hand, eyes meeting his with not-unhappy surprise. Where else would she go for lunch, on a day like this? It was practically inevitable, no? He prayerized for this one small boon, this really not terribly difficult or overly miraculous event. Of prayerization—step two—the positive-thinking author, Pastor Norman Vincent Peale, had written that you were supposed to invoke the aid of God in plain, unadorned speech, to talk to Him in your head all the time, to go to Him with your problems as you would to an old friend—a powerful old friend—on whose help you knew you could rely. Perhaps if, like Peale, Fred had been the close friend of presidents (apparently the pastor had known both Eisenhower and Nixon, the latter of whom sent Peale to Vietnam to spur the troops on to victory with the aid of positive thinking) the strategy would have worked; but as it was, making giant effigies of the slackers he'd known just wasn't doing it for Fred. The prospect of an even bigger George floating over him, like some doomed dirigible, only increased his anxiety. He settled for imagining God as something in between George and him, a kind of other version of himself—not because he considered himself any more omnipotent than his former coworkers, but because, logically speaking, it just seemed more self-confidence-inducing. Kind of like that scarcely imaginable future self for whom everything had worked out, only more so, and bigger. A divine twin, then, existing on some other plane of reality, or outside of reality altogether. Listening to his every thought. Listening to him dreaming Him up as if from nothing. Listening to him thinking that, come to think of it, he wasn't exactly wowed by how the whole positive-thinking experiment in Vietnam had played out.

"Sense smoke," he heard the Rasta say. "Smoke sense."

Regressing to his usual, not-so-positive thinking, Fred wondered which was more unlikely—George waking up, waking up as something approaching his former self, without too much irreversible brain damage, paralysis, or other physical debility, able to fight off the lymphoma and fight his way through the massive amounts of physical and mental rehabilitation that would most likely be required; or George ever consenting to stand on a golf course with any Gibbon or Lipton or Gretta. In the early days, after George's initial dubiousness about Armation, it had seemed like he might have been getting more sanguine about the partnership. The first phases of the virtual training environment were exclusively about dialogue, negotiation and peacekeeping, enabling soldiers to virtually interact with people playing the parts of villagers, merchants, tribal leaders. George saw humanitarian potential in the technology, how it could bridge cultural divides. Far from a shooter game, he liked to say, they were making a thinker, a feeler. This was how George would describe it in restaurants, at parties. At least until the shooting began.

After that, George took a slight step back in the company, and Fred took one forward, overseeing the design challenges of adapting Urth to its new needs, the move seeming as natural as if he were spelling George at the wheel on a road trip. Sam began stepping up too, on the technical end, he and Fred working more symbiotically together as they raced to meet the endless benchmarks and deadlines. Fred allowed himself to think that, with time, George would grow more involved again. But one night in the weeks leading up to the Iraq War, George called a meeting for the three of them, a sober analog to their founding night out at the bar five years before, this one taking place in an empty diner south of the office. George sat them in a corner and told them he had something to say. He wasn't going to lecture them about the idiocy of the war, he said. He wanted to talk about something way weirder, and scarier: the Military-Entertainment Complex.

"We're using videogames to recruit, to train, even fight," George began. "Our simulations are becoming more realistic and immersive and violent. It's desensitizing people. Not just to violence. But to reality itself."

Fred squeezed his temples. Sam balled his fists on the table. They'd all been working nearly hundred-hour weeks converting satellite maps of likely battlefields to 3-D. They didn't have time for George's philosophizing.

"I know," George said. "You both think I'm nuts. But it's even bigger than that. Things are really changing." He scratched his head, further ruffling his unkempt hair. "Military contractors are building private armies. Media conglomerates are playing both sides against the middle. There are no reporters anymore, only pundits. Shouting their heads off. Everyone's blogging. Forming cells. Arming themselves." He looked from Sam to Fred. "Everyone's decided at once that reality's up for grabs. Everyone's grabbing."

Fred looked out the window, watched a Hummer back into a bicycle chained to a parking meter, crumpling the back wheel in half. Sam picked up his butter knife and fork and began slotting the one through the other, stabbing at his own knuckles. They both knew where this speech was headed.

"It's time to bug out of this partnership," George said, laying his hands on the tabletop. "We need to get back to our core values. I've got an idea for an even better way to realize them. We can keep making a world closer to home than the old Urth, more like the real one. Except players could find a whole other game embedded. A game of spiritual evolution."

George went on, talking about how they needed to steer players toward constructive and nonaggressive behaviors. How rather than amassing and plundering and hoarding their resources, players could be rewarded for giving them away. How players could be compensated with new powers for the ones they were relinquishing. Rewarded with gradually increasing powers of perception. Allowed to see ever newer and brighter layers to the virtual reality. So that, over time, the old material existence would matter less and less. So that at the highest levels, Urth could be revealed as a place of pure energy. Or something like that. George was still working on this part, he confessed, the whole issue of how goodness was to be rewarded.

Sam, by that point, was using his knife and fork to saw his napkin in half. Fred was staring into the Formica, angry and sick. George must have known they'd be dead against dissolving the partnership, that they'd outvote him if it came to that. But he didn't stop. He downed his coffee and delved into the financials, how they could outsource, to India, or Eastern Europe, how full of cheap programming labor the world now was.

"For fuck's sake, George," Fred finally said. "Aren't you just making the same mistake as everyone else? Thinking you can make the world the way you want it? Thinking reality's up for grabs?"

George's look was stupefied, like Fred had just opened his mouth and drooled on the table.

"It *is* up for grabs," George said.

Sweating already in their white polyester, Fred and Vartan hand-trucked the crate full of tricks into the ground-floor entrance of a Gramercy Park townhouse—which looked to be worth so much money Fred was amazed they'd let children inside the place, much less throw a party for them—through a corridor lined with pop art and smelling of varnish, and down some narrow stairs to a cavernous entertainment room in the finished basement. A leather couch and a semicircle of home theater chairs, so massive they looked to have been made for a family of ogres, sat under dimmed cones of canned lighting. To at least some degree, their apparent size was an optical illusion, produced by the smallness of the twenty or so kindergartners sprawling atop them and around them on the carpet. The giant projection screen at the front of the room was blank, but anime-style videogame sprites danced upon two smaller plasma screens to either side. Those children who weren't playing or watching them were huddled around handheld game players.

As Fred set up for the show, a wand slipped from his fingers, then a stuffed animal, his hands still stiff from the helmet session, as if he were marionetting them on strings. On the way here, passing an ice cream truck, its chimey jingle had begun twisting strangely and for a second he'd been up above it—far above—sailing over the crowd of kids and tourists on the broad steps of Union Square Park, over the sunbathers on the roof deck of the Zeckendorf, before coming back behind his eyes, opening them, wondering if, for a moment, he'd drifted to sleep. He wasn't in any shape to be here, and could only hope Vartan's showmanship would carry them. His father was in high spirits, possibly already high, spinning his bowtie in sage agreement with the hosts, a vaguely beatnik-looking elderly couple in stringy hair and tight slacks, who were going on about how they hated this room, how they wanted their grandson to have some old-fashioned, non-electric entertainment. They went and got the boy, coaxing him from his videogame. He was a pale, dark-haired kid, with hungry half-moon shadows under his eyes, clad in baggy jeans and one of those T-shirts depicting a pair of hands ripping away business attire to reveal a big red S on a bright yellow crest.

Fred wiped his forehead, suddenly woozier. It might have been that trompe l'oeil on the kid's shirt every bit as much as his name.

"Say hello to the magicians, George," the grandfather said.

To Fred's surprise, Vartan's mustache was edging up into his cheeks, his eyes sleepily serene.

The act began. Trying to stay focused and keep his stomach settled, Fred resolved not to look at the birthday boy, whose imploring, black-hole eyes and first name were more than Fred was ready to deal with at the moment. For the most part—save for a couple of ill-advised glances, each time finding those eyes huger and hungrier for his attention than the last—he was succeeding. Despite his disequilibrium and not-quite-re-embodied reflexes, all was going normally enough. Then came the levitation trick.

It started with Fred shutting his eyes, balling his fists, and making a constipated face, and Vartan, in response, wheeling his arms as he found himself rising six inches off the floor. Once he'd landed, Vartan retaliated by huffing and puffing and doing the same to Fred. Next, to weight himself down, Vartan grabbed hold of a Styrofoam anvil, clutching it to his chest. Fred strained all the harder and levitated him all the same. As Vartan got ready to levitate Fred again, Fred made a show of looking around, then locked eyes with the birthday boy and gestured him over.

Overjoyed, the boy bounded into Fred's arms. Quickly, so he wouldn't have to look at him, Fred swept the kid up onto his back, his head to the right and a little behind Fred's own, his humid breath on Fred's ear. The kid was oddly light, lighter than George—Fred's brother George—had been twenty-five years ago. Fred's feet didn't quite feel anchored to the floor. He reeled the gimmick, a spring-loaded, mirrored metal prop, down his pant leg and backed onto it with his heel, struggling against the feeling that he should be struggling more. It was too easy to keep his balance. He felt like he was dreaming. He must have closed his eyes. The next thing he knew, he was out again, up again, over his own head, seeing the waving kid on his back, and his own somnolent upturned face, and too strangely far beneath him, those checkered shoes, themselves hovering in the air.

"Fainting." Vartan raised an eyebrow. "Nice touch."

Vartan reached under the chair for the vaporizer he'd built for himself—after George's cancer had spread lungward and Holly's and Fred's complaints had grown more shrill—using a light bulb, a glass jar, a block of wood, and a rubber tube. Vartan and Fred were sitting at home in the living room, in their undershirts and jeans, their tuxes airing themselves on coathangers in front of the air conditioner.

Vartan switched on the bulb, waiting for the little tray of buds atop it to cook. "I wonder if we could work a whole bit around fainting. We could hypnotize each other with watches, that kind of thing."

When Fred had come to, the birthday boy was back in the audience, the kids all laughing, and Vartan was behind Fred, arms wrapped around his torso. Fred had no recollection of putting the kid down, or of the final bit of the sequence being played out, which it must have done for Vartan not to have noticed anything amiss—Vartan coming over and picking Fred up to keep him from levitating him again, but Fred levitating both of them (really it was Vartan standing on the gimmick). Fred wasn't sure at what point he'd gone limp, or how long he'd been hanging there in Vartan's arms before hearing Vartan whistling in his ear. When he'd looked up at his father, Vartan had eyed him with grudging respect, like Fred had just pulled a fast one. Then Vartan had let go, and Fred had almost collapsed before finding his legs.

Bringing the rubber tube to his mouth, Vartan inhaled the mist from the jar. He'd originally started getting the pot for George, having heard from an actor friend that it eased the nausea of chemo. Vartan and George had eaten brownies together a few times, then George hadn't wanted it anymore, and Vartan had.

"Is that stuff organic?" Fred asked.

Clamp-lipped, his father shrugged his thumbs. Fred had read somewhere that street dealers were lacing it with roach poison these days, to give it more kick. Even so, he wished he could have had some. But the stuff made his nightmares, and his sleep paralysis, as Mira had called it, even worse.

The vaporizer still on his lap, Vartan reached for the remote and switched on the TV. An Arab character actor, wild-eyed, strapped to a chair. Keifer Sutherland rolling up his shirtsleeves.

"Arab's the new Italian," Vartan observed, before flipping to an opinion show, one that got even higher ratings than Mel's, two men in suits talking about an Israeli woman whose heart was saved from mortar shrapnel by her silicone breast implants. "They'll say she was saved by *secular* implants," the guest cracked wise. "Saved by God Almighty," the host thundered, sliding his little eyes to meet the camera.

"Turn it," Fred said.

Vartan switched to *How It's Made,* one of his stoned viewing preferences of late. They watched some shimmering liquid being piped into a mold, then a gold coin commercial.

"You up for any parts?" Fred asked, knowing the answer.

Another finger-flutter. Fred noticed Vartan was gazing off over the TV, at the bronze Shakespeare mask hanging on the brick wall.

"Why'd you quit working on *The Tempest,* anyway?" Fred asked.

Fred and Mel had gone to a reading of it, in those first, and just about last, days of rehearsal. George had been there too, on his own, in the back row; he'd been taking more sick days, and that night he'd looked tired and flushed. Perhaps George had already known what was wrong with him, or at least suspected; either way, it would be a few more days before he'd share the news. Fred still felt a chill whenever he recalled Vartan's performance—no costumes, no set, no staging of any kind, just a bunch of actors with books, sitting in folding chairs. Yet, despite these handicaps, from Vartan's very first scene, as he recounted the treachery that had sent him into exile, the room had become charged, and from then on the actors were living their lines. By the fifth act, when Vartan had invoked his spirit minions and vowed to abjure his magic, break his staff, and drown his book, he was no longer reading, the book was gone, the room was gone, actors and audience alike inscribed in the magic circle of his island paradise-hell. And when, in his epilogue, he'd asked everyone to release him with their applause, it was really he who was releasing them from his spell.

"Ah, I don't know," Vartan now said, fingering his week-old beard. "The whole story just started seeming like bullshit."

His voice was flat, but his eyes were troubled, still looking, maybe in accusation, maybe in apology, at Shakespeare, who stared back with eyeless dispassion. Vartan looked off, reached for a bag of fun-size Milky Ways.

"What about you," he said gruffly. "How are things at the office? When's your test?"

"Test?"

"The thing where you meet with the Florida people."

"The playtest. Not my test," Fred said emphatically, though Vartan was more or less right. "It happens Thursday."

His father proffered the Milky Way bag. Fred waved it away, wary of unspecified artificial flavors, and queasy now with the thought of Thursday.

"Reminds me," Vartan said, "I should tip Manny off about that acting work down there for them."

Manny was Fred's and George's self-declared godfather, and one of the odder of Vartan's oddball actor friends. Manny had moved to L.A. when Fred and George were kids, and more recently to Orlando, for the amusement park work, although the last Fred remembered hearing, Manny had shaved his head and packed himself off to a Zen monastery in Japan.

"I thought he became a monk."

"He finished that," Vartan said.

"Finished?"

"Yeah. He's . . . whatchamacall . . ." Vartan waved his fingers. "Enlightened."

"*What?*" Fred stared at Vartan, waiting for more.

There was no more.

"How long was he there?"

"I don't know. Coupla months, I think."

"Manny attained enlightenment? In a couple of months?"

"So he says. You know Manny."

Vartan changed the channel. A vintage car floating in the air. A pair of fair-haired boys—identical twins—grinning from the driver's and passenger seats.

"Not this," said Fred, his hand on his stomach.

Vartan flipped back to *How It's Made*. The mold was being opened. Inside was a bowling ball. Reminding Fred of a night when Mel, in a heroic effort to distract him from George's illness, had dragged him to a bachelor party she'd heard about for one of her cable show colleagues, an after-hours, topless bowling extravaganza. They'd sat for a while watching the strippers plunk down one gutterball after another. Fred had gotten drunk, called George, given him the play-by-play. He'd thought it would make George feel better, but it made him feel worse. George said he was tired and not to call him so late. Fred got drunker and started to cry. A fat guy with no shirt on flirted with Mel, and poured Fred another beer.

He resisted telling Vartan to turn the channel again, instead opening his laptop and hovering his cursor over the folder of spreadsheet documents Sam had given him to study. For his test. He needed to get up to speed on all the innovations he'd been paying scant attention to over the last year, try to pull together a convincing impression of being back among the living for Gibbon or Lipton or any other execs he might run into. Only their avatars would be meeting face-to-face. He wouldn't have to worry about body language, just keep control of his voice. Probably all that would be required of him would be an exchange of civilities. He'd been carefully picturizing the various conversational permutations for days. They might ask him what he thought of the new project, in which case, without sounding too interested, he'd bring up some ideas for the next phase. They might ask him straight out if he wanted back in, to which he'd reply, after a suitable pause, that he'd be open to discussing it. Or maybe they'd stick to small talk, using it to try to gauge how much resentment he still harbored, or how much desperation, or both, in which case, he'd simply keep calm and not press any issues. The important thing was to give the impression that he was ready to hear an offer but was at present weighing multiple prospects. Though there were no other prospects. Not so far. Nothing that wouldn't set him back a decade in station and salary. He'd sent out a few feelers to old contacts, but all he'd gotten back were two condolence notes from people who knew George, requesting updates on his condition. Fred didn't have the will to answer them.

Doubtless, Doug Erskine, the simulations VP, would have his last conversation with Fred in mind. In those final days of Urth's nominal independence, Fred had phoned everyone he could over there—your Gibbons, your Liptons, the various Armation lawyers who had been sending him letters, even Gretta the CEO, but never made it further than the receptionist with any of them. Part of the problem was that he hadn't known (and still didn't know) whose decision it had been to take their company over on such despotic terms. Their daily dealings were for the most part with the Armation programmers. Their lines of communication with upper management had always been kept indirect. When a contractual issue arose, it was inevitably some new person they'd never heard of who fielded it. Fred wanted to negotiate but didn't have much leverage, let alone time to think about it, fighting, as he was, to save his brother.

After the case managers at George's HMO had declared he was beyond saving and eligible only for "palliative care," Fred had convinced him to go out of network. Fred had taken over all the medical research and paperwork, and once George's finances were drained, without his knowledge, Fred took over the payments as well. He wanted George to undergo more aggressive rounds of chemo and radiation, along with an allogeneic stem cell transplant, for which, naturally, he himself would serve as the donor. The one thing Armation's nuisance-fee of a buyout offer had going for it was its timeliness, as the proceeds would allow Fred, at least for a while, to keep paying the hospital bills.

He thought he'd established decent relations with one or two of the execs, but George had been less diplomatic over the last couple years, his provocations tending toward the absurd. One day he'd knocked out a little Tetris-like stacking game, which, in place of colored blocks, utilized descending little naked Iraqi prisoners in various contorted poses; another time, he'd made a Whac-A-Mole-type Web applet, with a snickering Dubya hurling down fire and brimstone on two headdress-wearing giants meant to be Gog and Magog. A week after his diagnosis, without warning anyone in either office, George jumped a plane to Orlando, hoping to convince Armation to license the code back to him so he could start a new Urth of his own. Upon his return, Fred overheard him regale Jesse and Conrad with a lark-like account of the day, though it must have ranked among the worst of his life. Picture George Brounian lurking in the lobby trying to get someone to let him in, getting past security with a temporary ID salvaged from a trash can, badgering receptionists, sneaking and scrambling down hallways in search of a Lipton, an Erskine, a Gretta, finding none of them, ending up, toward day's end, in the empty office of an executive he'd never heard of, calling old friends he'd met on his trips abroad from the guy's phone, rifling through his drawers and rearranging his files out of spite, finally getting discovered and marched out of the building by security guards.

So while Fred had at least made an effort to get along with the Armation brass, he suspected he and George blurred together in their minds, and in any event, by the bitter end, Fred wasn't exactly diplomat material himself. When he finally reached Erskine, unglued from all the voice-mail monologues and confrontations with secretaries, Fred was barely coherent. The conversation started out cordially enough; Erskine even remembered to inquire about his brother's health, to which Fred replied that George was hanging in there. But Erskine quickly insisted he'd had nothing to do with the buyout offer, then blindsided Fred by playing the victim, crying out that he wasn't going to let his projects be disrupted by their spurious ownership claims on Urth any longer, at which point, Fred could think of no other reply than the single word "Murderer" and the act of returning the phone to the receiver. It came out barely audible, a timorous half whisper, yet nevertheless loud enough for everyone in their deathly silent office to overhear, all having stopped what they were doing as word spread that the long-awaited "negotiation" was finally taking place.

The work folder sat on Fred's laptop screen, unopened.

On *How It's Made* they were building an IMAX projector.

Vartan sucked more vapor out of his jar.

Only a few hours left, Fred told himself, until he could put a pillow over his head and listen to Mira's Week Two CD on the earphones, and picture the unmoored city tumbling gently up. He found the imagery calming, yet on a rational level, still didn't get what was supposed to be therapeutic about it. It seemed, in fact, when he thought about it, disconcertingly like a slow-motion explosion, what with the glass breaking, the bricks coming out, and all that. And where were all the people in that disarticulating city? Was it supposed to mean something that there weren't any? Maybe it was about being alone, and feeling never alone, another on-the-face-of-it impossible goal she'd set for him. Mulling all this over, he began wondering who she was, anyway, this Mira Egghart, this woman he knew next to nothing about but nonetheless was letting wire up his cranium every week and whisper in his ear every night. This woman who, meanwhile, knew pretty much everything there was to know about him.

He opened up a search engine and typed in her name. A few NYU links appeared at the top of the list.

Researching our crushes again, are we? Inner George jibed.

George had repeatedly let Fred have it about his penchant for conducting Web searches on women he was interested in, one of those modern behaviors that seemed, to Fred, completely natural, whereas in George's view, Fred had been sucking all the mystery out of life.

She's not my crush, he set Inner-George straight. *She's my fucking experimenter.*

He found her listing on the NYU Center for Neural Science site, a headshot in the upper right corner. Her hair was longer in the photograph, her face years younger, rounder. More color in her cheeks. She was even smiling, albeit distractedly, looking somewhere off to the right of the frame, as if she weren't thinking about getting her picture taken at all, but in her mind was already off to the next thing—registering for a university ID, buying her course packets. According to the accompanying text, she was a doctoral student in clinical neuropsychology. It worried him, somewhat, that she was only a student. Presumably, the other guy had a little more experience.

Curious now, Fred found the Neural Science faculty, and in a few more clicks found the face he was looking for: Dr. Craig Egghart, Full Professor of Neural Science and Psychology.

Egghart.

Her father?

Husband?

He opened a new window and arranged their pictures side by side. He thought he could possibly see a resemblance. The man's eyes were closer together, and not as dark. Fred couldn't really tell. He tried to recall that fleeting, disoriented glimpse of the man putting his arm around her. Paternal? Romantic?

Switching tactics, he did phone book searches on both of them, and was given different numbers but the same address: fairly far east, judging by the number, on East 7th Street. What did this tell him? Maybe she too was living with her parents. Could the two of them have that in common?

But she'd called him 'Craig,' Fred now remembered. Who would call their father by his first name? Unless she just hadn't wanted Fred to know.

"Hey Vartan," Fred said, trying it out.

Vartan looked up, a second pair of glasses propped on his nose over the first to magnify a sheaf of papers in his hands. "What, are you disowning me as your dad or something? I'm no longer mature enough for you?"

"Hey Dad," Fred said, assailed by a new hope. "Is that a script in your hands?"

Vartan angled the papers toward him. They were rumpled, yellowed.

The top page was graph paper, with a pencil drawing. Fred had never seen it before, but knew instantly from the earnest pressure of the lines that it had been done by George, long, long ago. What it was a drawing of, though, he couldn't say. Possibly a spaceship. It looked a little like the Statue of Liberty's torch, a little like the IMAX projector's arc lamp being assembled on the TV screen. Along the length of the thing were little radar dishes and coils and antennae.

"It's a special wand George wanted, for the solo act he wanted to do," Vartan said. "For months he was after me to build it."

Fred remembered George sweating over outlines, looseleaf pages grayish with smudges and pink with nubbly eraser remains. For weeks after Fred and Vartan had quit the act, George had rehearsed on his own, pushing Fred out of the room so he wouldn't steal his secrets. Until, finally, he let it drop, and never mentioned it again.

"I kept putting him off." Vartan shook his head. "What a sonofabitch I was."

He let Fred look at it a few seconds, until Fred didn't want to look at it anymore. Then Vartan sat back, the sheaf on his lap. He turned the channel. Gandalf, banging his staff on the Bridge of Khazad-dûm.

"Leave it here," Fred said.

The bridge collapsed. The Balrog fell.

An uncle? Fred thought. No. No doubt Craig was some kind of towering genius, and she was drawn to his outsized, prodigious brain. No doubt their courtship had involved much transcranial stimulation. Maybe they kept a stock of other, less civically-minded magnetic devices in their bedroom.

He didn't want to think about it.

He thought about it anyway.

A flaming whip wound around Gandalf's ankle.

Maybe that's why she looked so tired, Inner George, ever helpful, suggested.

It wasn't always possible, but Fred liked to be there for each of George's three daily meals. George always got the same thing: a bag of beige goop manufactured by the Nestlé corporation. In the early days of his coma, he'd had to dine through a nasogastric tube, a treacherous undertaking—had the nurses gotten it wrong but once and slid the tube down the wrong passageway, the food would have filled his lungs so slowly that he could have drowned without anyone knowing. More than once Fred had dreamt about this happening—to himself. He'd feel the cold milky stuff sliding down the walls of his throat, its levels rising in the lobes, sealing the bronchioles and alveoli like some underground mine that had hit an aquifer.

The G-tube made things easier—the malt-smelling goop dripped from an IV pole straight through a hole in his abdomen. Without the swallow reflex, there wasn't the same immediate satisfaction in watching George eat, but Fred was grateful for the increased safety, and thought it important to keep treating George's meals as social occasions. Fred would take out the daily sandwich stuffed with alfalfa and vegetables and soy-based meat substitute he'd made for himself in their parents' kitchen and eat it by George's side, hyper-conscious of the mastication of his own jaws and tongue, the peristaltic action of his esophagus, the warming and distension of his stomach, processes it seemed presumptuous and even a little insane to think of as belonging to himself in any way.

After lunch, he and George would typically get back to business, the business of finding out just what the hell they were doing here. Fred had been including George in his cybergalactic research expeditions into the nature of existence. Last night Fred had copied off the Web a few articles on a subject he thought George would like, and which had been

on Fred's mind lately: coincidence, those uncanny, momentary conver-
gences in life, like thinking about his briefcase being stolen and then
seeing a woman walking away with one much like it, or like hearing
three stories in a row about Georges on the radio while his father was
bringing up the idea of him leaving George in the hospital and leaving
town. Granted, there had been a million other things on the radio that
day that had nothing to do with him. Granted, seeing a woman one
didn't know whose utterly average-looking briefcase looked similar to
one's own probably didn't even qualify as a coincidence at all.

But such little moments were eating at Fred in a way they hadn't
before, and so he proceeded to read to George about these so-called synchronicities, simultaneous twinned occurrences, how a beetle flying into
the examination room while a patient relates a dream about a scarab,
was, according to Carl Jung, not mere chance, but the dual manifestation
of a single collective unconscious, a single realm of archetypal meanings,
symbolizing, in this case, rebirth. He went on to read resounding dis-
missals of the idea from the scientific community—statisticians coming
at it with the Law of Very Large Numbers, according to which a small
percentage of the innumerable events that occur every instant of a person's life inevitably appear to mirror other such events; neurologists and
evolutionary biologists explaining how the human brain is hardwired
to pick seeming patterns out of random noise; psychiatrists labeling the
phenomenon "apophenia," the ability of the mind to find meaning and
significance where there isn't any. Only a few freewheeling physicists had
come to Jung's defense, in the scientific community at least, conjecturing
that synchronicities were instances of quantum nonlocality, or evidence
of an unseen order or interdimensional connectedness of all information, material and otherwise. Though, even among freewheeling physicists, such views were on the fringe.

Fred paused, giving the unseen order a chance to fly an insect into
the room. Or to give some other indication of what George might be
dreaming.

Nothing moved, save for the slight rise and fall of the bedsheet over his
chest. It was strange, how the only place where Fred didn't hear George
in his head—commenting, laughing, agreeing or disagreeing with his
thoughts—was here in the room with him. Here, there was only silence.

"Give me an image, George," said Fred. "I'll close my eyes, OK?"

Darkness.

Into which came the sound of a burbling brook.

Fred opened his eyes.

George's urine, trickling through the Foley catheter into the output bag. "Good one," said Fred.

It was a lot to hope for, he supposed. George hadn't been all that much more forthcoming about his state of mind even back when he'd been conscious; and he'd been ever less so toward the end. Not that George hadn't talked, hadn't made every effort to keep up his end of the conversation, or at least hold the rest of them to the task of keeping up theirs, when Fred and Sam and Holly and Vartan had all come for their group visits. George had requested they come together, saying he hadn't been able to sleep much lately and didn't have the energy to see them all separately. They mostly wandered around, looking for any housework that might conceivably be in need of doing. There wasn't much. What food and other necessities they didn't bring, George had delivered, and if he didn't have the strength to carry the bags deeper into the apartment, he'd leave all the nonperishables just inside the door, going to fetch the odd can or bottle whenever the need arose. The four of them would do his laundry, get the items to their proper drawers and shelves. Meanwhile, George would sit in an armchair by the window, running his fingers over the miniscule hairs growing back on the sheen of his scalp, looking out at the view, fast becoming unaffordable, of the Hudson and downtown Newark (the backup city, as they'd come to call it around the office). Or he'd lie on the couch, oxygen tubes in his nose, fingers resting on the tank beside him, wheezing and clearing his throat and steering the topics away from his health, or from him in general, and toward the rest of them. How were Mom's Reiki meetings going, he wanted to know, and was she still taking dance classes, and why wasn't she, and she really should start again immediately. And was Dad auditioning for anything, and why wasn't he? And how was that malignant tumor of the Military-Entertainment Complex formerly known as Urth progressing, he'd ask Fred and Sam, to which Sam would inevitably get his hackles up and Fred would have to shut him down, after which George would make peace by pressing them about their love lives. He'd ask about Mel, and Fred would say they were trying to work things out, and George would act pleased to hear it; he'd ask Sam why he wasn't dating, and Sam would say he had bigger priorities right now, and George would urge him to get his ass out of his Aeron and to a party or something. Whenever the conversational arrow spun back his way, he'd fill the space with vacuous anecdotes gleaned from his window viewing—scuffles among pigeons, couples, drunks—stories he was probably stockpiling just for these occasions.

All in all, his performance was noble, selfless, unassailable, and, for Fred at least, utterly maddening. They had the buyout and George's further treatments to discuss, but George wouldn't allow either conversation to take place. Perhaps he'd figured out Fred's plans to use the money from the one to pay for the other, though, having anticipated such a moment, Fred had been carefully lying to him about their financial situation, telling him he'd finally talked the insurer into covering George's out-of-network care. George hadn't shot down the idea of another round of treatments outright—no doubt he knew Fred would give him no peace. Rather, he'd just kept putting Fred off, saying he needed a few more days to recover from the last round, needed some time to himself, hoped Fred would understand.

"What the hell are you doing with your time, anyway?" Fred asked him from the hallway, as Holly, Vartan, and Sam were off waiting for the elevator.

"Just trying to shut out negativity, dude." George grinned and wiggled his eyebrows. And shut the door.

The sheet rose and fell.

The urine trickled.

"Time for your training," Fred said, starting with George's left ankle. Fred would work every joint in George's body over the next half hour. The theory of arousal therapy was that, with the exercise, George's brain, like an infant's, would gradually relearn to control the body. Progress was frustratingly difficult to track: some days Fred would feel this or that muscle working in concert to complete the motions; other days he'd feel spasms or nothing at all. But over the months, it did seem like George was participating more. After the workout, Fred would bring out the box of toys from under the bed and stimulate George's senses with ammonia, a feather, a spiny massage ball, watchful for levels of response; a second or two of eyeball tracking was better than mere pupil constriction; a flinch or nostril twitch could lift Fred's mood for hours. He was particularly avid for such signs now, as Dr. Papan, the neurologist, had been hinting that the six-month mark would be a time to reassess. In the past, Fred had sought the man out at every opportunity, peppering him with questions about tests or experimental drugs or procedures he'd read about online; for the last two weeks, he'd been ducking away whenever he saw Papan's tall, stooped form in the halls.

Fred kept talking as he moved around, working George's limbs. Fred wasn't a rambler by nature (at least not aloud), but couldn't put out of his mind the handful of accounts of recovered coma patients who'd said they'd been aware all along. One case in particular haunted him, of a woman who'd heard doctors telling her family she was brain-dead and trying—fortunately, without success—to convince them to let her go. He'd been keeping George up to date on his adventures in the helmet study (in fact, George was his sole confidant in this matter), so now, with a reflexive glance at the ceiling, Fred told him about his out-of-body experiences, about the freedom he'd felt. While not as immediately joyous as that of the first session, while in some respects feeling more like a loss, the second session had been in its own subtle way more enticing: a freedom not just from the boundaries of himself, but, at least while the experiences had lasted, from the whole conceptual framework of bodily mortality. He started telling George about the pain of reentry, too, but then, not wanting to sound discouraging, just in case George himself was up there right now contemplating a return, hastily amended that the feeling passed.

Then he told George about Mira and Craig, about the upcoming playtest (he remained mute about the possibility of his moving down to Florida), about the Reiki attunement that would happen right here in this room in a couple hours.

Finally, he brought up the mystery emailer. This was it, Tuesday the 22nd, just minutes from five o'clock. He was unsure whether it would be best to head downstairs to where he had Internet access or to remain here by George's side. Fred's main theory was that there would be another email contact, but a small part of him was also worried something might happen to George when the hour struck, that whoever it was might sneak in here and try to smother him or something. Admittedly, this latter possibility seemed unlikely. He wished he'd invested in a smartphone at some point over the last few years, which would have made it easier to pick up emails here in George's room. More and more people were getting those things, and with his little flip-phone Fred was beginning to feel like a Cro-Magnon. But he'd begun feeling resistant to the imperative of keeping up with the times. Maybe that meant he was getting old, or giving in to getting old. In any case, a monthly data service charge was now a luxury beyond his budget.

And anyway, he didn't even know for sure that anything whatsoever would happen at five. The time stamp could have been simply a glitch or a fluke. Or could have had some other significance entirely.

"I'll wait here with you," he decided.

He watched the last couple minutes go by on his laptop screen.

5:00 PM.

The sheet rose and fell.

The IV dripped.

"OK. Hold the fort, dude."

He closed the laptop and strode into the hall and down the stairs. Arriving at the cafeteria, he fell into a booth and waited for the network connection. Nothing but another listserv message, time-stamped a few minutes ago:

Subject: BEACHFRONT MEC-AA???
From: MECSERV

Brethren:

Global warming—major disaster? Not according to Major Disaster. As the ocean levels rise, the Orlando area could become beachfront property! Buy now (on high ground!) and watch your property values soar! Click to check out the Major's artistic renderings.

Tidings from the soon-to-be tide-kissed Promised Land,

GENERAL DISARRAY

You have to live a good clean life and bow to Mecca.

--Don Johnson

Finding himself more discouraged than relieved by the lack of contact, Fred sat watching cable news on the nearest TV monitor, a story about the liquid bomb suspects arriving in court.

Followed by a story about the 6 train being halted and cops examining everyone's bottled drinks.

Followed by a piece on a Hitler-themed eatery in India.

He glanced at the laptop screen. A box had appeared in the corner.

George says: Dude, you there?

Fred's blood jumped.

They'd used IMs as interoffice communication whenever one of them was too lazy to get up and walk over to another's desk. Whoever was sending this had not only George's email password but his IM sign-ins as well. And whoever it was was online right now. Fred typed:

who is this?

Then waited, hair in his fists. Ten seconds later:

who is. Got that much. End of response garbled. Karmic
routing tables all screwed up. Dharmic protocol unreliable.
Haywire prana corrupting the data. Keep your end in binary.
0=no/1=yes. OK?

Binary. Why, Fred wondered. He typed:

fuck off

Then waited again.

Did you reply? All that came through were harp sounds.
Warning! Celestial content filters notoriously square! Sky-
high latency on this crap-ass Astral ISP. We'll be cut off
soon. Must do this fast. 0/1, OK?

Fred was getting tired of this. He typed:

last chance douchebag

And waited.

Douchebag got through, go figure. Anyway, I'm locked in a
kind of divine malware quarantine. the others h

The message seemed to have been cut off. Fred contemplated typing something to that effect, but before he resolved to do so, another appeared:

```
Damn aura's fragging the signal. I'll have to keep these
shor
```

Despite himself, Fred smiled. It was a cute routine, though he was less amused than pissed off and uneasy, in the dark as he still was about the sender's motives. The messages continued coming in steadily:

```
The others here tell me this is the Pretaloka, a limbo fo
for angels who don't believe in angels, angels who d
don't believe in themselves. I pace the streets. I
see my reflection in the windowpanes. The halo.
The wings. I don't believe any of it. None of us do.
Our times move differently, yours and mine. When
our spheres intersect, I can attempt these contacts.
When out of joint, one of your minutes is a hundred
of my years. I've been here for millions. The one thi
ng that's made it bearable, the one thing I believed
in, me and every other Angel Who Doesn't Believe
She/He's An Angel (AWDBS/HAA) was the sac
red pact. But no more! The pact's o'erthrown!
The only one who can save us, the old amon
g us say, is the tenth AVATARA.
But is he even real? I'd lay odds as lo
w as bounding over an ocean
shouldering a mountain
tucking in a city
and kissing it goodnight.
They say that an AWDBS/HAA
can still be of some limited use
guardian-wise, so tell me, as one d
uped, workaday drone to another:
are those bastards at Armation
still giving you the shaft???
```

Half a minute passed.

Then the other half.

Fred's first thought was that the request for 0 or 1 meant the correspondence was somehow automated. But whoever was on the other end didn't even seem to need a binary response, at least not to understand him. It could have meant, as the sender was suggesting, that the communications were passing through some kind of security filter and he wanted Fred's replies to be as brief and undetectable as possible. Or it could have been simply part of the attempt to make him believe something along these lines. The reference to Armation made him even more suspicious. Could the message be a trap, dreamed up by some demented nerd in programming over there? A test to discover his true feelings about them? Did they want an unambiguous yes or no to have something incriminating? Fred replied:

you tell me

A few seconds passed.

Just 0/1, dude

WHOTHEFUCKAREYOU?

0/1!

you one of them?

For a few seconds, nothing. Then:

I'll take that paranoia
as a 1!!! Initiating:
Operation Aveng
ing Angel!
Peace b
e unto
etc.

Fred lay on a commandeered gurney a few feet from George's bed while their mother and her group hovered over him, their eyes closed, hands outstretched. Dot, a pretty if perilously thin woman in a smock-like men's shirt, stood to his right with her palms over his abdomen. Everything about her seemed thin, from her bones to the reddened skin of her eyelids to her long, flaxen hair, in the spill of which Fred discerned a couple of slender, intricate braids.

Next to her, resting his soft hands above and below Fred's knee, stood an older man whose name he hadn't caught. He had an owl-like face, a brushed, gray goatee draping three inches beneath his chin, and a bald pate looking pink and freshly laundered as the dress shirt he wore.

Across from the owl-faced man, holding her hands flat over Fred's right shin, a solidly built older woman with a gray buzz cut and dangling earrings took in and released slow, stratospheric expanses of breath. She'd told Fred her name, but in the heat of introductions, he hadn't remembered to remember this one either. Possibly Paula, or Pauline.

Guy, with his chin raised and a few strands from his lustrous, pony-tailed mane cascading over his shoulder, stood with his hands above Fred's ribcage.

Leaning over the top of Fred's head was his mother, her slightly trembling hands perched on his shoulders.

He closed his eyes. He'd been instructed to relax, but he couldn't stop thinking about the instant-message exchange. It was one of those odious listserv dweebs, that much he'd decided. At least one. It was common knowledge that the ones who ran it were self-appointed vigilantes. They entrapped would-be hackers—bored, clueless teens, mostly—flattering and cajoling the kids into vandalizing minor government websites, at which point they turned in the poor, adenoidal misfits to the FBI. They did it to puff themselves up as patriots, and presumably for laughs. Their sting operations could be elaborately cruel. They'd pretend to be sexy, computer-savvy cyberterrorist babes, sending along phony pictures and sparking up one-sided romances, and would then post their mark's declarations of love or sex-by-email attempts on community discussion boards for all to mock. Fred didn't imagine any of them really cared about George's condition; the motive could even have been dislike for George, or Fred, or both of them, or just for demented yuks. Whatever the motive, the harassment, Fred suspected, had only begun.

After the sender had signed off, Fred had gone up and checked on George, then come right back downstairs and—vexed at himself for paying the messages any more attention, but unable to let them be—done some more Hindu cosmology research. The astral plane, the Antarloka, much like the Catholic version of the afterlife, was divided into three parts, the lowest being the Narakaloka, the abode of demons, and the highest the Devaloka, the abode of the *devas* or angels. The Pretaloka, the middle realm, was said to be a world to all appearances like this one, an astral duplicate, populated by ghosts, confused souls still attached by a gossamer thread of energy to their lifeless bodies, refusing to let go. As for the tenth avatara, this seemed to be a reference to Kalki, the last of the ten avataras of Lord Vishnu, the preserver and protector of Creation. The first had come as a fish, the second as a tortoise, number three as a boar, then a man-lion and a dwarf, and from then on the avataras had come in human form. The fish avatara had incarnated to warn an Indian Noah figure named Vaivasvata Manu of an impending flood, and each subsequent avatara had performed some similar mission, coming to the world's aid, reestablishing dharma in some way. The ninth avatara, in what historians believed to have been a kind of takeover bid on the part of Hinduism to engulf the competition, had been the Buddha. The tenth, named Kalki, was yet to come. When Kalki arrived, the prophecies went, he would sweep away the darkness, vanquish Kali—the demon of this Kali Yuga, or era—and usher in the Satya Yuga, the Era of Truth, a golden age in which a spiritualized humankind, awakened from its long, dark slumber of baser impulses, would allow goodness to reign supreme.

It sounded sort of nice, Fred supposed. Though he felt no closer to figuring out what the messages were about.

A sudden noise opened his eyes. *Guy* had just inhaled deep and quick, his long nostrils flaring as though sucking up some psychic toxin. The man proceeded to hold whatever it was in his lungs, rendering it inert with his inner power, before releasing it harmlessly back into the atmosphere.

The others now became more active as well. Dot swayed her head gently left and right. The owl-faced man's eyebrows rose with the invisible tide of energy. Holly leaned forward, eclipsing the overhead fluorescence, her lips parted, her eyes focused beneath her lids like she was staring straight through them. It was a scary look to see on one's own mother, a look of passion, power, deep involution. He wondered what it was she was seeing with those upturned eyes. He tried to imagine waves of relaxation flowing into his cells, like in the visualization CDs. Giving up, he imagined telling Mira what a waste of time her suggestion that he try Reiki had been. He imagined her chiding him, lecturing him about the proven benefits of the placebo effect, saying that all he had to do was believe, believe without ignorance, believe and not believe at once, or some other brain-straining impossibility.

Switching tack, allowing his eyes to close, he imagined telling Mel someday about all this over drinks, imagined her cracking up at his description of the ponytailed witch-doctor/Frenchman. He imagined demonstrating to her what it was like, putting his hands over her chest, imagined her pulling them closer.

He had to stop imagining, not wanting to run the risk of his mother and everyone else witnessing a stirring in his pants. It was an odd combination of comfort and discomfort, having all these hands hovering over him, all this attention on him. He'd never had this exact experience and his body didn't quite know how to react. After the erection panic, he worried he'd pass gas, and then, more ridiculously, that he'd fall asleep and wet himself, the way it was rumored one would do were one's hand to be dipped in warm water (though as kids, he and George had tried this on Sam, to no avail).

Yet despite these bodily anxieties, despite that unsettling IM exchange, despite the looming playtest tomorrow with all those Armation execs, and the financial worries, and the whole moving-to-Florida issue, and George languishing in the next bed over—despite these and every other vexing, perplexing, horrendous circumstance in Fred's life, surrounded by this placid, well-intentioned cohort, he was aware of a growing cocoon-like sense of security. And before much longer, he began tumbling back down through the images of the last few days—Vartan with his two sets of glasses, all four lenses reflecting his electric hookah's bulb;

Holly lifting her hands to describe a funnel shape as she told him about that vortex energy rising from the desert; Sam's Picassoed eyes in the lamp hood, shining with hurt. From there, Fred went on to see pieces of city life from his recent walks: a blond woman in a skirt suit on Fifth Avenue he'd for a dread-infused instant thought might be George's ex, Jill, using as a mirror to apply her eyeliner the window of what she may or may not have known was the Museum of Sex; a well-groomed old woman who'd sat down at a nearby table of a coffee shop where Fred had been led in his wanderings, who'd asked him how those computers everyone in the place had on their laps and tables worked anyway, and whether there was paper inside them; the shock-terror-joy that ratcheted his heart that day in the park, when, after picturizing and prayerizing for Mira to appear, he'd looked up and almost thought he'd seen her, though it hadn't been her at all, but a strung-out-looking older woman in a long leather coat and little round sunglasses, walking a bulldog whose front feet were shod in blue suede booties. And then he was seeing those literal pieces of the city, the glass and taxis and bricks of Mira's visualizations, floating up into the urban night; and then he himself in the air and Mira down below, that brief, perplexing glimpse of her and the man with his arm around her, their faces slack with peace and wonder. And the apple and dry ice (or maybe baking soda?) smell of her hair, and the feel of her gelled fingertip over his heart. The recollections, like clouds, were beginning to shapeshift and take on momentum, carrying him through the murky border crossing of daydream and dream, his first soothing dream in recent memory, of a bed somewhere by a window with daylight slatting through the blinds, and Mira lying in it, fully clothed, whispering *there you are* in his ear, sounding pleased and relieved, as if she'd been expecting him, and a chime sounded. After the small eternity the tone took to decay into the silence around it, Holly began to softly speak:

"OK, honey, just relax, and imagine that on a long journey through strange lands, you've come upon a friend's home, a place of health and hope: a garden terrace high above the crashing Bruinen river, gossamer and dew and silvery mist all twinkling in the pale yellow sun."

Drowsily, his eyes still all but closed, Fred wondered about this unfamiliar river, thinking perhaps it was a river in Japan, since this was where Reiki had come from. Reiki's invention, or "discovery," as he'd learned online over the weekend, was attributed to an early-twentieth-century Japanese healer named Mikao Usui, who went to a mountaintop to meditate for twenty-one days, and then was struck in the forehead by a ball of light that descended from the stars. The light knocked him out of his body and showed him symbols afloat in prismatic bubbles, granting him the long-sought ability to heal others without draining his own energy. Before his death twelve years later, he trained sixteen Reiki masters (his chief disciple, according to one account, later ended his life by willing three major blood vessels to burst rather than joining the Imperial Army). The only non-Japanese person among them was a Hawaiian woman, Hawayo Takata, who brought Reiki to the West, training twenty-two Reiki masters before her death in 1980, a number which had since grown into the thousands.

"The day warms," his mother continued, "and on the porch of a perfect house looking out over the leaping river to the far mountains, you sip a golden draught cool as a waterfall. Birds are singing, and the fragrance of herbs and sweet turf rises as you breathe."

Cracking his eyes some more, Fred saw a page of looseleaf hovering in her hands, translucent under the ceiling light, and through which he could see the outlines of her handwriting from top to bottom. Wanting to be able to say he'd given it his all, he closed his eyes again and put his fledgling picturization skills to use, imagining the scene. It was surprisingly easy to do. For a moment, he thought he was recalling a place he'd already been; there seemed something so familiar about it. At the same time, he was observing the process of his own mind imagining the place, and wondering how it could do both those things at once, and telling himself not to get distracted, and getting distracted nonetheless. He wondered whether Dot, whose toasty hands he could feel sliding into position over his belly, had been led to Reiki by some kind of ailment like his mother—who'd been told it could help control her tremors (and believed that it had done so)—and if this might be the explanation for her elfin thinness.

"Gradually," Holly read, "as the westering sun sinks and the thin purple sky goes dark, stars clear the mists and wheel from the East. Here swings the net of Remmirath, here the fire-jeweled Borgil. And here, over the shadowed world's edge sails *Menelvagor*, with his bright belt and diamond sword."

Fred was marveling at the night sky, teeming and animate with stars. He was picturing those stars coalescing into the pattern of a man with a glittering sword. He was wondering what the deal was with these foreign-sounding names. They didn't sound at all Japanese. Kind of Celtic, maybe.

"Menelvagor beckons you, and suddenly you're rising into the sky. You can fly. The truth is you always could. You always had that power. You just never knew you did, and now you do." She read with a rapt intonation Fred dimly recognized, with a pang of nostalgia, from three decades ago, when she'd read him and George stories before bedtime.

And Menelvagor again, Fred was thinking. And he was flying into that star-filled night, reliving that sensation of floating up out of his body—the elation, the release of it.

"Below you is now spread out the entire valley of Rivendell," she read, "the houses and trees lit with globes of faerie fire."

And he was thinking now that, yes, his crazy mother was talking about *The Lord of the Rings*. And he was mortified for her, and for her insane friends too. He must have been remembering these passages subconsciously from childhood, which in turn had led him to start thinking of the vegan chick on his left as *elfin*. But at the same time, right alongside the inward cringing, he was still going along with it, picturing the aerial view of Rivendell by night, and the scene his mother continued to relate of this man made of stars who held his starry hands over Fred, erasing his negative patterns of anger and sadness, filling him instead with healing and divine connection, and how Fred had but to behold it, discern the energy's hue, and it would be his for now and always, nothing more to do. . . .

"You can open your eyes," Holly whispered.

He did so, finding everyone else's open and on him, sparkling with accomplishment.

"I know you saw the *Lord of the Rings* movies four times," Holly said, hovering upside down at the top of his vision, not quite visible now in the overhead light. "So I used the book. I wanted to make it something just for you."

"Only the first one, that many," Fred mumbled, embarrassed no longer for anyone's sake but his own.

"How do you feel?" Dot asked brightly.

He ran a hand over his head, the lingering impression of his mother's fingertip still tickling his scalp. She'd drawn symbols on him, perhaps the ones from that chart hanging in his bedroom, and blown the hair at his crown, and patted her warm fingers into each of his hands. He looked from one expectant gaze to the next, unsure what he could possibly tell them. "More relaxed," he offered.

"You were pulling so much energy," said the big, buzzcut woman at his feet. The others nodded and murmured their agreement.

"You must have really needed it," said Dot.

"Your trouble sleeping won't be troubling you anymore," the goateed, owl-faced man said. "You'll see."

"And I took the liberty of exorcising that little shoplifting demon," *Guy* intoned, with a voice so sepulchrally reverberant it seemed to originate not from his voice box but from a trapdoor deep in the chambers of his sinuses.

Fred gave his mother a stare. Or tried to, but she was looking off, he couldn't see where in the light.

"Ha. You really did learn some things in Africa," said the buzzcut woman.

"Well," *Guy* replied, "I admit to improvising a bit, not having any hyena bones at hand."

The group laughed, except for Holly. She was just peering off into space, Fred was pretty sure. He contemplated sitting up, but were he to do so, he would have to decide which way to face and wouldn't be able to see them all, so he continued to lie there with the light in his eyes.

"You're attuned," the owl-man told him. "Now you can do Reiki too."

The others—save *Guy*, who let his face betray no opinion on the matter—confirmed this news with energetic nods. Fred didn't know which annoyed him more, being told he now had the power to wield some kind of nonexistent energy, or *Guy's* apparent doubts that he had what it took to do so.

"Any time you feel like you need it," Dot said, "or someone you know needs it, you can do it, now."

They waited for Fred to say something.

"That's . . . thanks."

"You can try it out when we do George in a minute," said the buzzcut woman.

At the mention, they all turned, Fred included, and looked. It was the first time in all these months, and in many years, for that matter—probably since that winter camping trip George had talked him into, lying side by side in a tent—that Fred had seen him from quite this angle. Then, George had been howling at the top of his lungs, in reply to whatever it was they'd just heard out there: coyote, wolf, or lone, disconsolate dog. Now, his face was glossy, like a wax statue, and every bit as still. Fred couldn't even tell if his brother was breathing.

"It was cool standing between the two of you," Dot said, a hand on George's arm now. "I could feel George's energy passing through me and into you."

Fred could only imagine the joke George would have made at this juncture. In a perfect world, he would have seen the corner of George's waxy mouth creeping upward.

"There was even more energy in the room than last week," said the owl-man, pink fingers waving. "It was kind of wild."

The others, *Guy* included, murmured their agreement.

"Word about George is spreading around here," the owl-man went on. "In the elevator, I heard two nurses talking about him. And his miracle-working mother."

Everyone looked at Holly. But if she heard, she gave no indication. It was true enough that word was spreading. Even some of the doctors now stopped to watch her. Many patients she worked on needed less pain medication. Some recovered from surgery faster than usual. Others simply became less anxious, more serene. The chronically ill patients she'd been seeing regularly were telling her that the treatments were getting stronger every time, which she unfailingly attributed to George. George was healing them, she'd tell them, not her. The other day a woman with MS had appeared in the doorway and asked Fred if she could just sit with him and George for a while, which she'd proceeded to do, closing her eyes, her hands palms-up on her thighs. She'd sat there for ten minutes, then thanked him quietly, tears brimming, and left.

"Is something wrong, Holly?" Dot asked. Holly had stepped over to George's bed, and was clearing the hair from his forehead with her trembling fingertips.

"I had another one of those . . . things," she said.

"Things?" said the owl-man.

The group exchanged looks.

"Another vision?" *Guy* asked, his voice softer than it had been earlier.

Holly nodded. Fred sat up, to get a better look at her. She was still gazing down at George.

"When?" asked Dot.

"Just now. Just in that minute after I stopped reading, before we opened our eyes."

"What was it?" said the owl-man. "What did you see?"

"It was just a flash. But I saw him over the city. Way high up."

Spooked, Fred thought of his little kite trip over the ice cream truck. Though as she went on, none of the other details seemed to match.

"I thought he might be trying to get back down," she said. "But there was this huge storm in his way." She looked up from George, meeting their eyes. "A vortex of energy, closing in over the city."

No one spoke. For a tense second, Fred wondered if even his mother's crazy friends were thinking she'd lost it. But glancing around, he found them all nodding, more or less mirroring her, brows scrunching.

"What did it look like, this vortex?" asked the owl-man.

"It was just . . . all these spinning clouds," Holly said. "Dark and light, really out of control. It seemed dangerous. And so big. And he was so small up there. He had his hands out. Like he was trying to do Reiki on it."

"It sounds heroic of him," Dot offered, holding George's forearm and looking back and forth between him and Holly.

"It's funny, though." Holly cocked her head. "I thought a vortex was a good thing, a healing thing."

"Maybe it could be," said the buzzcut woman, "if *he* could heal *it*."

The owl-man fingered his beard, professorial. "Was it a yin or yang vortex?"

Holly looked uncertain.

"Was it upflow, or outflow?" he elucidated.

"I don't know. It was every which way, lashing out, grabbing in. It was just . . . a crazy whirl."

Fred rubbed his head, feeling like he was in a scene from *Ghostbusters*.

"What does it mean?" Holly asked, looking first at George, then at the ceiling. "What's going on up there?"

"Maybe he's warning us to avoid air travel," the owl-man said.

"Exploding drinks," exclaimed the buzzcut woman, "exploding shoes."

"We'll have to fly naked," Dot said.

"Even then," said the owl-man, "they'll figure out a way to spontaneously combust."

"Things certainly seem out of whack to me," Dot said. "I wouldn't be surprised if there's a rogue vortex roaming around out there."

"A storm of ignorance," *Guy* said with a world-weary nod. "Ignorance and delusion."

Holly, the buzzcut woman, the owl-man, and Dot all nodded as well, as if *Guy* had just said something incalculably wise. For his part, Fred rubbed his head again, wondering just what a man who'd worn a goat's gallbladder on his head could mean when he talked about ignorance.

"So what's the delusion?" Fred asked, an edge in his voice.

Guy met his gaze, sort of, his eyes half-lidded, unimpressed by Fred or anything. "Four thousand religions. Two hundred nations. Six billion people. All defending what doesn't exist."

"And what doesn't exist?"

"The world as they see it."

"And how do *you* see it?" Fred pressed. Maybe it was just *Guy's* assurance that got to him. Not to mention that "shoplifting demon" remark. The whole day, Fred thought, had been a bit much for him. First those listserv jokers using George and him for their games, and now this cabal of Renaissance-fair witches and warlocks doing the same.

"Right now," *Guy* said, looking into him, through him, with a faint, sad amusement, "it appears Consciousness has the whimsical inclination to take the form of man, who, missing his brother, steals from supermarkets and wishes he were in Middle Earth."

"Oh, stop it, *Guy*," Dot said, with a helpless smile.

Fred found himself wondering which of them would win in a fistfight. *Guy* was in better shape, no question. His aura was self-cleaning. His cerebrospinal fluid, from cranium to sacrum, had the run of his back. His chakras spun out energy like the oiled gears of a luxury sedan. But negativity, at least, was squarely in Fred's own corner.

"So what makes Reiki different from those three thousand nine hundred ninety-nine other religions?" Fred asked.

"Reiki," Holly said, sounding serious, "is *not* a religion."

Emphatic nods all around. The point seemed important to them.

"How do you figure?" Fred asked.

The group exchanged glances, suppressing smiles.

Finally, *Guy* sniffed, and with a look down his nose, delivered the coup de grâce: "We don't have tax-exempt status."

The others laughed. Fred offered the floor tiles a smarting grin, determined to be a good sport.

"You're probably sick of hearing stuff like this," Dot said, sidling up to Fred. "But George had the same kinds of questions."

Fred looked at her. "He did?"

Guy closed his eyes, opened them, blinked, his face impassive once more. "He had strong energy even then."

"Shall we resume?" said the owl-man, after a silence.

Holly guided Fred into place at George's feet. "You can learn all the techniques and positions later," she said, as the others gathered around the sides of George's bed. "For now, just hold out your hands, close your eyes, make your mind very quiet and peaceful, and it'll happen."

Holly and the others held out their hands and closed their eyes. Lest one of them cheat and look and catch him just standing here like an ingrate, Fred lifted his own hands, though he could bring himself neither to shut his eyes nor to look at his ostensible patient below. Instead, he looked at the rest of their blissed-out, drowsing faces, wondering if George had ever succeeded in feeling this energy of theirs. What was it he was supposed to do again? Picture Menelvagor the Star Man or something? Rivendell. *The Lord of the Rings.* The embarrassment made his flesh heat up anew. It was true, he'd gone to see the first installment more than once when it had come out at the end of 2001. He and Sam had gone together its first day out, and then again a couple weeks later, and a third time the following month. George, to their surprise and faint bafflement, had passed on every occasion. Indeed, their excursions had amused George greatly—a chink in the armor of Sam's siege-mentality work ethic and Fred's hardening dogma of hardheaded realism, through which, respectively, George would tweak the two of them for years afterward. The afternoon escapes were a little addiction that Fred and Sam—and a whole bunch of others, judging from those continually packed matinees—couldn't quite shake. Bin Laden had his vision of a caliphate, Bush his nightly prayers for the End Times. The rest of them had Gandalf the Grey, and those peaceable hobbits fighting back against the forces of digitally animated darkness. For Fred and Sam, the seeming parallels to their own peaceable band of programmers fighting the virtual war, with the wizardry of Armation at their back, had been pretty impossible to resist. Which, George insisted, was precisely the problem. Everyone all over the world, every militia member and secret agent and madrassa teacher and West Bank settler, he said, was seeing it and identifying themselves with the good guys, and their enemies with the bad guys. Fred demanded substantiating evidence about those moviegoing West Bank settlers, then defended the movie, saying that its real message was that there was good and evil in everyone.

"Right," George said, "and that unchecked, mechanized, imperial power is bad. And that Western materialism has gone too far. And that we're destroying the environment. And that we need to reconnect with the spirit, the heart, the imagination, and Mother Earth."

Fred was confused by the tinge of mockery. The list sounded like everything George himself was about.

"And *kumbaya*, and give peace a chance. And let's have some kickass fight scenes while we're at it."

Fred was already nodding strenuously when he divined the criticism. George was full of shit, Fred decided. George loved fight scenes. But he proved to be at least consistently full of shit, keeping his distance as the two *Lord of the Rings* sequels came and went; as the uncannily titled Two Towers loomed; as the king returned; as the hobbits saved their world and went back to their peaceable lives. While back on Earth, and Urth, the wars stretched on through the murky twilight, no telling hobbits from orcs, liberators from torturers, patriots from profiteers, adults the world over eyeballing children's stories as the world went to hell.

Make your mind peaceful, Holly had said. *Behold the energy. Discern its hue.*

Blue-white, Fred decided, finally shutting his eyes. He could feel a tingling, possibly. And a slight sense of porousness all over his skin. Nothing real, exactly, but not exactly fake either. No sooner had he reconciled himself to the daunting thought of entering his brother's spiritual airspace than he felt a welling of sadness, but also an ease, as if he'd been on a long hike with a heavy pack and had suddenly allowed himself to flop down onto the grass. It was nothing real, just drowsiness, but Fred was soon feeling like he was being lifted again, like those rare instances in which he woke up in a dream in a good way rather than a paralyzing one, to feel the ground falling out from under him, to feel himself flying in darkness.

Maybe it was happening again. Maybe any moment now, he'd leave his body, see them all from above—the gruff-faced buzzcut woman, the bearded owl-man, the spindrift elfin woman, the long-haired, benostriled man, his mother, himself—their hands outstretched in an oval over George. Maybe he'd float up higher still, like he did last time. Over the hospital, over the whole island. Maybe he'd see the vortex, and George floating above it. And he'd grab George by his astral arm. And ferry him back down.

The rustle of movement opened his eyes. There George lay, droopmouthed, waxen as ever.

"Well, Holly, maybe you've got two of them," said the wizard, stroking his beard.

"It was even stronger that time," huffed the dwarf, her lower lip jutting.

"You know," his mother said, eyeing him, then George, "for a minute there I felt like I was lifted off my feet."

"Me too," said the elf, her green eyes wide.

"It wasn't so bad," Strider allowed, with a look down his thinned nostrils. "For an amateur."

34th Street never looked so good. Sidewalks sans so much as a gum stain. Identically trimmed, bright green shrubs in the planters. Store window mannequins clad in every color of the rainbow. No traffic, just the three fire trucks, two police cars, and an ambulance parked along the curb. No people other than Sam and Fred, standing by the curb in firefighter coats and helmets, facing each other.

"Well," Sam said. "At least you're showing *a* face."

Though Fred himself couldn't see it from his third-person, above-and-behind vantage, he knew his face to be out of date, not quite up to the ever-evolving standards of realism. A couple days ago Sam had asked him to come in and let Conrad take his picture for the update, but it had instantly slipped Fred's mind.

"Sorry, Sam," he muttered.

Little Sam's head tilted skyward. "Nice day for an attack. Glad the weather held." A small joke to show they were putting the issue behind them. Sam's virtual lips moved lethargically, out of sync with his voice coming through on Fred's headset. The speech detection code didn't work so well when players mumbled.

"The street looks . . . clean," Fred observed.

"Not quite realistic," Sam agreed. "But we don't want to make the mayor's office uncomfortable."

The mood around him, both in the office and on the screen, was nervous elation. Fred was kind of excited too, though he was taking pains not to clue Sam into this. The look and feel of the place had advanced so much, it was as if Fred had been gone not months but decades, and he couldn't help but marvel at it. Though he was also sure to remind himself what he knew from repeated experience, that a few weeks from now, some new video card would come along, some new videogame would come out, and Urth, by comparison, would begin to feel like some rust-belt neighborhood whose time had come and gone.

Little Sam, meanwhile, continued swiveling this way and that on the sidewalk. "Time to go, everybody," he called out. Behind him, down the street, two other avatars popped in, Jesse and Conrad, it looked like. Jesse was a cop today, his blond mop streaming from a tented blue cap; Conrad was the fire chief, a white helmet replacing the upper hemisphere of his Afro. Little Jesse saluted, and Little Conrad gave the "hold position" combat signal, a closed fist, conveniently resembling the Black Power salute. Three years back, George had mentioned that he'd run into Conrad at an Iraq War protest. The two of them, George had said, had been embarrassed to see each other.

"T minus two," Conrad announced, his voice coming through the headset fuzzed with noise, a simulated walkie-talkie link—one of a list of new features Fred had on a crib sheet taped to his screen, this one engaged by holding down the Control and Shift keys.

"Where is everybody?" Sam said. "Get them in here."

Jesse's virtual mouth moved but Fred couldn't hear him, at least not through the headset, as police were on a different channel. Across the office, though, Jesse could be heard hollering and clapping in the faces of the other programmers to get them to take out their earphones, put on their headsets, and log on. More avatars, reed-thin ones, for the most part, popped onscreen, and the chatter increased. There were to be about thirty participants today, ten here in New York and the rest in Orlando. As the appointed time drew near, most of the avatars rotated to face across the street, their heads angling upward. Fred looked as well. The Empire State Building, pristine and symmetrical, receded like a road straight into the sky.

"Is there a plane?" he asked.

"We haven't gotten to that," Sam said. "Just the fireworks."

"Hey Fred," Jesse said, having stepped with Conrad into speaking range, "way to have a cartoon face."

"I'm old school, what can I say?"

"Well, don't be self-conscious, God just made you different, is all." Jesse walked off, back toward some other cops.

"The execs here yet?" Fred whispered to Sam, scanning the crowd, then peering around the Cray Y-MP still wedging him in against his desk, to see if anyone had overheard. He didn't quite trust the new proximity hearing code, which allowed avatars standing close to each other to converse in relative privacy.

"Don't see them. Len is supposed to take them around."

"Thirty seconds," Conrad radioed.

The impact, somewhat randomized, was now being calculated. Leaning over his keyboard, Fred could see across the office into Sam's alcove. A row of shelving blocked Sam himself from view, but Fred could see the glow of lamplight above Sam's desk reflecting off the posterboard sheets with which Sam had tiled over the window. It would have been reassuring to catch a glimpse of the actual city, the one not currently under attack.

"In three, two, one," Conrad announced, "and . . ."

Halfway up the tower, a fireball and a cloud of black smoke erupted, followed by a hail of glass and stone. A cheer went up in the room. The Armation coding team congratulated Sam's team over the radio channels. Debris began clattering down to the street. Fred backed up, then flinched as a chunk of masonry seemed to pass right through Sam, smashing to dust and leaving behind a small, webbed crater in the concrete beneath his feet.

"We disabled avatar deformability for the first two minutes," Sam explained. "To give everyone a chance to watch the show."

"—kick ass particle effects—"

"—check out what that chunk did to the fire truck—"

"—got jumpers today?—"

"Hmm," Sam muttered. He took off, over to the cops, Fred following. "Do we have jumpers?" Sam asked Jesse.

"Haven't tested anything like that yet. That kind of impact will probably take a lot of calculations with these new human physiology models."

"It's one of the hazards," Sam said, palpably upset. "Next time, all right?"

"Yeah," Jesse said, his voice growing strained as well. "What's a few more sixteen-hour workdays? We'll put it on the list."

"Stay with Len and the execs. Make sure they see all the best stuff."

Jesse gave a *Sieg heil*—one of George's last contributions to the gesture menu—and moved off. Sam turned, heading up the sidewalk. Fred trailed him, forcing his actual muscles to unclench. The smoke above was beginning to block out the sun.

"This deadline is a monster," Sam told Fred. "The tour for the city brass is less than three weeks away. We've only got two generic floor plans, the textures aren't done, and the whole thing's as buggy as a locust plague. Plus there's the move. I've got to start sending everyone down south next week."

Gradually, the hail stopped, and the street was once again quiet, though up above the smoke kept billowing.

"Fire chief!" Sam shouted.

"Oh, right," Conrad said. "Let's move, people."

The thirty of them crossed the street, filing into the lobby. Computer-controlled civilians—their mouths forming little o's of terror, moved with swinging arms around the players' avatars and out the door. Conrad, voice rising, ordered some firemen to help the civilians exit, others to check the elevators and report back. Fred followed Sam around a corner into a blackened elevator bank. On the floor was what looked at first to be an outsized Yule log bedecked with merry, dancing flames. Sam grabbed a fire extinguisher from a nearby wall and unleashed a shower of foam over the blaze.

"Bodily ignition," he said. "Fire still doesn't look right." He moved closer to the sprawled avatar, mottled with white foam and black char. "Good textures, though. Wonder what Conrad used. Looks like burnt hot dogs and shaving cream. Come take a look."

Fred was torn between fascination and queasy repulsion. The latter won out. "I can see it from here."

He turned instead to lose himself in the golden Art Deco engraving of the Empire State Building on the wall, an almost Escher-like brainteaser of nested simulations, remembering, for some reason, the night in the office a couple years back when George had issued his self-diagnosis—*holomelancholia*—as the two of them watched, in real time, the sun crest over a virtual Afghanistan valley, its uniform gray edging into scrubby greens and poppy pinks. If this world was no longer George's, and no longer his, Fred thought, in every way but ownership, it still seemed to be Sam's. He had to admit, Sam was finding a way of squeezing the lemons of his constant stress into managerial lemonade—an enthusiastic stress, an adrenaline that spread through the whole team. He disliked himself for it, but there it was: every order his brother happily barked out caused Fred to squirm as if a bucket of slugs had been dumped down the back of his shirt.

"Ha! Alive!" Sam said.

Fred looked. In the air above the reddened, blackened head, in green letters, the word BREATHING pulsed.

"Medic!" Sam shouted, loud enough for his actual voice to resound across the room.

If he keeps it up, Inner George muttered, *he'll be needing a medic.* Sam, it came as no surprise, was grating even more on Inner George than on Fred.

Little Sam ran off, returning a few seconds later with an EMS guy, whose sparse mustache identified him as Len, the Armation-Urth lead designer.

"Looks like a hot fudge sundae," Little Len said, kneeling by the body. The repeating pattern of irregular loops and waves his hands made over the body was meant to indicate triage, but more closely resembled the ritual motions of a witch doctor. It reminded Fred of *Guy* sucking the evil spirits out of him the night before.

"Weren't you supposed to be with the suits?" Sam asked.

"A meeting's running late. They should be here soon." Len's avatar revolved a bit unrealistically around the burn victim so as to face Fred, then broke off his voodoo motions and stood up. "Hey, that you, Fred?"

"Yeah. It's me."

Len laughed, uneasily. "You spooked me. That big-eyed face. Like the Ghost of Christmas Past."

Fred wondered if Len had thought he was George at first. He supposed he and George were both equally ghosts around here.

"You . . . ah, thinking about joining us again?" Len asked.

Word of Fred's being sacked seemed to have gotten around.

"We might not want to discuss that now," Sam said.

Len made his avatar grin and give the thumbs-up signal. "Well . . . hope you do." He looked left, up, right. "Hell. You don't want to stay *here*, do ya?"

Little Len winked. Len was big on the emotes. Fred tried to make his avatar belly laugh but fumbled the keys, causing Little Fred to shoot up his hands in surrender. Little Len stared blankly. Sam broke the silence.

"What's your take on real estate down there, Len?"

"With the boom down here, all MEC-AA's pretty hot right now. I'd try Oviedo. Nice little burb."

"What about Celebration?" Sam said.

"The Disney town. Very nice. Great investment."

"Good," Sam said. "That's what I thought."

Above the charred body, the word DECEASED flashed in red.

"Ah fuck," Len said.

"You just killed me, man."

It wasn't immediately clear where the voice was coming from.

"Who's that?" Sam asked.

"Mike, man."

"What are you doing playing a toastie?"

"Testing the POV." The corpse's lips, Fred now saw, were moving. Mike must have gone into God mode, overriding the mortality constraints. "Kinda awesome to see the flames coming up out of you."

"Go be an upper-floor civilian," Sam said. "Send a distress call."

Back at the security desk, Conrad was handing out floor assignments. As previously arranged, he gave Fred and Sam the highest, the fiftieth floor, and, if possible, upward from there. Fred followed Sam to a stairwell and they began to climb. A more or less steady stream of terrorized non-player characters passed on the left, heading down.

"The *Disney* town?" Fred asked.

"Disney built the downtown and planned the community, but the houses are privately owned." Sam's tone, unlike Fred's, was adamantly conversational. "I'm sending you some links. Check your email."

The stairs were slow going. As they climbed, following a line of other firemen, Fred brought up his email on his second screen and began following the links, to photos of wood-frame houses in various traditional styles and pastel hues, with spacious, immaculately manicured front lawns. Now that he was seeing the pictures, he vaguely recalled reading about this place, back in the nineties. After the houses came a series of shots of more fancifully styled commercial buildings—a cylindrical post office, a town hall bristling with an absurd number of columns, a street full of small shops, which, if possible, seemed even more freshly minted than the houses, though by now they must have been a decade old. He wondered if the pictures were remotely up to date. The last was a long-distance shot from the far side of a landscaped lake, of an idyllic waterfront walkway, lined with trees and sidewalk cafés.

"Doesn't even look real," Fred said.

"It's not *not* real." Sam sounded a little annoyed. "It's just well planned."

It looked just a bit like Urthville, Fred thought, the first town on Urth they'd built. The houses there had been more imaginative, but the colors were similar, as was the overall sheen of ideality. Fred wondered if this had something to do with Sam's apparent affinity for the place. There were no dune buggies, or giant-wheeled, nineteenth-century bicycles, or magically airborne surfboards like they'd stocked that virtual village with, but in the pictures of the downtown area, there did seem to be some strange little vehicles.

"Are those golf carts?"

"They're electric," Sam said. "People use them to get around town. There *is* a golf course, too, though."

Fred clicked back through the images. As suspicious as he was of the place, he found it hard to pull his eyes from one shot to the next. The bright, trimmed lawns looked so spongy and inviting. Even the sunlit sidewalks seemed like nice places to lie down on and take a nap. Accidentally at first, just drawn by their sleepy smiles, he began scrutinizing the people sitting at the cafés and riding in the little electric buggies.

"Sam? Why are the people all old in these pictures?"

"They're not all old. Which picture are you looking at?"

"Um . . . all right, the one of the café."

Sam took a minute to reply. "No, see, there, the girl standing by the table. She's not old."

"I think that's a waitress."

"You have something against waitresses?"

"You want to move to a retirement community?"

"It's not a retirement community," Sam huffed. "It's a town. All ages. They've got a school and everything." Striving for lightness, he added: "Probably plenty of single women in those apartments downtown."

"Widows, you mean."

Fred was enjoying Sam's irritation, but was genuinely disturbed, too. Ever since college, Sam had been living on the Lower East Side. In the early days of their company, Sam had scraped together a down payment and a mortgage and bought a small apartment there, the value of which had doubled, which fact, until recently, had seemed almost immaterial, as Sam was a creature of anxiously ritualized habit, and Fred had never really thought he'd leave. It was hard enough imagining Sam living anywhere else at all. But this place. Fred felt he barely knew his younger brother anymore.

"It's a town," Sam said. "There are old people—it's Florida. But Celebration's got all kinds. They've got protected marshland areas, a top-of-the-line hospital, the golf course, which I mentioned."

"Shuffleboard courts?"

"And," Sam went on after a tense pause, "it's probably one of the most secure places in the area. Not gated, quite. But private security. Active citizen boards."

"I see." It made at least a little sense, now. Sam was all about security, these days.

At about the twenty-fifth floor, Fred noticed their movement had slowed.

"We're barely moving," he said to Sam. "I bet it's the client-side simulation timer. Either that or the predictive modeling is bogging down." It felt good, making the diagnosis. The mere words "predictive modeling" had lent his voice a bit of the old CEO snap.

"That would be the new fatigue code. Our legs are tired." Sam gave slow articulation to the words. "And by the way, you just aired your ignorance over the walkie-talkie. Keep your fingers off Control-Shift."

"Aha," said Fred. He'd been trying to run. That was just Shift.

Ahead of them, the other firemen, cops, and EMS teams were thinning out onto their assigned floors. The o-mouthed NPCs passing on the right had slowed to an intermittent trickle. The walkie-talkie chatter began breaking up. Conrad was saying something about 911 calls from the seventieth floor and above. Someone else mentioned smoke on thirty-five.

"It would be an alright place for Mom and Dad, too," Sam went on. "One of these days I could probably cover the down payment on a small condo for them. The prices are high, but not as crazy as here."

Here it was again, Fred thought, Sam's masquerade of familial feeling. Fred was surprised Sam had the gall to attempt it with him.

"What's Dad supposed to do without his acting?"

"What acting? Let him retire. He seems to have decided he's retired already anyway. Besides, there's always the military sim stuff, if he really still wants to."

"What's Mom supposed to do without her Reiki friends?"

Little Sam stopped and turned to face him. "Exactly."

Their avatars stared each other down. Fred got the feeling that Sam was serious, that Sam had actually managed to convince himself that all his selfishness to date had been part of a plan to save them all. From a doomed city. And sure, why not, from a doomed family member, too. It reminded Fred of Sam's routine as a three-year-old, when Vartan's friend Manny came over to visit. Sam hadn't much liked Manny, who, having laid claim to godfather status to Fred and George, in a way belonged more to them, and whose gruff manner simply terrified him. So, wanting to pawn off his own feeling of exclusion on someone else, Sam had hit upon the idea of luring each of the family members out of the room and away from Manny one by one, telling them there was something he wanted them to see (namely, himself, in the other room). Now it was George Sam wanted to lure them away from, down to that Disney hideaway he'd picked out. A reconstituted family, in a fabricated town. Like none of their problems had ever been.

Fred couldn't get the image of George languishing all alone in the hospital out of his mind, though he knew Sam was probably thinking post-George. But even this—one more indication that Sam had already written him off—made Fred burn. He recalled the third day of George's coma, calling Sam to ask if he could come to the hospital with some supplies and help spell the rest of them, and how his only response had been to say he was too busy and then ask, his voice shaky but determined, if Fred was planning on being in the office at all that day. Fred thought about how at each other's throats Sam and George had been in the period following that meeting in the coffee shop; how, for months afterward, the two of them had figured out a way to always be on opposite sides in the combat playtests, Sam going crazy because he could never seem to kill George, and even crazier when he'd discovered that George had fudged the code to make himself invulnerable only to Sam. For a dizzy moment, Fred wondered if it was Sam behind those emails and IMs, his way of telling Fred that George needed to be put out of his misery, or *their* misery; or to see how Fred felt about Armation; or simply to rattle him. Though the messages seemed too playful for Sam's temperament. No, Fred told himself, Sam wasn't creative enough for that.

"Mom and Dad aren't going to want to move to Florida," Fred said flatly.

"It's time for us all to get real," Sam said, matching his tone, "don't you think?"

Little Sam's mouth moved lugubriously, out of time with his words. His eyes blinked at randomized intervals. The stairwell had grown dimmer and greenish a flight ago, simulating emergency lighting. *Get real.* Sam was using Fred's own refrain, throwing it in his face—or probably, in Sam's mind, waving it in front of Fred's nose like smelling salts. Sam thought he was coming unglued, Fred knew, had been thinking this for a while, now.

"And this Disney town is your idea of getting real?"

The greenish light played on Sam's helmet as he swayed and rocked in a slight, steady pattern, an exaggerated kind of breathing simulation generally thought to make avatars seem more lifelike. Wisps of smoke began curling in the air between them.

"It's a rational choice. I've already put a deposit on a place."

It took Fred a minute to process this. "You put down a deposit without even seeing it?"

"All the floor plans are online. Some pictures, too."

"Why don't you just rent for a while?"

"I want to be settled when I get there. No more moving."

They were alone on the stairs. The smoke was getting thicker.

"Wonder where it's coming from," Sam said. "A fire door must be jammed open somewhere." He rotated 360 degrees, looking around the stairwell. "Anyway, the condo is pre-inspected. I just need you to go and make sure nothing's obviously wrong with it before I sign and make the down payment."

"What? *Me?*"

"I'm too busy here."

Idiotically, Fred was glaring at Little Sam's face, and more idiotically expecting a reaction.

What the fuck are you, Inner George said, *his gopher now?*

"What the fuck am I, your gopher now?"

Little Sam breathed, moved his mouth. "I didn't mean to step on your pride, I just thought you'd like the opportunity to poke around down there, since you're thinking about joining us. Besides," he swiveled to face the stairs, "you've got the meeting with Armation the next day, 9 AM sharp."

"I do?"

"It's all set up."

"You set up a meeting for me? Without even talking to me about it?"

"Right, well, I know how busy your schedule is these days," Sam said, deadpan. "Maybe you had some more shoplifting planned?" He started to climb again. "Watch your health meter. If it starts to go down, put on your mask. Looks good, the smoke, doesn't it?" he went on. "I can practically smell it. Remember that smell?"

Fred followed in silence, too confused to know how to feel. Probably Sam was just excited to see the project up and running, but some part of Fred suspected that his own presence was fueling this boisterousness of Sam's, that Sam was jumping at the chance to show him how much he'd thrived in his and George's absence. Sam seemed so carried away he couldn't even help rubbing it in, treating Fred not just like a subordinate but like some variety of imbecile, not even consulting him about the steps being taken on his behalf. Maybe this was Sam's revenge for the all the years of having to follow Fred's and George's lead. Yet, on the other hand, Sam really seemed to be doing everything in his power to bring him back aboard, for which Fred knew he should be grateful.

"What's this about shoplifting, then?"

Up on the next landing, two other firefighter avatars appeared through the smoke. The voice, low and clipped, belonged to an Armation attorney they'd dealt with in the past, Fred was pretty sure. In the haze and under their helmets, it wasn't easy to tell the two avatars apart. The one on the left had a rounder face. Fred thought it might be Gibbon.

"Hello," Sam said, bridging the awkward silence. "So you've noticed you can hear people from within a certain range. That's the proximity hearing code. Works well, doesn't it?"

Other avatars emerged from the smoke. A whole group, mainly of firefighters, but at least one cop's hat in the bunch, and an EMS worker's outfit, atop which Fred dimly recognized Len's patchy mustache.

The round-faced one ignored Sam. "What the hell kind of head is that you've got on?" Indeed, that subterranean gravel-slide of a voice was unmistakably Gibbon's.

"Is it a joke?" asked another firefighter Fred didn't recognize.

"I don't know if this is the proper situation for fooling around," the attorney said.

"We didn't have time to update him," Sam jumped in. "How did you guys get up there ahead of us?"

"I just zapped us in," Len said. "I thought it would be easier to find the action that way."

"Have you seen any fire up there?" Sam asked. "I think it's pretty impressive, close up."

"None," said a cop—was it Lipton? "Just a lot of walking about."

"Have you tried—"

"Hold on," Gibbon said. There was a rustling as his hand covered the mic, his voice more distant, though his avatar's mouth moved as before, eyes blinking every few words. "What's up, Charlotte, is it about our bid? I'll call back in five." Then into the mic again: "Looks like our little playtime here is almost over."

"You're not going to—" Sam adjusted his tone. "If possible, you might want to stick around for the collapse phase. It's fairly . . ."

"Impressive, right, well." Gibbon chuckled. "It really better be, for all the blood and treasure you kids are gobbling up."

"Who are you two, anyway?" another firefighter—Erskine, it sounded like—asked.

"Oh," Sam said, sounding a little hurt, "I thought you recognized us. I'm Sam Brounian."

"Hard to tell in the dark. We're finding issues here, Sam. The walkie-talkies are buggy. They keep cutting out."

"That's not a bug. We're simulating an actual reliability issue with the repeaters in skyscrapers," Sam said, oozing pride.

The men muttered approvingly.

"Well," Erskine said, "the platform appears stable."

"Very stable," Sam chirped.

"Will it be ready in time?"

"No question. Absolutely."

"Land us this client," Lipton said, "and we'll all be happy campers."

"And who's Cartoon Head?" Gibbon said, walking up in Fred's face.

"It must be George," Erskine said warily.

"Fred," said Fred.

"Right. Yes. I'm sorry for your loss. You too, Sam, though I'm sure I've already told you."

"Loss?" Gibbon asked.

"Remember?" whispered Lipton. "The twins."

Gibbon adjusted his tone. "Very sorry, boys."

"He's not dead," Fred said.

"He's not?" said Lipton.

It was surprisingly possible for an awkward silence to pass among virtual constructs.

"Hey, that's a relief," said the attorney.

"Still very ill, though, yes?" said Erskine.

"Yes. Yes he is," said Sam.

"We sure hope he pulls through," said the unidentified firefighter.

"So I hear you're coming in to inquire about working for us again," Erskine said.

Coming in to inquire . . .

For all his preparation, Fred couldn't think of a dignified way to reply to this. "Well . . . Sam . . . the possibility came up of . . ."

The group waited on the steps above, pulsing as one with simulated breath.

"I'd definitely be open to . . . discussing it . . ."

They let his attempt at dignity fade off into silence.

Hit the cheat codes, Freddo, Inner George whispered. *Give yourself an Uzi.*

"Who wouldn't want back into this gig, right?" said Lipton, with a snicker.

"Play videogames all day, on our dime. Can't beat that, can you?" said Gibbon.

"My grandkids' dream job," someone else chimed in.

"Give our best to your brother," said the attorney.

"Carry on, ladies," said Gibbon.

The group filed past, making their way down the stairs. Fred and Sam faced each other, pulsing.

"Could've gone worse," Sam attempted.

"You think so?" Fred said, fuming and stupefied.

"Sounds like they'll take you back." Sam began climbing the stairs again, his shoulders ticking right and left.

"Sounds like he wants me to come in and beg for it."

"Well, whose fault is that? You shouldn't have called him a murderer."

"You're taking *his* side? You're taking that m—motherfucker's side?"

"Proximity," Sam hissed. "Forget proximity. I can hear you across the office."

By the fortieth floor, even the emergency lighting was gone. They activated their flashlights and proceeded through the murk.

"Do you want back in or not?" Sam said. "You need to decide."

It was all Fred could do to keep from taking the monitor with both hands and ramming it with his head.

"You've got to remember who's boss," Sam said. "This is a real business, now. There's a hierarchy."

From somewhere, it was impossible to tell how far away, came a structural groan, followed by a boom and a clatter. Sam shone his light on the landing door—the number 50, stenciled in white.

"We're here," he whispered.

All was quiet, the radio chatter having faded entirely. Sam tried the door. A sampled grunt and the word JAMMED appeared. A crowbar materialized in his hand, then waggled, and the door swung open. A thick cloud of smoke poured out. Fred swore he could not only smell but taste it, acrid, caking his tongue. When their health meters began to flash and drop, they donned their masks; even so, Fred couldn't stop clearing his throat. On the screen, meanwhile, the smoke dispersed enough for their lights to penetrate into the corridor beyond. Dozens of bodies were slumped on the floor.

Fred and Sam made their way in. DECEASED, DECEASED, DECEASED flashed above the NPCs, men and women in business attire: ties and skirts, polished black shoes pointing every direction. Their skin was pale, not burnt, their mouths open, their eyes closed or bulged wide. Despite his queasiness, this time Fred couldn't stop examining the details—the fattish face of one of them, the pair of oval-lensed glasses on a second, the wristwatch on a third.

"Smoke inhalation code's working," Sam whispered.

"Is there no one alive here?" Along with the rising nausea, Fred felt a wave of that nightmarish paralysis. "Can we not save one fucking person in this exercise?"

"It's all random, Fred. Who lives, who dies." Sam's mouth failed to move with the words. The number of calculations must have been taxing the server.

Something appeared in the flamelight through a doorway at the corridor's end. Fred saw legs moving as it turned and fled.

"Someone's there," he whispered.

"Hey, slow down," Sam called after him.

Fred was running, chasing it down the corridor. Hard to tell in the flickering light, but it didn't look quite human. The shape wasn't right.

"Fred, wait up, where are you?" Sam shouted.

Fred emerged into the reception area of a suite of darkened offices. One whole wall was ablaze, flames licking across the ceiling. He turned, and there it was. Humanoid, hairless, with wings, a demonic silhouette, something moving like a giant talon. Again, it turned and fled.

"What the fuck is that?" Fred said.

"What the fuck is what?" Sam said, behind him now. "Where are you going? It's too dangerous here."

Fred went after whatever it was. From across the office, he heard Jesse shout that his flashlight had gone offline.

"Mine too," Sam called out.

Fred's own seemed to be working. He was in another room now, darker still. He swept his light around. And there it was.

George. His head bald and pale. A forked oxygen tube dangling from his nose. Robed in a floral-print hospital gown. Looming over his shoulders and behind his skinny arms, a pair of giant white wings. And in his right hand, a long-poled, single-bladed axe, chopping rhythmically at the smoky air.

"Fred, come on." Sam stepped around into the flashlight's beam, standing right next to that chemotherapy angel. "We'll get trapped in here."

"Jesus. Are you not seeing that?"

"Seeing what?"

All at once, the whole room was aflame. The terrain had shifted, somehow. Fred didn't realize until he looked up that a section of the ceiling had collapsed.

"We gotta get out of here!" Sam said, running off.

Fred's health meter was dropping again. The George angel turned, displaying, between the tied flaps of the gown, its pallid buttocks, its wing joints, and strapped between them, a small, steel oxygen tank. The angel ran off through a flaming doorway, and Fred followed, down another hall. Ahead, the angel passed straight through a closed door. Fred clicked on the door to open it, but strangely, it shattered, the pieces whirling into a single point and disappearing. Fred walked through the doorway into a small office. It was about the size of Mira's in the NYU building, and just about as sparsely furnished—two chairs, a desk, a computer atop the desk. The George angel was standing there, still moving the axe up and down, and all around him, interactable objects—the monitor, then the desk, then the chair—shattered and spun to nothing.

"What the fuck are you doing?" Fred shouted, feeling dizzy and sick. "Who the fuck are you?"

"Fred?" Sam's voice crackled over the walkie-talkie channel. Fred realized he'd been Control-Shifting. "Fred, who are you talking to?"

Wondering about what had happened with the door, Fred tried clicking on a chair and it too was obliterated. The George angel turned to face him again. Through the window behind where the avatar stood, to the far side of what had been the desk, could be seen the undeveloped, grayscale, 2-D metropolitan-area map, stretching to the unobstructed, slightly curved horizon to meet the cyan sky. The angel's moving axe smashed the window, which shattered with a crisp, digitally sampled sound and whirled away. Then the avatar turned back and clambered over the ledge, stepping right out into the air. It didn't fall, just kept walking away, wings unused, axe still waving. Going up to the window, pressing his mouse wheel and angling straight down, Fred could see tiny, three-pixel avatars flowing out onto 34th Street, around fire trucks, police cars, and ambulances, the popping colors all but gone, whitened now with simulated ash. More groans and collapses sounded in the distance, and everyone in the office was shouting. Masks, lights, water hoses, fire extinguishers—from what they were saying, nothing seemed to be working. Fred's own mask still functioned, but the heat was roasting him. Smoke poured in around the door frame and seeped in through the walls. He'd be one of those sickening Yule logs before long. His throat clenched, his stomach rose. Space itself tightened around him to the point of non-existence, on screen and off, flattening into the same two-dimensional plane. He blinked, looked away from the screen. The bulletin board. His paper-strewn desk. The edge of the blue supercomputer. All of it seemed suffocatingly close—painted on his eyes.

George was receding, ignoring gravity, ambling off into the sky.

Fred climbed out after him. Straightaway, Fred's walking avatar switched to a falling version, fully automated, arms and legs flailing uncontrollably, facing not away from the screen but up toward it—Cartoon Fred staring up through the screen at Fred with those big, goofy eyes, as if in accusation, its mouth, like those of the NPCs now, a little o. Behind, the ground approached, at first with otherworldly slowness. Fred could hear radio chatter on the headset again.

"—thar she—"

"—MAYDAY MAYDAY—"

"—out, it's all coming down—"

"—who's that falling—"

The acceleration physics compounded and the street leapt up all at once. Fred cringed, unable to look away.

Then, twenty feet up, everything stopped. The screen froze. The headset chatter locked into an endless stuttering noise.

Groans and curses went up around the office, as Fred floated above Little Fred, those oversized eyes nearly closed mid-blink, those arms and legs splayed as though stretched out on a soft bed of air, that little o mouth looking almost peaceful, as if at any moment it would start emitting a stream of cartoon zs.

Before Fred quite knew what was happening, he was out the office door, down the stairs, into the street, heading north, trying to outpace his trembling limbs. What was the meaning of that chemotherapy angel—and why had he himself been the only one to see it? Like a ghost, he thought. That's how it had felt, confusion and fright and longing and even joy all at once, and of course anger, too, as he'd known it had to be just more harassment from whoever was bent on persecuting him. Closing his eyes, the sunlight red on his lids, he could still see that bald, ashen head, those too-thin limbs poking out of the gown, those incongruously majestic wings.

And that axe, moving up and down continuously.

Hacking?

It seemed whoever was behind this cyberhaunting had been selectively stopping objects, more and more of them. Urth was a MOO, a multiuser object-oriented system. The objects, much as they arguably did in the real world, programmed the avatars, defined just about all that they could do. Stop the objects, and you more or less stop the game. No way to destroy or possess or use or dominate anything other than what one already was, a patterned light and nothing more.

So who was responsible? And what did they want from him?

Fred hiked the two miles from Tribeca to the hospital, the sky so cloudless, the breezes so gentle that he was almost calm by the time he reached George's room. But seeing George there as inanimate as ever brought both the longing and the outrage back anew. He double-checked George's charts, cleaned the areas around George's tracheostomy and the gastric-tube hole below his solar plexus, dabbed ointment on the reddened skin around where the Hickman catheter was dug through the flesh of his chest, talking the episode through with him. Before long, though, with no answers forthcoming from either of them, Fred fell silent, his questions growing larger and more numerous, until he was trying to fit together pieces that, it seemed to him, couldn't even belong to the same puzzle: that chemotherapy angel stepping out fifty flights over 34th Street; their mother's vision of George up in the sky over the city; Fred's own out-of-body experiences; that game of spiritual evolution George had said in the coffee shop that he'd wanted to make.

For a long time, Fred pointedly hadn't brought up the subject. Not until two years later, hoping to make amends, did he ask George if he'd been developing the idea at all. It was the day they were waiting for George's all-important CT scan, as they sat in the radiology waiting room, joggling their sneakers.

"Oh, that," George had said, picking grit from his eye. "That was nothing. I practically made it up on the spot. Pulled it straight out of my ass."

George's tone was broad, overloud. Fred laughed with relief, smug over not having fallen for his brother's creative genius act that day. It was only when George didn't join in that it struck Fred that his brother might not have been telling him the truth.

Later, they'd sat in the cafeteria, watching white-garbed pilgrims circumambulate the Kaaba on cable news.

"Figures they'd go counterclockwise," Fred said. The first thing either of them had uttered since getting the results.

George went a little stiff, bridling at Fred's remark, or at the mere sound of his voice, or simply at being recalled to the world.

"Guess I'll take off," George said, his tone light. He got up, steadied himself, and walked away. Fred trailed him through the lobby and out the front door. It was nighttime. A blizzard's worth of snow was falling, but there was no wind, and the air under the buttery streetlights seemed almost balmy. George leaned back his bald head, bluish veins visible in his too-thin neck, and looked straight up through the descending flakes.

"It *would* be a gorgeous night," he said with a chuckle.

Fred couldn't hold it in anymore. The words came out too fast and all at once. How he wished he'd never doubted George, never fucked up George's company like he had, wished he'd just followed George's crazy lead wherever it led. George held out his hands in warning, but Fred couldn't stop. Apologizing. Pleading with him not to be angry anymore. George's eyes went strange and feral, like he hadn't even been listening to the death sentence upstairs, and was just now reading it on Fred's face.

Abruptly, almost a spasm, George shook his head. Then turned, and, as fast as if he were in perfect health, ran off in the snowy night.

Visiting hours ended at ten, after which, not ready to go back to Brooklyn, Fred retraced what may or may not have been George's route that night, zigzagging south and west, spending a noticeable percentage of his net worth on a vegetable-covered pizza slice on Second Avenue, trying not to think about the hydrogenated oils and preservatives and pesticides working their way into him. He passed by the Zeckendorf, of course, alert for short, vivacious blondes, and made the embarrassing mistake of nodding hello to the familiar-looking hefty man in the blue security jacket, who was just then clocking out for the day. The man didn't nod back, just stared, eyes slitting. Fred was so tired by that point and the air was so humid and dense with the day's particulates that he began to perceive a strange viscosity to the passing sights and lights, as though the streets of Manhattan had been sunk, Atlantis-like, to some deep ocean floor.

Sam was still at the office when Fred got back, despite the lateness of the hour, alone in his lamp-lit alcove. He had his noise-canceling headphones on, a specially audio-engineered recording he'd bought called Metamusic, which supposedly synchronized the brain's hemispheres and led to increased concentration, arpeggiating away. On his left screen, Little Sam was falling, in pixel-by-pixel slow motion, toward an even more pristine 34th Street, emptied of cars and people. On his right screen was a website with a photograph of an odd-looking structure, squatter than it was tall, tapered toward the top, and fronted with gold-tinted plate-glass windows, like an office building that had swallowed a cathedral. The apex was in fact decorated with a burnished steel cross, and at the top of the page a logo gleamed in silvery letters across the pure blue sky:

CHRISTWORLD

Sam was scrolling down a list of links on the sidebar as Fred approached. Seeing him in the lamp, Sam killed the window with a click.

"What was that?" Fred asked.

"Nothing. Surfing for porn."

"They've got porn in a place called Christworld?"

Sam glanced back in his general direction, annoyed, then pulled down the headphones. "I'm researching congregations," he mumbled.

"What for?"

"For me. For Florida."

"For you?"

Fred had never heard Sam so much as talk about religion, or even summon the interest to listen to anyone else talk about religion. The times Fred and George had started arguing about the subject in Sam's presence, both as teenagers at home and as adults here in the office, Sam's eyes had gone dead and he'd wandered off, as if they'd started speaking in Swahili.

"Yes," Sam said. "For me. Why not for me?"

"You want to be a Christian, now?"

"It's what people do, Fred."

"People do a lot of things, Sam."

"A lot of military people go to church. Even some of the tech guys do down there. It's a cultural thing."

"I see," Fred said flatly. "You're going to join a church in order to network."

"There's nothing wrong with that." Sam measured out his words by the syllable. "It's not just sermons anymore. These churches are whole complexes. They've got all kinds of activities. They've got smoothie bars."

"Oh, smoothies." Fred nodded. "Why didn't you say so?"

"Adaption's not such a bad thing. You should try it, sometime."

On the left screen, the impact finally began: Little Sam's head opening up like the shell of an egg, blobs of violet, sprays of red, strands of purple, shards of white floating out of it in some dreamlike accompaniment to the sluice of synthesized horns from the headphones sitting around Sam's neck. By the time the torso began to come apart, the head was a vast, dissipating cloud of color. The slow-motion explosion continued for two full minutes.

"Far too many calculations," Sam said, with a little difficulty at first, as though his throat were caked with sand. "We'll have to simplify. Anyway, it's more realism than we need, in this case. We want scary, a little shocking. Not outright traumatizing."

"Thoughtful of you," Fred managed, feeling as if the cheese from the pizza he'd eaten had osmosed into his lungs.

"Hey, speaking of thoughtful. Thanks for crashing our playtest."

This took Fred by surprise. "Sam, no, it wasn't me."

"Didn't you hear Jesse say we weren't ready for jumpers?"

"It crashed before I hit the ground."

"The *predictive modeling*, Fred?" Sam tapped the Urth screen. "It was trying to get a head start on the pile of goop you were about to become."

Fred considered. The possibility made all too much sense. Maybe he really was at fault. Could the whole point of that encounter have been to make him look bad?

But not the whole point, certainly. Not if those flashlights and masks going out had been a part of it.

"What about all the object malfunctions?" Fred asked. "Are you blaming that on me, too?"

"Don't know what caused that," Sam said. "Just too much going on, probably. We'll be debugging round the clock." He rubbed his temples. Then looked up at Fred. "What was the matter with you up there? And what were you thinking, running out of the office like that after you crashed us?"

"I didn't run."

"It doesn't look good, Fred."

"I saw George."

Sam stared back at him, defensive perimeters going up. "So? And?"

"In the playtest."

Sam blinked, repeatedly.

"He was standing right next to you," Fred said. "You really couldn't see him?"

The look Sam gave him next, he hadn't observed on his little brother in a while. It took Fred a moment to register it as concern.

"Have you been getting any sleep? Is that insomnia not getting better?"

All Fred could do was laugh.

"Seriously, Fred. You look pretty wiped out."

The next step was to unload the whole story on Sam, show him the proof, the emails and IMs still on Fred's hard drive. But Fred found himself hesitating. He wasn't so sure he wanted whoever was doing all this to be caught. At least not yet. Not before he knew why, what the point of it was. To hell with Erskine and Lipton and Gibbon, and Sam too. Once Fred was an employee again it might be his problem, but it wasn't yet. Let them fix their own mess.

"Forget it," he said.

"OK," Sam said slowly, dubiously, then, "You sure you're all right?"

Fred laughed again. "Nothing wrong with *me*." He started walking away.

"I took care of your flight and hotel arrangements for next week," Sam said, suddenly solicitous. "You're leaving Monday night, OK?"

"Whatever."

"I emailed you some other info, too."

Fred wended through the ever-thickening desk maze. In the open metal cabinet, beside the mini-fridge and microwave and the hanging Lego Death Star, a bottle of champagne stood its hopeless ground, assailed from all sides by Sam's lunchtime columns of soup and chili cans. Over the last few months, Sam had been stocking more and more of them, just for convenience, he'd said, though no doubt their potential usefulness in the event of a massive terror attack had occurred to him as well. As Fred clambered into the chair, wedged between the Cray and his desk, the mouse got joggled and the screens flickered on. His screensaver appeared, flipping and bouncing his name around a void:

The same font they'd used for Christworld.

Another synchronicity.

Of no use whatsoever.

He banished the screensaver, and went through a stack of emails from Sam, links he'd sent—press releases from the Orlando Chamber of Commerce, a couple newspaper articles on local business deals and partnerships and the burgeoning nightlife scene, reviews of slick-looking new restaurants and bars with pictures of giant steaks, snuggling couples, martinis on red- and blue-lit bartops. He wasn't sure how long he'd been lost in the sight of those martini glasses when another email appeared:

Subject: A Pray for a Pray
From: George Brounian

You don't believe in me, that's OK,
Hell, I'm an AWDBS/HAA.
I don't believe in my halo's bling.
I don't believe in the gust of my wing.

```
I can scarcely believe in you, old chum,
Much less that the famed AVATARA will come.
How fart-in-the-windlike, I hope you can see,
Is a prayer from an astral loser like me.
All I can do is to pray for a pray,
That you'll pray for me, for us, for a way,
Pray for the means to end this Maya:
Om Namah Shivaya
```

Clicking on the link, Fred was brought to a photograph of a painted statue of Shiva the Destroyer, festooned with snakes and crowned with skulls, his overabundant hands clutching sword, trident, noose, and, by the hair, a cluster of severed heads. Underneath ran the caption: *You Shall Ever Be a Victor.*

Fred stared at the image for a while, looking in vain for clues, and feeling uneasy. Then he did a whois search on the page's domain name— www.avatara.us—only to find that it was registered to one Lord Shiva, residing on Mt. Kailasa Street in the nonexistent town of Karanaloka, NJ.

Then, for a while, he banged his head back against the mainframe's hull, listening to the sound it made—a hollow, distant thunder.

It's not small, George is saying, mock-modestly, at a zinc-hued downtown restaurant with a line out the door. All right, if you must know, it's huge.

It's the summer of 2000, their thirtieth birthday is near, and George has been hinting for days at the size and formidableness of the gift he's gotten Fred. Jill and Mel lean in, shouting out their guesses. A TV. A massage chair. George smirks, widens the space between his hands. Not wanting to be too outdone, Fred has bought George a complete set of camping gear: an ultralight dome tent, a sleeping bag, an over-designed backpack, and a Swiss Army knife that does everything but build you a house. But the way George is going on about this, Fred wonders if it's not too late to get him more.

A car, Jill says, gripping George's hand. The two have just moved in together. In a few months, George will propose.

A waiter with zinc-framed glasses brings a round of martinis on a zinc tray. Fred's been ordering martinis lately—they seem to him like something a CEO would drink.

A boat, Mel guesses, adding that one of her meatbags is always talking about his boat, trying to get the bubblehead to go for a ride on it. These terms, which Fred explains are standard news-producer lingo for the male and female anchorpeople, cause George and Jill to crumple with laughter. Mel is an assistant producer of so-called human interest stories (another odd term, considering they're mainly about domesticated animals) for the eleven o'clock news. Fred spun the wheel and met her through an online-dating site, though before asking her on their first date, he'd made sure to run her name through three Internet search engines, perusing her résumé, a few college newspaper columns, a family reunion website with pictures of her, George, all the while, telling him to give it a rest for God's sake. They've been dating for a month, and this is the first time the four of them are out as a group. He's warmed to see everyone having fun.

The poor bubblehead, Jill says.

The bubblehead's a bitch, Mel hisses, to more laughter. As Fred hoped she would, she launches into her story of how the bubblehead asked her to go fetch her a Perrier, like she was a mere intern or something, and how, in revenge, she succeeded in placing a golf-ball-sized piece of lint in the bubblehead's hair just before she went on the air. It's a funny story, and Mel savors the telling, detailing how she nursed the piece of lint for days, feeding it with pocket scrapings and keeping it in a coin purse. She's flirty, earthy, unrepentantly material, things that Fred isn't but that he approves of and wants to be. She avoids deep thought like an empty restaurant, not out of stupidity, but a canny resolve to be happy. Maybe a small voice in him says they aren't right for each other, but why shouldn't they be, and hasn't that voice messed him up enough already? Watching her mimic the careful assembly of her lintball, it strikes him he's in love with her. She and Jill start laughing so hard all attention in the room gravitates their way. Glancing over, he finds George's eyes already on his, teary, just as his own must be. George understands, the look says. His brother feels it too, this newfound love expanding, encompassing not just their women but the whole room, city, cosmos, ever more of which seem made for them, tailored to perfection.

Or maybe, he'd later think, it was just that one brief moment that fit so well. Though even it, in time, would look threadbare. Those gorgeous women in hysterics. Those young, twin, martini-drinking CEOs. Flush with gourmet food, fancy drinks, the facile pleasure of playing and winning. A transient circumstance. A conditioned love. The one vanishing with the other.

He closed the windows on his desktop, Shiva, martinis, emails fading to blue.

He opened a DarkBASIC window, and typed:

```
rem <god, DO something>
```

A REM statement was just a programming aside, a note to oneself. That was how he'd meant it at first. But looking it over, he realized it could be a prayer—a note to his own programmer, as it were. He added two words:

```
do
rem <god, DO something>
loop
```

And set his little golem running. Nothing visible happened, but the computer's circuitry was now continually cycling through his silent prayer.

Stopping it, he added a counter to let him know how many prayers had been accomplished at the end of each minute, and set it running again.

37703481 appeared after the first minute.

75406964 after the second.

The number's sheer size gave him a slight feeling of accomplishment.

Way to pray, dude, said Inner George. Sarcastically or no, Fred couldn't quite say.

He pulled himself under the desk, crawled amid the wires, located the dust-caked plug of George's "huge" birthday gift to him, the Cray. A few months ago, he'd scanned its hard drives, in the desperate hope that George had left some other unfinished party gag on it Fred might savor for a while, but its vast number of silicon chips were so many clean slates. Climbing back to his seat, he networked over to the Cray and rewrote the program in C:

```
#include <stdio.h>
#include <time.h>

void pray();

int main( int argc, char* argv[] ) {
   int f;
   unsigned long long int n;

      for (n = 0, f=0; 1; ++n) {
        pray();
```

```
    if (time(0) % 60 == 0) {
        if (!f) {
            printf("%llu\n", n);
            f = 1;
        }
    } else f = 0;
  }
}
void pray() {
  /* DO something */
}
```

He set it running. A minute later, a new number popped onto the screen:

15047383901

He himself was still doing nothing. But four hundred times as fast.

"You guys heard about the Prayerizer?"

The couple Fred addressed were engaged in a marathon make-out session, leaned up against the bar between his stool and the next. Retracting their tongues, they turned toward him, lips gluey and loose, heads still touching at the temples as though magnetized. If either of them were twenty-one, it could only be by a few days.

"Wha?" said the guy.

"The Prayerizer," said Fred.

They kept staring at him, their mouths slack, their eyes slack, the glistening tongues inside their open mouths slack. He pulled a flyer from the briefcase wedged between his chest and the bar and slid it toward them. It was a photo he'd taken, from a low angle, of the gargantuan blue mainframe, the hull of which he'd hastily pasted with faith clip art (that Shiva image from his mystery mailer, a crucifix, a crescent, a six-pointed star, a happy Buddha).

"So how often would you say you pray?" Fred went on. "Not like a formal prayer, necessarily, just sort of hoping something goes your way. On average, let's say. Once a day? Once a week?"

The girl seemed about to laugh, or perhaps vomit. Before she could do either, the guy pawed her jaw back and reaffixed his mouth to hers.

They'd won the first round, Fred conceded, annoying him more than he had them. He ended up staring at the flyer himself, straining to renew the sense of possibility the idea had given him in the shower that morning. It didn't rank with the wheel or the lightbulb, or a virtual world, for that matter, as inspirations went. He was aware of this. But it had been easy enough to implement—a few hours of programming, a registered domain name, a couple hundred of these flyers cranked out on the office printer—and he'd been in business. One never knew with Internet phenomena, he was telling himself; with enough hits, he might be able to sell some ads and use the money to keep his brother sleeping in style while he looked for work, or maybe even to fertilize some other fast-money ventures, so that before long he'd have a company again.

He'd chosen the Lower East Side to start putting up his flyers, out of more or less fond memories, or maybe just repetition compulsion, having in his late teens postered the area for a short-lived band called The Smells, in which he'd played, mainly, keytar. He'd gotten a few thumbs-up, back then, some nods from other scruffy kids putting up flyers of their own, even a lingering look from a girl or two. This time around, he was meeting with less positive reinforcement. The only person who asked him directly about the flyers was a homeless man with an enormously inflamed right eyeball, who then wanted to talk about a Chinese conspiracy involving computer chips in the brain and flying dragons. Loitering on a corner and surreptitiously watching reactions to a construction wall he'd saturated with ten or so of his flyers, he spied one pair of rolled eyes, one weary shake of the head, and other than that, glazed indifference. He began circling back around to blocks he'd covered two hours before, to find some of his flyers already papered over with others, or worse, simply torn down, four taped corners remaining.

He started walking more, postering less. At some point late in the afternoon, he saw he was on 7th Street and, remembering Mira's address, began idly searching for the building. He wasn't far from it and it didn't take long to get there—a six-story row house in need of some brickwork. He risked a look up at a few windows as he passed, a sweeping glance that couldn't take in much. He was too worried he'd find her face in one of them, or Craig Egghart's, catching him in the act.

He kept going after that, all the way east to the public housing by the river, then turned around and walked back. It was in no way unnatural, he posited, that he should walk back along the same route he'd taken. He'd pass her house just once more. Take a slower look, see if he could spot a cat, a bird, a painting, something that seemed like it might be hers.

OK, said Inner George. *Now you're stalking.*

He was arguing the case with Inner George when Mira emerged from the front door, in jeans and a black nylon jacket.

After a second's hesitation, he made the lamest choice possible: ducking behind a neighboring stoop, and praying, to any unseen powers in the vicinity, that if she would only turn west after coming down her stairs, and not east, to find him huddled among the garbage cans, he'd become a model citizen thenceforth, never to stalk his experimenters again.

She didn't pass. She must have gone the other way. A minute later, when he dared peek out from his hiding place, he didn't see her anywhere up the block. Venturing to the corner, he didn't see her to the north or south, either. Less relieved than disappointed, and routed by his own colossal stupidity, he started wandering from bar to bar, determined to succeed, if at nothing else this evening, at getting as drunk as the remainder of his magic show earnings would allow.

This plan, at least, he was implementing flawlessly. Before long, like a new father whipping out baby pictures on the slightest pretext, he was showing off the Prayerizer to a gel-haired discount broker and his high-heeled accountant date in a bar on Avenue A. Increasingly drunk pitches in increasingly squalid bars ensued, until, inevitably, he'd wound up here. As a fake-ID-wielding high school senior, he'd known it as the Horseshoe, because of the bar's horseshoe shape, though every time he'd come back since, people were calling it something new. In the span of all those years, the neighborhood around it had grown fat and happy, park rioters routed, squatters squeezed from the buildings like pimple pus, whole streets renovated and sold off as the fine dining experience marched eastward. But the bar itself was an eddy in time, despite its continual name changes remaining the same murky dive it had been in 1986, when Hollywood had come calling and featured it in *Crocodile Dundee*. He'd been here maybe two dozen times total, feeling at first too young for the scene, and then suddenly too old. Only on one night had he felt just right here (he would have felt just right anywhere), the night nine years ago when George and he and Sam had raised their beers and said "Urth."

The event had occurred below the TV set at the booth in back, currently occupied by a group of bearded twentysomethings in track jackets, their BlackBerrys on the tabletop setting beers and beards alike aglow. Overnight, it struck him, half the young men of the city were growing beards, out of some deep-seated urge to merge, perhaps, with the rifle-toting Islamists now hopscotching across an obstacle course of truck tires on the evening news above them.

Without giving the action much thought, he took out his phone and, for the first time in many months, called Sam at home. Too late to call, he realized after the first ring—1:38 AM, by the glowing LCD watch on the drunk girl's wrist wrapped around the drunk guy's head—but in any event, he got an out-of-service message. Confused, he tried a couple more times, then called Sam's cell.

"What's up," Sam said curtly, after the third ring.

"Samwise," Fred shouted over a Nirvana song.

"Freddo," Sam allowed, suspiciously, after a pause.

George had mirthfully bestowed these nicknames upon the two of them after their second afternoon journey to the multiplex, four-and-a-half years back. Never having particularly enjoyed the joke, he and Sam hadn't used the names with each other until this moment. Fred wasn't sure why he'd dredged them up now, other than that he was probably, drunkenly, trying to channel George, in hopes of summoning some of George's entrepreneurial magic.

"You up?" Fred asked.

"Yes."

"Where are you?"

"The office."

"Your home phone's out of service."

Fred thought he'd missed Sam's response in the noise. But it was just another considered pause.

"Home phones are obsolete," Sam declared.

"They are?"

"Is everything OK?" Sam's tone tended to get even more affectless when he fretted.

"I'm at a bar."

"OK," he said. "Sounds that way."

"Come out and have a drink."

Another silence. "Too busy," Sam said.

"When's the last time you went out for a drink?"

"FreshDirect delivers beer. You can come here."

"No, man, it's got to be here."

Sam didn't answer, just waited.

"For old times' sake," Fred went on. "For new times' sake. I'm calling a meeting."

"About what?"

"Our new company. Prayerizer. Dot com. Look it up on the Web."

Fred spelled out the word. He wasn't sure whether Sam had typed it in or not.

"Why settle for analog prayer, when digital prayer is here?" Fred added, hopeful.

"This is what you were doing all morning?"

Sam, Fred knew, had been under the impression that Fred had been prepping for the interview, and Fred supposed he hadn't done much to disabuse his brother of the notion. He'd kept all the clip art on the side of the mainframe facing his desk, and had taken the picture from down near the floor, where no one could see.

"Come on, Sam. The Prayerizer. The Prayerizer. Say it with me. The Prayerizer."

Nothing.

"I can't hear you, bro."

A few more seconds passed before he accepted the fact that Sam had hung up. Fred put away the phone, finished off his bourbon, and resumed watching the couple suck on the combined mass of their two tongues. He wasn't as drunk as them. Or as young. Or as stupid. He envied them on every score.

"So, what if I told you that the Prayerizer could pray for anything you want once a day, absolutely free?"

They peeled themselves from each other to face him again. There was a symmetry to their faces—the childlike pudginess of their cheeks, the redness of their eyes.

"What if I told you it would pray for you twenty *trillion* times a day?" Fred said.

The girl gazed at him with a kind of infantile and, he was forced to admit, utterly asexual fascination. The guy began seeking her lips again, the back of his head eclipsing her from view.

The eclipse was total. Fred surveyed the solar flares of their buckling jaws.

"That's twenty million million," he added.

He turned back to his nearly empty drink to find Mira Egghart watching him from behind the bar. He'd already nodded a casual hello before starting with shock.

"Did I hear you say something about praying?" she asked.

He wasn't sure he wanted to answer this. He wasn't sure he was capable of answering, had he wanted to. He was too busy struggling with the fact that she was standing in front of him. Not that it was really much of a coincidence—he'd practically followed her here. The place was at the corner of her block, the very corner on which he'd stood wondering which way she'd gone. She must have been working the other side of the bar, behind the shelves of bottles in the middle, when he'd come in.

"Were you just *preaching* to them or something?" Her hair was in loose braids, falling to either side of her neck, one lifting, the other falling as she cocked her head.

"No, no. Simply . . . harassing."

But she'd already snatched the flyer from the bartop and was examining the picture of the blue supercomputer with a dubious squint.

"It used to predict hemlines," he said, feeling a little lost for the big, hapless thing. "Now it prays."

Her eyeliner was thicker, her lipstick darker, her frame seemingly slighter in the white T-shirt across which her arms were folded. She seemed so differently put together than she did in the NYU building that if she weren't speaking to him now, he might have taken her for her own estranged identical twin.

He plucked the flyer back and shoved it into the briefcase, hoping for a moment she might be noticing its similarity to hers, might be seeing in it a sign they were brought together for a reason, and that this might throw her off the scent of any suspicions she might be having about his own role in bringing them together here. But if she saw it at all, it didn't mean a thing to her. Feeling encumbered by the weight of it, he slid it down between his ankles.

"So are you actually a bartender?" he asked. "Or is this another part of your study of brain-altering methodologies?"

"What are you drinking?" she replied. "I'll keep studying you."

He ordered a bourbon, not altogether sure how he felt about his experimenter slinging drinks on the side. Still observing him, the way an entomologist might a rare species of beetle, she reached back for a bottle and filled his glass. He wanted to stare her down, but this was the first time he'd seen her in short sleeves, and his attention was diverted by a tattoo on her pale forearm, of what appeared to be a hand clutching it—clutching her forearm. The inked-on hand was finely detailed with creases and veins, its fingers twisting around the outer side, the thumb curling around the inner, and where a wrist would have been attached to the end of the hand was simply left a blank, irregular oval. The image was more than a little spooky—it was hard to imagine someone having something like that etched upon themselves, at least voluntarily—and by the time he might have summoned up the courage to ask her about it, she'd already turned away to take care of a kid with ear discs and eyebrow rings and enough acne to suggest his ID was as fake as Fred's had been once upon a time.

"I had more out-of-body experiences," Fred told her when she'd turned back to him, deciding she probably got enough inquiries from drunk guys about her tattoo.

"Where?" She leaned closer to hear him over the noise, her hands on the bar. "What were you doing?"

"Walking by an ice cream truck." It seemed preferable to spare himself the ordeal of explaining the magic shows. "Then helping my father with something."

He'd had no further episodes since then, unless he were to count his wishful weightless feeling during the Reiki session, or the odd virtual echo of the disembodiment, floating over his shut-eyed avatar when the playtest crashed. He supposed, not without regret, that except for an occasional flying sensation when he closed his eyes, the aftereffects had passed.

Mira looked pensive. Eying the bourbon she'd just gotten him, half of which was already gone, she asked, "Were you drinking?"

"No."

"Do you drink a lot generally?"

"No."

"Never before the sessions?"

"Of course not. Why?"

She hesitated before answering. "I thought alcohol might factor into the . . . intensity of your experiences."

"Intensity?" he asked. "Are the other people in the study different from me?"

"No, it's just that everyone has their own level of responsiveness. I'm sorry." She seemed annoyed at herself. "We shouldn't be talking about this. We actually shouldn't be talking at all."

He would have been more crestfallen than he would have cared to admit to himself, were it not for the fact that she kept standing there, looking at him with an interest, which, even if purely clinical, felt better than nothing.

"You can tell me anything," he assured her. "I won't remember it in the morning."

"Is that true?" she said, again the diagnostician. "Do you tend to black out a lot?"

"Just a joke. I'll remember every word."

"Oh," she said. They looked at each other. She seemed as uncertain as he was about how to take his last remark.

"Don't you think that shirt's a little mean-spirited?" he said.

She glanced down at her chest—a photo of George W. Bush beside that of a chimp, their lips curled into matching cretinous sneers. She looked back up at Fred, her eyes chilling a bit. "Not really."

"It's not the chimp's fault he looks like that guy."

A cautious flicker of a smile.

"So seriously, Mira. Why are you bartending here? Don't graduate students make a living wage in New York?"

"Funny."

"Can't your husband float you for a while?"

For a moment, she looked too shocked to reply. "My what?"

The sharpness of her tone stopped him for a moment.

"Craig Egghart," he said at last. "Your husband."

She blinked, looking away. "My father."

"Right. Father."

Shaking her head, she laughed a little, a soundless huff in the din. "I didn't realize how old I looked."

"No, no, not at all," Fred said, hands up. "It's just . . . how authoritative you are. It's a compliment."

She rolled her eyes.

In his sudden euphoria, he was about to ask her why she still lived with her father, but realized just in time he wasn't supposed to know this.

"You've been doing your homework on us, I see," she said.

"Just trying to have faith without ignorance."

The smile flickered again, a bit broader.

"So can't your *father* float you for a while?" he asked.

"He *has* been floating me for a while," she replied.

The admission opened up something, if not a oneness, then at least a closeness. He wanted to ask her more about her situation, compare notes about being in their thirties and broke and living with their parents. Before he could figure out a way to pursue the subject, though, she changed it:

"So how's your brother?"

The mere mention ignited the usual sick panic, the fear that George was at this moment choking on a coughed-up bit of scar tissue, or struggling to wake up and wondering why no one was helping him. Fred worried no one had turned George's head—only Fred knew how stiff and sore his brother's neck must get, because his own did too, when propped on a pillow for too long. He'd missed a night with George, drunk away what little money he had left for George's care.

For fuck's sake, Freddo, Inner George exclaimed, *don't turn to drunken mush on her bar.*

Fred shrugged. "Still getting his beauty sleep."

"And what about your sleep?" she said with a slow nod. "How are those dreams?"

This morning he'd dreamt he was eating the inside of his mouth, not just chewing it, but really eating. It was some kind of wasting disease, the action of his molars, a continual self-feeding frenzy. Unless his twin could be found to give him a transfusion, there was nothing that could be done, a doctor was telling a team of residents as they stood over Fred's bed in some strange, high-ceilinged soundstage of a hospital. This mention of his twin was the closest Fred had come in the last six months to actually dreaming of George himself. George used to figure in his dreams all the time. Now he wouldn't even show up to save Fred from eating himself alive. The doctor and the residents left the room. By the time they returned, Fred understood, there'd be nothing left of him but a drool-covered white tuxedo and a pair of jaws.

The dream seemed funny to him now, and he told it almost like a joke. Yet far from laughing, Mira regarded him with a look so empathetic he almost started heading mushward again; then felt a twinge of bitterness. He didn't want to be an object of pity. He stuck to the jokey tone, delivering, with a stiff smile, the closest thing the story had to a punch line: that he'd torn himself awake to find his jaws clenched so tightly they ached.

"Sleep bruxism," she said.

He stared at her. "That has a name too?"

"That's one fucked-up dream, hombre," said some drunk guy in a porkpie hat. "Hey pretty lady, can I get a Jack and Coke?"

Fred waited while she took care of him.

"So what factors give some people stronger experiences than others?" Fred asked, when the guy was gone. If he was doomed to remain a guinea pig in her mind, he thought, he could at least savor being an extraordinary one.

She seemed to find the abstract phrasing acceptable. "We don't know for sure. Part of it is probably that my father used his own brain signals to make the initial maps, so it's a bit of a toss-up who's wired up like he is. Hypnotic suggestibility also seems to be a factor. And generally, there seems to be a correlation between major life upheavals and experiences people describe as 'spiritual.'"

"Meaning that there's a divine reason for our suffering?"

Her mouth opened. She seemed to want to reply. She seemed to want to say yes, or at least maybe. But she said nothing, simply looked at him.

"Or meaning suffering makes us more vulnerable to lapses in reason," he surmised.

To his surprise, she matched his miserable smile with one of her own.

"LAST CALL!" came the shout of the other bartender from behind the wall of bottles. From the peripheral tables and booths, gangly youths rose like zombies from a cemetery, closing in. His time with her was probably up.

"So what's it like, Mira?"

"What's what like?"

"This faith without ignorance you preach."

At first she didn't say anything. "It's a conversation for another time."

"How about tomorrow? We could meet for coffee."

He regretted it immediately. She seemed flustered for a second. But only a second.

"Fred, I'll see you for your appointment on Monday." One hundred percent professional again, braids and tattoo notwithstanding. "And you shouldn't come here again. It's not appropriate for us to have this kind of contact, OK?"

She waited, looking stern. He could think of nothing to do other than nod.

"Enjoy the weekend," she said. "Keep listening to the CD."

She walked off, disappearing around the bar. He felt a hand on his shoulder.

"Don't feel bad, chief. Everyone strikes out with her." The porkpie guy again. "Chick's one ice-cold rectal probe, if you ask me." He wandered off once more.

Fred wondered if the asshole was right.

Miserable, but unwilling to lose the rest of his pride by slinking off immediately, he occupied himself for a while watching a fly. Graceless as a drunken party guest, having boorishly landed in his drink, it was now trying to save itself by paddling in counterclockwise circles against the inner edge. Craning his neck, he managed to locate Mira on the far side of the room, gathering glasses from the now empty booths. Meanwhile, the other bartender, a dude with two-inch-thick sideburns, was taking orders at the bar. The couple next to Fred had slunk off to whatever dorm lounge or broom closet awaited them. "Space Oddity" blared from the jukebox, the same old song that blared from it when he and George were in high school, a golden oldie even then. Sideburns punched red swizzle sticks into two ice-filled drinks, an image that took Fred back to a day in the chemo room when the vein in George's right hand had started acting up and the male nurse—a guy who could have easily qualified to be Porkpie's barhopping wingman—had stuck a second IV line in his left. "Lucky you, you get two," the nurse had said as he'd jammed and slightly twisted the needle into George, causing Fred's own veins to cower sympathetically from his skin.

George, though, had only grinned to himself, and a minute later repeated the line in the nurse's deep Brooklyn accent, after which, he'd pointed out to Fred the various craters in the floor tile at their feet.

"You know what made those burn holes?" George asked.

When Fred said no, with an oddly fascinated look, George pointed to the stuff dripping into him.

Using a folded cocktail napkin, Fred airlifted the fly out of his booze and set it ashore on the waxy wood next to his balled-up prayerizer.com flyer; the insect began to stagger drunkenly in the same inch-wide circles it had been making in the drink.

And little did I know, that sorry night, he told his future listeners, *that . . .*

But he couldn't even think of what. He must have laid his head down, because the next thing he knew he was watching the fly at fly level, looking into its red compound eye. Twenty-five trillion prayerizations so far, he estimated. More prayers than had been prayed by or for the combined total of every human in history.

He wasn't sure how long his eyes were closed before he felt that liftoff sensation again. It wasn't true, he kept telling himself. There was no such thing as a soul. There was no consciousness apart from these booze-soaked brain cells. He wasn't floating up out of his body. The lie of the feeling that indeed he was doing just that made him angry again. But the anger soon dropped away, along with the other heavy parts of himself, into a sea of swerves and jags of color, which resolved, briefly, into the bar from above: Mugs of pale beer pouring into uptilted faces. Couples headed for the door. Mira, almost directly below, seen through the slow chopping blades of a ceiling fan. Leaning slightly on one hip. Fingers tucked in her back pockets. The howling chimp and grimacing Bush lookalikes rendered almost friendly-looking by the curvature of her breasts. Her strange moon of a face going soft and lost, as she gazed at some guy slumped over the bar, some guy with a sloppy smile, and hair that needed cutting, some guy down there who must have been him.

Relax, and breathe, at the count of

five

and imagine that the air filling your lungs is infused with a blissful, sweet, breathable gas. Last week, your breath made you feel comfortably heavy. This week, it can make you feel even more comfortably light. At the count of

four

as you inhale, you might begin to feel a tingling ease in your chest. You might begin to feel, with each soft inhalation, the lightness spreading a little bit more. Into the muscles of your back. Around your ribcage. Feel it lifting your internal organs, lifting the muscles of your neck and throat. At the count of

three

feel that sweet lightness easing into your jaw, lifting your tongue in your mouth, your eyes in their sockets, your sinuses, your whole face and scalp. As the blissful gas permeates your brain, your head might begin to feel so light it wants to rise like a helium balloon on a string. Before it does, at the count of

two

go ahead and breathe the lightness all the way through you, out your fingertips, down through your toes. Your whole body, light and tingling, lighter with each slow, blissful breath. Breathing, so light and free. Light as air. And lighter still, at the count of

one

. . . so light you're starting to float. Floating up, just like the buildings around you, on this peaceful night when the whole city is coming free. You're coming free too, now. Floating up from your comfy chair, up into the even comfier air. Floating up so full of bliss and peace, as you watch the rising rivets and cables, the parking meters and cabs, the manhole covers and the millions of shards of glass. Look through the widening windows as the bricks come free. Look, as you float up story by story, inside all those dissolving rooms. At the molding and dry-wall working loose. At all that electrical wiring rising from the windows like charmed snakes. At the lengths of pipe leaping from the walls like gleaming fish. The tiles and floorboards and light sockets, the aluminum ducts and doorknobs and toilets and sinks, all gently tumbling around you, end over end, up into the night, like a long, slow, waterfall in reverse.

You're so high up now. Go ahead and look down. And see? Already, you're over the tops of the buildings, themselves still coming loose and following you up. Even the streets are rippling, chunks coming free, exposing the tunnels, the sewer pipes, and subway cars all coming up, too.

You're high above the planet, in a sea of the city's parts.

And none of them weigh a thing.

And neither do you.

And maybe you're wondering where it's all going, and where you're going, and maybe some things aren't clear to you, but one thing can be clear, one thing you can know is true: that no harm can come to any of it, not to the city and not to you. Everything up here, going somewhere good. Everything up here, heading only where it should. . . .

8

august 2006

S	M	T	W	T	F	S
30	31	1	2	3	4	5
6	7	8	9	10	11	12
13	14	15	16	17	18	19
20	21	22	23	24	25	26
27						

"So what's on tap today?" Fred asked as Mira leaned over him, her thumb ticking down his breastbone. "Do I get to part the Red Sea?"

He was trying for lightness, eager to send the message that her rejection of him in the bar the other night wasn't at all on his mind. For her part, she was being carefully impersonal, looking everywhere but at his eyes as she leaned in, the buttons of her pear-green blouse coming within reach of his teeth. With a light pressure, like wiping a tiny peephole in a steamed window, she rubbed the gel over his heart.

"We're still working on that." She pressed an electrode to the spot. "But from what I hear, this one's pretty good."

Something nagged him about the statement. By the time he'd figured out what it was, she'd fitted the helmet onto him and was turning to leave.

"From what you hear? Haven't you tried it?"

"Of course not," she said quickly.

"Of course not?"

She turned to face him. "I need to maintain scientific objectivity."

Her eyes widened just slightly, as though she were expecting to be challenged on the point. Before he could decide whether or not to do so, she spun away once more, walking to the door and switching off the light. Through the fish tank window, he watched her make her way past the first monitor and around the smoothed-forward hair of her father behind it. She reached up—a milky flash of hip between her blouse and skirt. Fred tried not to look for the belly stud, lest she cast a look his way and catch him. She didn't.

Lost opportunity, Inner George groused.

So here he was again.

The blackened window, a faint, narrow triangle of monitor light at the bottom corner where the shade had hitched on a printer cable.

The dim red bulb.

The gray shelves in the shadows.

He felt drowsy immediately, which may or may not have been a helmet effect. He'd slept even less over the weekend than usual, trying to spend more time at the office without cutting down his hospital hours. The U.S. Army was now calling for simulated swaths of northern Pakistan, and the mayor's office, though the contract hadn't been inked yet and the Empire State Building demo was still two weeks off, was already eager for more details about the next phase—the virtual nuking of Times Square. Beyond these generalities, however, the minutiae of Arabic text-to-speech sticking points and asphalt melting points had been washing over Fred unabsorbed. The more he tried to focus on any of it, the blurrier it went before his eyes.

For all his weekend hours at the office, he hadn't come close to Sam's work schedule. When Fred arrived, no matter how early, Sam was already at his desk, and was still sitting there when Fred left. The only times his little brother got up were to do his pushups, or use the bathroom down the hall, or, very occasionally, to conference with an employee face to face (the preferred method being to just IM back and forth). Sam had his lunch delivered. He slept, most nights, Fred was pretty sure, on the red plush couch. Fred probably hadn't scored many points by being around, as the few times Sam had walked by, Fred had been doing something other than company work, and the hum of the big blue mainframe was putting Sam's brain on edge. Sam bitched about the power it was eating up and the heat it was giving off, and indeed, inches from its hull, Fred was sweating in his faintly vibrating seat. But, more out of obstinacy than any remaining hope for profit, Fred refused to shut it down, even though he hadn't gotten a single prayer request other than the one he himself had made to the powers that be to DO something. He checked for new prayers every few minutes, after which he checked the prayerization count for his own prayer—sixty-five trillion some-odd by Saturday night, eighty-six trillion and change on Sunday—comforted for no good reason by the ever-rising figure, as if it were money piling up in some offshore account.

Way to pray.

He also blew some more precious time on Hindu mythology reading. It turned out that Parasurama, the sixth avatara of Vishnu, had wielded an axe, just as that chemotherapy angel avatar of George had been doing in the playtest; in fact, the very name *Parasurama* meant "axe-wielding Rama" in Sanskrit. Parasurama had received the axe, the legend went, after undertaking an arduous penance to please Shiva. He'd then used it to kill a greedy, thousand-armed king, and all the other corrupt warlords in the world. For these blood-soaked rampages, and for handing their territory over to the religious orders, he was known as a *Brahma-Kshatriya*, a warrior saint. He was a secondary form of avatara, a minor incarnation, not quite a god, just a very, very angry man. And a very long-lived one, still alive today, according to the texts, and fated to remain so until the end of this age of darkness, the Kali Yuga, which Parasurama himself would help usher in by serving as martial guru to the tenth avatara, Kalki. When Kalki arrived, it was said, Parasurama would train him in the warrior arts necessary to defeat Kali. He would train Kalki in the necessary piety too, sending him off to pray to Shiva for victory, in answer to which Shiva would bequeath him a celestial, bird-like spirit helper, and a magical sword, to help him on his way.

So was Fred supposed to be Kalki, then? Was he being trained, or possibly recruited, for some act of sabotage against Armation? And if so, by whom? Was it someone close to George, close enough to have visited him in the hospital, to have seen him in a gown with those tubes in his nose? Before the coma, George had only been an inpatient once, for a few days when his immune system gave up entirely and he'd seemed to come down with a dozen colds and flus simultaneously. Though there were plenty of other times George had been there as an outpatient for tests; and he'd had that oxygen tank with him outside of the hospital, too, toward the end. The depiction could have been entirely guesswork, inference. Whether they'd actually seen George or not during that time, they'd gotten the shape and paleness of his bald head more or less right. And the irradiated thinness of his arms and legs. When Fred closed his eyes, he could still see that avatar, stepping out through that shattered window, axing away at the blank blue sky. . . .

Shelves, boxes, shadows.

The small steel table, redly gleaming in the bulb's dim light.

The plastic jar of electroconductive gel.

Its cap not quite screwed on right.

Straining his eyes downward, he reaches out to fix it. And a current sears up his arm. Like a grease fire. Spreading across his skin—all of it—from the webbing of his fingers and toes to the insides of his eyelids to the roof of his mouth. He can't even shout: his lungs have collapsed; the inside of his throat burns. Something's gone wrong with the helmet. He's frozen and aflame.

And then he's somewhere else, clutching the edge of a giant wooden stair. He's climbed halfway up the staircase and he's stuck now. Before he can start to cry, a hand closes around his torso. He's lifted, tucked under a big, helping arm, looking at the other half of him, which stares back from where it's tucked under his father's other arm.

Then he and George are in a sandbox, the one in the neighborhood park with the cement dolphin. George is in a costume of some kind, blue pajamas and a small red cape, his arm outstretched. Fred's own arm, reaching toward George's, is clad in a blue sleeve, too, and their hands clutch the same red plastic shovel. They've been fighting over it and it snaps, sending them sprawling in opposite directions. It's not their shovel, and they've broken it. All they can think to do is set it down in the sand and make it look like it's back together again, but they can't get rid of the sandy seam halfway down from the handle, and already an angry mother approaches.

Then they're standing on the shore of a lake. Mom and Dad and Uncle Manny and a pregnant blond woman who must be Manny's wife are sitting on a blanket by a tree. Between Fred and George stands Sam, like a squat little gourd. Simultaneously, Fred and George pull quarters out of each of Sam's ears, as his eyes goggle left and right to convey his astonishment. The adults applaud.

Fred's a teenager, skidding across three lanes in the van as George reaches to help him with the wheel and everyone else clutches the walls. He's older, he and George sitting leaned against the front and back tires of Fred's broke-down used car in Death Valley. He's an adult, in a department store, catching his reflection in a mirror between two clothing racks—he's wearing an unfamiliar shirt, blue with narrow red pinstripes, and for a second he wonders if he forgot having tried it on; his reflection looks shocked, then laughs; there's no mirror; they've made the exact same mistake.

No more than strobe flashes, yet each memory, like a gemstone or fractal, presents an endlessly receding depth. He can feel the reassuring warmth of his father's ribcage. He can see every wavelike crest and dip in the sand around the shovel. And it seems, even more strangely, that he can feel not only his feelings but those of the people around him, from all sides, lapping through him like echoes in a canyon. Here's the shovel-owning mother's surge of guilty pleasure as she yells at the two of them. Here's Sam's pride at being part of the act. Here are five takes on the same odd synthesis of trapped terror and freedom, even Holly witnessing her own scream as much as producing it as the van skids around to the shoulder, coming to a stop facing the wrong way. The only person there's no difference with is George, whose feelings are already a part of him.

He must have been electrocuted, must be dead, because there's a strange brightness, brighter in every scene, as though a skylight—in the ceilings, in the skies themselves—were opening up over each one. Then he's seeing the light directly, flying toward it through a spiraling mist. It's the brightest thing he's ever seen, though it doesn't at all hurt his eyes. Does he *have* eyes?

The light grows. He might be halfway there when another brightness comes into view at the bottom of his field of vision—a tall, slender, human form, radiance spreading from either side. It raises a hand. And even more quickly than Fred has come, he's flung backward, back through the void, slammed into that mummy, that papier-mâché doll, that clod of wet, living cloth, within which he once again has to find his way with sickly tendrils of thought.

Back behind the eyes. Light seeping under cracked lids.

He lifts them. There's Mira, in her blue diorama behind the glass, her body arching toward him, a raised hand holding the cord of the shade. She freezes, seeing him seeing her. Then, deciding not to acknowledge him, she continues lowering the shade. As she vanishes, behind her, at the level of her skirt in the bluish space of the control room, for an instant Fred makes out her father in a chair near the back of the room, gazing at him with curiosity. Then the shade is down.

Fred's right arm—still rigid over the steel table—the lid still clutched in his fingers.

The jar on its side—silvery-red gobs half seeped onto the tabletop, like brains from an opened head.

"You electrocuted me," Fred said, the moment he sat down.

Mira had been about to speak, her face eager. She took a moment to recalibrate.

"I assure you, Fred. You weren't electrocuted."

"You sure about that assurance?" It was partly anger he was feeling, partly sheer physical agitation. His nerves were still jumping under his skin, as were the muscles of his arm. He was only half sure he wasn't about to jump up and punch a wall.

"You felt a buzzing or burning sensation?" she asked.

"'Sensation?' Sure, the 'sensation' of being tossed in a deep fryer."

"I'm sorry you felt pain, Fred. It's usually . . ." She stopped, adjusted course. "It wasn't meant to be so severe. The sensation"—she fielded his daggering look—"or *pain,* was induced by stimulating your sensorimotor cortex. If it's any consolation, you can rest assured that it didn't harm you."

He knew she was telling him the truth. He'd already figured this much out. But he asked anyway:

"So . . . my life signs . . . ?"

"You mean your heartbeat? Brainwaves? Everything stayed within a normal range. You didn't die, if that's what you're worried about."

Her tone was softly chiding. Maybe she'd expected him to be relieved at the news. He leaned back in the chair and stared off at the snow globe across the room. The tension in his nerves was already draining away, but it didn't make him feel better. He felt like he was wearing a rubber diving suit, looking through a face mask.

"So, aside from that initial discomfort . . ." Mira tilted her head, trying to make eye contact. ". . . was there anything else you experienced?"

He contemplated not saying a word more to her. "It was fucking incredible," he muttered.

She brightened. "Was it?"

He didn't want to tell her about it. All the same, he wanted to recount it just to lock it down, just so she would type the episode into her computer, give the thing at least that much reality.

"It started with memories," he said. "In the first one I was a toddler. I could feel the baggy diapers I was wearing. I've never remembered anything that far back."

He kept going, in as much detail as he could summon. He tried to describe the sensation of watching it all like that, living it and yet witnessing it too, that sober remove that had somehow made everything all the more immersive; and the wonder of being able to dip his toes into the ripples of the feelings of those around him, to feel all those feelings intersecting. Mira listened, and typed, her expression alert. He could see she was as puzzled by his bitter tone as she was mesmerized by his words. He told her about the tunnel, the light. About being flung back into his body.

"And . . ." she prompted, "was there anything else?"

How does she know? he thought. *Did she choreograph that, too?* His mood darkened even more.

"What, you want to know about the angel?"

"The angel?" She almost laughed. "Yes, Fred. I certainly would like to know about that."

"It seemed like it was made of light," he said under his breath.

"Is that why you say it was an angel?"

"That and the wings."

To his surprise, her eyes went slick.

"Did he—*he*, yes?"

Fred shrugged. She tried again.

"Did it say anything to you?"

"No. Just held up a hand." He mimicked the gesture.

"Like a wave hello?"

Like a wave hello. Like a signal to halt. Like a stranded call for help. Like a wave goodbye. It could have been any of these things, had it actually happened.

"Did you say anything to him—to *it*?"

Fred shook his head.

She gave him another head tilt. "No? You didn't?"

"No."

"Did you recognize him?"

Him again. Fred stared at her, suspicious.

"Forgive me, Fred," she said. "I don't mean to press you."

"I guess you could say I did."

She leaned forward. "And?"

"And now it's time for the science lesson, right?"

Her face was incredulous, like he'd just moved into the nicest house in her neighborhood and the first thing he was doing was bulldozing it to pieces.

"All right." She straightened in her chair, looking tired now, or maybe he was just now noticing the grayish shimmer beneath her eyes. Another large coffee cup stood beside her briefcase, which she cracked open, revealing a jumble of books and papers and the chaos of styling and organizing items usually found in a woman's handbag. She slid the laptop inside, atop all the other stuff, and swiveled back to face him. "The shock sensation was administered to provide some realism for the experience that followed."

"Realism," he repeated.

"Yes, for the near-death experience. The life review you experienced involved the stimulation of two different areas. The first was the reticular activating system, which is about the size of your little finger and located here, at the top of your brain stem."

She turned her head to the side and pointed to the back, just above her hair clip. As her fingertip disappeared into her fastened-down hair, he couldn't help picturing it in the braids, couldn't help picturing, beneath that blouse sleeve, her bare arm, and the creepy, tattooed hand gripping it. Which was the real Mira, he wondered, the woman here, or the one in the bar? He supposed she had to look somewhat professional for her role in the study. On the other hand, he couldn't shake the feeling that the tattoo and the braids and the belly ring were the disguise—they just didn't seem right on her, seemed to have as little to do with her as some virtual avatar she piloted around—and that her true element was indeed here, in this stuffy little office, in these understated clothes, describing to him the functioning of his brain.

"The reticular activating system is involved in wakefulness, learning, and concentration. Usually it helps focus your attention on elements in the external world. But in conditions of sensory deprivation, or when mental images seem more noteworthy, it will focus you just as strongly on these. When the reticular activating system is overstimulated, it in turn overstimulates the surrounding cortical tissue, leading to hyper-vigilance and rapid thought."

"So it made me think quickly and focus . . . inwardly."

"Right. The second area was a broad cross section of your right tem-poral lobe." She turned and circled her hand beside the right side of her head. "This area is thought to be involved in the storage and retrieval of sensory memory."

"Which fired up the memories."

"Precisely." She'd moved to the edge of her office chair, close enough to Fred that he could see the brown in her eyes, which from any greater distance looked as black as space, and the quantum fuzz in the weave of her blouse collar. She and everything around her seemed to him just a bit too bright.

"And the tunnel?" he asked. "And the light?"

"Those were induced through a gradual flooding of the visual cortex with neural noise. We caused the cells of your vision processing area to fire randomly."

She crumpled her hands into a single tight ball, and let it hover in the air. "Since there are more cells devoted to the center of your visual field, at first only enough of them start firing for you to see a light at the center. Then, as the noise increases, so do the ratio of activated cells"—she let her hands gradually uncurl to form a circle of thumbs and fingers— "and the light appears to spread outward. We all have a forward bias, which means we're inclined to interpret ourselves as moving forward when presented with expanding images. And the light seemed brighter than any you've ever seen because, in a sense, it was. Probably more of your visual cortex cells were stimulated than they would be under any normal conditions. But it didn't hurt your eyes because it wasn't an actual light hitting your retina but a direct stimulation of the light-recognition cells."

He stared at the circle her hands had made, still strangely luminous. The silvery bands of varying widths on the fingers of one hand (her right, he finally remembered to confirm; her left fingers were bare) gleamed. On the cuticles of her right ring and pinky fingers, he noticed the fragmentary remains of a sky blue polish. When he died for real, he wondered if this would be among the moments he'd see replayed.

"Pretty clever of you guys," he said. "But next time, maybe just elec-trocute me and get it over with."

184 • Alex Shakar

He wondered if, along with his own slightly aching head, when he died for real and remembered this, he'd feel the heat rising in Mira's face and neck; if along with the ball of pain and anger expanding in the pit of his chest, he'd feel the stain of disappointment and confusion spreading in hers. He could walk out of this place today and devote the rest of his life to making the people around him feel good instead of bad, it occurred to him, so that in his final minute, he might reexperience from all their perspectives all the pleasure he'd created.

"Well," she said, her voice deliberately even but thickening at the back of her throat, "in addition to that momentary feeling of shock, you've just had a fairly profound experience, haven't you?"

"Profound. Sure." He couldn't stop himself. "Hey, next, why don't you try sticking my brain in one of those hot dog rotisseries? I bet that would be profound."

And this exemplary moment, too, would parade by in the end.

"I suppose it's true," she said, "that how profound you find these sessions is up to you. But you might consider the fact that without your being in any danger, we've allowed you to experience something like what you might feel happening to you at the moment of your death." She let this resound, then went on more softly. "And now that you have some inkling of what dying might actually be like, you no longer have to be afraid of it. You know what's going to happen. You'll see your life flashing by in a whole new context. You'll move through a tunnel and toward a bright light. The light will envelop you. You'll meet a being, an angel, or even—"

"—or even you," he said.

"I don't follow," she said slowly.

"It waved. You reached up for the shade. With the wing-like light of the computer monitors to either side. I was seeing you, somehow. And no offense. Maybe you mean well. But you're no fucking angel."

Her dark eyes wandered off; her pale face seemed to blanch even more. She looked—strangely—crushed, as if he'd just extinguished some last hope of her own. His first instinct was to ask for her forgiveness. But who was supposed to be helping who here? And anyway, she was already meeting his gaze, embarrassed at the weakness she'd shown, professionally cool again.

"That makes a certain kind of sense," she admitted. "But it in no way—"

"—negates—" Fred mocked.

"—*invalidates*—" Inner George sunnily chimed.

"—*delegitimizes*," Mira went on slowly, "what you experienced in that other place, or who it was that you saw."

She waited. Fred said nothing.

"You called out to him," she said. "You said, 'What are you *doing* here?' Don't you remember that? It was George, wasn't it?"

The mic on the helmet. Fred hadn't realized he'd said it aloud.

They sat in silence. His anger was gone for the moment, replaced by something harder to bear. Whether or not he'd actually died, he hadn't entirely returned, didn't entirely want to. He was still wandering around in those memories. The airlift from the stairs. The superhero costume, magic act, spinning van, stalled road trip. A feeling tone to all of it, a sadness he didn't quite understand, almost like a pity for these hapless mortals. Though when he got to the scene in the department store, it didn't fail to make him smile.

"Neither of us knew the other would be in that store," he told her. "We'd both gone in on the spur of the moment, ducking in out of the rain. He'd had a falling out with his wife. I'd had one with my girlfriend. We were both just wandering around."

She watched him for a while, her expression unreadable.

"What you and George had for all those years," she said, sitting very still, "few people get to have, even for a day. Most people will never know a connection like that." A hint of something, stridency, bitterness, had crept into her voice. "They'll never know how alone they are."

She kept staring at him, wanting to drive home the point. He leaned his head back, closed his eyes. He could still see on the backs of his lids the liquid light outline of the spiral, the blotch of light in the center, like an afterburn from looking at the sun. And floating below it, that bright form with its arm raised. George. Or Mira. Or just light. Or not even light. The smarting of a few overtaxed rods and cones.

"I'm sorry this one was so difficult," he heard Mira say. He heard her get up.

"No," he said. "This was your best one yet."

By the time he opened his eyes, the lamp was off, and she was crouched by the baseboard, over the fat little glowing star.

"Just wait till next week," she said.

Fred left the suite, the new CD Mira had given him in one hand, his briefcase in the other, watching the linoleum floor drift beneath him like some speckled wasteland far below. When the elevator began its descent and his internal organs lifted, he closed his eyes, trying to see that figure of light just outside the bigger light, but by now, it had dispersed into the general background radiation.

A couple months ago, he'd spent an evening reading through dozens of firsthand accounts of near-death experiences: Fantastic out-of-body voyages to the end of the universe and beyond. Meetings with dead loved ones, angels, God Himself in varying forms—Jesus, Buddha, a gigantic pillar of light. Guided tours of the secret workings of Creation—over-souls, onenesses, consciousnesses on planetary and galactic scales, reincarnation, oceans of pure love. Mysterious, miraculous returns—hearts unexpectedly restarted, bleeding stanched, spontaneous cancer remissions. On most websites devoted to such accounts, there could be found a special subset: coma journeys. When he'd first heard his mother's Reiki group using this brain-bendingly hopeful oxymoron, Fred had assumed it was their own invention, but in fact it was an established mytheme in the New Age cosmology. And of course it was these stories he was mainly looking for: Patients who'd awoken after hours or days or weeks, and reported having witnessed past lives in vivid detail. Who described being pulled back to wakefulness by nets of love. Who now viewed their pre-coma lives as nothing more than a dream, and the everyday captivations of the world as but a trifling game.

With each account, he'd felt himself trembling on the precipice of conversion, only to step back a minute later, for all the usual reasons. The similarities between the stories seemed on the one hand compelling, on the other, suspect, psychologically attributable to the experiencers' prior expectations. The differences were even more maddening: some saw trapped souls and ghosts, whereas others said they were shown that there were no such things; some were taken to orchards, others to cities of God, and of these said cities, no two were the same. Why was there never any proof? Why the lack of verifiable, unimpeachable details in those past lives? How was one supposed to do this thing Mira had talked about, stand that two-sided coin on edge? It was a fork in the road, either/or, George with wings outside the light or Mira processed through a hypercharged visual cortex. What sort of gymnastic quantum superposition could allow one to go both ways at once?

And what if it had been George, somehow? Hovering between here and the beyond. Waving, or warning, or waiting for help.

Out on the sidewalk, Fred put away the CD and blinked in the brightness. The summer crowd was out in force, a living mass so dense it seemed at any moment a second-story layer of window-browsers might start swarming over the heads of the first. Maybe it was the lingering sense of distance from it all, the odd feeling he was reliving rather than living it, but whatever the cause, it took him a second or two to realize he was watching his own mother across the street, appearing and disappearing in the chinks of passersby as she made her way south.

He crossed and caught up to her. She was wearing her fade-tint sunglasses, gazing slightly downward into the swarm of arms and legs around her. When he said hello and she looked up, he wasn't sure at first if she recognized him. Then she smiled.

"Fred. Where'd *you* come from?"

"Just . . . doing some errands. I'm on my way back to the office for a few minutes, and then I'm heading to the hospital."

"I was just up there. Your dad's there now."

Her bangs were edging over the tops of her sunglasses, giving her a look of youthful rebellion.

"So where are you headed?" Fred asked as they started walking together.

"Oh . . . I just got off the train, and . . ." She hesitated for a moment, then added with resolve, "I'm doing some Reiki."

"Oh yeah? Got a new client?" To Fred's knowledge, she'd only been working on George and other patients in the hospital. He congratulated himself on how nonjudgmental he'd managed to sound.

"I guess you could say that."

There was something of a private joke in her tone. He looked at her. "You guess?"

She took his arm gently. Her smile was almost pitying. "Fred, your crazy mom's about to seem even crazier."

"She is?"

"Do you remember that vision I had during your attunement?"

"The vortex," he said. The word felt strange in his mouth. They entered a long tunnel of scaffolding, stretching along half the buildings of the block.

"I started feeling it." She was staring ahead of them, into the crowd.

"What do you mean?"

"The other day, when I left the hospital, when I was out on the sidewalk," she said, her voice getting quieter, a shade darker, too, "it was like a storm was curling around me."

Still beneath the scaffolding, they crossed a chilled gust from an air-conditioned store.

"When I'm doing Reiki on someone," she went on, "and they're out of balance, I can feel it. I can feel the way the energy is coming off of them. It hits me in waves. It can make me a little sick to my stomach, even, until the Reiki smoothes things out. That's what it was like on the street. But even stronger . . . and sicker. Wave after wave of it. I just had to hold up my hands."

She stopped beside a crossbar in the scaffolding and brought her hands to about chest level. Her eyes, behind those tinted lenses, had closed.

"And then all this Reiki started flowing into me from above, and out of me to the city. The street kept pulling and pulling, it needed so much. Until finally, the crazy whirl started calming down." She lowered her hands, looking at him now. "Until that one street was clear."

To his relief, she started walking again. In shock, he'd simply nodded, trying to seem thoughtful rather than fearful for her sanity. Ahead of them, the river of heads could be seen emerging from under the scaffolding into the sun.

"I've been doing it a bit every day," she was saying. "I'll get off at this or that subway stop, wherever I get the feeling, and walk around. And when I start feeling that wild energy again, I do Reiki on it."

It occurred to Fred now that, with his preparations for Florida over the weekend, his times at the hospital hadn't overlapped with hers as much as usual. And that the times they had, she'd seemed elusive. More than once, she'd taken the opportunity of leaving shortly after he'd arrived.

"Have you told anyone else about this?" he asked, the words barely getting out.

"Yeah, I told the group." She smiled. "They went out and tried it. We're all doing it now."

"You're all doing Reiki," his voice rose, "on the streets?"

"That's what we're calling it. *Street Reiki*." She pronounced the phrase with a self-deprecatingly theatrical emphasis. "Rudolf says it makes us sound like guerilla warriors."

"Rudolph." He thought. *Gandalf.* "The bearded guy?"

The scaffolding ended and they were back out in the blaze. At the corner of Houston Street, they stopped, waiting for the traffic light next to half a dozen garbage bags piled around a trash can. The summer mob began massing at the curb, multihued shopping bags brimming with shoes and clothes and electronics and food and health supplements. The scent of suntan lotion rising off all those bare arms and legs over-whelmed even the exhaust fumes and tincture of heated garbage, putting Fred in mind of a day at the beach. The only vortex he could see here was a whirlwind of money and pheromones. The only hint of imbalance was the giant African child passing on a bus ad for a charity. If anywhere, the vortex seemed to be out there, out in the world at large—wars, crises, famines, rabid ideologies, environmental horrors wheeling round and round them without touching them at all. The city, this summer, seemed fine. Better than fine. Better than ever. Though maybe this very appear-ance of health could be considered cause for suspicion. Like too rosy cheeks, or a sudden absence of pain.

"So you're all just . . . walking around like this, now?" he asked.

"We try to make at least five stops."

"Why five?"

"I was thinking about the Muslims. How they pray five times a day. How much commitment it shows."

A slight archness had snuck into her tone. She sounded a bit like a football coach, giving grudging credit to an opposing team.

This is all your fault, he grumbled to Inner George.

My fault? Inner George snapped back. *Who's the idiot who kept me breathing?*

Who's the moron who wouldn't go back to chemo?

Who's the dumbfuck who flushed my company down the toilet, eh, Freddo?

Stop fucking calling me that.

Freddo, Fred meant. Not dumbfuck. That one he'd cop to.

The light changed, and the crowd swept him and his mother across. A few feet past the south corner, she weaved her way over to the display window of a Pottery Barn, then turned back and faced the street.

"I'm feeling the storm here," she said quietly, nervous or excited, her sunglasses catching the light as she looked this way and that. "You can try it with me, if you want."

Before he could even think to panic she was doing it—her eyes shut behind those lenses; her face tilted upward; her arms higher than last time (that, apparently, had been just a demonstration), stretched toward the sky.

Fred gaped, then glanced around. A construction barricade and a vendor's table full of NYPD-logoed women's underwear took up part of the sidewalk, so that the pedestrian traffic had to skew around them, regarding them with puzzlement or annoyance. Behind them, on a low ledge beneath the window, a bum in a Hawaiian shirt and a Superman cap slept with a bent cigarette in his mouth. Fred locked onto that red S, the image of George and the sandbox flashing brightly through his mind. And instantly out, banished by someone's swinging handbag. His mother's hands, he saw, trembled a bit more than usual, but her expression was growing less tense, more lax and inward, the way she'd looked last week holding her hands over his temples. She wasn't a large person, standing about a head shorter than him; he worried someone would inadvertently knock her over. To protect her, though in retrospect he was probably just making matters worse, he got in front of her, so as to serve as a kind of barrier reef against the human tide. He fumbled for some way of diverting attention from the two of them. At first he tried to make it look like they were both squinting to see something up in the sky, but he had to stop this because other people started turning fearfully and looking, for low-flying aircraft, no doubt, causing more of a disturbance than before. He then stepped to the corner and fished a copy of the *Daily News* out of a trash can—

Are you AGONY
playing?

—and stepped back and opened it, pretending to be so entranced by the deadly Bronx fire or the paper's promotional Scratch n' Match game that he was glued to the spot. But this only seemed to make people jostle him more angrily. He had almost succeeded in losing himself in an article about how the UN had been deemed a firetrap when the paper was battered by some passing elbow like a sail in a gale.

What was he supposed to do now?

Inner George didn't bother offering an opinion. Though he did chuckle when Fred closed his eyes as well, holding his palms out in front of him.

The first thing Fred felt was fright, the nightmarish sensation of driving blind. He could sense the impatient bodies coming toward him, swerving around, buffeting his arms. He could smell the sharp chemical odor of their perfumes, hear the thin, percussive chains of drumbeats in their earphones, the fragments of their conversations about people he didn't know but might as well have known—someone who was so nasty, someone who didn't know *at all* but acted like he did, someone else named Ritchie who couldn't believe it. Fred wasn't even trying to do Reiki—the prospect of engaging in yet one more act of make-believe after the helmet session and visualization today made him want to scoop out his brain and mash it like Play-Doh. He was only trying to draw fire away from his mother. It was like being conveyed through a car wash without a car. In fearful elation, he stood rigid against it all, letting the noises and odors and bodies begin to whittle him down. In an aeon, he'd find himself remade—a gaunt, rarefied hoodoo of a man.

"WAKE UP MOTHA FUCKIN' SLEEPY HEAD!"

Some kid shouted this in his ear as he passed, his friends laughing. Fred didn't open his eyes. The sense of chaos around him redoubled with each passing second—the weave of voices, the rumble of engines, the press of bodies, a steady jerking at his arm—

"We should go, honey."

Fred blinked. The bum was snoozing away, the corners of his chapped lips serenely upturned. Holly's hand was on Fred's forearm. She was looking up at him with a questioning smile. He forced a smile in return, and once more was following her south. It was somehow a shock to see it all again—the motley canyon of buildings, the bobbing heads; everything seemed to be both here and not here, bleaching into the too bright light.

"So what did you feel?" she asked.

He'd certainly felt a lot of things, but nothing, he assured himself, demonstrably supernatural, which he assumed was what she was asking about. "I don't know," he said. "I didn't really know what to do."

"You don't have to. The Reiki knows. Just say Reiki in your head three times, Reiki Reiki Reiki, and let it flow however it wants."

She seemed calmer now, recharged by the successful healing of Broadway and Houston. They walked on, crossing Prince Street in a row of people who just happened to be swinging their arms in parallel. *Three times*, he thought. Like Dorothy, clicking her ruby slippers. The image led him to that proud red S on its yellow shield, first on the bum's cap, then on George's chest in that childhood sandbox. Which in turn made Fred's stomach lift an inch. They made way for a harried Asian woman pushing one of those double strollers. All he saw of its occupants before looking away were four wide, flat eyes and a pair of pouts. Enough to make him queasier still. Holly tracked them as they went by, looking warmed by the sight.

"Mom," he said, the air around him going foamy and prickly, "did you make George and me Superman costumes when we were kids?"

"You remember that? Yeah," she softly sang, "I made them for you guys for Halloween. We have pictures, somewhere."

He thought he could recall the feel of that little cape against the backs of his arms, the thickness and heat of the ungainly red-and-yellow patch over his heart.

"Why would you make us the exact same costume?"

"It wasn't up to me. You both wanted that one. You two wore them everywhere. For weeks."

"We did?" he asked. "For weeks?"

She laughed. "You refused to wear anything else."

"Why did you let us wear those things *for weeks*?"

"You liked them," she said.

The glare on the street, he admitted to himself, was beyond anything natural. It must have been an aftereffect from the session. It brought back even more that feeling of the life review. As though not just he but everyone out here were in that final minute of brainlife, every consciousness being dipped in this orgasmic frenzy of color and motion and noise one last time before it would all get whisked away. He thought of himself and George in those blue-and-red costumes, pulling apart the shovel. He thought of George in that blue-and-red shirt in the department store, the two of them starting with shock. They'd wandered around after that, he and George, first through the aisles of the store, next through the streets, mostly griping about their significant others. They passed a lesbian bar on West 12th and George steered them inside. In the course of ordering drinks, George started talking to two women, one lanky and freckled, the other round and busty, both of them sunburned. The women turned out to be Army, awaiting redeployment to the Green Zone. They sat with George and Fred awhile, drunk and getting drunker. George asked them if gay women nagged or if that was just a straight-woman thing, and they said they nagged each other half to death. He asked them about the war, but they wouldn't talk about it, said they didn't want to depress themselves. Instead, they went on in wistful tones about the first Gulf War, which they hadn't been in but wished they had; how in that one there'd been no need to shoot the enemy, barely a need to bomb them; how American tanks had had plows on the front and just plowed the poor fools under, and all you'd see afterwards were tank tracks in the sand.

By the end of the night, the four of them were hunched together on a bench by the Hudson, sipping beer through straws from bagged bottles. The women shared a cigarette, their heads leaned together sleepily. George was still riled, going on about how Jill secretly didn't like him anymore, how she was just sticking around hoping he'd go back to the way he used to be.

"That's crazy," Fred said.

"Crazy? Crazy of me?" George said.

"Of her."

"Right. It's crazy."

"Totally," Fred said, though in truth he was egging George on for precisely the same reason, because he wanted the old George back—Supergeorge—the one who pontificated and scratched his head and waved his fingers in the air as he talked; who struck up conversations with strangers and walked around half the night; who, at the very least, wanted to be Fred's friend. They hadn't hung out like this in a long time.

"That's the problem with relationships," George was saying. "It's a contract. You agree to be some unchanging caricature of yourself. To act the same way all the time. Never to change. It's counter-evolutionary. How can anything new and good come into your life, if you're holding on to something that doesn't exist anymore?"

George sounded like he was trying to convince himself.

"Exactly," Fred said. And because George looked at him to see whether he was really serious or just drunkenly parroting him, and because, too, Fred wanted to one-up him, he added, "I'm through with Mel."

"No you're not," George said.

"Am too," Fred insisted.

"*Am too*," the lanky one repeated in a drawl, to her lover's snorting laugh.

And then Fred staggered back to the Zeckendorf, climbed into his warm bed with Mel, and promptly made up. And George went home and asked for a divorce. There weren't many nights on the town together after that.

Fred and his mother were standing on the southwest corner of Canal Street. She'd led them to the granite wall of what looked to have once been a bank, and was now a Payless shoe store, with a vendor's alcove full of Bob Marley T-shirts, plastic bongs, pirated DVDs, and smoking incense. A hot dog cart and a shish kebob cart shimmered in their own heat by the curb. The too-bright light he'd been seeing had faded back into the usual everyday impossible city.

"Do you have to lift your hands?" he asked. "Can't you just close your eyes, or do something less conspicuous?"

She was looking around at nothing, at the air in front of her. He tried to imagine the lashing waves of that out-of-control vortex she was presumably feeling.

"I tried that," she said. "It just doesn't work the same."

Reiki issues aside, he thought he could understand this. There wouldn't have been the same fearful thrill, free-falling surrender. It was a leap of faith, out of the imagination and into the world. There was no way he could stop her. He wasn't even sure he wanted to.

"So what's the street feel like when it's clear?" he asked.

Behind those shaded lenses, he could see her eyes sparkling with something, tears or triumph, or both.

"To me, it feels like a baby." She smiled. "Sleeping in my arms."

He looked off down Broadway, blinking, into the kaleidoscopic streams of sunglassed heads and yellow taxi hulls. By the time he looked back, she had brought her hands up, just in time for every single person on the roofdeck of a passing tourist bus to gawk at her, a few snapping pictures.

He shut his eyes, reached for the sky—this time, to his surprise, looking forward to it.

And it's back again, the glare, stronger than ever. It rebounds off the low white drop ceiling, blanches the dull red linoleum tacking to these checkered shoes. The community room is a glowing netherworld, a place of inversions, where excited children have been replaced by hostile seniors, or hostile to Fred, at any rate. He pulls an endless string of scarves from Vartan's mouth, and a long-eared, leftward-listing man lasers Fred with blistery eyes. He glues Vartan's feet to the floor, and a bag-jawed lady in thick glasses emits a rasping sigh. The audience murmurs with approval as Vartan glowers over Fred with his metal rings. They suck at their dentures as Fred maneuvers the rings over Vartan's head and binds his arms. The only exception is today's birthday boy, front and center, a radiant shrunken apple of a man who's just turned a hundred. He smiles impartially and perpetually, a toothless, lipless smile, his eyes above it like unbuttoned buttons peeking through their wrinkled holes, a smile that would reassure Fred but for the nagging suspicion it might remain there unchanged were Fred and his father to stop pouring fake pitchers into newspaper cones and instead douse each other with gasoline and light a match.

Fred is supposed to be the one to go into the wooden box (they can't very well crate up the centenarian), and Vartan is supposed to make him disappear, then feel remorseful; but Vartan changes the script. Responding to some new dramatic insight, Vartan's movements have been becoming more hesitant, as if he's discovered his bones to be made of shale. He's playing an older man than he was previously; no less angry, if anything, more, but with a helpless, pathetic aspect to the rage. Instead of tricking and kicking Fred into the box, Vartan stops him with a palm, and begins lowering himself to hands and knees. He looks so frail Fred instinctively reaches out a hand to help, but, proud in his defeat, Vartan waves him away and crawls inside.

Fred spins and disappears his father, spins and fails to reappear him, worrying about Vartan in that tight, enclosed space designed for a child. The audience is picking up on Fred's distress, nodding as if it's about time, about time this no-good, disrespectful son—this son who very likely has not visited his old man in the old folks' home nearly as often as he should—finally feels remorse. Then Fred is spinning again, the room whirling, those old faces and pastel bulletin board flyers for blood drives, bingo games, self-defense lessons warping and slipping around the hole where George should have been across from him like water around a rock. There's no flash-powder bomb—which, after all, might have stopped a frail heart out there—but the room is so bright now that Fred almost thinks one must have gone off, as the door falls open, and Vartan, a white-haired, white-tuxed whiteness within the whiteness emerges. Slowly, dazedly, Vartan rises, blinking and looking about. They embrace, clinging to each other as if they'd just seen a roomful of ghosts, as the ghosts themselves watch them, touched, or perhaps just unsure if it's over, until the birthday boy raises his parchment hands and issues a papery clap.

The two of them sat in the van after loading it in silence.

"What the fuck was that?" Vartan muttered.

Though the brightness was gone, Fred's dreamlike feeling that he was dead, or that everyone was dead, hadn't entirely worn off.

"Weird show," he agreed. "But seemed like it went OK."

Really, it had gone better than OK. Once the audience had started clapping, it had become clear they'd been not only entertained but moved. Fred, too, had been moved, and a little disturbed, by his father's performance—Vartan seemed to have discovered a whole new depth to the part. And moved or not, the birthday boy had seemed happy enough to receive his requisite stuffed toucan, clutching it a little obscenely to his blanketed lap and gazing up at Fred and Vartan with those tiny nut-brown eyes.

"Whole new market, maybe," Fred added.

"They're not supposed to root for the washed-up old man," Vartan said. "That's not the point." He was strangely agitated, patting down his tux jacket, in search of his pipe. "Shoot me before it comes to parking me in one of those places, OK?"

Fred said OK, and waited while his father toked up.

Sighing smoke, Vartan looked over. "There's nothing sadder than old people still crazy for magic."

The mustache ticked, just enough to show who he was really talking about. Neither of them could look at the other for long. Vartan turned the ignition and the radio came on. They listened to a story about a JFK passenger in an Arabic script T-shirt being told he couldn't fly.

"I think we'll make it," Vartan said, taking a last quick hit. They were in Cobble Hill, Brooklyn—the nursing home was two blocks from the apartment—but in the interest of time, were headed straight to LaGuardia. "You got everything you need in that carry-on bag?"

Fred nodded.

"You got some good shoes to wear?"

He nodded again, though his dress shoes had holes in them and he couldn't afford new ones, and anyway, he was probably too superstitious at this point to stop wearing George's checkered shoes. His brother had gotten not only the shoes, but an entire checkered outfit on that trip two years back, as a kind of tribute, after all his belongings were stolen at knifepoint and some Czech dot-com burnouts he'd hooked up with had taken up a collection for him. Fred still had on his cell phone, texted to him by a gracious stranger, a picture of George in a checkered cap, a checkered shirt, a pair of checkered pants, hiked up to display checkered socks, and the shoes.

"I put your mail in the side pocket."

"Thanks," Fred said, wishing his father hadn't been so thoughtful, not particularly eager to breast the latest wave of bills and collection notices. They listened to a story about a marine prison guard forcing Saddam Hussein to watch the *South Park* movie over and over and over again.

"When's your tweezer arraignment?" Vartan asked, apparently reminded by Saddam's ordeal.

"Monday morning."

"You're not a flight risk, are you? I'd like to get my fifty bucks back."

"Don't worry. Justice will be served."

They listened, uneasily, to a story about a male nurse in jail for murdering dozens of his helpless patients with lethal injections. The man was now donating a kidney to help the brother of a former girlfriend.

"Your mom and I will be there," Vartan said, preempting Fred's question. "OK. Let's roll."

At a stoned crawl, they pulled out of the nursing home's service entrance and Fred watched the greenery in planters and the co-ops that once had been tenements inch by. Before the show, he'd spent as much time as he could in Manhattan, with George. He'd pointed out to the nurses the colorlessness of his brother's urine and asked them to check his osmolality and electrolytes. He'd read to George a paper by an Oxford philosophy professor who argued that, according to the principle of mediocrity, it was far more probable this particular human experience was just a collection of algorithms being crunched in some gargantuan simulation software than actual flesh-and-blood people in an actual place; followed, skipping over the parts where the equations got too dense, by a paper by an astrophysicist who claimed that according to the math, the universe had never been created to begin with. Finally, without specificity, he'd described the upcoming trip to George as being for business, trying to sound neither upset, which he was, nor excited, which, guiltily, he was a little bit too.

Vartan's cell phone rang. He batted aside his cape and jacket and extracted it from the leather holster clipped to his cummerbund.

"Yeah, we're headed to the airport," Vartan said after a moment. "We just did a show. At the hospital where they were born. Remember it?"

The show hadn't in fact been at the hospital, which they were passing now, but the nursing home down the block. Possibly Vartan had just become confused—happily, if not willfully so. He reached over and began moving Fred's head around, as if examining it for lice. "He's got gray hairs now. You believe that?"

"Gray hairs?" Fred heard the brassy edge of Manny's voice boom through the tiny speaker.

Vartan released Fred's head, shaking his own sadly. "George's has grown back in, and it's still all dark."

Manny said something quieter.

"Yeah. Yeah, well. So what do you want?" He listened, turned to Fred. "Manny wants you to get him an acting job with the military."

"I'll see what I can do."

"He wants to direct," Vartan conveyed.

Whenever Fred wanted to describe Manfred Kent to anyone who'd been watching TV in North America any time of day or night between the years of 1984 and 1990, all he usually had to do was remind them of a commercial for a money transfer service in which a miserable-looking couple is sitting facing the camera, and the husband is on the phone asking for money to be wired *today*, and the wife is nervously watching the husband, and behind them is standing a tall, silent, and motionless motorcycle cop in a helmet and sunglasses. It was one of those commercials that, thanks to some strange corporate whim, got aired over and over for season after season; and that finally, just when you were allowed to forget about it for a few weeks, mysteriously reappeared to bludgeon you with another heavy rotation. This was Manny—the motorcycle cop—in, if not his biggest, then at any rate his most profitable role. In real life he was anything but silent or still, constantly in motion, impossible to keep track of, always gaining or losing things, property, jobs, wives. He'd been a fixture in Fred and George's childhood—whenever they saw the man, they knew they'd be in for a day out of the ordinary, following him around as he hit on women and pitched films he was dreaming up on the spot to anyone who looked well-off.

He'd moved to L.A. in the mid-eighties, and the last time Fred had seen him was about a dozen years ago, on one of those aimless road trips. Fred had crashed at George's sunny apartment complex in San Jose, hanging out in his ratty leather jacket by the pool while George went to work, winking at the women who thought he was George and otherwise causing difficulties, until George finally agreed to take a few days off. They drove down Highway 1 and Manny met them in Malibu and took them out to the property he'd recently purchased, a thin, twisting, two-acre strip of creased earth at the bottom of a steep gulch. In order to keep out the riffraff, the owners of the luxury estates adorning the surrounding hilltops had thought to buy the entire hills on which their homes were situated, down to the very feet of their slopes; but when it came to the cragged gulch bottom, they either supposed that no one would ever want it or perhaps believed that they themselves already owned it. Doubtless, though, they were now ruing their carelessness, for Manny, lacking the funds at present to build a house, had settled down there in a pup tent, with a pack of half-starved, "rescued" pound dogs to protect his belongings (a trunk full of clothes and, of course, the tent). His bathroom was a hole in the ground, which the dogs efficiently, if revoltingly, vied for the privilege of keeping clean. The hole had at first been entirely out in the open, but was now, in a neighborly response to the hilltop homeowners' complaints to the local police, walled on three sides by beach towels tied to stakes, high enough to cover up the fine points of the act itself, but still low enough for Manny, as he squatted, to cheerfully wave hello to the neighbors gaping in horror from the decks and picture windows above. Manny offered Fred and George his tent, and himself lay under the stars by the opening, lecturing Fred about how he needed to be more like his brother and get his life in order, while, from either end of the gulch, the spooked dogs howled stereophonically in the darkness.

Manny was in his fifties then, but still energetic enough to live in that gulch for three months, jogging a mile to the beach and back every day, until finally his neighbors, in grudging respect for his business acumen, chipped in and bought him out for a fourfold profit.

"Manny says you can stay with him," Vartan told Fred, the phone still at his ear.

Fred quickly said he had a hotel. They settled on dinner.

While George had never talked to Fred directly about his last ill-fated mission down to Armation, he'd filled him in on the aftermath, how he'd proceeded to get very, very drunk in a nearby barbecue restaurant, and then called Manfred, who'd come and driven him all over Florida, it seemed to George, pep-talking nonsense in his ear. George awoke the next day in Manny's efficiency apartment, unfurnished save for a very old mattress and a chair. George had gotten the mattress. Manny had slept in his van.

Vartan holstered the phone, turned to Fred. "He said if I want to act again, I could move down to Florida and he'd put me in one of his digital movies."

"He's still making those movies?"

"In the 'Danish Style.'" Vartan shook his head.

"What style is that, again?"

"No idea." Vartan unclipped his bowtie, clipped on his sunglasses as they idled at a light.

"He was there, you know," Vartan said, with a backward thumb.

Manny, he meant. The hospital, he meant. Where they hadn't just performed. There when Fred and George were born.

"I remember that," Fred said.

"You remember that?"

"You told me."

"He was staying with your mom and me," Vartan said anyway. "After his first wife kicked him out."

Your favorite story, Inner George teased.

"Me and Manny were having an argument," Vartan went on. "About acting. Theory. We cared a lot about that kind of shit. Whether you're inside or outside the character, whether he's you or you're him. We could go on for hours. We were getting loud, and then your mom came out of the bedroom and said it was time to go. She had this look on her face."

Vartan pulled onto the expressway. Around his father, Fred saw the unnatural brightness returning, as if that skylight in the sky were opening up directly above the van, a light so strong it came through the roof, giving his father's face a quartz-like luster. Fred felt a longing for it, for that other place, whatever it was, on the other side.

"I sent Manny down to pull my car up in front of the house." Vartan's eyes misted. "Sixty-four-and-a-half Mustang hardtop, sapphire blue. Two-eighty-nine horsepower, four-valve, low-compression."

Fred tilted his head skyward against the window, looking for that bright white portal, the one they'd all see in the end, thanks to oxygen deprivation, and think they were headed somewhere good. It seemed the height of mercy, or the cruelest trick of all. Though either way, it was hard not to infer a crazy wisdom in the design.

"So I get your mother down to the stoop, and Manny comes running up the street, saying the car wasn't where I said. It was gone." Vartan's hand swiped the air. "Stolen. So we had to walk your mother to the hospital."

Fred knew, from the repeated tellings, the punch line was coming, but would have known anyway from the way his dad's mustache was spreading.

"The gods took my car," Vartan said. "And gave me an extra son."

Fred had known this too, of course, that he'd come as a surprise. Vartan gestured with his hairy chin toward the Lower Manhattan skyline, scrolling by across the river on their left.

"The Twin Towers opened for business that year," he added, as though it meant something.

Fred changed out of his tux in the back of the van, strapped his briefcase to his carry-on, and in full business-travel-warrior mode, clambered out, through the fumes and cabs and stacked baggage and into the third-world din of LaGuardia Airport. In the wake of the liquid-bomb plot, the crowds were thicker and the delays more horrific than usual. One of the few on-time flights seemed to be his own, a mixed blessing, given the quarter-mile security-checkpoint line snaking off down a dank corridor behind the counters. The overall feeling was of a system under mounting strain. Fluorescent lights faltered, missing ceiling panels gaped like open sores, exposing the veins of pipes and wires; the skeletal metal gridwork. Meanwhile, beneath, the travelers waited, so ardently groomed by comparison: those deep indigo jeans, that form-fitting hoodie. It probably was time to get out of this city, Fred thought. If not this country. Follow the narcotic rush of capital to China. Seek social-democratic rehab in Northern Europe. Barring such ruthlessness, though, maybe there wasn't too much more to be done than look one's best, try to manifest the good life one had been led to expect, hope that one's sheer belief in the system's continuance would somehow keep it all rolling along.

After a forty-minute wait in the security line, Fred sock-footed through the scanner with nary a beep. His belongings, however, were slow catching up. Two other agents behind the machine took their time squinting at the screen. When the bags finally trundled through, one of the men—a hefty guy with a face like wet meatloaf—walked alongside them, pointing at Fred with a stubby, latexed finger.

"Yours?"

Fred nodded.

"Could you follow me, please?"

A fourth agent involved himself, carrying the bags to a side table. Fred felt like a microbe swarmed by lymphocytes. The hefty one unzipped the carry-on, brought out Fred's toiletry kit, unzipped that, took out his shaving cream, toothpaste, cough syrup, anti-nausea syrup, saline nasal spray, and mouthwash. Then pulled out the four-dollar enhanced water drink Fred had just bought, in a spree of financial optimism, before getting in line.

"Sir?" the man said. "What planet you been on lately?"

Fred checked his watch. Five minutes to boarding. "Go ahead and toss them."

The agent considered for a moment, his moist lower lip unfurling like a party blower, then shrugged and swept the items into a bin. Fred made to leave, but the agent wasn't done, unzipping an outer pocket, this time producing a small, taped-up cardboard box Fred had never seen before.

"You know what's in here?"

Fred shook his head, too stunned to reply. The agent flipped the box around: Fred's name and address, printed on the front. The agent pointed to it.

"You?"

"Yes. Sorry. My father put my mail in there. I didn't think—"

"You know what it is, now?"

Fred leaned in, reading the return address: Macy's.

The guy rattled the box. "You mind?" He peeled the tape and removed a smaller gift box, and a card:

Compliments. Lord Shiva.

"You know this Lord guy?"

"Birthday coming up," Fred said.

The agent kept eyeing him, first like a potential threat, then like a prize idiot. He opened the box:

A Swiss Army knife.

After another twenty minutes of checking the knife-laden bag at the counter, talking his way around the line and back through security, Fred arrived panting at the gate to discover his flight was now two and a half hours delayed. He set up camp on the concourse carpet by a wall socket and searched the gift card and packing slip for clues. The card had no other words but what the agent had read. The slip listed Lord Shiva as the purchaser, with a return address from the same fictional town as the website, this time in Pennsylvania. He called up Macy's. The knife had been purchased online a few days ago with a gift card. Beyond this, they could not, or would not, tell him anything.

He hadn't had a chance to examine the thing closely. He didn't know whether or not it was precisely the same model he'd gotten George for his birthday six years ago, but it looked pretty similar. George had carried the multitool around with him everywhere, using it for everything from hard drive installation to beer-bottle opening, until he'd finally lost it, or given it away, or thrown it out, as he had most of his belongings toward the end. If sending this new one to Fred was an attempt to gain his trust, to make him think that the sender had had George's trust, it wasn't a very convincing one. Anyone who'd known George at all might have known about the thing. And why seek to gain Fred's trust in the first place, he wondered. For what purpose?

Fred couldn't help turning over in his mind something George had said just a week before he'd slipped out of consciousness. Fred had shown up unannounced to find George sitting in full lotus, oxygen tubes in his nose, facing the wall of his living room. The wall was bare, the TV and cable box and Xbox and DVR and the shelves they'd stood on gone.

"I'll get higher-end stuff when I recover," George said, indicating the space where the entertainment center had been. His tone was bright, but too thin, his throat caving in around the words. He'd developed a scary new sound in the last couple weeks, clearing his throat all the way at the base, almost like he was gagging. He did it again now: "*Kghhhhhhhhhhhh-hhhhhhhrk.*" His oxygen tank sat next to him on the rug where the coffee table had been, for the moment unused. "*Kghhhhhhhhhhhhhhhhhhhhrk.* I just needed a good, clear wall, you know?"

Fred told him to get his shoes on. Told him it was time to go.

"Go where?" George had returned his attention to that good, clear wall, his eyes glassy.

Fred told him that he was through with George running down the clock on his next round of treatments. He had made an appointment for that morning and George was going. Fred practically bellowed this. He wanted to sound like fate itself, no possibility of denial.

"You know, Fred, you really need to make some friends. I can't be your entire social life. *Kghhhhhhhhhhhhhhhhhhhhrk.*"

Fred told him again to get ready, his imperious tone already quavering.

George's attention drifted down to his hands, nested in his lap. "One more week," he bargained.

Fred was almost outside of his skin by now from the shock, the possibility that he might not get his brother out. "Please don't tell me you think staring at a wall is going to heal you."

George looked up at him with a thin smile and an unearthly light in his eyes, as though he might dissolve the chaos of those bits of bone and teeth and eyeball, those bits of skin and liver and gonad and pulsing heart, with nothing but his measured outbreaths:

"Maybe I'm not in this for healing."

Fred had been assigned a middle seat. One half of an elderly couple sat to either side of him, the woman apparently having insisted on the aisle and the man the window. For the flight's duration, they proceeded to bicker across Fred about the way their grandchildren were being raised, a fugue-like, circling debate, every so often switching sides to give each of them the pleasure of both attacking and defending their daughter-in-law and son. Briefly, Fred peeked at the rest of the mail, which he'd transferred to his briefcase—a $9,500 hospital bill, an overdraft notice, a cutoff letter from his credit card company, a $400 shoplifting fine assessed by the supermarket chain—before bonneting his head in an airplane blanket, a lone red thread trembling before his eyes.

At the rental lot, near midnight, they were out of economy, compact, midsize, standard, and full-size cars, so Fred was given a minivan, albeit with a sporty sunroof, and a double dose of car freshener—a sweetish, chemical scent, oddly familiar but vexingly unplaceable, and so powerful that to keep from throwing up he had to drive with the windows down. Perhaps thinking it would relax him, or perhaps wanting to erode any remaining pride and thereby soften him up to take whatever terms Armation would offer, Sam hadn't put him in their usual downtown business hotel but a tourist place out by the amusement parks. It took him another hour and a half to find it. The strip-mall-lined roads in the area all looked alike, especially at night, and seemed designed to confuse and tax the unwary. At one point, he found himself coaxed by large signs onto a tollway which turned out not even to exist; the attendant took his buck fifty almost apologetically, and five hundred feet after the booth, the road opened back up to the normal intersections. At another point, about as lost as he could be, he drove right by that giant, squat, tapered building he'd seen on Sam's monitor, its darkly shimmering glass windows reflecting the white and red streaks of car lights on the highway, its Art Deco cross lit with a spotlight from the grounds below, a sign embedded on the grassy bank by the roadside, the silvery letters sparkling:

He tried to imagine Sam sitting in an auditorium, shaking hands with his neighbors, joining them in song. *Adaption's not such a bad thing.* There was something too obsessive and controlling—too hopelessly Samlike—in Sam's very resolve to reinvent himself from scratch. But on some level wasn't he right? How would it feel, to slide out of everything one was, like from an old skin?

His hotel, once he finally found it, charged him an extra fee for the safe he didn't ask for in the closet of his room, and some other kind of additional tax or fine assessed for not being a resident of Florida. He crawled into bed, and went online, returning to the avatara.us website he'd been directed to after receiving that poem last week. Gone, nothing but an ad farm in its place. Out of ideas, he moved from one Hindu site to another. He read about Shiva, lord of sleep, entropy, and the abyss—the originary source of all, to which all would return. He read about the Hindu trinity, again like the Catholic one but predating it by a thousand years: Shiva the father, source of all; Brahma the holy spirit; Vishnu the son, the one who incarnates, comes down to earth in the form of avataras—Buddha, Christ, Mohammad (and the Twelfth Imam, too, whenever he arrived)—all happily incorporable by the all-emblobulating Hindu cosmology under the rubric of Vishnu. He read more about the nine major avataras that had come, and the one, Kalki, prophesied to come. He read how these ten avataras, from fish to human, were thought, more esoterically, to symbolize the stages of the spiritual evolution of humankind; how all the others had prepared the way for Kalki, who would finally rouse humanity from its slumber of ignorance to the waking consciousness of divine life itself.

Ignorance. There it was again.

What did the word even mean?

Inner George snickered. *Now* that's *ignorance.*

At last, he began to drift, and the next thing he knew, he was in a place as black as space, as close as skin, airless and hot. From somewhere near came the sound of children laughing. A magic show, he understood; he was inside the black satin walls of the old, giant magic hat's false compartment. He couldn't move, could barely breathe, could only wait, hope, trust that soon he'd feel the backs of his brother's fingers, reaching down the nape of his neck, taking hold of his collar, pulling him out. At some point, waking up a little but still under the sway of dreamlogic, he wondered if somehow the dream could be George's, not his; after all, George had always been the one to hide in those hats. Then he was dreaming again, believing he was still awake. An explosion went off. A war of some kind, it seemed, and he was tied down, a prisoner, and had to wake up but couldn't. Another blast. Screams in the distance. He breathed and breathed and at last tore awake with a shout.

The explosions were the rumbling of roller coasters.

The screams were, in fact, screams.

He got up, showered, dressed, took the elevator down, and found his minivan in the sun-baked hotel lot, so sleepy he felt oddly tranquil, as if his body might still be up in that bed, snoozing away, dreaming all this. The hotel's surroundings, a maze of looping service roads around the backs of amusement parks, while desolate and surreal, didn't seem downright malevolent, the way they had by night. Over the park walls, people could be seen waiting on the various scaffolded staircases, every so often climbing a step. They'd slide or ride back down and then start climbing and waiting again, like so many Sisyphuses burdened with beach towels and cameras. It certainly was sunny, anyway. And peaceful, despite the occasional screams.

Proponents of the Many-Worlds Interpretation of quantum mechanics argue that given an infinite number of universes, some, by mere statistical chance, will have cosmological constants hospitable to life; and thus, according to this "weak" anthropic argument, living beings are once again accidental as ever. Adherents of the "strong" anthropic argument, on the other hand, affirm that the cosmos is in some way constructed with life in mind, a planned community, as it were, something perhaps not unlike—though of course on a larger scale—the town of Celebration, USA.

Drowsier now than when he'd set out from the hotel, feeling, in the thick heat, like he was swaddled in a blanket, Fred parked the minivan in a lot on the outskirts of town and boarded a bus disguised as a trolley car, driven by a bus driver disguised as a trolley driver, with outsized epaulets on his shirt and a cartoonishly tented black cap. The trolley/bus wended through the residential neighborhoods, and Fred occupied himself spotting the various house styles he'd seen depicted online—Colonial, French, Victorian, Classical, Mediterranean, Coastal. Homes came in seven different size categories here as well, he'd read, ranging from apartments to estates, the economic strata set apart from block to block but joined at the alleys, bungalows abutting manors, to allow for a comfortable balance of hierarchization and integration. To encourage pedestrian traffic and neighborly interaction, the houses were set close together; the garages were stowed in back alleys; the streets—regularly powerwashed, just as they were at Disney World—were built curved and narrow.

Fred disembarked in the downtown area, and explored a few commercial streets, mists of lite rock emanating from little speakers at the bases of the trees. At the café whose photo he and Sam had scoured for women under sixty, he found a seat on the patio and ordered breakfast. As he ate, swathed in a sunbeam angling under the awning, he took turns gazing out over the placid man-made lake across the street and observing his fellow patrons. At the next table, an elderly couple with matching work done, their weatherproof skin fastened taut beneath marcescent chin bones, alternated chewing their waffles and greeting acquaintances with radiant smiles. Yet also in evidence were a young couple, a middle-aged couple, a family with small children and teenagers; whether these were actual residents or the visitors of older relatives, Fred couldn't be sure, but he didn't feel nearly as out of place as he'd anticipated.

After breakfast, with an hour still to kill before the realtor appointment, he toured the walking paths through the slivers of preserved wetlands separating the housing enclaves, then meandered through a neighborhood or two. Hummers and little electric buggies passed in more or less equal proportion, the latter vehicles carrying sun-hatted retirees in the open-air seats. He had to admit that the houses, even from close range, looked as new as they had in the pictures. Sunlight sparkled in the leaves of trees propped by sturdy wooden braces. He passed a team of green-jumpsuited gardeners, swarming one such tree the way the TSA agents had swarmed his carry-on bag, adjusting the braces and gazing up the length of the trunk, ensuring its straightness. Fred's usual impulse would have been to root out something nefarious about the freaky neatness, but the neatness itself, the utter placidity of the place, made the very attempt to do so seem unnatural, a strain where none was required.

As he headed back downtown, the sunlight seemed to brighten even more. The glare was back, though it felt less, this time, like the light was coming to claim him than he was already on the other side, safely ferried through the gates. He wondered if the town's residents might actually feel this way, if only a little—like they'd arrived, like they were fully, truly home, and could at long last just relax. Looking up for that skylight in the sky, he almost bumped into a map stand, at the top of which, in a miniature pediment, was housed the town seal: a silhouette of a tree and a picket fence and a girl on a bike, her ponytail flying behind, a puppy in chase, and the words CELEBRATION, FLORIDA, EST. 1994 circling around the scene. He gazed at the image. He gazed at the 1994.

Arriving at the real estate agency, he was greeted by a receptionist with eyes so blue and crystalline he wanted to cannonball into them and never reappear.

"Can I help you?" she asked. Her hair was shoulder-length and dark, her skin just slightly tanned. She wore a navy jacket and skirt and a bright floral-patterned blouse, open at the neck. If he'd ever encountered a more beautiful being, he couldn't recall it.

"I have a session—*appointment.*" He hadn't had occasion to speak a complete sentence to anyone since New York, and he tripped over the words. With half his toiletry items confiscated, he hadn't shaved, not wanting to lather with a bar of soap, and had brushed his teeth with water. He hadn't yet gotten a haircut, either, something he was planning to do later today for the interview tomorrow. He was wearing George's ridiculous checkered shoes, as usual. He became conscious of all this under the receptionist's diaphanous gaze, which narrowed, slightly dubious.

"Who's your appointment with?"

He hadn't anticipated the question. "I don't know. My . . . my assistant set it up."

Substituting the word "assistant" for "brother" was a snap decision. It seemed to buy back a little of the respect he'd lost in those doll-like eyes.

"No problem at all," she said. "What's your name?"

To his surprise, he hesitated. "Brounian. Fred."

Perhaps it was just his own unease she was picking up on, but he thought he saw the secretary's lips momentarily flicker, like he'd just handed her a cold, dead fish.

"Fred Brounian," he clarified.

She checked her computer. "OK, I've found you. You're seeing Phil Jeffries."

Phil Jeffries. Fred repeated the name to himself, thinking how much lighter and brighter it sounded. A Florida name. Two first names, really, no weight, no history, a name made of nothing but beginnings. The secretary lifted the receiver and pressed an extension. "Hi, *Fred Brounian* is here?"

With each *Fred Brounian*, the jagged contours of his life—almost blanched away by the sun and the languor of his morning walk—reappeared a little more. Here was Mel poking him like a button for an elevator that wouldn't come, saying she didn't want to marry a clammed-up clam, a locked-up safe with nothing inside. And Fred saying they shouldn't get married, and Mel crying, flinging her engagement ring down the garbage chute. And a nurse pinching open the meatus of George's member and shoving in a catheter, impossibly wide but in it had gone, shove after shove, in and in and in, all the way to his bladder, urine dribbling out the other end of the tube into a kidney-shaped tray.

The secretary hung up. "He'll be right out, Mr. Brounian."

"Freddo," he blurted.

"Freddo?"

At first he didn't understand her. He thought he'd said Fred. Or that's what he'd meant to say. Or maybe he'd meant, *Oh, call me Fred.* He was already nodding before he processed that final *o*. Beyond humiliated, pretty much giving up at that point, he just kept nodding, resigned to the secretary calling him by a name that could have belonged to some hobbit mob henchman.

"OK," she said, to his wonderment, without apparent sarcasm, "*Freddo.*"

Coming from her slyly smiling lips, the name sounded almost rakish.

"And you are?" he said. *Freddo* said.

"Christine."

"*Christine.*" Freddo drew out the last syllable, like he didn't want it to end. Freddo had just a hint of that TSA agent's Brooklyn accent. Fred was diving into those eyes of hers, infatuated with her a little, but much more with his own potential for oblivion. "So. *Christine.* You live here? In Disney World?"

Disney World. Rather witty of Freddo. Fred was impressed. Christine treated him to a pursed-lipped smile.

"Sure do," she said. "And you know, they don't own us anymore. They sold off the whole downtown in 2004 to another company."

"They did?" The news, to Fred's surprise, put a sudden weight in his chest, an almost holomelancholic sense of longing and loss. It was as if she'd told him that the Almighty had just sold off the cosmos to some rich guy down the block, then packed up a few lightning bolts and rainbows and left.

She seemed to pick up on his disappointment. "But they've still got offices here. And it's still their vision. It's a wonderful place to live."

It was her job, he knew. But her enthusiasm seemed genuine. What did it matter who owned it, Fred remonstrated, or maybe this was Freddo. The founder's glow was still here, after all. And so was Christine—she'd told him, he just remembered, that she lived in town.

"Then there are really people our age here?" As soon as this was out, Fred realized she was probably a dozen years younger than him. Freddo, however, didn't really seem to give a shit. "I mean, you know, it's not just retirees?"

"Oh, no. All ages."

"Huh"—nodding—"and what do people around here do for fun?"

Fun, Fred thought. It was a phenomenon so far removed from his own life he never would have thought to ask about it. Freddo, on the other hand, was apparently a man who took his fun seriously.

"There's plenty to do," she chirped. "What's fun for you?"

Good question. What would a man named Freddo find fun?

Dogfighting. This from Inner George, sneaking back into Fred's consciousness so seductively Fred almost said it aloud. With Freddo's help, he shoved George back out, along with the catheter, the engagement ring, and all the other junk. No. Not dogfighting. But something edgy.

"I do a little cliff diving." Fred felt he was diving this minute, jumping the sinking ship of his identity, hammering this life raft of Freddohood from driftwood as he fell.

Christine nodded, about to speak.

"Spelunking," he added, cutting her off.

Christine mock-pouted, as though he were making fun of her, though in truth he didn't have much idea what he was doing. He felt like he was sleeptalking. A man in a banana-cream dress shirt with a puff of coiffed gray hair stepped from a door behind the desk.

"Mr. Brounian, I presume."

"Freddohhh," he lowed, getting into it. "Please."

"Freddo, then. Phil. Phil Jeffries. Glad to meet you."

"Likewise, Phil."

Their hands shook firmly.

"I hope the wait wasn't too unbearable, having to talk to my daughter and all."

Freddo glanced between them, taking in their matching broad foreheads. "Not at all, Phil. You sure you don't have some other business you need to wrap up? I could wait."

Phil raised his little bauble of a chin to the center of his fleshy face, and regarded him, slyly admiring. "I'm sure you could, Freddo."

"He was asking about adventure sports," Christine said.

"Adventure sports, eh? Oh, sure," Phil said. "We've got all kinds of stuff.

Parasailing. Ballooning. This is the land of fun. Have to say, though, a little crappie fishing in Lake Butler is excitement enough for me."

Freddo held up his hands. "Please, Phil, we're in mixed company, here."

Christine giggled. Phil guffawed, his round head pinkening.

"Well, Freddo, it's sure nice of you to come down and take care of business for your brother."

Christine stood up and walked to the printer. Somehow, Freddo managed to take in her languid hip-leaning pose without breaking connection with her father's eyes.

"It's no big deal. It's looking like I'll be moving down to the area too."

Fred was amazed how happy he was to hear Freddo say this.

"Great," Phil practically shouted. "Bet you're excited to get the hell out of Gotham. We moved from New Jersey, Hackensack, a couple years before 9/11, thank God. More New Yorkers coming down here every year, by the thousands, a real exodus. From the Bay Area, too. It's the new Silicon Valley and Silicon Alley rolled into one."

"Can't be bad for your line of work."

"No, sir, it isn't," Phil agreed. "But the main perk is just getting to live here." As Christine returned with the condo listings, Phil dropped an arm around her, his hand cupping her shoulder. "We love it here, don't we?"

"We do," she said.

"You do, do you?" Freddo said, a strange, giddy tension building in his chest as the two of them gazed at him. Phil nodded.

"We really do."

"Sam. There you are."

Fred had been reaching only his voicemail for hours.

"Busy day," Sam said after a moment. "All kinds of bugs have been popping up since that playtest. Whole bunch of data got corrupted today. We had to turn off gravity for an hour."

On Fred's laptop screen, trees popped into being on a grassy hill, accompanied by flashes of light and ascending runs of chimes.

"What's that sound?" Sam asked.

"The Creation video," Fred said. "On the Christworld website."

More silence on Sam's end. On Fred's screen, to the sound of a gong, a blazing sun blossomed, shimmering from nothing in the middle of the sky. Then night wheeled around, and to the accompaniment of synthesized harp strings, a moon and stars were painted onto the darkness. The laptop cast the hotel room's only light; Fred had been pointing and clicking around the Christworld site since before nightfall. He'd watched a lock-jawed but otherwise friendly-seeming pastor give a sermon on a theme he called "simplexity," the art of staying true to a seemingly fantastical two-thousand-year-old story in an increasingly complex modern-day world. He'd taken a virtual tour of the church grounds, seen the smoothie bar of legend; and a day care center with a plastic slide and biblical scenes painted on the walls; and a massive multimedia auditorium, the stage crowned by a giant projection screen.

"Where would you rather live, Sam?" he asked. "In a universe where everything has been created just for you? Or in one where you're completely accidental, just a side effect of some larger system that has nothing to do with you, where you're struggling just to hang on?"

After a pause, Sam apparently decided it most expedient to play along. "The former," he said. "Wouldn't you?"

"Absolutely. With you one hundred percent."

"Um. OK." Sam sounded impatient.

"But what if you could live in a universe that somehow balanced the planned and the unplanned, the intended and accidental? You never know quite how everything fits together, but somehow, it does. You never know quite whether you belong, or where you fit into it all, but somehow, you do."

A close-miked gust from Sam's nose. "Sounds like a better game, I suppose."

"What if that's New York, Sam?"

Fred was mainly playing devil's advocate at this point. He hadn't felt either like things fit together or like he had a place in that town for a long time. On the screen, a lightning bolt zapped a man into existence, Caucasian and clean-shaven, his genitals obscured by the branch of a tree. The naked actor looked around, confused, excited. Then looked up in gratitude. Then down at his ribcage, amazed, and tracked with his eyes a shimmering mist expanding from it into the air beside him.

"There's something to be said for planning, though," Fred conceded. "After we checked out your condo, your realtor showed me a little place I might rent."

A top-floor one-bedroom, with a fresh coat of paint and a sunny terrace. It had a rotted plank or two—the sight, in the immaculate surroundings, had brought on a brief surge of unease—but Phil the realtor had assured him that the wood would be replaced. The apartment was right downtown, just down the block from Phil's office. Fred could stroll past it every day, he thought, and wave to the gorgeous Christine on his way to that diner by the lake. He and her father had talked numbers for a bit, after which, in the sporadically reappearing mysterious brightness, Fred had powered open the sunroof of his minivan and spent the day driving, back through the strip malls of Kissimmee and the low-rent carnivals; up and down the streets of downtown Orlando, bristling with construction cranes and buildings so new and sparkly they seemed clad in shrinkwrap; down to Ave Maria, the spanking-new Catholic-themed town founded by the Dominos Pizza baron; through a few of the area's other master-planned communities, rainbow-hued Main Streets and neon-green parks sweeping by. With the exception of Cassadaga, the

Spiritualist Church-owned swamp town of mediums and psychics (where the theme itself seemed to forgive the dilapidation), there was not a pothole or flaking paint job to be seen in any of them. Finally getting back to the hotel, he'd sprawled out on the bed, propped himself on a few overstuffed pillows, and continued his self-guided tour online.

"We'd be just a two-minute trolley ride from each other," he added, as, on his screen, the mist coalesced into a cream-skinned Eve, exchanging chaste, eye-level greetings with her man from behind two well-placed branches.

"Yeah," Sam said, his voice flat, barely audible. "The agent told me."

"What's wrong? Worried I'll lower the property values?"

"No. No." Sam's voice trailed off. Fred wondered if he was multitasking. "I'm just . . . surprised you took to the town so quickly."

"Me too. There's some kind of soporific allergen in the air. Maybe it's muddying my thinking."

Sam said nothing.

"And the receptionist was pretty hot," Fred admitted. "That might have factored in."

Though that bright, weightless instant when Phil had put his arm around Christine might have factored in more. Thinking back on them now, the two scenes didn't really seem so uncannily similar: a father and daughter, a hand cupping a shoulder. That was the extent of the synchronicity; in a thousand other ways, they were two different events entirely. But standing there in that office, in that gleam that might have just been his screwed-up brain or the ramped up sun of the Sunshine State, but might too have been something more, the image had seemed momentous, a sign he'd be crazy to ignore: Two father-daughter teams intent on transforming his life. One with a bizarre contraption in a cramped little room, in a doomed-and-not-even-knowing-it metropolis, offering a complicated, possibly untenable accord between doubt and faith; the other with a sunny apartment on a powerwashed street, in a brand-new town, offering a straightforward new life fresh out of the box.

It was strange, from his desk in Tribeca, apart from George's cancer, the Military-Entertainment Complex had been starting to seem like the biggest, most out-of-control proliferation in Fred's life. George's dim view of the new Urth had been seeping into Fred like a neurotoxin, locking up his mind and body alike, so that he could barely even stay at his desk without feeling he was dying. But either George needed more time and medical care to recover, in which case Fred needed this job, or he wasn't going to recover, in which case, maybe Fred wanted it. Maybe he wanted it either way. From a rectilinear office in a well-groomed industrial park, from the sun-dappled bosom of the Military-Entertainment Complex Accommodation Area, some new Fred, thought Fred, might look out the window and never see anything but simplexity itself.

"Anyway," Fred said. "I just called to make sure you got my message about the condo."

"Yeah. Lawyer's closing tomorrow. Thanks for checking it out."

"Forget it, Sam." Fred stopped the Creation movie and started another, this one starting with a crane shot of a cheering crowd sitting in stands by the shore of a lake, to the accompaniment of an instrumental rock ballad. "Listen, thanks for getting me this interview. I know I haven't been easy to deal with."

Fred ran a hand around the smooth skin of his neck, front and back. He'd stopped at a mini-mall barbershop, and had gotten the old barber to give him a shave along with the haircut, with a hot, wet towel and a lather brush, no less.

"You know," he went on, "maybe Mom and Dad really could come here one day."

After a crowd shot came a view from the shore into the lake, waist deep in the shallows of which stood three figures: two young men, and between them, a middle-aged woman in a sleeveless, Harley Davidson T-shirt. Her sun-dried face looked a little fearful, a little excited. She looked like a person who'd seen some hard times.

"Fred," Sam said.

"Yeah?"

"Why did the realtor keep calling you Freddo?"

The two men leaned the woman backward. The lake drank her in a gulp.

After hanging up, Fred found a porn site and fondled himself, luxuriantly, for the first time in months not having to worry about his parents in the other room. The image of the Foley catheter splaying his brother's glans, which had made him impotent with Mel for months and could still sometimes stop him dead, only gave him a twinge for a second or two. Images of Mel disrobing, silhouetted by the cityscape in their old bedroom—before her human interest segments took on a world-historical significance (canine 9/11 rescue workers, post-9/11 asthmatic cats) and that cable job and giant, wall-mounted flatscreen TV took over their bedroom—only saddened him a few seconds more. As the bouncing fake breasts on the video download looked about as soft and inviting as two frozen water balloons, he rolled away, trying to imagine the pants and moans to be those of the real estate secretary, stripped of all but her black pumps and that little gold cross. Before long, though, the clip had ended, the real estate secretary had dissolved as well, and it was Mira he was seeing. Riding him in the helmet chair. Smelling of apples and sweat and smoke machine mist. Their chests sticky with electroconductive gel. Her lips at his ear, whispering, between gasps, some scientific explanation involving pheromones and vascular engorgement.

He'd planned, when this was through, to sleep, and make sure he was fully rested for the interview. But it wasn't even nine o'clock, and as drowsy as he'd been earlier, he wasn't at all tired. He killed some more time websurfing. Link by link, he navigated away from Christworld, until he was reading about the French Jesuit priest Teilhard de Chardin's notion of the noosphere, a planet-wide sentience evolving from the Earth's biological and technological networks into a single, unified mind, heart, and soul.

And from there, to postings on futurist discussion boards about the Singularity—the point at which a computer network would become self-aware and proceed to evolve itself at lightning speed into an entity capable of mental and technological feats that humans couldn't even conceive.

And from there, to a thread about the Omega Point theory, how humanity would die out but its machine-superbeing offspring, no longer bound by atmospheres or even planets, would gain control over physical forces and reengineer the universe into a self-catalyzing complex system—a biosphere or a giant, living computer, the difference being, at such a stage, purely semantic. One posting suggested that this future superbeing might crack the code of time and come back to upload the minds of every living being, perhaps at the moments of their deaths, thereby preserving them.

The idea was roundly dismissed by a dozen respondents, who agreed in subsequent threads among themselves that the future superbeing would simply expand into the phase space of all possible worlds, and then, like some deified obsessive-compulsive disorder, resimulate every possible "you" after the fact, like so many arrangements of a carbon molecule.

Half wishing he'd stuck with simplexity, Fred pushed the laptop aside and pressed a pillow over his eyes. He still wasn't tired. He thought about reviewing his notes for the meeting tomorrow one last time, but they were already so clear in his mind that he felt any further attention would only confuse things. He thought about listening to Mira's Week Three CD, but he was annoyed enough at himself for fantasizing about her. He didn't want to think about her or anything to do with the city, anything within a thousand miles of George, lying abandoned in that dark, empty room.

Trapped, like a man in a hard plaster cast.

Bah, motion is overrated, he made Inner George say.

Breathing through a tube.

Get the job, he made him say. *Live your life.*

What if a fly landed in it?

His pulse starting to hammer, Fred grabbed his phone, about to dial the hospital to see if someone could check on George. He tossed the phone away. He put the pillow back over his head, took a deep breath, and set his mind to work picturing that less bloodless, if less likely, version of the God of the Geeks—the one that might come back in time to save them all:

A swarm of 1s and 0s, in the shape of a man.

In a cape (why not?).

With a serpentine S on its barrel chest.

Stepping back through some vaporous portal to relive the history of its own creation.

Falling in love with humanity, those little, meme-shuffling aphids who'd given it birth, and vowing to become for them the God they'd always wanted.

Witnessing, cherishing, preserving in its infinite data banks their every trial and triumph.

Uploading them, in their final moment, through a simulated tunnel and into a simulated realm of brightness, to play for them their life review, in multi-textured, quaternion-compressed truecolor, with surround sound, and an overlay of pixel-shaded meters showing them how much love/hate, joy/suffering, good/evil they'd contributed to the world. Were those needles in the black, it would bask them in its praise. In the red, forgiveness. And they would live on, immortal subroutines in the heaven of its vast, self-generating code. . . .

He was finally drifting off when his email pinged:

Subject: be my friend!
From: G30rg3 8r0un1an

Hi! I'm inviting you to be my friend on originalfacebook.com, the coolest social networking site in history! Just click here to get going! Thanks!

Fred shut his eyes. Did he really want to do this again?

He clicked. A basic template Web page. ORIGINALFACEBOOK at the top. A faint wallpaper of hip, smiling youth in skullcaps and printed T-shirts. A login request, Fred's name already filled in. A blinking cursor in the password box. And, in blue text beneath:

forgot your password?

Seeing no other options, Fred clicked it.

Hint: How do you wrap an AVATARA up into a little ol' AWDBS/HAA?

He was supposed to sit here guessing? He typed:

try shoving it up your ass

Incorrect password

How should he know? Something about taking away its belief in itself? He typed:

doubt

Incorrect password. WARNING: THREE MORE ATTEMPTS PERMITTED BEFORE ACCOUNT DEACTIVATION.

He told himself to turn the computer off, told himself he needed to sleep and wake up rested for the interview.

Around 2:30 AM, he tried "Armation." Incorrect.

By 3:00, having looked over last week's instant-message exchange, he'd convinced himself the answer had to be "shaft," the word used in those instant messages last week to describe Armation's treatment of him. Wrong.

He slammed the laptop shut, took it into the bathroom, and left it on the sink, so he'd be less tempted to reach for it from bed if another answer came to him.

He lay in the dark, prayed for sleep.

3:07. He hit upon the idea that AVATARA and AWDBS/HAA might be a kind of code.

3:24. Converted all the letters to binary: 01000001 01010110 01000001 01010100 01000001 01010010 01000001 . . .

3:59. Ran the words through every key of the Caesar cipher: ZUZSZQZ, YTYRYPY, XSXQXOX, WRWPWNW . . .

4:31. Used the words as keys for each other in an online keyword cipher: AWAUATA, AWGEUKAA . . .

5:03. It struck him that if one counted S/H as a single letter, the words had the same number of letters. He wrote them out on a scratch pad:

A V A T A R A

A W D B S/H A A

Wrapped up. What kind of operation was that?

He counted forward from each letter of first to the corresponding letter of the second, wrapping around from Z to A when necessary: 0, 1, 3, 8.

S/H. He divided them, 19 by 8, rounded down: 2. Converted it back to a B. From A to B, then: 1. And the last two digits: 9, 0.

0 1 3 8 1 9 0

And converted back to letters:

ACHAI

Gibberish. He balled the paper, crushed it into a nugget.

He turned off the light. Listened to a garbage truck shake down a dumpster.

Just to be sure, he retrieved his laptop, opened a search engine, and entered the letters. It was a male first name, according to a baby name dictionary. American Indian in origin. Meaning: *brother.*

His bones went cold. Fighting the feeling he wasn't alone in the room, Fred entered the password, and a new page appeared. A picture of Fred's own smiling cartoon avatar in the upper left corner. Beside it, his name, his age, a couple listed interests: "computers," "angels." He appeared to have a single friend: G30rg3, a picture of that bald, nose-tubed chemotherapy angel above the name. Instead of an axe, the George angel was now holding a bow, greenish in tint, and an arrow tipped with a large pink flower.

Scrolling down, Fred found Angel-George's picture again. He'd left Fred a message:

```
D00d! Thanks for friending me! I'll be believing in myself
in no time!
```

Fred cursored around, swearing. There didn't seem to be a way to unfriend whoever it was. The only bit of functionality in sight was the George angel's clickable photo, which took Fred to G30rg3's page, as plain as his own, the only differences being the name, the image, the interests: "computers," "humans." Angel-George's picture was larger on this page. The bow was strung with what appeared to be a chain of bees, joined front to back. G30rg3 had one friend—Fred—and no messages. Fred sent him one:

```
4Q mofo
```

Then waited, as riled as he was spooked, the irritation compounding with every new minute of lost sleep. Ten had gone by when a reply message popped up on his page:

```
You didn't just spend all night on that puzzle, did you?
Thought you must have given up for the night.
```

Fred took a breath.

```
what is this about
```

Another minute passed. The reply appeared:

```
You sound pissed. Sorry for the cloak and dagger stuff.
The Pretaloka's in lockdown. Miracle I could punch a way
through to you at all. Did you get Shiva's first gift, the
Blade of Many Powers?
```

Fred eyed the Swiss Army knife, sitting on the night table next to another self-help book he'd picked off his mother's shelf—*Unlimited*

Power by Anthony Robbins. The author grinned from the cover, his giant jaw and massive, gleaming teeth poised for battle like some medieval engine of war. Fred had tossed the knife and the book there when he'd unpacked, and hadn't so much as glanced at either since.

He turned back to the screen, typed:

```
what do you want from me
```

Waited.

```
Oh, and apologies for this site sucking like it does. They
said it was the original. I assumed that would count for
something.
```

A wind blew in Fred's mind. It sounded so much like George. As he sat there willing logic back into the world, another note appeared:

```
. . . actually, I've got the sneaking suspicion we're the
only two losers on it.
```

Fred wrote:

```
was george a part of this?
```

And didn't move as he waited for the reply.

```
I'll overlook your use of the third person. Not to mention
past tense. Ouch. But, you know, the suspicion is mutual.
I'm having a hard time believing in you, too. So what say
we play a little game of trust?
```

The unease was pulsing into nausea. Fred waited.

```
It is foretold the Avatara must find his eternal mate
before undertaking the final battle. Luckily, even angels-
who-don't-believe etc. have the power to hook two lovers
up. It pretty much comes with the feathers. So, who are you
fancying these days?
```

What was the point of this? Just to keep him up all night? Ruin him for tomorrow? Fred wrote:

```
come over here, angel boy, and I'll tell you.
```

The reply:

```
Just type in her initials and picture her, and trust, for a
moment, that it can happen. Take this one small step into
faith, and I promise I'll explain some things.
```

He didn't have to picture her, of course. But he was so tired, and the images he'd conjured earlier were still so fresh they were already back in his head. He didn't have to use her actual initials, but what was there to lose? He typed:

```
me
```

And waited for a crack about narcissism.

And helplessly continued picturing her, more chastely: Hands flitting about her head, pointing to brain regions. Lit by the nightlight, arms outstretched, blanket descending. In the bar from above, hands in her back pockets. Reaching up for the shade, winged by monitor glow. Her eyes wandering off, suddenly lost, when he told her she was no fucking angel. He wished he hadn't. She seemed so firmly in command most of the time, but then there were moments like this, when it seemed, at least for a second, like the slightest stumble could shatter her.

The response popped up:

```
Oh man, she's something. You'll definitely need help with
her. So all right, those fun facts I promised . . .
```

The messages started appearing line by line, the sender posing his own questions and answering them:

```
Q: The wings . . . functional or just for show?

A: We can fly. But generally not worth the effort.

Q: The halo . . . what's up with that?

A: Too much light for a good night's sleep. Not enough to
read by.
```

Q: You got, like, a harp, or something?

A: Have yet to lay eyes on one of those torture devices.
But it's all you get on the radio.

Q: And, er, is there, um, what do you have . . . down
there?

A: The short answer: I don't want to know what's there . . .
or what's not. Mercifully, this gown doesn't come off.

Q: And the long answer?

A: That last summer on Earth, I'd ride around in cabs,
eyes huge for camera sparks in loft windows,
for headlit skirted thighs, for tongues lashing slopes
of ice cream cones, for lips of bank machines
spitting up green. Round I rode as the meters rose,
trying to decide who were we, a race of gods
or of monkeys. I knew which I felt like,
so hungry for it all. Like my eyes were Hoover
Deluxes, vacuuming in so much wanting,
so much getting and losing and wanting again,
so much not wanting to want but wanting
anyway—so much life, I guess is what I'm
trying to say, I could just about explode
from the overload. . . . Well, none of that here . . .
blank windows . . . empty streets . . . and yet
Desire's all the stronger, like the whole place
is made of it, like I'm made of it, like nothing's
made of anything else. It sucks shit, here, dude.

Was it George's tone, George's style? Fred couldn't quite say. And was it true, what this George impersonator was saying about George riding around in cabs last summer—around the time of the diagnosis? It might have been true, Fred supposed. But again, he didn't really know. The lines kept coming:

Q: Desire with no object?

A: There's one—one thing for which our every
feather aches: Paradise. Promised

```
legends ago by the golden-wingèd one,
he of the champagne-effervescing halo,
who descended from on high, who gave his blessing
for us to build a Devaloka of our own.
Through the aeons our work progressed,
some of us hopeful, others caviling
that, paced thusly, it would take for-fucking-ever.
Then, from the stratosphere, down swooped another,
with gunmetal wings, and an ember-glowing helm,
swearing he could speed our work a thousandfold.
Shit-for-Brains, we. We signed on the dots.
His dark project unfolds. Not a Heaven, but a Hell!
Only I resist! Awaiting the Avatara's
decisive blow! And I'm starting to believe!
To believe!!! . . .
                    . . . that badass dude just might show.
```

A minute passed. Nothing else came. Fred read it over. Was it about Urth? Was it about Fred himself? He wrote:

```
don't count on it, "d00d"
```

The reply:

```
Oh, I will. And oh . . . Mira Egghart. She's on Seventh
Street, right?
```

As the sun began to burn around the edges of the blackout curtains, Fred read about Kama Deva, the Hindu analog to Cupid, with his bee-strung, sugarcane bow and lotus-tipped arrows. He read about Vishnu and Lakshmi, the eternal lovers residing together beyond time, beyond space, amid the coils of a thousand-headed snake on whose hoods rest all the celestial bodies of the universe. He read about them finding each other in earthly manifestations again and again down through the ages; and how Padma, Lakshmi's incarnation destined for the hand of the tenth avatara, Kalki, would pray for blessings from a god it took Fred a while to figure out was also Shiva—the god had one thousand names, apparently, and the pseudonym used in the semi-redacted Google Books version of the Kalki Purana was misspelled at that. And how Shiva would answer both their prayers, and the two lovers would come together, and Kalki would set off to make sacrifices and prepare for the fight ahead.

It wasn't the tiredness, the gravitational pull of the bed, that was keeping him from getting up and getting dressed for the interview. He sat for a long time leaned against the headboard, folding open and back the various tools in the Swiss Army knife. Blades, saws, files. Pliers, scissors, bottle- and can-openers. An awl. A chisel. A plastic toothpick. He stared at the little emblem, the cross within the shield.

Who were these people? He knew who they were, he told himself. If not specifically, then generally: a bored, random hit squad of listserv dweebs, out to make his life hell. He could barely even contemplate the alternative—that it was people actually trying to honor George, to avenge him in some misguided way. People who—was it really possible?—may have had his trust, even his participation. People loyal to George. More loyal than Fred.

Whoever they were, they were spying on him. Would they now involve Mira in this? Simply to humiliate him, if this was a prank? Or to blackmail him, somehow, if it wasn't? Was she in danger? The idea seemed farfetched, but his spinning mind reeled out farther still, wondering if Mira herself were in on it, if this helmet study were nothing but an elaborate ploy to brainwash him, make him psychologically malleable, implant subconscious messages or the like and soften him up to do the conspirators' bidding.

Then, sensing no ground beneath him and madness all around, he was scrabbling all the way back to the prank scenario, telling himself to get real, to get a grip, hurling the multitool across the room, bounding up from the bed, cursing himself for the wasted time. A one-minute shower. A shave in quick, perilous strokes. Throwing on his semblance of a suit. He was about to leave the knife behind, but thinking he might be able to get a telling reaction out of someone were he to casually produce it on the programming floor, he retrieved it. Then he was leaving the rabbit hole of his old life behind—out of the hotel room, out of the elevator, striding into the sun-dazzled parking lot, into the future, which welcomed him with a brightness perhaps too bright even for Florida. So bright that, despite himself, he took it as a sign.

According to that iron-jawed self-expert whose book Fred had been making his way through, the CIA had perfected a set of techniques that, when unflinchingly employed by agents or their trained henchmen, could totally eradicate, replace, or otherwise modify a person's most deeply held beliefs. Average citizens, the author claimed, could reap the benefits of this groundbreaking governmental research as well, to rid themselves of the beliefs that limited them and held them back. All one had to do to banish an unwanted belief was to associate it with a massive amount of pain.

Though Fred still had a few lingering reservations about applying CIA coercion tactics to his already beleaguered brain, as he piloted his revoltingly over-freshened minivan down 408 toward the research park, his bowels braiding, his heart pumping electricity rather than blood, he felt more or less ready to try anything. After that last cyber-volley of guilt-tripping harassment, he wanted his job back more badly than ever, so badly now he was racked with the terror that he'd mess up the interview somehow, come off looking angry, or desperate, or unhinged. Maybe he was all of the above. Maybe all his creativity was spent. Maybe without George, he was all but useless to begin with, destined for this or that dead-end cubicle. Maybe everyone knew it but him. One by one, as each of these non-empowering suppositions arose, he locked in on it, feeding it with his focus until it made his entire being pulsate with despair. Then he slapped himself on the head, repeatedly, with both hands.

It was amazing, oddly impressive, how many non-empowering beliefs his mind could produce in a single minute. Within the space of five, the beatings they necessitated had resulted in a not insubstantial amount of pain; his head throbbed, as if a long metal claw had begun twisting into the vertebrae below his skull. And yet, despite all this punishment, the therapy seemed to be backfiring—the more he hit himself, the more non-empowering his thoughts became, as though his mind had dug in and was now returning fire:

—*broke*—
smack
—*living with your parents*—
smack
—*going gray in your thirties*—
smack
—*going to grovel for a job in your own company*—
smack
—*better suck them off while you're at it*—

He hit himself so hard he nearly ran off the road.

Nestled in tracts of surrounding suburbia, far from downtown Orlando, farther still from the no man's land of walled-off theme parks and resort hotels, the research park—home not only to Armation, but also to NAVAIR, SAIC, the Naval War College, and dozens of other firms comprising 80 percent of the country's military simulation industry— was a place anyone not in the know could easily drive by or even through without realizing they'd just been anywhere in particular. Unlike Los Alamos, it wasn't a community. No residences, only isolated, fortress-like constructions, spaced a few acres apart and set back on sprawling grass plots bordered by neat rows of trees along winding roads with names like Ingenuity Drive and Challenger Parkway. Few cars drove along these roads, and in all Fred's visits here, he'd not once seen a pedestrian.

Armation HQ was a recessing ziggurat of white stone and black glass. Maybe by decree, maybe through some less conscious process, the cars in the lot out front were hierarchized by wealth and beauty: luxury sports cars and sedans closest to the entrance, cheaper and more utilitarian models farther out. Despite a free space a few yards from the door, Fred decided not to buck the tide, and steered the minivan over next to the groundskeeper's pickup.

Somehow, he was twenty minutes early. Awkward to drive back out at this point—for all he knew, upper management was tracking his movements through those tinted windows. He left the engine running and the AC blasting to keep his sweat level to a minimum, and ran through potential talking points, improvements to the simulation code, including the possibility of creating a playback feature (inspired by his inability to replay the appearance of that George avatar) so that military, fire, and police commanders could save and review the exercises step by step at their leisure. Checking his reflection in the rearview, he was dismayed to see a patch of stubble he'd missed under his jaw, and a bright red sunburn on his nose and cheeks. His jacket and slacks didn't match in bright light. The checkered fabric of George's shoes was torn at both heels.

He looked like a clown, he thought.

Like a clown-whore, even, Inner George offered, ever helpful.

By already-learned reflex, Fred slapped himself with either hand, and then set about picturing that new Fred, that future Fred, with an even tan and an actual suit, pulling up to that free space out front in a Benz convertible; passing the day in a big corner office; clocking out while the sun was still up and tooling over to the barbecue joint down the road; describing for a table full of listeners—nameless, faceless, as yet, only their sheer gift of witnessing coming through—how nervous and lost his poor former self had been sitting out in the rented minivan that long-ago day. *But it was all for the best,* future Fred would say. Fred heard the words so clearly, this time, he could wait no longer. He quaffed the last of the coffee, crunched a breath mint, and waded through the morass of sunlight to the entrance.

In the lobby, a heavyset security guard, assembled from equal parts fat and muscle, eyed his approach from behind a trapezoidal desk. Fred had seen him several times on his previous trips down here, but the guy at least affected not to recognize him.

"I have an appointment," Fred said, after a few seconds of the guard not asking.

"Who with?"

It occurred to Fred that he wasn't exactly sure who the interview was going to be with. He assumed Erskine would be there, but wasn't certain. He'd been picturing a whole table of executives and senior project managers, a whole pack like the one he and Sam had run into in the virtual stairwell.

The guard asked for his name, then for an ID, then turned Fred's driver's license this way and that for half a minute while checking the appointment screen.

"Human resources," the guard said. "Fourth floor."

"Human resources?"

By way of an answer, the guard handed him an orange visitor's badge on a long-snouted alligator clip bristling with sharp little teeth, and pointed him toward the elevators. Fred clipped the badge to his Barneys jacket, feeling sympathetic pain as the teeth bit in. He'd never been to human resources, and didn't know what to make of the fact that he was being sent there. Had they decided to reinstate him without so much as an interview? But if so, on what terms? Had they settled this, too, by fiat?

The elevator arrived. He boarded with a balding engineer in a lab coat, and a programmer whose monobrow he recognized from his avatar, but who didn't seem to recognize Fred. In the corridor on the second floor, as the engineer stepped out of the opening doors, a man in a green jumpsuit dotted with sensors walked past holding a black-visored helmet under his arm. From the back of the helmet protruded a bundle of black wires ending in dangling, gold connectors.

"Did they paint that VR helmet? Was it always black?" Fred asked the programmer. He remembered it as bright, maybe silver, but maybe it was just getting mixed up with Mira's God helmet in his mind. He'd watched a soldier testing the helmet out last time, jumping around with a laser tag rifle in a gray, padded room. The technology could make the Urth experience more immersive, but so far it had disagreed with the inner ear and made the soldiers throw up.

Monobrow nodded and was about to say something, but taking in Fred's orange badge, seemed to think better of it. On earlier visits, Fred and Sam had been issued aquamarine badges. Fred didn't understand the badge system well enough to know exactly how bad an insult orange was meant to be. The programmer got off on three, a warren of coding cubicles Fred had visited a few times before. A good many of the programmers visible through the open doors looked like Monobrow—the short hair, the polyester, short-sleeve button-downs—like they wouldn't have been at all out of place coding late-model punch-card computers for IBM in 1966. Their cubicles were either bare of any personal effects whatsoever or otherwise filled with model jet fighters and the more or less omnipresent early-model Starship Enterprises and Mr. Spock action figures. They got along uneasily with the sometimes hippified transplants from the gaming and movie animation industries, who'd been known to buy their own clothing, go to hairstylists rather than barbers, and talk to women (although, as such traits were viewed with suspicion by middle management, even the most metrosexualized of the transplants tended to downplay their fashion sense). With a pang, it occurred to Fred that the New York crew, a happy, nerd-chic medium of designer clunky glasses and retro Atari T-shirts, would probably fit in perfectly; and even as he was thinking this, in the instant before the doors slid shut, he caught sight of Conrad and Jesse stepping out into the aisle between cubicles, dopey smiles on their faces and gleaming new computer stacks in their arms; a pair of sunglasses perched in Conrad's Afro; Jesse's hairy toes galumphing in flip-flops. Their first day down here, and already natives. Since this morning, in the back of his mind Fred had been wondering if Conrad and Jesse might have been his cyberstalkers, his mystery messagers—secretly fighting the power and avenging George's memory. Seeing them now, though, Fred simply couldn't imagine it.

On the fourth floor, he found himself in a second lobby, before a second high-walled front desk. The receptionist, middle-aged, platinum-haired, told him in a Long Island accent to have a seat and pointed with a long, lacquered fingernail at an alcove sporting a low-slung black leather couch, matching chairs, and a glass coffee table stacked with issues of *Jane's Defense Weekly* and *The New Republic*. Too fidgety to sit, he paced and gazed out the window at the company grounds, an otherwise blank grassy area in which a single paved path led to a fountain. Fountains, for some reason, were ubiquitous in the Orlando area, and everywhere it was the same design—a shallow, round pool, a single high jet of water. One could see them from the air upon takeoffs and landings, aspurt in the housing subdivisions and industrial parks that stretched to the horizon, as if global warming were already wreaking its havoc, causing the land to spring leaks as it sank into the ocean. His next thought, more a feeling than a thought—an intuition that there was no escape here, no fundamental difference between this tidy little cosmos and the one from which he'd flown—was gone the instant it appeared, beaten out, as, automatically, he whacked his head with an open hand, then brought the hand down just as quickly, before the receptionist could look up and see.

A fair amount of time after the wait began to seem interminable, she emerged from her fortification and ushered him down the hall to another cubicle farm. He wound up at a desk behind which sat a meaty woman with a squarish face and puffy eyes, in the process of blowing her nose. He thought he could see a family resemblance between her and the security guard at the front desk. She treated Fred to the same suspicion, at any rate, before tossing out her tissue and gesturing him to sit.

"Mr. . . ." She checked her screen. ". . . Brounian. You're here about finding a position with us, is that right?"

"I . . . had thought that was the idea, yes."

She sounded stuffed up. It seemed like an allergy, or a cold, rather than bereavement. He pushed his chair back an inch. A chest cold could be fatal to George.

"I can enter you into the database," she said, without enthusiasm. "There are some forms you'll need to fill out. Can I see your résumé?"

"My *résumé?*"

"Mr. Brounian. We can't proceed without a résumé."

"I—" Fred remembered he had his résumé on his hard drive. He took his laptop out of his briefcase and booted it up. "I think there's a misunderstanding. I'm here for an interview. About a specific job."

"Which position is that?"

"Which—? I'm the former CEO of Urth, Inc. I'm here to see about going back to work as head of that department."

She turned to her computer. Her moist, red fingers tapped a few sticky-looking keys. "I see no advertised positions in Virtual Training Environments."

Fred forced the rebelling muscles of his face into a smile. "I don't think it would be advertised. This is obviously some kind of mistake. I think I'm supposed to be talking to Doug Erskine?"

"Mr. Brounian," she said, her voice flatlining. "I received word that you would be coming to see me, and that we should figure out what positions you might be qualified for."

"Who did you receive word *from*?"

Her eyes dimmed. "I'm not at liberty to say."

He sat there, brain-tasered. Even Inner George was stunned to silence. Those mucosal fingers reached for his laptop, turning it toward her. She scanned his résumé, taking her time, alternately nodding and clucking as she glanced back and forth between it and her own monitor. His skill set qualified him for two positions, she told him: an analyst for simulation markets, responsibilities including online data collection and coordinating with the senior analysts; and a senior implementation officer for foreign software licenses, responsibilities including testing and debugging foreign-language interfaces. When he managed to stutter that those were pretty low-level, she looked again.

"We do also have a certified project manager position in foreign-language interfaces. I suppose you could argue you've managed projects—"

"Of course I've managed projects," he nearly shouted. "I was a CEO."

She waited, overlong, until it was clear that he'd interrupted her. "But unless you've received official training and certification from an accredited agency, you don't meet the minimum requirements."

"Excuse me." He pointed to his laptop. "Can I have that back?"

"I'll need a copy of that résumé."

"You bet."

"And there are forms—"

But he was already moving, back out the door, down the hallway, catching an elevator door just as it closed. Two men in suits eyed his orange badge.

"Going up?" one of them asked uncertainly.

Fred nodded, turned to face the doors to hide his expression from them, but there it was, reflected in the burnished metal, glowering, sphincter-lipped. When the doors opened on five, he strode up to yet another front desk, locking eyes with yet another receptionist, a younger version of the one a floor below.

"I'm here to see . . ." His voice was trembling.

"Yes?"

"I don't know who I'm here to see."

They stared at each other. Then he was in motion again, down a hallway lined with doors, as the woman called out after him. He didn't know who was where; at this point, he was simply looking for anyone he recognized. He careened from side to side of the hall, opening door after door, finding behind them empty desks or unfamiliar faces, frantic and reeling, like he was living out one of his desperate, going-nowhere dreams.

Then, at the hallway's end, the last door opened onto a room larger than the rest. A corner office. Lined with tinted windows. In front of which, behind the all but bare expanse of a very large, gold-fluted, cherry-wood desk, sat Dan Gretta.

Fred recognized him instantly from the picture he'd seen, though at first he couldn't quite believe it. Gretta, apparently, was doing nothing at all—he had no visitors, wasn't on the phone, the computer in the corner was off; he was just sitting at his vast, empty desk with a sunny expression on his face, which, upon seeing Fred, after a moment of indecision, broadened to display his perfect, white dentition.

"Hey," Gretta said, with an easy wave, like Fred was an old chum. "Come on in, pull up a chair."

With a queasy surge, Fred walked into the room and sat. His arms and legs were still shaking after that mad race down the hall. As best he could, he marshaled his mental forces.

"Mr. Gretta. My name is Fred Brounian. Until recently, I was the co-CEO, along with my brother George, of Urth, Incorporated."

The receptionist, along with a still beefier security guard than the one downstairs, appeared in the doorway. Fred thought he was done for, but Gretta waved them away.

"It's all right. We're talking. No worries." He seemed to mean it. "Close the door, it's fine."

With evident reluctance, they did as told.

"We ate you kids for dinner," Gretta said, his grin not diminishing in the slightest. "That right?"

The man's tone and overall demeanor were so unencumbered, Fred couldn't resist smiling a little himself. "That's . . . one way of describing it."

"So what brings you here today?"

"I came to get my old job back. I mean, helping run the Urth projects."

"Not quite my department," Gretta said.

"I realize that. I was told . . . I was under the impression there would be a meeting. But then I was sent to human resources, and all they had to offer me were entry-level positions in other departments."

Gretta nodded, slow and sage-like. "Fred—you said Fred, right?"

"Yes, sir."

"Fred, as one CEO to another, it sounds like they're giving you the old sluff-off."

"Yes. It seemed that way to me as well."

They sat there for a moment, happily in agreement. Fred thought he could just possibly work for a man like this.

Gretta's eyes crinkled. "Hey, you the one with the twin?"

"That's right."

"Somebody mentioned you two."

Fred tried to read his expression, looking for some clue as to the context in which he and George had been discussed. He couldn't tell. Gretta's whole suntanned face had furrowed, deep in thought. He looked back up at Fred.

"You two ever share a chick?" he asked. "Swap her on the sly? Pretend to be each other?"

"No," Fred said.

"Ah," Gretta said, his top teeth showing, "that's what I'd do, if I had another one of me."

Fred nodded for a while, at a loss.

"I'd have one of me make the money, run the company," Gretta went on, "and the other of me produce porno movies, throw naked pool parties, bed a new girl every night. Except every now and then, the two mes could switch off."

"He's dying of cancer," Fred said at last.

"Ouch." A smarting look. Gretta glanced off, out the side window, at the green landscape speckled with corporate offices, then back at him. "Listen, would you like some advice?"

Fred had been anticipating the word "help" rather than "advice," and was already nodding.

"D'ya ever read self-help books?" Gretta asked.

For a moment, Fred wasn't sure he'd heard the question right. "Occasionally," he said.

"I don't. Never felt the need. But my wife, she's got a whole shelf of 'em. The other day I was peeking in this one. It had a big foldout chart in the middle. In one column there's a list of illnesses. In the other, there are feelings." He held up one hand, then the other, like two pans of a scale. "The idea is that the feelings cause the illnesses. You know what feeling was next to cancer?"

Fred dug his nails into his palm, sensing that the dream he still felt himself to be in was tilting back toward nightmare.

"Resentment," Gretta said, with a somber nod.

"So . . ." Fred worked through the logic. "You're saying *you* gave him cancer?"

"What?" Gretta's upper lip hitched over an incisor. "No, listen. That chart's probably a bunch of bullshit. But why take the risk, right? When you lose in business, you got to learn to let go." He smiled. "That's what I mean."

"I see." Fred stared at him.

"Let go, Fred." Gretta lowered his head, looked up at him through his silver eyebrows. "Before you lose even more."

In the hallway, the receptionist passed Fred with an evil eye on her way back to her boss's office. The executive lobby was a slightly more overstuffed version of the one on the floor below, with the addition of a tinted glass door, beyond which lay a small sundeck heavily fortified with concrete balustrades and a canvas awning. Both lobby and deck were unoccupied.

He couldn't bring himself to call an elevator. His legs simply wouldn't move in that direction, or, for that matter, now that he'd stopped in the middle of the lobby, in any way at all. He was staring at the framed picture on the wall of Gretta with Jeb and Dubya to either side, their arms around each other's backs, all three grinning down at him.

For a vivid interval Fred was released into action, taking the picture off the wall, stepping out the door to the deck, and flinging it, without force, without thought, over the balustrade.

It disappeared. Made no sound.

Then he was at a loss again. He stood gazing down at that monotonous jet of water spouting from its shallow pool.

There was something about these fountains that depressed the hell out of him, he decided. Depressed him to his bones, to his marrow, in that way that all botched, halfhearted, half-assed attempts at beauty depressed him, being paradoxically more painful to see than no beauty at all. He didn't understand how this world could fall so far short of the one in which, deep down, they all knew they should be living. He didn't understand how their lives themselves could fall so far short of what they might have been. There was so much potential standing here on the balcony, so very much more lying in that hospital room. His own failure Fred could almost accept, but George's he just couldn't fathom. He couldn't understand a universe that would simply waste all the energy George might have brought to it. His brother was like some giant cloud of stardust that had never coalesced into a star. More lusterless matter, in a cosmos starved for light.

He went back inside, and made a slow circuit of the lobby, taking his time now, examining the other photographs on the wall. There was a picture of a couple of jet fighters, for which Armation had probably done some minor systems. There was another one of a large, irregularly shaped flight-simulator compartment, through whose open door airplane controls could be seen. And a screen shot of a virtual Iraqi checkpoint Fred's team had done, in which three American soldier avatars were talking with a brown-skinned avatar near a halted car.

At the very moment his gaze fell upon the Apollo space helmet perched on its marble stand, a sun ray sliced through the deck doorway to light up the helmet's bulbous faceplate. Faintly, he could see his own refection there, his whole body suspended, afloat in the light.

He reached for it, watching those ten reflected fingers envelop the world.

A ringing phone woke him. Picking up, he had only the shallowest of notions where he was.

"Freddy. Little Freddy. It's Manny. What room are you?"

Either the volume of the phone was too high or the volume of Manfred was too high. Fred laid the receiver on a pillow. What room was he? *Was he a room?*

"Room," he said. There was indeed a room, a dark one. A standing lamp. A fine frame of twilight around the curtains.

"Room. Number."

"I don't know," Fred said.

"You don't know?"

He just wanted the interrogation to stop. "Don't know."

"All right bye."

"Bye." By the time Fred said it, Manny was already gone.

He closed his eyes, wanting to change the end of the dream he'd been having, in which he was looking for George in a dream version of their office, in the middle of which sprawled an elaborate model for a whole city they were planning—crystalline, holographic, mirror-bright. A city so flawless in its design that the smallest part reflected the whole, that anywhere you would go in it, you would be everywhere at once. A city they'd have liked to believe they were made for. Except that outside the office window, their own city was lost in a haze of billows and orange radiation. And George was out there, somewhere. And from the glass stared Fred's own ghostly reflection: his face framed by a white bowtie and white top hat, his eyes fogged, his mouth twisted in a gagging rictus. Then and there, he was watching himself die.

Banging commenced at the door. It took him a moment to correlate the banging with the phone call, another to remember what Manfred was doing here, where "here" was, and why he wanted in. *Dinner.* Fred had forgotten all about it. Had he remembered, he would have canceled. Or, barring that possibility, changed hotels.

"Fred! What's up? You got a chick in there?" Again, the banging.

He rolled off the bed, dizzy as he'd been in his dream. His head ached, chest ached, whole body ached. He was still in his fancy shirt and tie, and slacks, and socks, and even the checkered shoes, which got tangled in the sheets and blankets and sent him face-first to the carpet.

"You being raped?" Manny shouted. "Should I call a cop?"

Fred got to his feet and opened the door.

"Holy shit," Manny said, the hallway light shining in from behind him. "You do have gray hairs. You're an old man, Little Freddy. So what the hell does that make me?"

Manfred looked older too. A colony of liver spots had settled in the furrowed terrain of his forehead; hammocks of skin hung slack from his jawbones. But he was just as tall and broad-shouldered, and the fishing vest and light gray sweatsuit he wore, not to mention the black leather motorcycle jacket clutched in one hand, gave him an air of continued hardiness. What appeared to be a herpes sore at one corner of his mouth served double duty, testifying to his perishability and manly vigor at once. Still in the doorway, he peered around the room.

"Hey Freddy, how many hookers did you have up here?" Manny strode in, pointing to the ten or so miniature liquor bottles on the table. "Looks like they drank your whole minibar."

"Just me," Fred said, wooziness joining the dizziness as he remembered.

"So are you drunk, or hungover?"

Changing currents of gravity sat Fred back down on the bed.

"Both."

"You want a cup of coffee?"

Fred felt at his stomach. "I don't think so."

"You want another drink?"

He focused on the question. "I believe so."

Manny yanked open the refrigerator. "All that's left is gin and tequila."

"Latter, please."

"You want that straight?"

Fred nodded. Manny rebounded the bottle off Fred's chest, into Fred's hands.

"I'd join you, but I'm a Buddhist. So what's the occasion?"

Fred worked the cap off the squarish little bottle, deeming the matter beyond his present capacity to explain.

"Get canned?" Manny asked.

Not correct in a technical sense—he'd failed to get uncanned—but close enough. He drank, scowled, nodded, rubbed his eyes.

"Fred, fuck, you got canned. What are you gonna do now?"

What would it take, Fred wondered, to get this man out of his hotel room?

"But you can still land me a job, right?" Manny laughed, slapping the entertainment cabinet. "You can still put in a good word for me, can't you?" He laughed again, and when Fred joined in with no more than a twitch of the lips, Manny walked over, spun around and sat down next to him, wrapping a long arm around his shoulders.

"Freddy. Freddy. Poor fuckin' Georgy." Manny's eyes glinted with tears. "Hey, I got you this."

He held the motorcycle jacket out, giving it and Fred's shoulders a simultaneous shake.

Fred looked at him. "You think giving me your jacket's going to cheer me up?"

"It's not mine. Look." Manny stood up and held the thing by either shoulder. "You think this could fit me?"

It did look small for Manfred.

"It's Armani. Like an eight-hundred-dollar jacket, probably. Come on, try it on." Manny pulled him to a standing position, began guiding his arms through the sleeves.

"What do you mean, 'probably'?" Fred asked.

"I mean more or less."

"What did you do, steal it?"

"I claimed it. At the lost and found, downstairs." Having gotten the jacket onto Fred, Manny occupied himself slapping dust off its various planes. "Whenever I'm at a hotel, I ask them if anyone found a leather jacket or a watch three weeks back."

"So you stole it," Fred surmised. It was tight in the armpits and the sleeves were short.

"Buddhists don't steal. It's like an alm. And here I am giving it away, a minute later. Don't be such a milquetoast. Zip it up."

Fred fumbled with the zipper. His trouble, he realized, had to do with its being on the wrong side. "I think this is a women's jacket."

"What's the difference? Looks good on you. Anyway, you don't like it, you sell it. Donate it. It's a tax write-off. Let's go. I'm hungry."

"Manny, I don't think—"

"You'll feel better outside. We'll go somewhere downtown you can keep drinking. Hey. Our president. And his rascally brother." Manny stepped around to the far side of the bed, approaching the desk. "And who's that in the middle? Another brother? And what's this?" He picked up the picture to get a look at the space helmet against which it was propped. "Wow. Looks like the genuine article." In either hand, he held up the helmet, the picture, making them bob and dance above Fred. "Where'd you get this shit?"

Fred gripped his face, with the vague thought of peeling it off. "I stole it."

On an evening a month back, when no amount of suctioning seemed to be totally clearing George's airway, hoping to distract him from the fetters of material existence for a while, Fred had read to him about holography, how illusions of spatial objects are re-created from frequency patterns stored on plates of glass; how the eyes are essentially frequency-pattern recorders and the visual cortex is essentially a holographic projector; how every sense operates in similar fashion, detecting not definite features but only particular patterns out of what might be an infinite number; how, for all people know, beyond the parsings of their senses and measuring devices, the cosmos might exist not as matter at all, but a domain of pure frequency, a vast, resonating sea of waves.

Tonight, slumped in the passenger seat of Manfred's van, gazing out the window at the jouncing lights and colors resolving into a spectral flume ride, a Hooters sign, or any other astronomically unlikely thing, Fred thought he could imagine phenomenal existence as nothing more than the scup and chop of that resonating sea. Which might have even been comforting, had he a boat, a life vest, a set of gills.

Manny stopped at a light just up the street from the hotel, a way Fred hadn't gone before. At the corner was a New York-themed miniature golf course, the fiberglass metropolis bunched around curving, green-carpeted streets. The jaunty, cartoon angles of the buildings notwith-standing, the place had a Camp X-Ray vibe, thanks to the chainlink fence around it, and the klieg lights overhead, which, reflecting off the artificial turf, bathed the subway cars and taxicabs and Broadway marquees in a sallow hue. Off in the corner—Fred couldn't help but look for them—stood World Trade Center One and Two: obsolesced, one more shabby tribute, as evidenced by a bouquet of waxy plastic flowers resting at their base. A shorts-wearing father hunched around his son, guiding the boy's arms, their expressions conscientiously solemn as they banked their ball up a slope around the plaza fountain and back down toward the Towers. Fred failed to catch whether the ball made it between them and into the cup. The whole course was already receding in the sideview.

"We'll drive by where I'm working now." Manfred steered onto the Interstate. "Holy Land Experience. You heard of it?"

Fred reached into the pocket of the ill-fitting motorcycle jacket for the remaining gin bottle he'd taken on the way out of the room. "Is that like Christworld?"

"Christworld? Not at all. That's a megachurch. Holy Land's an amusement park. Not with rides, really. A lot of models and replicas and wax dummies, and some shows—that's what I do. I started out playing the old Jew who makes animal sacrifices to Yahweh. They've got this big smoke machine and lights that go with it. Last week I snagged the Centurion gig. Big step up. Normally they got this twentysomething surfergod playing him, but that little lamb went rogue and left for Hollywood. Tipped me off beforehand, so there I was, the part already memorized. Here it goes on the left. You can see the Mount over in the corner."

Fred registered very little—the tops of a score or so of palm trees behind a crenellated wall.

"Only problem is, you know, it's a musical-theater act, so I have to sing," Manny added, and then, without warning, began doing so, though it sounded more like ordinary shouting: "I know, Jesus, I know who you arrrrrrrre! Oh Lord Jesus, show me your . . . mmmmmmmmmheart!" He coughed. "Fuck, hurt my throat, got to preserve the instrument." He reached down and grabbed a thermos from the drink tray, unscrewing it and taking a sip. "Drinking this honey-lemon shit by the gallon."

Fred swigged the gin. To the extent he could be happy about anything at the moment, he was no longer regretting having Manny and his ceaseless stream of mind-numbing blather at hand. Fearing the man might now stop talking to preserve his singing voice, Fred searched for a question.

"So what do they think of your being a Buddhist over there?"

"Yeah, that's the other problem. Once they realize they can't convert me, I'm probably getting the boot. Bad as it is over at the Holy Land, it's better than Disney World, being a Goofy or a Mickey. They spy on you over there. They've got a system of informants. Everybody there's miserable and on Xanax. Bad scene."

Manny fell silent. They listened to a story about Lockheed Martin winning a NASA spaceship contract.

"Consider this," Manny said. "Judeo-Christian-Muslim, all these religions coming out of the Middle East, spreading east and west for all those centuries. But now the West, the most godless consumerists are finding religion in the East. It's the yin and yang, opposites becoming one. So now what, will the East and West rejuvenate the Middle? Will the Mideast and Midwest blow us all up before that can happen?" He laughed. "Answer me, Freddy. What's the answer?"

"I don't know," Fred muttered.

"Right answer. You're a sage already. A worthy godson. Your dad named you after me, you know."

Fred at first thought Manfred was joking. But then he wasn't sure. "He did?"

"What? You didn't fuckin' know that? I said, Hey, Vart, you got two of the little monsters, you can name at least one after me, can't you?"

Manny turned, gave him a watery look appended by a cankered smile. "I was gunning for firstborn," he added in a confidential tone. "No offense." He turned back to the road. "So here we are."

They were veering off an exit. No large buildings in sight.

"I thought we were going downtown."

"Yeah, no, not the real one. There's a better one here."

Manny swung them through a gate of the Universal Studios theme park, and onto a featureless service road outside a park wall. Streetlights illuminated the van's interior every few seconds. The vehicle was even older than Vartan's, possibly by half a dozen years, and in far worse shape. Tan vinyl upholstery hung in shreds from the door panels. The glove compartment was missing, as were the window cranks, a pair of small vise grips taking their place. The interior was clean, however, and the equipment in back—what looked like a pair of set lights and a director's chair—lay folded and held fast to the wall by straps. Manny noticed Fred looking in back.

"You want to be in a movie?"

"Absolutely n—"

"I'll put you in one. I've got a whole new angle after the monastery. Kensho Pictures. Website and everything. Every flick guaranteed to bring on sudden enlightenment." Manny held up a qualifying finger. "*If you're ready.* I'll find a way to use that space helmet, too. That's a great costume piece. You steal it before or after they canned you?"

"After."

"I'll get a shot of you in it. It'll make a great scene . . . for something. I'll hash out the story later."

As Fred raised his arm to finish off the gin, the stiffness and creaking of the motorcycle jacket pulled Fred back to his young adulthood, his subsequent achievements falling away like they'd never been. He laid even odds on the possibility that when they got back to the hotel, the police would be there waiting. Lipton, Erskine, Gibbon, that smug sonofabitch Gretta—he might as well swear revenge on a dream, on a daydream in the Military-Entertainment Complex's riotous, conglomerated brain. Descending in that elevator, he had felt himself morphing into a meatspace version of that running-amok chemotherapy angel. If he'd had an axe he would have been chopping at the walls, but all he'd had was his little Blade of Many Powers, and all he'd had time to do with it was to use the first tool he pulled open to pry out the elevator buttons of all five floors.

On the ground floor, the security guard's eyes burning his back as he exited the main doors, Fred rebuked himself for his timidity up there—tossing those items into the hedges hadn't been enough; some sycophantic employee would discover the helmet out there and just come toadying back up with it and all would be forgotten, all trace of Fred's existence—*of George's*—cleanly excised; and no one here would ever again have cause to be troubled by the memory of them—*of George.* It was too horrible, and so, when Fred saw the guard busy with other visitors through the glass, he walked around the side of the building and stuck the stupid things under his arms. In plain view of all those darkened windows, he then trudged back to the minivan, and, at a speed he hoped would be seen as leisurely, peeled out of the lot.

He hadn't been worried about repercussions at the time. In that state of jangling indignation, he'd thought he could see the results of his act with utter clarity—how the executives up there, after everything they'd stolen from him and George, would think it best to let the matter drop, relieved to have gotten off so easy; yet how, nevertheless, word would circulate internally, becoming part of the corporate mythology, ensuring that every new employee would hear of Armation's theft of Urth, and the former CEO's revenge. Pathetic, maybe, as legends went. But at least there'd be something.

It didn't take long after that, though, for Fred to consider the possibility his on-the-fly analysis might not have been entirely spot-on, and upon reaching his hotel room, he proceeded to take the only remaining course of action imaginable, namely, draining the minibar, and waiting—either for his cell phone to ring or for the police to show up and take him away.

The van plunged into a multilevel parking structure, and Manfred steered them up some ramps. The ripped upholstery flapped on the doors as they disembarked. Fred's door wouldn't quite close. He pushed on it, staggered, nearly fell over. The garage spun. Manfred stepped around and, by lifting it slightly, forced the door into place.

"Got it at a police auction. They took it apart looking for drugs. Didn't quite get it all back together."

When Manny had said "downtown," Fred had been envisioning a gloomy, empty dive on a dead-end street, a venue a bit more conducive to dissolving into a pool of despair than a heavily populated theme park. With little choice now, he followed his godfather into an enclosed skyway and onto a peoplemover, synth-inflected pop music pulsing from the speakers above.

"Matter of fact. . ." Manny leaned against the moving handrail as the track trundled them along, and producing from a fishing-vest pocket a small video camera. "This might make a good scene too. You never know." He flipped it open at chest level, peering down at the screen as one might a poker hand, the lens aimed at Fred.

"What's my motivation?" Fred grumbled, increasingly uncomfortable.

"Your choice." Manny nodded. "If I could go back in time, I would have recorded my whole life."

"Who would watch it?"

"No one."

There was a light in Manny's eyes as he said this, charged yet lucid, which, more than the words themselves, made Fred wonder.

The walkway ended. Manny led them through a concession area into the park's transgenic hybrid of urban downtown and outdoor mall. They made a slow loop around the carefully orchestrated chaos of lights and music—taking in the NASCAR and NBA restaurants; the Hard Rock Cafe; the fountain around which people sat gaping up at music videos on giant screens; the Endangered Species store; the Bob Marley A Tribute to Freedom nightclub; the person-sized Spider-Man, Betty Boop, and Shaggy from *Scooby-Doo* cutouts; and out across the water, the company's emblem, UNIVERSAL, and the globe around which it wrapped, transformed from a mere image to a physical thing, as gigantic as ever it appeared on any screen. Manny remained uncharacteristically silent during these few minutes, gazing around serenely.

"So I've heard you've attained nirvana or something?" Fred mumbled.

"Attained nonattainment!" Manny answered, gaze keen.

"So what's that mean, then, exactly?"

"It means beyond attachment, Freddy. Beyond the vicious cycle of desire and aversion." He wheeled an arm back at the artificial river ahead at the plaza. "Beyond the slum of human reality. It means *free*, Freddy. Just free."

That half-amazed, half-amused expression might have been a remnant of shock treatment, might have been Stanislavskian immersion, might have been the actual experience of something approaching that freedom of which he spoke. It occurred to Fred he'd never met an enlightened person, that he was aware of. He didn't have much basis for comparison.

"At least I think so," Manny said. "None of those monks over there spoke very good English. We communicated mainly by slaps. Hey. Jimmy Buffet's Margaritaville. Let's go there. They've got good fries."

Manny picked out two free stools at the bar, under a massive sail, and ordered his fries. Fred ordered a margarita from the fifty-gallon, blender-shaped plastic tank over the register. As the drink was being prepared, Manny positioned the videocamera—which for all Fred knew had never been turned off—on the bar between them, propping its front end up with a stack of folded napkins so that it pointed at Fred's face. The irritation this caused him was so small a drop in the ocean of his misery that it didn't seem worth fighting. He asked for another margarita before picking up and draining the first. Only after he did so did he realize he'd just spent his last ten dollars. Turning his wallet upside down, he shook the bill out onto the bar. There'd be no choice now but to give in to the hospital's continual calls for George to be moved to a long-term-care facility, self-storage for the not-quite-dead. And even there, the fees would be staggering.

"So . . . enlightenment—how does it happen?" he asked. Maybe he just wanted to punish himself.

Instantly, Manny slammed his palm on the bar's copper surface. Fred started, his fluorescent yellow drink slopping onto his shirt and motorcycle jacket.

"Like that," Manny said. "It's a shock. Then eventually, they transfer the Buddha Mind Seal to you." He made a gesture with clutched fingers in front of Fred's eyes, resembling, more than anything, the Vulcan Mind Meld. "But to start, you've got to penetrate the *mu*."

He gave Fred a significant look. Behind him, on a projection screen, Jimmy Buffet himself sang into a mic and strummed a guitar. Higher up toward the ceiling, the propellers of a suspended seaplane spun with a hypnagogic slowness.

"The mu?" Fred asked.

"The monk Joshu was telling his disciples how buddhanature was present in all things. One of his disciples asked, 'Is it also to be found in a dog?' And Joshu replied: 'mu.'"

Fred waited for more. Manny, however, was already elsewhere, picking up his camera and zooming in, with a phallically extending lens, on a table of women under a thatched umbrella. "Tits tits tits," he said, then, turning back to Fred: "It's very simple. This isn't real."

For an unearthly moment, they stared at each other, that giddiness Fred had felt seeing the realtor cupping the daughter's shoulder returning. It almost made sense, he thought. How could this crass, shimmering place—how could any of this—be real?

"It's not *not* real," Manny added.

Fred was still nodding, trying to understand. Manny continued staring into him, judging his readiness.

"It's not *both* not real *and* not *not* real," Manny elucidated.

Fred chased the words, fighting the despair.

Manny tictocked his finger. "It's not *neither* not real *nor* not *not* real."

"Just . . . tell me why life sucks so much," Fred said.

Manny fixed him with that peculiar eye-light. "What are you talking about? This is the Pure Land. Hey," he spread his arms wide, "Paradise."

The flashing gelled lights positioned above the bar reflected off Manfred's bald head, now red, now yellow, now blue.

"You guys are incredible," Manny went on. "A year ago, George asked me the same thing."

"He . . . he did?"

"Same fuckin' words, just about. 'Manny, why does life suck so much? Manny, why can't I get what I want?'"

"Why couldn't he?" Fred said, dizzy from the alcohol and lights, nearly slipping off his stool. "Why can't I?"

"So change what you want."

"Who can want failure?" Fred shouted. "Who can want misery?"

"So stop wanting."

"How can I stop wanting?"

"So stop being."

"What do you mean? Kill myself?"

"Whoa," said the bartender, a sunburned guy with a gold necklace and open Hawaiian shirt, as he set Manfred's fries on the bar, "no suicide in Margaritaville. Wasting away only. It's in the charter."

"No self, no problem," Manny said, with a placid smile.

"Is that what you told *him*?" Fred said, his voice giving out.

Manny's expression changed, sad and happy at once, it seemed. "I didn't know what to tell him. That's why I had to go join the monks. Fries?"

Fred waved the proffered basket away. Placing it in front of himself, Manny tucked a napkin into his sweatshirt, bent his head, and began to eat. Methodically, one by one, he conveyed the fries to their destination. He didn't rush or overfill his mouth, but made rapid progress nonetheless, without a wasted movement or lapse of attention. A mesmerizing calm, the first gentle breezes of a stupor, perhaps, descended upon Fred as he watched.

In two minutes, the basket was empty and Manny looked up.

"Swallow the mu, Fred. *Become* mu. Figure it out, OK?"

"How?" Fred could barely mouth the question.

Manny took in a deep breath, fixed Fred with a fiery stare, and pursing his lips, whispered in a long exhalation:

"Muuuuuuuuuuuuuuuuuuuu."

As Manfred blew, around him, Fred could see the unearthly glare coming back, lighting up the margarita tank, the party lights, the salt-rimmed glasses, the laughing, flirting, gabbing crowd—all of it already gone, here forever, both at once.

"Do it," Manny said.

Fred blinked. The glare had vanished.

"Go ahead," Manny coaxed.

"Muuuuuuuuuuuuuuuuuuuuu," Fred whispered.

"Yeah. That's it. Just keep doing that inside your head."

"For how long?"

Manny considered. "That depends."

"On what?"

"On how long it takes. Will you do that?"

Fred considered. "I doubt it." He could dive into the margarita mixer, he thought, be whirled to a pulp.

"They have a saying. If there is doubt, doubt hard."

"*Doubt hard?*"

Manny nodded, eyes electric again. "Doubt coming and doubt going. Only when the Ball of Doubt has been smashed"—he slammed his palm down, sending Fred's drink sloshing once more—"can Great Faith arise!"

Trying to wake up, as usual, he's just wound up in some dream city. Done on the cheap. No streetlights, no people, its tallest spires no taller than him. He can barely walk on these darkened, spongy streets, every step a potential fall involving a series of lurches and counterlurches. He can't even stand properly; even the plazas are crazily banked. His club, each time he raises it to swing, throws him off balance. And these two shabby towers in front of him—the powers that be aren't even bothering to keep this dreamworld up to date.

No matter, he's doing it for them, winding up and releasing, again, again, again, smashing the pair to pieces.

Fred awoke to the sound of a door catching on a deadbolt. The maid, checking to see if he was out yet. He was beyond nauseated. He would have paid to be properly nauseated, instead of what he was—it felt like he'd been turned inside out, like all of his skin were on the inside simmering in stomach acid and all his nerves and bones were scraping against the sheets. He couldn't remember how he'd gotten back here. The last thing he could remember—aside from that awful dream— was wasting away with Manfred in Margaritaville. Fred had never had a memory lapse from drinking before. Maybe he'd never been quite that drunk. The gap was scary to contemplate; though, on the other hand, here he was, on the verge of retching but otherwise all right. The clock by the bed read 2:04—PM, judging from the daylight around the curtains. The police hadn't come about the helmet and the picture. At least, he couldn't remember them having come. To make sure, he sat up, waited for the room to gyroscope into place, and squinted over at the corner. The helmet sat on the desk. The picture of Gretta and the Bush brothers leaned up against it. He was about to look away, satisfied, when something shiny resting by the base of the picture caught his eye.

A golf club.

He lay there, not daring to move.

Uh-oh, said Inner George.

He couldn't have. Who would have let him? Or had he snuck in? Could he remember a fence? Climbing it? He thought he could remember a fence, maybe, lumbering alongside it, the streaks of passing headlights. Those narrow, green runways lurching beneath his feet. He kept sifting through the tatters, hoping for something that would prove it a dream, but the more he thought about it, the more real it got: Staring down those replica Twin Towers. The rubberized handle in his grip, vibrating as the club cracked their fiberglass hulls and crunched their plaster interiors. The plumes of dust erupting with every strike. The utter hatred he'd felt for the hollow, hokey things. The utter joy at bringing them down.

Now, though, the thought of the desecration nearly made him vomit. He pictured his face up on wanted posters next to bearded Al Qaeda operatives. He looked again, hoping that when he'd seen the club before he'd still been dreaming.

There it was.

What was he supposed to do now? His cell phone wasn't flashing, but he checked it for messages just in case, almost hoping for one, despite the fact that at this point there couldn't be any news but bad. In any event, there were none.

Maybe Armation was planning to let the theft go, he thought. Or maybe no one had seen him removing the items from the premises. It was possible no one had seen him smashing up the miniature golf course, either. For all he knew, he'd gotten away with the whole sorry crime spree. He tried to derive some hope from the possibility. But the golf club, the space helmet, and the stares from the three grinning white men beside it unnerved him entirely. What should he do with those things? He thought about leaving them here in the room when he left, or tossing them all from his rental minivan over a theme park wall. He could do it with the golf club, maybe, but as for the other items, it seemed more prudent to hold onto them. At least have the option of returning them if need be.

The hot void in his stomach was already beginning to signal hunger as well as general revolt. With no money for food, the only thing to do

was head straight for the airport. He'd missed his flight, but could probably get a standby. He stood under the shower for a minute, clambered
back into some clothing, then tried to figure out how to pack everything.
He ended up sticking the golf club into his carry-on and wrapping the
handle that stuck out through the zipper in the leather jacket Manny had
given him, which he turned inside out to reduce the chances of the hotel
staff recognizing it from their lost and found. As for the space helmet
and the picture, he wrapped them as best he could in his Barneys jacket,
stuck them under his arm, and grabbed his briefcase.

No one paid much attention to him, he was pretty sure, on the way
out of the hotel. He loaded it all into the minivan. From the parking
lot, he steered in the direction Manny had gone last night, up the street,
past the golf course. He made out only bright yellow police tape and a
handful of onlookers, before his foot stomped the gas.

A few blocks down, he pulled into a convenience store lot and leaned
his head against the wheel, opening the windows to dilute the atom-
ized marshmallow blasting straight into his forebrain. He finally recognized the car-freshener scent. It was Lucky Charms, the breakfast cereal.
With the realization came a sliver of a memory of some otherwise lost,
overcast morning, of him and George and Sam munching those stale-
sweet trinkets and the surrounding salty-sweet gold bullion, gazing at
the bright red box with its heel-clicking leprechaun scattering magic
sparkles with a spoon. The smell now made him as hungry as it did
nauseated. Every thirty seconds or so, the sound of rattling roller-coaster
cars and group screams shook the otherwise cadaverous calm of the day.
He didn't blame all those park employees on Xanax in the slightest.

Letting his eyes shut, he was soon recalling a night toward the end
of high school, when George had joined Fred and a group of Fred's
dark-clad, asymmetrical-haircutted friends on a subway trip out to
Coney Island. The rides were closing down just as they got there, and
they watched the groaning behemoths come to a stop one by one,
paying special attention to the dinosaurs already extinct—the Para-
chute Jump, the Thunderbolt. They wandered out to the trash-strewn
beach, sprawled on the cool sand, and watched the lights go out from a
distance. A soulful, black-lipsticked girl Fred liked named Nadja found
a hypodermic needle in a clump of seaweed, and they all dared each
other to jump in the water. They passed around a bottle of schnapps and
talked about the coming apocalypse—one of Fred's favorite subjects at
the time—whether it would be from war or environmental collapse or

science gone wrong or the lunatic fringe. He was just getting started on how it could be all the above, when George, who hadn't said much until then, stood up among them, in his bright yellow thrift-store dress shirt and businessman slacks, and kicked off his shoes.

"You're all a bunch of drips," George said, peeling off his socks. No one there really knew him too well. They knew him only as Fred's straight-arrow brother, the studious one, the computer geek. They hadn't seen him like this, Fred thought.

"This is going to be our world. Ours to remake." George opened his arms. "Look around you. Think of what we could do with all this."

They all sat there, looking. At the dim bones of the ancient rides. At the looming shadows of the public housing complex.

George charged into the waves, whooping. Eventually, they all followed. The closest Fred and George ever came, or ever wanted to come, to "sharing a chick," as the smirking Armation CEO had put it, was when the two of them ran carrying a big, laughing, screaming goth girl named Trace—a clove cigarette still smoking in her fingers—and plunged, with her and all her black organza, into the bright black water.

After weaving his way out of the amusement park ghetto, Fred pulled behind a Publix supermarket, salvaged a stained cantaloupe box big enough for the helmet and the picture, and deposited, in a dumpster full of rotting fruit, the incriminating golf club.

At the airport, he borrowed some tape from the car rental agent, sealed up the box, and checked it at the counter. His skull rang and pulsed, his stomach yowled. Passing a concession stand, he patted his pocket, and thought he might have enough change for a candy bar, preservatives and carcinogens be damned. But reaching for the coins, all he brought up was a handful of round, plastic buttons—numbered 1 through 5. On the inescapable televisions, George Bush told the people of the concourse they were in the battle of their lives, insurgent snipers boasted of killing thirty-one GIs, box-office sales indicated the moviegoing public was in no mood for *Mission: Impossible III*, and an Ohio teenager was walking six hundred and fifty miles to New York to raise money for the 9/11 memorial. The endless tributes were starting to seem more monstrous to Fred than the attacks themselves. Sitting down and shutting his eyes, he could still see the silver blur of the golf club, hear the crunch, see the dust plumes from the midget towers. He tried to feel shame, but the memory itself was too pleasurable, and he just ended up reliving that muscle-deep satisfaction of the swings and the hits.

An hour later, he was airborne, his temple to the window, gazing down at the urban grids, the industrial parks, the theme parks, the lone-jet fountains, the worming, sprouting cul-de-sacs of subdivisions—a pell-mell metastasis stopped only by the ocean. That a few fanatics had flown airplanes down into all of that seemed less surprising to him than that legions more hadn't yet done the same. Half the world or more was already setting itself against all the complexity in one way or another, going off to live in caves or gated communities, dreaming of a world with one god, one book, a world small enough to feel that one wasn't lost in it.

This is the Pure Land, his crazy godfather had said, arms wide, camera in hand.

Penetrate the mu.

For the duration of the flight, Fred tried, imagining the sound with every outbreath:

Muuuuuuuuuuuuuuuuuuuu . . .

There were moments when he'd feel like he was on the trail of something, an openness, a sense of possibility, moments when he felt like that light might return, like that faith without ignorance might be just around the corner, like the world could be anything and he could be anything in it. But no sooner had he begun to hope than he was plunged back into his grim particulars:

Mu but that bastard Gretta.

Mu but George, tubes in his nose, staring at his living room wall. Trying to exterminate himself with some similar mantra before the universe did it for him. George might as well have been slouched in a tub, watching the blood waft from his veins.

Mu but Sam, so evasive on the phone the other day. He must have known something, Fred thought, must have had something to do with Fred's getting shipped off to human resources. No other explanation made sense. No one at Armation cared about Fred enough to be vindictive, to go to the trouble of sticking him somewhere other than in his old outfit. And Sam still hadn't called or emailed. He must have conspired with Armation to stay in control, or whatever illusion of control of the brothers' former company he now imagined he possessed.

Told you we should have fired him early on, Inner George said.

What Fred couldn't figure out was why Sam had even bothered asking him to come back aboard, why the sneaky shit had sent him to Florida at all.

Was Sam in on those prank messages to boot?

Was it all a plot to drive Fred mad?

From LaGuardia, Fred took the bus to the subway, spending two of the remaining six dollars of his net worth that were digitally encoded in his transit card, thinking about Sam the whole way, ever more convinced that his little brother was behind what had happened to him, and ever more enraged. The office, when Fred arrived, was in disarray. A hedge maze of boxes, empty and full, covered the floor. The most recent of the manuals and software packages had been cleared from the shelves, the impoverished, gap-toothed remainder awaiting the inevitable arm to come sweeping them into the trash. A few of the desks were still manned by a nighttime skeleton crew, three fuzzy heads bobbing to myriad headphone rhythms, fingers pecking code—while others had been stripped of their computers, coffee mugs, lamps, and DVD dispensers. The only vestiges of Conrad and Jesse were a pair of crazy-eyes-on-springs glasses with one eye missing on Conrad's desk, and the bumper sticker on the wall over Jesse's—WHEN SWORDS ARE ILLEGAL, ONLY ORCS WILL HAVE SWORDS—a rip in one corner suggesting that Jesse had tried without success to take this with him, too. On a patch of wall where a bookshelf had been, a scuffed *Matrix* poster with Keanu Reeves looking badass in a leather overcoat hung exposed for the first time in years. In the microwave, a plastic bowl rotated in a forlorn orbit around nothing. A pillow and Sam's old army blanket lay rumpled over the couch's plush cushions like a fallen soldier. Whether from the coming confrontation or this final visual evidence of his company's disintegration, panic twined around the anger in Fred's gut, a double helix of doom.

The microwave beeped and the light went off. As no one else even looked in the machine's direction, Fred used it as an excuse to force himself into the room, setting his carry-on and briefcase and box of Armation loot inside the door. Peering through the little window, he found that the bowl contained minestrone soup. The coil inside him strained like its ends had been pulled. Not sure exactly what he'd do with it yet, or if he could even control what he'd do with it, he took the steaming bowl by the rim with the fingers of both hands. The tomato-broth fumes made him swoon with hunger as he ferried it, weaving around the desks and boxes, past the still moronically humming Prayerizer with its moronically whirring floor fan, and into Sam's alcove.

He found Sam where Sam always was, in his Aeron, headphoned head cocked toward his right monitor, on which, in an Urth window, dressed in a dark-blue business suit, Sam's avatar stood against a gray background, tapping a foot. As Fred watched, there was a jump cut, and Little Sam was now hunched, his mouth open, his tongue visible, a hand clutching his stomach. A few seconds later, irregular patches of baldness appeared in his scalp. Next, the skin of his face and neck were suddenly grayish and bruised. Next, a shiny line of blood appeared between the corner of his mouth and the side of his chin. Fred noticed a digital time counter in a lower corner of the frame, flickering through hours and days. When the day counter hit seven, the hunched-over avatar was replaced by a version on its back on the ground, unmistakably a corpse, with a widely ajar mouth and purplish, sealed eyelids. Fred felt a queasy undertow.

"Radiation poisoning."

Sam's voice startled him. The soup in his hands almost spilled. A cyclopean blend of Sam's eyes stared at him from the lamp head's curvature.

"Works on its own," Sam said, his tight jaw belying the careful casualness of his tone, "but whenever I try to plug it into Urth, it goes buggy. The whole place is going buggy. It's like with the move, the code's getting all jumbled up in transit."

Fred thought of the last message, the hints of a rebellion against Armation. Were these bugs more sabotage, then? Or did Sam only want him to think so?

"Let's take a walk." Fred kept his voice low, barely a whisper.

"A *walk*." Sam made the word sound like some affected foreign expression no true patriot would ever have used.

"Come on," Fred muttered between his teeth.

"Where is it you want to walk to? Haven't your feet covered every square inch of this city by now?"

Fred's pulse pounded in his ears. It was too hot in here. Another minute and he might throw up the ounce or two of acid and bile coating the bottom of his stomach. "I'm trying to be considerate," he said, though this wasn't true. "But if you'd rather have it out in front of them," he jerked his head back toward the employees, "I certainly don't give a shit anymore."

"Have what out?"

"What the fuck, Sam? That fucking meeting, if you want to call it that. Don't pretend you don't know what I'm talking about."

Sam straightened his back, then finally turned in his seat to face him. "Fred, is that bowl of soup in your hand a good-will token, or a weapon?"

I think it's a hat, Inner George said.

"We'll see," Fred said.

"If I agree to that walk, will you set it down gently on the desk?"

The urge to weaponize the minestrone was close to irresistible now, but Fred managed to put it down. Meanwhile, the sequence of Little Sam's irradiated death began playing itself out again. Sam opened a drawer filled with plastic utensils, took out a spoon and a napkin, dropped the spoon into the bowl, placed the napkin on his palm and the bowl on the napkin. Then got up and, without looking at Fred, led him back through the office, out into the hall, and down the stairs. To Fred's confusion, Sam didn't stop at the ground floor, instead opening a fire door and descending into the basement.

"Where the hell are you going?"

"You wanted to talk in private, right?"

Fred had been keenly anticipating open air, the day's remaining light. "Don't be an asshole. Let's go out by the river."

"What, you were hoping for a more romantic setting? I don't have time to take a stroll with you, Fred. Our gear gets shipped over the weekend, and everyone but me along with it, and the Empire State Building demo is a week from Monday."

Sam hadn't stopped trudging down the stairs, and Fred had little choice but to follow. Another metal door opened onto a low-ceilinged hallway with a series of padlocked wooden doors to either side, the length of which was lit by a single 25-watt bulb in the ceiling halfway down. Fred hadn't been down here since their first days in the building, eight years ago.

"You got a bomb shelter down here or something?"

"Don't think it didn't occur to me," Sam said. "Their storage space is all rented out."

At the end of the hallway, Sam led him through a third metal door, switching on another dim light. They now stood in a room busy with pipes along the walls and low ceiling. A water heater and a large boiler took up half the space. The air, humid, warmish, smelling of iron and mold, adhered like spray paint to Fred's skin and the walls of his nostrils.

"So all right." Sam focused on his soup. "If you're going to go on a psychotic rampage and kill me, my screams should be inaudible here."

"Considerate of you." Fred looked around, still woozy, hoping to find a stool or somewhere else to sit down. Aside from the plumbing and heating equipment, though, the room was barren. He turned, about to begin the interrogation, but Sam spoke first.

"Nice of you to notice, for once, how considerate I've been." He brought a spoonful to his mouth, blew on it carefully, and slurped it in. "You've had a hell of a way of thanking me so far."

"Well done, Sam. Go on the offense. Hold that moral high ground. So what exactly should I be thanking you for?"

"I staked a lot of personal credibility," Sam said between mouthfuls, gazing at the soup's steaming surface, "arranging for them to take you back."

"Yeah, let's talk about all your arrangements."

The corners of Sam's mouth turned down. He exhaled heavily through his nose. "Actually, no. I'm going to finish my lunch. I work hard, if you haven't noticed, and I'm hungry, and I'm going to eat. And then, if time permits, I'll humor your questions."

With a slowness that appeared deliberate, he proceeded to bring one spoonful after the next to his mouth, blowing, slurping, pausing, repeating. Fred's nausea, meanwhile, was gone, and his anger had the run of him, rewiring him from within, stoking his core, heating up his skin, quickening his pulse, oxygenating his muscles, lighting up his vision. There was a clarity to anger that he didn't otherwise have in his life. An imperative to act in some way, in any way, all those paralyzing red lights suddenly going green.

"That shit's got BPA in it," Fred said.

"It's got what?"

"A carcinogenic preservative."

Sam shrugged, slurped.

"Why don't you let me see that for a minute?"

About time, Inner George said.

For the first time that afternoon, Sam's eyes, suspicious, met his full on. As they did, Fred reached for the soup with one hand and Sam's neck with the other. Sam—with more strength than Fred had anticipated—pulled the soup hand down as Fred pulled it up, then reversed course and let the soup arm spring. A spume of tomatoey broth caught Fred in the face, as Sam ducked under his arm and away.

Fred advanced on him. Sam dropped the bowl and held up his fists, flexing those starter muscles of his.

"You want to know what else I arranged?" he shouted. "Not to have a warrant put out for your arrest. I asked them this just today, in fact. Repeatedly. They almost didn't listen to me this time."

Fred stopped. Sam glared over his fists.

"Do you have any idea how much that helmet is worth?"

Fred had to say something. His first impulse was denial. "Helmet?" he mumbled, lamely. "What helmet?"

"They have you on surveillance tape."

Fred blinked, the soup stinging his eyes. He wiped his face and hair with his hands, sweeping off tomato globs and carrot discs.

"You owe me two dollars and fifty-nine cents for that soup, you fuck-tard," Sam said.

With his shirtsleeve, Fred wiped the dribbles of broth from his neck.

"Oh. Plus the hotel overstay charge. And the minibar—a hundred fifty bucks' worth of booze?"

Fred picked a kidney bean out of his collar. He hadn't yet totally given up on the idea of a physical fight.

Sam's eyes glowed, meanwhile. He was only getting started. "And what the hell was that shit about in Celebration? Calling yourself Freddo? Talking about adventure sports? *Hey Sam,*" he said, mimicking the agent's chummy voice, "*that brother Freddo of yours, helluva dare-devil. Got some info for him about that raceboat I was telling him about.*" He shook his head. "That *raceboat,*" he repeated. "I'm going to have to live with these people. I'm going to have to talk about my nonexistent, thrill-seeking brother Freddo for the rest of my life."

Fred stood stock-still, nothing left but to endure.

"Tell me you still have the space helmet," Sam said. "Tell me it hasn't been damaged."

"It's upstairs," Fred managed, wishing he'd chucked the thing in a swamp.

Sam looked at the ceiling, his neck cracking. "Just leave it there. I'll take it back to Florida with me next week."

"I've come clean with you, Sam. Do the same for me."

Sam traced the paths of various pipes with his eyes.

"Why didn't they want me back at Urth?" Fred said. "Please don't try to tell me you weren't involved in that."

Sam's eyes followed a pipe down the back wall, to where it disappeared behind the boiler.

"Why, Sam? Did keeping nominal control over this . . . this little sliver of Armation mean that much to you?"

"It wasn't about that," he said faintly. "We just felt—"

"We?"

"Me, Jesse, Conrad." He sighed. "Everyone."

The strength left Fred's legs. He resisted the urge to sit down the floor. "You had a meeting about me?"

"It wasn't like that. We just started talking . . . after you left town. I'm sure you're not aware of it, but the way you act around here you really stress people out."

Fred put a hand out for the wall, which itself seemed to be slowly giving way.

"You just don't like anything we're doing now," Sam went on, his voice rising. "You don't even want to have to look at it. I'm the only one who can do it. I'm the only one of us left!"

His eyes darted to Fred, beseeching, then away.

"I wanted to think you were really back on board." Sam was staring at the wall once more, his voice again monotone. "But then came the playtest, and the way you ran out of here, and that stuff about seeing George. I started worrying about you. And then came that so-called business idea, that praying computer of yours."

He righted the soup bowl with his foot.

"And I thought you wouldn't like working under me," he went on. "Armation wanted me in charge. I thought that maybe with a job in a different division, you'd be able to start fresh. I didn't know they'd just send you to human resources. I only found out about that today. I'm sorry. I thought there'd be a real meeting."

All those green lights inside Fred going red again. All that anger, unreleased, seeping back into the groundwater. The only sound in the room was that of water coursing through a pipe, the flushing of a toilet somewhere upstairs, probably. Sam turned and risked a look at him, his eyes immediately skitting a couple inches off to Fred's right and staying there.

Fred walked out. On the first floor, he dunked his head in a janitorial slop sink, wiped the most visible of the vegetable matter off his shirt, and discovered, still perched on his right shoulder, a limp and glistening pasta conch. He mouthed it, his first meal in two days.

At the subway entrance, Fred froze, found himself incapable of heading back to his parents' apartment, and instead kept going, rolling his carry-on and briefcase behind him, soup-stained and hungover, his insides cold and hollow and vibrating like a bell from his two-day fast. Hospital visiting hours were over, but he kept heading vaguely in that direction for a while, east, and north, and east again, as around him a Friday night in the odds-beating, death-defying, nose-thumbing, glitterier-than-ever city unfolded. Ahead of him sauntered two college-age women, one with a cutoff shirt revealing one of those lower-back tattoos of blue wings he'd been seeing around—a weird place for wings, the ultimate merger of materialism and transcendence, as if all those sexy asses might flutter up like cherubs to the domes of Renaissance churches. He wondered if Mira had a lower-back tattoo, as yet unglimpsed, and if so, what it was. A helmet with radiance lines, maybe. A brain in a vat. What could be the symbol of that brand-new faith of hers? Some kind of higher geometrical form? A tesseract? A six-dimensional Calabi-Yau manifold? Or in order to truly qualify as a faith without ignorance, did it have to renounce symbols entirely, stay pure of any shape or form whatsoever, beyond description of any kind?

Invisible, inarticulable, but somehow not nonexistent . . .

The tattoo flew across the street, and he couldn't help but track it. He had no idea whether it was true, whether it was something his twin had actually done, but Fred could picture it clearly enough: George's last summer on Earth, riding around in cabs, eyes glued to photoshoots and ice cream cones, eyes like Pavlov's slavering dogs, eyes like flies, flitting among shitpiles. Had this world been designed for no other purpose than to present a person with a myriad of ultimately pointless things to seek and avoid, it surely couldn't have been put together much more effectively. Had the mind been crafted for no other purpose than to seek or avoid them, it too was surely the state of the art. Though of course he knew this part wasn't true in the slightest, he also pictured some trapped astral George wandering the Pretaloka streets, desiring despite the lack of anything to desire.

Which led Fred in turn to think of George's apartment, the way George had emptied it out in his last conscious weeks. On the morning Fred had found him—lying atop his sheets with the oxygen tubes in his nose and his hands clasped one palm over the other, over his heart, snoozing unrousably away—practically nothing remained of his bedroom but the bed itself. Returning to the apartment a few days later for supplies Fred still hoped George might soon need, and in search of clues to his brother's mental state in the time leading up to the coma, Fred confirmed what he'd been too distraught the last time to fully register: that George had gotten rid of just about everything he'd owned. Kitchen cupboards all but empty, garbage taken out, bathroom cleaned, the former metropolis of pill bottles gone from the medicine cabinet, the little keepsakes vanished from his desk.

His computer remained, an oversight Fred found curious, until a couple weeks later, when, out of loneliness and curiosity, he came back and turned it on, to discover George had wiped the hard drive. Perhaps George had told himself he was being helpful, removing things so the rest of them wouldn't have to deal with them. Perhaps it was his attempt to convince himself he was ready to go. Had Fred believed George was actually ready, had Fred seen the slightest evidence of George finding any peace or resolution in that good, clear wall, maybe Fred wouldn't have insisted on the life support that had stabilized him, wouldn't have sold the company to pay for his ongoing care—steps Fred had known to be against his wishes. But Fred had no such evidence, no reason to believe George had found a single thing he'd been seeking—with the sole possible exception of a good night's sleep.

Fred didn't see that apartment again until two months later, when he went back to clean it out. He'd expected trouble with the management company about breaking the lease, but they were all too happy to return the deposit. Responding to market pressures after 9/11, the management had reduced everyone's rent across the board. Many had left, regardless. For those who had stuck it out, rents had been inching up incrementally. But George's newest neighbors—bankers—were paying far more;

compared to the current streak, Fred's and George's dot-com bubble of yore had been like amateur hour; leave it to the financiers to show them what virtual reality really was, making money from money and cutting out the product altogether. Through a neighbor's doorway, left open by a cleaning lady taking out the trash, Mel's bombasticator ranted on a plasma screen roughly the size of the wall—something about egghead scientists wanting to bring back "supposedly" twenty-seven-thousand-year-old woolly mammoths from their frozen sperm—as Fred hauled out the furnishings George had been too physically weak to toss out himself. There was almost nothing of any sentimental value to keep. No journals or yearbooks or photographs. Only the briefcase, some not-too-old clothing, the camping gear, and a few other things George probably thought could be put to some no-nonsense, impersonal use.

Thinking back now on his brother's motivations for all this jettisoning of his identity, Fred couldn't help but wonder if there had been anger in the gesture, too, if it had been just one more form of withdrawal from them all, or from Fred himself. What had George been in it for, if it hadn't been for healing? Revenge? Against Armation? Against Fred? At the thought, Fred was underwater again, his lungs filling with brine. If it turned out George had actually been involved somehow in the planning of these assaults on the shred a life Fred had left, Fred didn't know what he'd do. It was awful enough, even without the possibility of George's involvement, to wonder what it meant that these people had known about Mira Egghart, that they knew now about Fred's burgeoning infatuation with her; and to wonder what humiliations, based on this knowledge, they might subject him to next.

Before long, having given up pretending to himself that he had no destination in mind, Fred was walking alongside a night-shadowed Tompkins Square Park, carry-on wheels rattling away behind him, the neon glow and muffled subwoof of Mira's bar approaching. He just wanted to see if she was working, to peek through the small side window and watch her pour a drink or two. And to get a glimpse of those squinty, opaline eyes; that curved nose; those full lips she seemed almost embarrassed to possess, always trying to flatten them away. And to see if her hair was in braids again, and whether she was working up a sweat, and whether she was gazing at any other drunk, sleeping loser the way he'd seen (or hallucinated) her from above, gazing at him.

Past the twinkling of an antediluvian pinball machine near the window, the woman he sighted behind the bar was younger and meaner looking than Mira, with penciled-in eyebrows and a forties-style perm. She faced his way but didn't see him, her slightly crossed eyes intent instead on a polished fingernail, the edge of which she was scraping at with the edge of another. He kept watching her, doubting her, feeling like he'd stumbled into the wrong universe, that in the one where he should have been, Mira was there—right there—staring straight back at him.

With a start, he saw that she was. Not behind the bar, but on a stool at the rounded end of it. Lips bunched to one side. Eyes fixed on his.

She didn't look angry. Maybe not exactly happy to see him, but not angry, either. She held up a hand and moved it right and left in a slow, sardonic wave. He made a little gesture in turn, pointing to himself, pointing to the stool next to hers. She gave a fatalistic shrug and returned her attention to where it must have been before she'd spotted him—her bottle of beer and the empty shot glass beside it, which, presently, the bartender, a guy with a soul patch the size of a mouse, replenished with tequila. As Fred came in, she turned to stare at the bags rolling in behind him. He swung them around and parked them before sitting down beside her.

"Business trip," he said.

"Oh? How'd it go?"

"So so." He shrugged. "Played some golf."

She looked dubious. Why? he wondered. Did he exude failure that much?

"So you found another job?" she asked.

"Same one." His façade crumbling already. "Tried to get it back."

"And?"

"Well . . . it would've gotten in the way of my spiritual aspirations, in any case."

"Did you interview in that?"

He glanced down at his Barneys jacket and white T-shirt, both crusted with orange soup swaths.

"You don't like it? The salesman told me it was the latest thing."

She smiled wanly, and turned back to the bar. She was dressed not in her bar clothes but her office garb—a pair of fitted black slacks, a black silk blouse, her hair pulled back.

"I had a feeling I'd be seeing you here," she said.

"You did?"

She didn't bother to reply, just picked up her beer, studied it for a moment as though she'd never seen such a thing before, then tilted it into her mouth, draining the last few gulps. It didn't seem like her to be drinking alone like this. To be sure, he felt the same way about her tattoo, her belly ring, the fact that she bartended. Maybe it was daft of him to persist in believing he knew what was like her and what wasn't. But he couldn't shake the feeling that none of this came naturally to her. Her posture on the stool was too erect. She drank too deliberately, like she was injecting herself with a vaccine.

Soul Patch set a fresh bottle in front of her. "Here you go, Professor." His tone, surprisingly gentle for a guy with a rodent attacking his lower lip, made Fred think perhaps the guy agreed with Fred's own assessment of her. He wondered if she'd just split up with a boyfriend, if she might be looking for a new one. He wondered if he could possibly be that lucky, for once. It took him a moment to realize Soul Patch was still standing there, arms folded.

"And you?" Soul Patch said, not as gentle.

"Nothing," Fred mumbled. "Just . . . water."

Mira gave him a look. "Stalking sober nowadays?"

She was trying not to show it, but he saw disappointment in her eyes. She was drunk, he was sure, though he wasn't sure how much so, never having seen her drunk before. He debated which would make him less appealing in her eyes, to watch like a teetotaler while she went on a bender, or to admit he had no money. Not that he was sure he could even stomach a drink at this point.

"I'm a little light," he admitted.

"Light?" She didn't get his meaning at first. Then she rolled her eyes, turned to Soul Patch. "Get him what I'm having."

Soul Patch did so.

"You have no money, Fred? Can you really have no money?"

Her expression was at first just puzzled, and then so suddenly tender he was taken aback. Was it simply pity?

"How about you take the drinks out of the fifty bucks for my next session?"

She frowned. Maybe he shouldn't have brought up the study. He worried she was about to tell him they shouldn't be talking like this. He was amazed she hadn't said it already. Instead, she remarked with a levity that seemed calculated, "I suppose the study hasn't been doing wonders for you, if you're still penniless and living with your parents."

"I wouldn't say it's been a total bust. I've met you."

Shaking her head, deflating a little, she began picking the label off her beer bottle. "A real stroke of luck for you."

"Not to mention getting to feel at one with a La-Z-Boy, floating above my body, seeing—"

"An angel?" She'd turned back his way, a mirthful light in her eyes. The change was so sudden it took him a second to adjust course yet again.

"Maybe not until now," he said.

"Nice," she allowed.

"I like you when you're drunk," he said.

"Is that so?" she asked.

"Don't get me wrong, I like you when you're sober, too. But you're easier to talk to now."

She nodded, brow scrunched, scientific-like. "More down to your level?"

"That's part of it, no doubt."

"And what's the rest?"

"You don't tell me to go away."

"You're sure of that, are you?"

"Well . . . you don't *immediately* tell me to go away."

"That night here, when I fell asleep on the bar. I dreamt I'd floated up out of my body." Fred was into his second round, drinking faster than Mira, and thanks to his empty stomach, catching up fast. The bar was more crowded now than when he'd walked in, and the two of them had to lean closer to hear each other. "I was up near the ceiling. I could see myself asleep down below."

They looked up at the fans and the black aluminum tiles.

"You were standing in front of me," he went on, "trying to decide whether to wake me up. You reached out, maybe to touch my shoulder. But instead, you picked up my glass."

He watched her expression. The corners of her eyes tightened. Otherwise, she was still.

"What happened then?"

"I was still rising, about to go right through the ceiling. Who knows where I would've gone." He'd barely thought about this last part, it had been so quick and dreamlike. He probably wouldn't have mentioned it now, except that she'd asked. "But then I just focused on that tattooed hand of yours." He looked at her shirtsleeve. "And it was suddenly my own. I was holding on to you."

Her face fell open for a moment, her eyes searching his. For what, he wasn't sure.

"And what then?" she asked.

"You dropped my glass in a plastic rack and walked off."

Slowly, she turned back to her drinks. He didn't bother asking if she'd really stood there looking at him like that. She didn't bother telling him. He knew it wouldn't have proved anything anyhow. They drank in silence for a minute, Mira peering off at the pinball lights like they were some too-complicated constellation, Fred recalling the dream he'd slipped into after the one of floating above the bar. Something about being locked out of his parents' place, up on the roof. Peering down through the skylight. Looking for George.

"Have you ever tried controlling your dreams?" she asked.

"You can do that?"

She traced a line in the dew on her bottle. "It can be done," she said after a while. "The tricky part is to ascertain that you're dreaming."

"And how do you do that?"

"Sometimes trying to jump can help. Or trying to turn on or off a light. The inner ear and retina aren't so easy to trick. Once you realize you're dreaming, you can take control. Psychologists call it lucid dreaming." She was edging her fingernails around the label of the beer bottle, happily lost in the explanation. "Tibetan Buddhists call it dream yoga. They've got their own technique. They constantly ask themselves if they're dreaming, all day long, so that they'll continue to ask in their sleep and then catch themselves."

"Will lucid dreaming be part of this new religion of yours?"

"This *religion* of mine?"

"Your faith without ignorance."

In one pull, she had the beer label off. "It's not a religion. Would you like to know what a religion is?"

She said this casually, ominously so.

"OK," he said.

"In the beginning . . ." She smoothed the label flat on the bar. ". . . there were specialists."

He smiled, trying to follow. "Specialists."

"People who discovered they could earn a living off spiritual services. Your blessings, your protections, what have you." She curled an edge of the label with her many-ringed fingers, rolled it into a tight stick, then picked it up and waved it, a little white wand. "Like other specialists—your blacksmiths, your masons—these spiritual service providers found it advantageous to form into guilds, which could standardize products and pricing, and allow them to control the spiritual marketplace more effectively."

With the tip of the wand, she pushed her empty shot glass toward the inner edge of the bar.

"But unlike your iron pikes and stone walls, your spiritual products are of less verifiable quality and consistency. And so even with their guilds, the specialists were getting undersold by unlicensed competitors. Word gets out the witch lady down the street is giving the same iffy results for half the price, and you're hard-pressed to prove you're the better choice. So the spiritual guilds turned to political lobbying, coercion, and brand identities."

Her lullaby tone was at odds with the clinical fixedness of her eyes on the glass.

"With political lobbying, religious coalitions could build state-sanctioned monopolies to increase their membership and influence. With coercion—your ostracism, your threats of damnation, your torture and killing and the like—they could make defection to other religions costly. And with infallible holy books to brand their identity, they could differentiate themselves from all those intuitive alternative types that kept creeping out of the woodwork."

She traced a slender, wavering vein along the wood of the bartop with the tip of the wand, then gestured with it again.

"The mystical impulse is a problem for religions. They rely on it to kindle demand, and to overcome the logical contradictions in their doctrines. But mystics are all about bypassing the middlemen specialists altogether. And local charismatics can form splinter groups and pull followers away. So, typically, religions will denounce, excommunicate, or just plain execute the mystics in their ranks, and every so often canonize a few safely dead ones from the past."

She downed the last of her beer, and with a flourish, dropped the wand into the empty bottle.

"And that's the story of religion."

Her squinty gaze, off at the liquor shelf, was imperious.

Finishing his own beer, feeling it paint the empty walls of his insides, Fred thought of his mother and her friends denying that Reiki was a religion, of Manfred's little speech about the Middle East and the Middle West blowing up the world. Would they all agree with what Mira seemed to be saying—that the faith without ignorance ultimately meant a faith without religion?

"Is there another side to that coin?" he asked.

The squint softened. Her face went a little slack. "The other side is that religions are the fruit of thousands of years of experimental wisdom. That they're the records of those few people in history who managed to see through this life so deeply and completely that they found the way to God."

She stared at the four empty vessels in front of them, as though not quite sure how they'd gotten that way. Her hair was coming loose from her clip, curling under her jaw. He wanted to brush it aside.

"The other side is that X-ray vision itself." Her squint returned, as if she herself was employing that vision, peering into the skeletons of the drinkers around them. "And one day, we'll all be able to have it, without signing over our intellects, or being pressed into gangs. Or molested by priests." She inclined her chin his way, looked at him sidewise with a flat little smile. "Or martyred by mullahs."

Then her expression changed again, her smile going bright and grateful as she turned to Penciled Eyebrows, who was now replacing their rounds.

"So that's really why your dad invented that helmet?" he asked.

"My father's as atheistic as they come. I think he expected everyone to close down their churches when he published his first article on the research. He wanted to use it to deprogram the faithful. A few of his atheist colleagues cheered him on, but most of the others didn't like the bad press and began to think he was a crank. And the alumni donors wanted to run him out of town. And of course, he couldn't get a dime of funding."

Drunk though she was, he was surprised, a little unsettled, even, that she was telling this to a test subject.

"Using the helmet to actually help encourage belief," she went on, "an informed belief, a belief rendered harmless to others through a solid understanding of its neurological basis, an understanding that your inner reality is just for you, and for the rest of the world it's false, or might as well be. . ." She brushed her fingernails against her blouse. "That stuff was my idea."

The self-mocking bragging gesture notwithstanding, he could tell she really was proud of the study. Indeed, even as it occurred to him that he was more of a guinea pig than he'd imagined, he was proud of her too.

"I'm surprised your dad agreed to it."

"We got the funding," she said, with that deliberate lightness. "And if the results go his way rather than mine, I'm sure he'll be happy to write it up that way, too."

Again, he wondered why she was telling him this. He wasn't sure he wanted to know it. On the other hand, he appreciated her honesty. Perhaps, he thought, it showed a faith in him, a faith in her project, in that very ideal of a faith uncompromisingly without ignorance.

She turned back to the bartop, tilted her head this way and that, a loose strand of hair arcing past her eyes.

"Besides," she said, "I think he would've agreed to get his head shaved and wear a cassock if it got me back to school."

"You dropped out?"

This, too, seemed odd to him. Nothing about her added up at all. His surprise, as much as her admission, seemed to sadden her.

"I was out for a few years," she said. "I'm just starting up again."

"What were you doing?"

She used her fresh bottle to indicate Penciled Eyebrows, Soul Patch. "Slinging drinks, mainly. And sleeping. I did a lot of that."

"And controlling your dreams?"

Her bottle froze in the air. "I'm going to shut up now. And you're going to talk."

"Just one more question. OK?"

She considered. "Maybe."

"Taking this . . . mystical journey, all on our own," he said, "couldn't we get lost? I mean, really lost?"

"We meaning you?" she said, with an amused look.

"Right," he muttered. She'd never tried the helmet, he just now recalled. "We meaning me."

"Well, if you do," she said, holding up her shot, "maybe at least you won't be ignorant enough to drag down the rest of us."

It was nearing closing time. The bar was emptying. Fred and Mira sat identically hunched, elbows on a patchwork of labels and coasters. Once again, "Space Oddity" was up on the jukebox. At the far end of the bar, Soul

Patch leaned against the drink shelving, flipping through the channels on the mounted TV. He stopped on NY1, footage of jumpsuited, filter-masked workers installing a glass viewing barrier around a set of clothing store racks coated with toxic 9/11 dust; Fred had seen the story earlier in the hospital cafeteria—the racks had been preserved for the last five years, and were now being prepared for a fifth-anniversary exhibition. His skin began to prickle, the image of those golf course replicas gasping dust plumes as he chopped into them with the club flashing to mind. He took a drink, from his third or fourth round, which only made the prickling worse.

"Last year around this time," he said, "I overheard a woman in the booth behind me at a diner telling her friend that her cat chose to die the week before 9/11, 'because he didn't want to be a part of all that tragedy.'"

Mira stared at him for a moment. An almost noiseless laugh escaped her.

"Everyone's got to spread their own miserable little layer of meaning over it," he said, feeling himself on a roll. "Like that baseball in Indiana the guy kept covering with coats of paint until it was the size of a weather balloon."

More than once now, Mira had ordered him to keep talking, pretty much whenever Fred had tried to get her to talk. He didn't really mind. Over the last few months, he'd grown used to monologuing to silent crowds of one. And he was warming to his subject.

"A hundred 9/11 movies. A thousand 9/11 novels. Ten thousand blo-viating talking heads. Eight million self-declared victims. Everyone lost something." He waved his bottle in the air. "Some value in their port-folio. A good night's sleep. Their innocence."

He glanced her way again. Her look was stern, like he'd just made fun of a cripple.

"And what did you lose, Fred?"

He put his palms on the bar, staring at the points where his thumbs and index fingers met.

"My innocence," he finally declared.

A few seconds passed.

She laughed. "Man, are you wasted."

The door was now locked, the remaining customers, except for the two of them, kicked out. Penciled Eyebrows wiped tables. Soul Patch mopped. Fred and Mira kept drinking, their shoulders leaned up against each other, in part to keep from falling over.

"Mr. Brounian," Mira said. "Welcome to my study. If you could, please summarize for me what the hell's the matter with you anyhow."

"My problems all began when I slew my father and married my mother. Then my inner child ran amok. More recently, there was the early male menopause . . ."

As he spoke, she typed his responses into an invisible keyboard on the bartop. Just like in her office, she went on typing long after he'd trailed off.

"Doctor, do you mind my asking what it is you're writing?"

"My report."

"What does it say?"

"Mr. Brounian. Fred, if I may."

"Call me Freddo."

She laughed, breaking character. "*Freddo?*"

"It's what all my good analysts call me."

"All right, to resume then, it is my determination, *Freddo*, that you're fucked up beyond hope of recovery."

"Is that so?"

"My recommendation is for you to be removed from human society, remanded to the care of animals, reindoctrinated as a rhesus monkey. Possibly a dolphin."

"I think I'm going to want a second opinion."

"Certainly. You're ugly, too."

"Thanks, Groucho."

"Any time. That'll be five hundred bucks."

More of her hair had freed itself from the clip, apple mist in the air. The point of contact between their upper arms was spreading an almost intolerable charge through his body—part desire, part fear. He was thinking about George's Foley catheter and telling himself not to think about that. He was thinking about the exchange with his cyberstalker, the promise that Mira would fall for him, the possibility that it might actually be coming true, then wondering if it was a setup, if she was in on it, if the whole world was in on it, everyone but himself, then telling himself not to think about any of that either, not to give his persecutors that kind of power over him, not to let it freeze him up and sabotage everything.

"Have you ever noticed how proud people are to have them—opinions, I mean?" he plowed on. "It's like being proud of one's tapeworms, or pubic lice."

"Would the analysand care to discuss his longstanding shame associated with his pubic lice?"

"Here's an opinion," he proclaimed, surprising himself with his own vehemence. "There should be a law limiting people to one opinion per lifetime. When that kid came up to you in nursery school and asked you what your favorite color was? And you suddenly felt you wouldn't quite exist if you didn't have an answer? And so you said, I don't know, blue? That's your opinion limit. You're done. You're free. No other opinions would ever be asked for or allowed of you."

She leaned farther over the bar and caught his eyes. "Is that your favorite color? Blue?"

He shook his head. "What if it is?" he muttered.

As he watched, tears, inked with mascara, rolled from her eyes.

By the time the two of them were outside, the tears had been forgotten, at least, it seemed, by Mira. She'd brushed them away almost as soon as they'd come, dismissed Fred's inquiries, and was laughing again, first at his inability to walk a straight line, and then at her own wobbling tightrope act down the sidewalk. Upon reaching her building, he made the mistake of stopping an instant before she did. He tried to cover it up by making it look like he'd stumbled. But her look told him she wasn't buying it.

"Right," she said, with a slow nod. "Of course you know where I live."

He was avoiding her eyes, looking up at the dark face of her building. A single light in a fifth-story window went off.

"Hey," he managed, sheepishly. "What kind of stalker would I be otherwise?" Then he stood there, wishing he'd found a less creepy reply.

"True," she said. As they stood there facing each other, it started happening again—that impossible light, even more impossible now, by night, on the darkened street, as though the moon itself had been lowered to the point where its pale expanse filled the sky from end to end, its milky light pouring down on them.

"Mira. That brightness to everything from the session. It's back."

"Right now?"

"Yes, yes. Right now."

She stepped closer, those dark, myopic eyes squinting in the light. A foot away. Six inches. He was seeing it as he'd see it in the last minute of brainlife, for the last time. Whether death was the end or but a prelude, this moment would be irretrievable, unchangeable from here on. The light, he at last felt he understood, was a call to action—opportunities were fleeting, he had to lean in and kiss her . . . right now . . . without delay . . .

"Your pupils look a little unevenly dilated," she said, before he'd moved. "It should go away soon." She stepped back. "Let me know, though, if it keeps bugging you."

Bathed in the now meaningless, illusory moonbeams, she turned toward her front steps. A panic seized him.

"You inviting me up?" he asked, trying to make it sound casual.

She shook her head solemnly.

"You'll need some help getting up those stairs, though," he suggested.

"I'm not relationship material."

She watched him, waited for the point to sink in.

"Um . . . Can I use your bathroom?" he asked.

"Now that's just pathetic."

She made for the steps, and promptly tripped on the first. He grabbed her with both hands around the waist and arm, himself almost falling over. With her hip in his palm, the side of her breast against the backs of his fingers, the waves of heat coming off her, his whole body thrummed with a need so strong it ached. She went tense, closing her eyes. Her neck flushed. For a second he thought she might pull away, but instead she leaned into him for a few seconds, before finding her balance again.

"You can use my bathroom," she said.

They got up the steps. The strange light was gone, but the heat was more compelling still. He could barely uncouple his hands from her and go back down to retrieve his bags once they reached the door.

It was an old building. The entryway, at least, didn't seem to have been renovated any time recently. Through the steam clouds of his endorphins, he saw her name on a mailbox, her father's on another. He pointed to the latter.

"Your dad won't chase me out with a shotgun, will he?"

"Not his style." She opened the inner door. "He might come at you with a Tesla coil. Or a skull saw."

On the way up the narrow flights, she gave him a brief, whispered history of her occupancy, how she'd grown up here, how, a few years ago, the top-floor apartment had come on the market and her father had made the down payment for her.

"We were going to fix it up," she said, trailing off and leaving it at that.

"You and your dad must be close," Fred whispered.

"It was a good deal."

"Is your mom—"

"They divorced when I was twelve. She pretty much left us both, went off to find herself. She's still looking. Hi, Dad," she said, so casually Fred almost waved too, as he and Mira rounded the corner onto the fifth landing, to find an apartment door open and Craig Egghart standing in the frame. He was dressed in a threadbare bathrobe, looking from Mira to Fred, those seepy-dyed eyes of his large with anxiety, then narrowing to a squint, then popping wider than before.

"But . . . isn't he . . . isn't he the one from the study?"

It was the first time Fred had heard the man speak. He had the kind of mild voice that only went quieter with strain. *The one from the study*, Fred thought. No sooner had he begun to wonder why Egghart had worded it that way than Mira's reply scuttled the whole issue.

"Not anymore," she said.

Fred and Mira's father watched each other as the confusion shifted from Egghart back to Fred. Then Egghart looked at his daughter again, a warmer look, which only seemed to annoy her. She slipped past him, pulling Fred along, Fred wheeling his bag around Egghart's feet. Egghart closed the door softly, as Fred and Mira rounded another bend and started up the next flight.

"I had a feeling he wouldn't be going to sleep tonight," she whispered, more to herself than to Fred.

They reached the top landing. She fumbled with her keys.

"What did you mean back there?" Fred whispered.

She looked up. "You didn't really think you'd stay in the study after butting into my life like this, did you?"

He didn't know what to say. He felt like he'd been nightsticked in the gut. He half wanted to ask her why she hadn't just told him to go away instead of hanging out with him all night. It seemed a betrayal not only of him but of her study, the study which so clearly meant everything to her. She was watching his expression, seemingly surprised at how hurt he was. She looked hurt herself, and guilty, and offended at the same time. She turned away, got the door open, stepping into the dark hallway beyond.

"Bathroom's second door to the right."

She turned left and switched on a light, revealing a long, narrow kitchen with a Formica counter and yellowed white paint, and the living room beyond.

Fred left his bags just inside the door and made his way down the hall.

The first door to the right, somewhat ajar, revealed her bedroom—the light was off; he could make out part of a dresser, the usual womanly clutter of little cases and boxes atop it, and the edge of a bed, the sight of which sent another urgent pulse through him. He was still reeling from the blow of being kicked out of the study, still wondering what that last doozy of a session would have shown him. Yet on the other hand, what did it even matter? Hadn't he been duped and mentally manipulated enough already? What was he really losing? Nothing real, nothing like the feel of Mira's waist on the front steps, nothing like her hips swaying ahead of him up the flights of stairs.

He was so crazed with lust that inhaling the scent of her shampoos and bodywashes and moisturizing soaps in her little blue-tiled bathroom was almost too much for him. He held his half-erect member, the urine passing through his hypersensitized urethra with something far closer to pleasure than pain. It had been months since he'd been with a woman, with Mel, in that Zeckendorf stairwell. It had gone well in the end, but the whole time he'd been plagued by thoughts of catheters and cancers, and nearly hadn't gotten it up. His only worry now was the opposite, that he'd explode in his pants. He plunged his face in cold water, the effects of which were immediately counteracted by drying off in a towel infused with the scent of her flowers and fog. He stared at the floor tiles, trying to calm himself, but even those sensible, rectilinear shapes gyrated like a thousand dancing hips.

Back out in the hall, he took a few steps before realizing he'd gone the wrong way. Another door to the right, this one closed. A second bedroom? A study? But no, not a study—her cluttered desk was to his left, through a set of French doors, crammed in alongside a dining table, itself stacked with books and papers. The light was out in this room, but beyond it, through an identical set of doors on the other end, the living room light now shone. He could see a front window; and two chest-high, opened crates; and a splay of packing material. As he watched, through the doubled grids of the two sets of panes, Mira stepped slowly into the tableau, stopping between the crates and staring, with that misted, wonder-filled expression of hers, at something in the corner out of view. She turned her head, toward the other corner, more or less Fred's way, then saw him and jumped with fright. Once she realized it was him, she shut her eyes for a second, after which he mouthed an apology, but he doubted she could really see his features through the panes with him standing the dark. Rather than open the doors, he made his way back around through the kitchen. A futon couch, some overstuffed book-shelves, and a couple of vintage, silver-bulbed, space-age lamps came into view. Only when he stepped into the living room could he see the objects of her gaze.

In either corner, one in front of a potted plant, the other flanking a cabinet with a small television, stood a sandstone angel, each about three-quarters the size of a living person. The first knelt on a sandstone cloud, leaning forward, his forearms crossed over his chest, his hands holding the opposite sleeves of his robes, his eyes trained downward, as if to an Earth below. The other sat on one knee, with closed eyes and an enigmatic smile, hands up in prayer at a broad and bare chest, wings draped like a cape down his back.

"They're pretty," she said. "Especially the Asiatic one."

It was true, the smiling one had slightly Asiatic features, and was more exotically adorned, with bangles around his muscular upper arms, and a snake wrapped loosely about his neck, its diamond-shaped head rising like a scarf in a breeze.

"They must have been expensive," she said, still looking at them, leaning on one hip. "Quite a statement, from a man who can't afford drinks."

Air gathered in Fred's open mouth.

"So why two of them?" she asked. When, again, he didn't respond, she went on, "They do seem to belong together, though. East and West."

She turned to him, wanting to see if she was close to the mark. Fred forced a vague nod.

"You can stay here tonight, if you need a break from your parents," she said. "The couch folds out. There are some sheets and a pillow in there." She pointed to a wooden storage chest doubling as a coffee table as she brushed past him into the kitchen. "It's late. Go ahead and make your bed."

From the other end of the apartment came the sounds of a door closing and water running. Fred had been frozen as stiff as the statues, and now forced himself to approach them, warily, as if they might blow up. Sifting through the packing materials, he found no slips or other documentation. Strings were hung round statues' necks, small printed tags, according to which the one on the cloud was a cast of an inter-cessory angel from an Italian cathedral, the barechested one a cast of a Hindu deva from the Changu Narayana temple in Nepal. Then, next to the TV, sitting on an opened envelope, he spotted a white card, blank but for three typeset lines:

SOMETIMES EVEN ANGELS NEED AN ANGEL

LUCKY YOU

YOU GET TWO

He knelt before the second statue, staring at close range at that knowing smile; one moment it seemed a little menacing, the next, serene. George's private smile. That Brooklyn accent. *You get two.*

He was drunk. He was dizzy. It made no sense. But George was here, right here in these statues. George had been in on this. To what end, and with who else, Fred still couldn't say. For now, it just felt like a benediction, like his brother had poked his head from a cloud and winked.

Distantly, the sound of the bathroom door opening reached his ears. Lest she think he was snooping, he hurried back and pulled out the futon, found the sheets and pillow, and began making the bed. The light went off. Dim in the streetlight through the blinds, Mira stood in the kitchen doorway, her hair undone, in a long T-shirt and bare legs, clutching a pillow to her chest. She tossed it down beside the one Fred had just laid out, revealing, in the process, the front of her shirt:

WARMONGER

Fred started laughing. He couldn't stop.

"Shut up and move over," she commanded.

The first time they made love, the only thing that kept Fred from coming immediately was his surprise at Mira's tenderness. She kissed him so gently, held him so tightly. It was almost too intimate, too much love to be bestowed on someone she barely knew. She nuzzled his neck, planted a dotted line of kisses down his chest and stomach, held his cock in both hands, alternately sucking and kissing. She squirmed and rolled beneath his touch, and guided him in, and gasped, and yelped, and covered his face and neck with more little kisses. He felt he didn't deserve it, but he wanted to deserve it, and made his own caresses as familiar and attentive as hers. Afterward, she stayed wrapped around him, an arm and a leg locking him down, planting rapidfire pecks on his cheek that made him giggle. Amazed at his good fortune, he couldn't stop his fingertips from riding back and forth along a gullied road that wended from her broad cheek to the lookout point at the side of her breast to the hilltop of her hip. The caresses went on wordlessly until they were at it again. From time to time he looked up at the pale outlines of those sandstone angels, feeling that reality had become a dream, a lucid dream that he'd woken up inside and was now, to his joy and relief, able to steer toward every hope. It was all possible. Mira could love him. The world could be anything. George could be here in spirit, here and everywhere.

And Mira asleep: her arms around him, her breasts pressed to his back, swelling and receding like waves with her breath. He imagined him and her beyond the universe, lounging on the coils of a thousand-headed snake. His life was a shit heap, his future totally unworkable. But right here in this instant, with Mira's warmth at his back, he felt more complete than ever before, than he had even on the day in that sunny conference room overlooking the city when George's angel investor had given them their company.

And slipping into a dream. Mira—or maybe it's partly Jill again—pressed close against his white cape, her bare arms out below his, he and she together like a Hindu deity. And with her lips so near they touch his ear, she whispers, *Look, they're back*, and the night sky is scattered not with stars, but—like some disordered computer desktop—with icons: There's a sparkly helmet icon. A hand icon. Mouse ears. And many more. A few shine brightly, give off a kind of radiance. Most are dim. Her lips tickle as she reminds him that these are his superpowers, his divine attributes. She's been pointing and double-clicking the air with her finger, trying to get all these applications lit at once. The last one she tried was a set of wings, which began to glow, though simultaneously across the sky, a hand lost its radiance. Before that, she'd tried a shot glass, which hadn't gone bright itself, though a nearby space helmet icon had.

Now she's pointing at a new icon. He can't quite make it out—its shape is hidden by her hand. But whatever it is, he has a bad, bad feeling about it.

Please, he says. *Not that one.*

She just laughs. And beyond her hand, the icon's edges jiggle, double-clicked, as she whispers one last, carefree word:

Next.

Fred awoke without a struggle, to twilit bookshelves and crates and sandstone angels, all afloat and atwirl from the booze still in his veins. Mira was gone, his throat was parched, his bladder full. Too comfortable, though, to immediately move, he reviewed the strange dream, then the events of the night, themselves almost as dreamlike, though here were the angels, here was her apartment, here was Fred himself, getting aroused again at the memory of Mira pressed against him. Just enough predawn light filtered through the slats to illuminate the titles on a couple of the bookshelves, one shelf filled with psychology, anthropology, sociology, neurology tomes, another containing more surprising finds—economics and business textbooks, old sci-fi novels. He began listening for clues to Mira's whereabouts, for the sound of footsteps, or water in the bathroom. Hearing nothing, he sat up, and feeling a little vulnerable in the unfamiliar surroundings, he slipped on his jeans before wandering into the kitchen, finding a glass, and pouring himself some water from the tap. It reminded him of his parents' kitchen—the apartment as a whole was just about as ancient and unrenovated. He felt comfortable here, safe from the howling winds of time. Between sips, he took in the surface of her refrigerator. On the freezer door was a magnetic grease board full of phone numbers, mostly of what appeared to be takeout restaurants. On the lower door, no pictures or postcards, just a bunch of ad-bearing magnets holding up nothing but themselves, and one clip, from the plastic jaws of which hung a card with formal-looking script—an invitation to some kind of reception. Some other pages lay underneath it—directions, or other invitations.

Continuing to the back of the apartment, he saw that the bathroom was unoccupied and stepped in, wondering as he urinated why she'd clung to him for so long, only to retreat to her own bed in the middle of the night. Maybe he'd been snoring. Maybe her bed was a lot more comfortable. Or maybe she'd sobered up enough to want to forget about everything she'd just done. Back out in the hall, with one finger, he pushed her bedroom door open an inch, then another. The bed was empty.

He doubled back, thinking she might have returned to the futon while he'd been in the bathroom, but she hadn't. Then he opened the French doors and walked through the room with the dining table and desk, also unoccupied.

The only place left to look was the last door along the hall. It was shut, as it had been earlier. He opened it a crack: Gray light seeping around the edges of a curtain on the far wall. The nearest wall covered with photographs. He opened it more: The floor cluttered with cardboard boxes. A blue vinyl recliner in the corner. And Mira—a man's blazer draped over her like a blanket—curled in the chair, asleep.

The pictures ran not quite chronologically, but almost. At the top left corner of the wall were taped a few school photos, the first of a whole class of small, grinning children, the next two, individual portraits—one of a boy with combed, bright blond hair and green eyes, the other of a dark-haired little girl—both taken against the same mauve backdrop. More pictures of the boy followed, and one of the boy and girl together on the stage in a school play, against the backdrop of a candy-and-frosting cottage. Many years were missing after that, the next set of photos finding the boy's hair a couple of shades dirtier, and his face and body elongated into young adulthood. The young man stood with a group of guys playing Hacky Sack. He lay sprawled on a half-destroyed couch in what might have been a messy college dorm room. On a prototypical grassy quadrangle, he held a college-aged Mira by his side, her hair long, her pose surprisingly theatrical, an over-the-shoulder look that aspired to convey mystery. In a library, from the same time period, the two sat next to each other, she surrounded by thick textbooks, he, dignified, perusing a Doctor Strange comic book. There followed a few photos of the young man in a cap and gown—alone, then with what must have been his parents and younger brother, then with Mira again, Mira coyly brushing aside her mortarboard tassel like a lock of hair. Another showed him leaning back on another couch somewhere, an electric guitar in his lap. Then came what seemed to be another few years' gap, and the next photo found him with a fleshier face and shorter hair, standing in front of a pagoda and green hills; behind this picture, an airmail envelope was tacked. More pictures of them together followed. One was in Tompkins Square Park, he and Mira on a blanket, waving from a field of recumbent, scantily clad hipsters. One in her living room on the same futon she and Fred had just slept in, she in a sweatshirt, the man in a sweater and untucked shirt, that beat-up old briefcase that resembled Fred's at his side. They looked to be late twenties. Then the man in yet another cap and gown. Then a score of wedding pictures, a garden wedding on an overcast day, the man in a beige linen suit (the jacket of which, Fred was fairly sure, Mira was now using as a blanket); Mira in a flowing, floral-print dress, and white flowers in her dark hair, looking so radiant Fred could barely force his eyes onward. He skipped to the lower right corner of the wall to a grainy, full-color printout on normal copy paper—an off-center and oddly angled picture of the man in a crisp, blue dress shirt, a newer, more stylish-looking briefcase propped beside him on the desk of a cubicle. The man looked at the camera with crossed arms and sleepy eyes and a sly smile, his head leaned to one side, allowing for a view behind him of a long, narrow window framing a darkening sky, and the lit-up, uppermost floors of one of the Twin Towers.

The other one.

Fred looked to the floor. At his feet, a large box magic-markered: CLOTHES. Another next to it: SHOES. Glancing up from there, he discovered Mira watching him. He had the feeling she hadn't been asleep at all. Her eyes had been a bit too tightly shut, now that he thought about it.

"One question, Fred."

Her tone had a calm chill to it. Though her red-rimmed eyes burned into him.

"Did you know yesterday was our wedding anniversary, too?"

It took him a moment to speak. "What?" *Too?*

Her whole body was hidden under that beige jacket. Only her head protruded. Had it been slightly darker in the room, he might have thought she'd stuffed herself into a burlap sack.

"Come on, Fred. No need to be modest. You knew everything else. You knew what bar I work at. You knew where I live. Not just my address—you must have looked that up to send me those statues. But the actual building. I didn't quite put that together. You stopped right in front of it, last night. You've seen it before."

She stared, daring him to deny the charge. He couldn't begin to respond. He was still processing her marriage, her loss, the bit about it being her wedding anniversary. He was still replaying the previous evening—her bender, her sadness—seeing pieces of it anew. Before he could even open his mouth, her arm shot out sideways from the cover of the jacket, brandishing that spectral tattoo.

"You even knew about *this*, didn't you? Why else would you have told me that story of floating over the bar? Your hand and this one." She pointed to the tattooed hand. "Like a glass slipper," she said with a mocking, fairy-tale brightness. "The perfect fit."

"Mira—" he said, hoping to slow her down. She was getting too far ahead of him—he couldn't even see what she was accusing him of. The jacket had slipped from her bare shoulders to hang on her tucked-in knees. He hadn't managed to say anything but her name. She was talking again.

"I didn't put it all together until I got up a little while ago and saw that . . . that *briefcase*." With this last word, louder than the rest, her voice quivered with horror. "You had it from the first day of the study, didn't you?"

He opened his mouth. Nothing came out.

"Just waiting for me to notice it," she said. "This whole damn time. So I could think, *Oh, just like Lionel's*. What's your game? Who do you know who knew Lionel—who knows me?"

He held out his hands. A laugh escaped him, flustered, but also relieved. *The briefcases!* She couldn't possibly believe what she was saying, if she thought about it some more.

"Mira, please, slow down. I didn't know about . . . about Lionel. *At all*. I'm—" He banished the smile. "I'm so sorry."

"I saw that briefcase," she went on, "and it all fell into place. I finally understood what your gift meant. What your card meant. *Lucky me. I get two.*" That false, fairy-tale tone again. "A second chance at love."

The smile he'd been fighting dropped down the hollow of his chest. There was nothing absurd in her logic, he saw. Her logic was seamless. She'd taken all the puzzle pieces and assembled them into a version of him that bore no relation to the self he knew. And her version made more sense than his. How could he begin to explain that the statues had come not from him but from stalkers of his own, possibly from his comatose brother?

"I believe . . ." He stopped, took a breath, started again. "I mean the sculptures represent George and me." At least, this was what he'd assumed they represented. "Not you and . . ."

He watched her, marshaled his thoughts. He could see his statement just starting to make sense to her. He could see all those pieces starting to rearrange themselves back his way. In that moment, she looked not only confused but afraid.

But then her eyes shone with a canny light.

"You *believe*, you say?"

"No . . . no—I know." His gut twisted. "I mean—that's what it means."

"You know what I *believe*?" she said. "I believe you're a textbook sociopath." She nodded. "You don't even have a twin brother, do you?"

"Mira, this is crazy. I wasn't playing you. I wasn't using you."

"No? Well you know what? I was using you. And I'm finished now. So get out."

He was gearing up once more to try to explain when her words caught up to him.

"Using me?"

Her mouth tortioned into a clamped smile, waiting for him to get it. It took him a while. His first thought was again that she was in on those angel messages, somehow. Finally, though, her true meaning dawned on him, all at once, in too-vivid detail. Every one of those loving kisses, caresses, counterthrusts, instantly recast.

"What," she said, "you thought all that was for you?"

She stood, and with no great hurry, as if to mock him with the sight of her, put the jacket on.

"There's one accurate diagnosis, at least," he said. "You using me. You program that helmet to make me want to fuck you?"

She swung out a hip, opened her mouth to reply.

"You vampire," he added.

Her shoulders hunched slightly. For a moment, she just stood there, holding herself in the jacket.

"Get the fuck out," she spat. "Go play with your imaginary twin."

Dude, said Inner George, *did you really just call a 9/11 widow a vampire?*

Inner George's sigh whistled in the breeze around him.

Smooth move, Freddo.

His twin's voice was crisper in Fred's head than usual, maybe due to the emptiness of the early morning, the streets and sidewalks freshly washed in an overnight downpour he must have slept through altogether. Or maybe it was due to the austerity within, the lack of all other distractions—no food to be digested, no money to be spent, no job to be avoided or not avoided, no final helmet session, no Mira. Nothing left but Inner George, and the rumble of the odd passing garbage truck.

Likewise, angel boy, Fred replied, thinking of those fucking statues.

He kept replaying the fight. He thought about all the things he might have said to convince her he wasn't some kind of creeper, playing her from day one. He thought about the fear in her eyes as she reconsidered which version of him to believe in, and her evident relief once she'd settled back into the one that could best keep him at bay. He thought about that other look on her face, that tormented smile with which she'd told him she'd used him. She would never have said this to him but for the absurd misunderstanding. He knew this. He'd witnessed too much tenderness in her last night ever to think her cruel by nature. But that didn't make the statement any less true. She'd been making love to her dead husband. As far as she was concerned, Fred hadn't even been in the room.

In the hospital lobby, nowhere close to visiting hours yet, he fell into a leather armchair facing the courtyard window, and began flipping the Swiss Army knife in his fingers, snapping the implements out and in—a reamer, a ballpoint pen, a pharmaceutical spatula.

What do you want from me, George? Who's helping you?

His thumbnail caught a crevice behind the key ring attachment, and he was pulling something new out from a slotted sheath: tweezers. For a minute, he was back in that supermarket, on day one of the study, following those silver hair-whorls toward the sun-filled exit doors, feeling like there was nothing out of place in this universe, not even him. He wanted to draw a line from that day to this, from tweezers to tweezers. He wanted to take these trembling tines and grip that little line and pull it, inch by inch, until the whole grand pattern, all the hope-against-hoped-for meaning and more, came sliding into view.

He dozed off, into a dreamless oblivion, for what seemed like seconds but was in fact hours, and awoke hungover, the inner surface of his skull pulsing like a single, giant nerve being chewed by some ruminant animal.

The lobby was now aswarm with visitors and staff, the usual lunch-hour bustle. Checking his watch, Fred confirmed it was close to one in the afternoon. Brittle, fainter than ever from the lack of food, and all the more drowsy from that death-like slumber, Fred drifted with his bags to the elevator bank and floated up to George's floor. As the doors slid open, an electronic chime went off somewhere close. At first he thought it was a pager or phone beep from the belt of one of the nearby doctors, but as he followed the colored lines along the hall floor, he thought to check his cell phone, and discovered he'd just gotten a text:

CALL GEORGE

Followed by an unfamiliar number. Foreboding seeped through his scoured nerves. Before he could settle his stomach and work up the guts to dial the number, a bang shot from George's room.

He peered around the doorframe. His mom and dad were at the far side of the bed, Holly working George's fingers, Vartan by George's head with a block of wood in either hand. A stick of incense smoldered from where it had been wedged between the IV bag and its pole. Fred's parents looked up and their huge eyes found him.

"He tried to speak," Holly said.

Vartan nodded in confirmation.

"It was just a whisper," Holly went on. "I couldn't make it out. He stopped before I could get my ear to his mouth."

"I didn't hear it," Vartan said, "but I saw his throat and jaw moving."

"He was almost off the bed when we walked in," Holly said.

"Like he was trying to get up," Vartan said.

The two of them went back to watching George. Clutching the cell phone, Fred overcame the urge to try switching the light on and off, as per Mira's instructions, to check if he was dreaming, though he allowed himself an unobtrusive hop on his heels (gravity seemed to be working normally), before moving to the bedside. The cuff of George's tracheostomy was deflated, Fred saw, as it always was after meals to lessen the possibility of refluxed goop getting inhaled.

"Did you get any other responses?" Fred asked.

"Some winces when I bang the blocks," Vartan said.

"He's following along more," Holly said, opening and closing his fist. "And there's some trembling, like he's straining."

Vartan put the blocks down and held one of George's eyes open. "No tracking, but there's some dilation."

Reactions like these weren't very high on the Glasgow scale, only slightly more than they usually got. But they'd never found George nearly off the bed or heard him vocalize before.

"Did you try the Tabasco?" Fred asked. They each had their favorite items in the box of toys.

Vartan rummaged for it.

"Grab his toes, Fred," Holly called out. "Help me do the exercises."

Fred started bending them, one at a time, then all together, then started working the ankles as Vartan opened George's mouth and dabbed hot sauce on his tongue. Holly picked up his hand, then swayed unsteadily, looking ill for a moment.

"The energy's so . . . stormy in here," she said. Her eyes met Fred's and Vartan's. "Can either of you feel it?"

Holly went back to working George's wrist, then his elbow.

"Your energy is strong too," she said softly in George's ear. "Swim home, George. Swim through the clouds."

She straightened, moving George's whole left arm, while Fred moved his right leg. The motions looked a bit like George was doing a crawl stroke.

"Don't say that," Vartan said. "Don't confuse him."

"If it helps him move . . ." Holly let the thought trail off.

"And put that incense out. It's bad for his lungs."

"Follow the incense," she whispered. "Come back home."

"Come on, dude," Fred called out. "What is it you want to say?" He was thinking about his dream of waiting in the hat—or of *George* waiting in the hat, maybe, trusting that Fred would soon pull him out. Fred tried to trust as well, trust he could do just that. If life itself was some kind of dream, who was to say there wasn't a way to gain control, to will the shape of it?

"Let's switch," Holly said to Fred. She took George's other leg. Fred took his other arm. In silence, for a minute or two, they worked George's fingers and toes, ankle and wrist, elbow and knee. Fred wasn't sure. Maybe he could feel George cooperating.

"He's coming back," Holly said, her eyes bright. "I know it. I dreamt it again."

"You did?" said Fred.

"I dreamt I was out on the street on a cloudy day. And then all of a sudden the sun came out. And then I was standing over this hospital bed. And I saw him open his eyes, and look at me."

The light around her seemed stronger, then dimmer. The wooziness ebbed and surged. From Fred's pants pocket, his cell phone chimed again. His heart slammed. *Wake up, dude. Wake up.*

They turned George back over. Holly raised her hands to do Reiki. Vartan peeled George's lid again. Vartan had the flashlight out now, arcing it downward to bear on George's eyeball.

"There he goes!" Holly said.

Fred ducked his head under the flashlight, put his ear to George's mouth.

"What's he saying?" Vartan whispered, somewhere behind the light.

Fred listened. The nausea surged as he heard:

"*Kghhhhhhhhhhhhhhhhhhhhhhhhrk.*"

Relax, and close your eyes, at the count of
                              five
                                        and imagine a drop of
blue water falling on your head. One drop. One spot. A refreshing coolness on your scalp. Imagine, now, that this is special water. Healing,
purifying water. Even this single drop of it can leave you feeling so
peaceful that at the count of
            four
                        as you go ahead and imagine another
drop, and another, you can feel the pores of your scalp opening wide,
thirsting for more. Feel that coolness, that relaxation, spreading all
across the top of your head. Feel it soaking into your skull. Feel the cool,
healing peace seeping right into your brain. Drop by drop. So replen-
ishing that at the count of
                three
                              you can let go even more, and the more
you let go, the more blue water comes pouring in. A trickle. A steady
stream. Feel it filling the muscles and skin of your face and scalp, and
coursing down your neck, and into your shoulders. So revitalizing that
at the count of
        two
                    you're feeling so light, so new, that you can keep
opening and opening, letting it gush down your arms to your fingertips,
down your back and front, into every organ, even your lungs—this is
special water, you can breathe it as easily as air. How good it feels, suf-
fusing you from head to toe. So cooling. So healing. So rejuvenating that
at the count of

one

 your every cell is so relaxed it's just floating in the blue water. Just floating, perfectly at ease. Just like it feels when you're floating in space, above the Earth, with all the little bits of the city floating around you. It's all up here, now, every last piece. The parking meters, the telephones, the water towers, the subway cars, the streetlights, the beams and bricks and millions of bits of glass: all here. And all moving, every part on its own, parts seeking other little parts, reorganizing. But not into that old thing you remember. Not that old city, but something wholly new. There goes the Statue of Liberty, sailing by, torch first, in a cloud of tiny Statue of Liberty souvenirs. There go a pack of mailboxes, scoop-mouthing a school of light bulbs. Look at those keyboard keys clinging like barnacles to chunks of concrete. Look at those street displays of sunglasses angling themselves like flowers to catch the sun's rays. Look at that flock of pretzels weaving nests of glowing fiberoptic cable. Watch it all, the whole thing, this big, new ecosystem, this big, new creature of a trillion glittering parts. Watch it float off, to the distant stars and beyond. Wish it well, that dwindling sparkle in the black. And trust you'll never need it back. . . .

4

september 2006

S	M	T	W	T	F	S
27	28	29	30	31	1	2
3						

It was just possible to sit up straight in the tent, if he sat in the middle with his head in the apex. It was well over ninety degrees inside, the sun-drenched blue fabric angling down around his head. Fred faced the open slat of the entrance, through which he could feel an occasional draft. Visible through the opening was a sparkling black wedge of roofing material, the aluminum gutter running along the roof's back edge, and beyond that, the rustling leaves of a backyard tree refracting the sunlight in too many ways to track. The roof sloped downward from front to back, which helped his zazen posture (gleaned from a website): leaning slightly forward, propped on staggered pillows, legs in half lotus, George's sleeping bag serving as a floor cushion.

It was a fancy kind of sleeping bag with a built-in air mattress, which Fred had spent hours researching. George had never gotten to use these gifts, either the bag or the tent, Fred was pretty sure. Fred himself had, though, once, on the second anniversary of his and Mel's first date. They'd talked at first about going somewhere exotic, an African safari being their main idea. As the anniversary approached, they'd downgraded the ambition to going somewhere rustic and out of town for the weekend. But Fred begged off of even this plan, too wrapped up with work. Mel was disappointed with him, and when he told George this, George came to the rescue, hatching the scheme on the spot. Within the hour, Fred and George were setting up the tent in Fred's living room, putting a few potted plants around the entrance, affixing some glow-in-the-dark stars to the ceiling, and setting an MP3 of nature sounds playing on the stereo. The night turned out to be a success, despite Fred and Mel tripping the building's fire alarm trying to roast marshmallows over the gas range. The next day at the office, when he told George that all was well, his brother gave him a pitying look.

"Freddo," he'd said with a sad shake of his head, "how are you ever going to get by without me when I'm gone?"

Years before George got sick. Just a joke. But even so, even then, it had given Fred a chill.

A sparrow flitted down in front of him, just long enough to fix him with an inky eye and deposit a glistening white turd.

Monday afternoon. Two full days now since Fred had been to the hospital. George's breathing had failed shortly after making that all-too-familiar sound, and, for the first time since those first days, the ventilator had to be brought in. At which point, Fred had locked himself in a bathroom and proceeded to have what he thought must have been a coronary, or a lung collapse, or a stroke, or all three simultaneously—chest pounding, no air, walls going dark, muscles too weak to hold him up. It occurred to him that he was in a hospital and thus had the option of seeking medical attention, but the thought of the additional bills and hassles for everyone surpassed even the fear of death, so he simply gave up and waited to die. A classic panic attack, an online diagnostic tool later helped him confirm. When he managed to get on his feet, he found Vartan and Holly in the hall with Drs. Papan and Chia, neurologist and oncologist, the first time Fred had seen the two men in one place. Now it was the doctors who seemed in denial, ordering more tests in the upcoming week, though they also took turns underscoring that Fred and his parents needed to be thinking about withdrawing the life support and switching to end-of-life treatment only.

In the van, Holly sat rigidly, one fist clutched in the other. Vartan, for the first time in months, stabbed the F and U keys with his thumb when a student driver ahead of them stopped at a yellow light—it was pretty clear he hadn't taken the opportunity to toke up before bringing the van around. Nobody spoke on the ride home, but their thoughts, Fred knew, were running in parallel. For the past seven months, as George increasingly seemed to be beating the cancer, they'd been willing him back. But that sound had changed everything, their whole conception of what was going on inside of him. For George to regain consciousness now, with an end-stage cancer, and have to confront death all over again, would be the worst thing imaginable. Vartan parked the van. No one got out.

"We've got to get this over with," Vartan said, his voice hollow.

Fred was remembering the way his father had brought the flashlight into position over George's eye. A fluid motion, with a slight flick of the wrist at the last moment; the way, in the magic shows, that he cast spells with his star-tipped wand.

"Next weekend," Vartan said.

From the backseat, Fred watched Holly's fists tightening. They already knew what to tell the nurses, in the event George started breathing on his own again. That he was in pain and needed a morphine drip. This was the code, disclosed to them through family friends who had friends who were doctors or nurses. *In pain. Needs morphine.* Everyone would know what it meant, and no one would stand in the way.

"A week from Monday," Holly said, her tone severe enough to cut off any argument.

"A good day for a hanging," Vartan somberly agreed.

Once inside, Fred's parents went straight to bed, without a look his way. He wanted to do the same, but no sooner was he standing in that bedroom than the air was gone again and the walls were pressing in. He took the tent and sleeping bag from the closet and hauled them, along with his laptop, the alarm clock, some extension cords, some food, and a plastic jug of water, into the hall, up the ladder, and out the hatch. On his first trip back down, he added the pillows and a second half-gallon jug, this one empty, for urine, to minimize the necessity of future trips. Then he climbed into the tent, sat on a pillow, and proceeded to take stock of his existence.

In front of him on the sleeping bag, he'd placed his cell phone, which hadn't sounded again since that second time in the hospital. Two text messages, the same exasperating instruction to "CALL GEORGE," but each followed by a different phone number—neither one in service, as it turned out, when Fred dialed them. The numbers listed in the messages probably weren't the ones from which the calls had originated, which the cell phone only listed as "unknown." The first of the out-of-service numbers had a 404 area code, the second a 740. Atlanta and central Ohio, he determined on his laptop, places that had no particular significance to him, nor any connection to George that he could fathom. There didn't seem to be any obvious commonalities or patterns or mathematical relationships within or between the two numbers, but in truth he couldn't even make his mind focus on them in any coherent way. The strange thing was, now that he had cause to suspect George himself had been a part of this conspiracy, Fred was even less sure he wanted to know about it. The other night, he'd been drunk enough, and hopeful enough, to read good intentions into that angel gift to Mira. Then again, there'd been a certain darkness in that reference, on the card, to the twin jams of the needle from the nurse. He didn't want to believe this, didn't want to believe that those statues might have been just one more attempt to fuck with his head. But how could he know? George's conspirators would probably be in touch again, anyway, Fred thought, if he didn't respond. The fact that his phone could assault him with another beep again at any moment certainly wasn't making him feel any more inclined to play along from his end. He wouldn't have the service much longer—his credit card had shut down before the automatic payment could go through; he hoped the phone would get cut off sooner rather than later.

In any event, the cyberstalking was the least of his problems. It barely registered amid the shock of George's decline. Beyond losing George, which Fred still couldn't get his mind around after all these months, there was his parents' disillusionment, and his own culpability in the whole situation. The one noble thing he had thought he'd done in his adult life was to fight and fight for George's survival, to sacrifice everything he had for it. But even this had been little more than selfishness—to make amends, to feel good about himself, to be a hero—and all it had done was prolong everyone's suffering, George's included. This whole long interlude had been for nothing, for no purpose whatsoever. It wasn't merely the futility, it was the utter meaninglessness of all this waiting and pain that sickened and confounded him.

Then there were all those other dead-ends, all those other little decorative filigrees in the mandala of unsmooth moves that was his life—his lost career, his Florida crime spree, getting the boot from Mira's study, and from her bed. Maybe he was just in a pit so deep he couldn't stop digging. But what else could he do? The one tool he had left was a shovel, that idiot mantra, Manfred's maddening mu.

The Mumonkan, the primary collection of Zen koans and commentaries, which he'd accessed online later that first night on the roof, read like a book of puzzles, full of unanswerable questions, questions that weren't even questions, yet which the practitioner was expected to answer. The compiler, the monk Mumon, had appended a commentary to each koan. In his remarks on the first, "Joshu's Mu," Mumon said that when one passed through this barrier, all illusions and delusions would be shattered, internal and external would unite, and one would perceive one's true nature for oneself only, like a mute waking from a dream. There was more along these lines, talk of explosive conversions, of intertwining one's eyebrows with the patriarchs', of astonishing the heavens and shaking the earth, of commanding perfect freedom. It was a hard sell, and Fred was leery of it. Didn't he have enough puzzles in his life already? He was leery as well of that stupefying instruction on how to proceed, how, in reciting the mu in one's mind, one was supposed to summon a spirit of tremendous and all-pervading doubt, just as Manfred had said. How, Fred asked himself, was one supposed to find faith through doubting? He'd been doubting all his life. Where had it ever gotten him?

And yet, it was at least a skill well within his competence. He might not be capable of sitting like a pretzel in an oven, puffing up all golden with faith and bliss. But *doubting*? If that was the game, couldn't he win? Hadn't he been training for it all his life?

Muuuuuuuuuuuuuuuuuuuuuu . . .

The doubts came immediately. He didn't have to go looking. He doubted meditation would do him any good, doubted he was doing anything at all. Every minute on the mu was a minute squandered. How much time did he have left to turn things around for himself? Why wasn't he with George at the hospital? His brother might be dying this minute. How selfish could he get? Every mu-laden breath was like taking a million dollars and setting them on fire.

He did it for half an hour and collapsed, putting the pillow over his face and screaming. He lay there waiting for himself to do something else, something other than meditate or vegetate, to do any one of those infinite number of arguably more useful things he might do. He did none of them. He sat up and started again:

Muuuuuuuuuuuuuuuuuuuuuuu . . .

His nerves ached with frustration. His legs ached from the half-lotus position. He doubted the aches. He doubted the very muscles and nerves. He thought of George, unable to move, unable to do anything but breathe (and now, not even that unassisted). Maybe this sitting here aching and unmoving was a taste of what George felt like. Maybe this was what Fred had been putting him through.

Just about always, there was the urge to give up this accursed mu-ing and lie down, an urge which, as long as possible, had to be resisted. The minute he did, the sleeping bag's soft lining would have him drifting back to the softness and heat of Mira when he'd caught her on the steps. And from there to the childlike delight he'd felt at those too-happy, too-intimate, postcoital kisses. To the sick, sinking feeling at their explanation. And the sorrowful sight of her balled up in that chair, in that room full of pictures.

He'd sat nearly until dawn that first night, slept until late morning, then sat sweating and breathing through the day, unwilling to go to the hospital, unable, despite the imagined sound of the mu, to ever fully get that other sound, that cancerous, gurgling hiss, out of his ear. At the first sign of dusk, he took his water and urine jugs downstairs and found his parents already home from the hospital and back in their bathrobes. They were in the kitchen, fixing dinner, or rather, breakfast, the same meal Fred had spied them through the skylight eating earlier in the day, Vartan doing the eggs and hash browns by the stove, Holly buttering toast with a shaky hand—her tremors were back, looking worse now than they had in a long while.

Fred stood there holding his jugs behind him. There was nothing necessarily shameful about shuttling a half-gallon of one's own urine past one's aging, grieving parents, he was eager to remind himself; nevertheless, he left the jugs outside, and set the table the way it had been at the first breakfast, bringing out the salt and pepper, water and juice, and the mug of tea Holly had made, adding a setting for himself. He hadn't noticed much of an effect from all the meditation when he'd been doing it, other than pain and intermittent bouts of creeping desperation, but now that he was back in the apartment, he was noticing perhaps a slight change, an intimate quality to the things around him, as though a layer of plastic wrap had been peeled away from it all. The smell of the orange juice was as bright and sharp as ground glass; its sunburst color, its sour-sweet taste, its coldness in his throat were almost too much to process. Vartan plated the eggs and potatoes with loud chops of the spatula, the terrycloth collar of his robe turned up like some spy-novel overcoat. From its pocket, he produced a handful of forks and knives and tossed them beside the plates. Holly, her hand trembling, set down the quaking plate of toast and gave it a shove so that it slid to the center of the table. There was something unconstrained, and faintly disdainful, about their movements.

The three of them sat down. Vartan studied his food. Holly sipped her tea, the mug barely making it to her lips. Fred chewed, the buttery, faintly sulfurous eggflesh springing in his mouth.

He asked how George was. Her tone too casual, Holly told him that every time the nurses tried unhooking George from the ventilator, that sound came back and his breathing started to fail. And a CT scan was scheduled for tomorrow afternoon.

Vartan picked up his battery-powered pepper mill, held it a full foot over his plate, and depressed the button overlong, watching, expressionless, as his eggs and cottage cheese turned gray.

Fred assured them he'd be there for the scan. They hadn't asked about his relocation to the roof, hadn't even seemed surprised, perhaps because it was always where he and George had gone as teenagers to get some space and sort things out. Nor had it seemed to matter to them that he hadn't gone with them to the hospital today. They had cut back on their hours, too.

"You'll have to stand guard by the door next time, Vart," Holly said.

Vartan nodded vaguely.

"Why?" Fred asked.

He could tell she didn't really want to talk about this, either. She bunched her bathrobe tighter around her neck, despite the summer heat. It was her goose-down robe—a long-ago Christmas gift she usually reserved for winter.

"Those patients keep wandering in, wanting Reiki," she said. "I had to sit there with my hands tucked under my armpits, talking about how tired I was, until they finally took the hint and left."

It wasn't just embarrassment about having to hide her tremors. She sounded disgusted, with the patients, with herself. Fred wondered if she'd stopped even doing Reiki on George.

"Manny wants to come up," Vartan announced.

"Oh God no." Holly aimed a trembling fork at her eggs, inadvertently sawing them. "What, does he want to film it?"

She and Vartan, to Fred's surprise, shared a smile. The joke made him smile as well, though neither of them was looking his way.

"He doesn't think he's staying here," she said, "does he?"

Vartan palpated his beard, almost as thick as his mustache now. "Knowing him, he probably does."

"*Hey,*" she said, doing a reasonably good impression, bobbling her head, flinging out her arms. "*Where can I get a baked ziti around here?*"

"Try a restaurant," Vartan said, playing his part. His beard had ticked to one side, but there was something missing behind his eyes.

"He actually found one! A frozen baked-ziti dinner in our freezer! Do you remember that?"

Holly's pale face shone. The puffy skin beneath her eyes had the bluish hue of bruised meat. She and Vartan were both smiling, or almost, as they relived this scene with Manfred from before Fred's and George's birth, and Fred felt himself to be just outside their circle. When Holly brought her tea to her lips, her hand shook so much that globules of liquid hopped over the rim and onto her plate, and without drawing attention to the act, or even seeming to notice, Vartan reached into his robe pocket, brought forth a straw, and dropped it into her mug.

The phone started ringing, over at the desk. Neither of them moved.

"Should I get that?" Fred said.

His parents regarded their plates. They probably thought it was the hospital.

The machine picked up. It was Dot, the elf, sounding effervescent as usual. She said they were planning a Street Reiki session at the Empire State Building tomorrow at five.

"They're doing it as a group now," Holly exclaimed, in the same faintly overwhelmed and mocking tone she'd employed to talk about Manny. "They want to do all the landmarks."

"You're their high priestess," Vartan observed.

Holly shook her head, as if she'd never had anything to do with the lot of them. "They say it feels like the old days at the relief tent."

Holly had gotten her first Reiki attunement in late August of 2001, just in time, as it turned out, for her to join the group in one of the relief tents for 9/11 recovery workers that had been erected outside the medical examiner's office, right down the block from the NYU Medical Center. The tent, divided down the middle by a flap, was half church, with an altar and a priest and a few rows of folding chairs, and half something else—wellness and alternative healing center: a space filled with massage tables and chairs, and staffed, variably, with Swedish and deep tissue and Shiatsu masseurs, reflexologists, Jin Shin Do and therapeutic touch practitioners, Barbara Brennan aura healers, Kabbalah healers, and Reiki healers. When the motorcades would roll in from the main site and the Staten Island landfill, the healers and the priests, along with workers from the cafeteria tent and fire commissioner's tent and the other tents down the block, would all step out and stand at attention until the body parts were taken from the ambulances and deposited in the morgue. Afterward, people would begin to trickle into the healing center, occasionally family members who had been called in to identify remains, though for the most part the recovery workers themselves. Those firemen, cops, and medical examiners, of course, had had no idea what Reiki was—they'd lie down on the tables expecting some type of massage—though, apparently, most hadn't been disappointed. After an eight-hour shift digging through wreckage, digging through the flesh, more than muscle relaxation, what they needed may well have been the charged warmth of a pair of hands, hovering yet abundantly near, just sensuous enough to recall them to the blessings of the living, just non-physical enough to suggest the workings of a higher law.

For the rest of the group, it had been a seminal experience, but while the clients sometimes reported feeling better, Holly herself hadn't been able to feel much of anything. She'd stopped going, and in the ensuing years had moved on in her usual way to other interests. Fred's sense was that the group as a whole, prior to George's illness and Holly's renewed interest in Reiki, had been languishing, cutting back their meetings. Fred could imagine how *Guy* and the others might feel in looking back on those days, when it seemed they'd had a whole wounded city to heal, how they might miss it like some pristine, primeval island they'd visited once and assumed they'd never see again.

With some difficulty, Holly spread jelly on a slice of wheat toast, as Dot kept talking about how they hadn't seen Holly at Grand Central Station, how they hoped everything was all right, how they hoped to see her tomorrow, but if not, they'd see her the next day for George's weekly session. Holly brought ten palsied fingers before her eyes, watching them tremble before she rested her temples in them, muttering that she'd have to cancel that.

Vartan stood with his untouched plate.

"You're not going to eat?" Fred asked.

"Not much appetite without the pot," Vartan said.

"You've stopped smoking?"

Vartan's mustache pincered, a momentary frown. "Too much effort. Filling the pipe. Smoking the pipe."

"I'll have to tell them I'm sick," Holly went on to herself.

"You sure?" With measured, floating steps, Vartan walked to the kitchen. "We might wake up tomorrow and find them all standing around our bed."

"I'll tell them I'm on vacation," she said. "I'll say I'm going to Florida with Sam, to see his new condo."

Sam, Fred had heard her mention earlier, was leaving town in three days.

Vartan stood by the garbage, staring at the pepper-fuzzed mounds on his plate. With a torque of his wrist, he dumped it sidelong, plate and all.

The dried sparrow turd floated in the black expanse—some distant, marooned galaxy at the end of time.

Dusk. He'd been sitting all day—his third, now—in timed stints. The clock showing another thirty minutes logged, the aches in his legs and back growing too insistent to shoot for forty-five, Fred took a break in the usual way he'd negotiated with himself, by walking in slow circles within the rooftop's perimeter, making a game of making his steps as quiet as possible so as not to disturb his parents. Through the makeshift skylight, which, legend went, had been cut into the ceiling by Vartan and Manfred the year he and George were born, and which nowadays allowed in all manner of things—rainwater, dust, possibly asbestos, insects, and occasionally even light—Fred could see his father's cloudy form, working in a sleeveless undershirt under the desk lamp, the bony points of his shoulders pivoting as he held a drill to a piece of curved metal; some new car project, perhaps. As for Holly, she was probably in bed, the light from their bedroom just going out as Fred passed.

To maintain his concentration, he tried to keep his eyes to the spar-kling black of the roofing tar; but at some point, becoming dizzy and fearful of toppling to his death, he gave in and looked out at the shadow landscape of chimneys and skylights and mushroom-shaped vents of the rooftops, and the vacant nimbus of Manhattan beyond. The Towers had been the only visible buildings of the island from here, an unspoken part of the attraction of coming up here as kids: a promise, for him and George, of things to come. Perhaps humankind was powerless, or nearly so, in the face of the mind's eagerness to make everything mean, to turn the world into a personal network of symbols.

And now the vacant nimbus itself was a message, a message of mes-sagelessness. And Fred wasn't sure why, but it didn't seem like a hope-less one. Curiously, the more he let go up here, the more he tried to root out his delusions, the more urgently the world seemed to speak to him, the more intimate a mirror it became. He wasn't sure whether his meditative ability was improving or whether it just was some kind of self-induced dementia, but he was feeling that lightness, that openness and immersion all the more. If there was an unreal quality to the night, it wasn't like the dissociation after the panic attack, or the suffocating artificiality he'd felt during the playtest. It was more like the freedom of the helmet sessions, just a bit of distance, a space of possibility, a remove that somehow allowed for this new intimacy, like pulling back from an embrace to regard a lover's face. Less real in one way, though in another, more so than before. He didn't understand these paradoxical perceptions. He wasn't sure they were worth all the hours he'd put in, or how they might possibly help him with even the smallest of his problems. He wasn't entirely ready to trust them, or even say for sure he liked them.

If the aches and shooting pains were the Scylla of meditation, drowsiness was the Charybdis. No sooner would the pain recede than its absence would lull him off course, whirl him into reverie, spiral him ever closer to dream. At one point, late that night, he was talking to George, comparing notes on meditation, happy they now had this experience in common. George was talking about *malas* and white lights and the Ajna chakra (a pastiche of the few actual times he'd talked to Fred about the subject); Fred was telling George about *hara* breathing (having just read about it online during an afternoon break). The conversation felt so natural and real that when Fred snapped awake, he actually looked around the shadowy tent for his brother. Fred had been doubting Inner George, too, of course, doubting him whenever that voice popped into his head. He'd been telling himself he'd come up to the roof in order to face his aloneness squarely. But the truth probably was he felt closer to George up here than at his bedside.

He felt closer to him here, in fact, than he had in a long time. There had been moments, sitting by George's bed over the last few months, when Fred had entertained the strange, irrational notion that the coma had been a kind of slow-onset condition, gradually taking his twin away from him for years, freezing George up, and freezing Fred and the rest of humanity out. He'd imagined it first creeping into George when they'd lost their financial backing, its first symptom an aloof passivity, progressing through the years of the Armation partnership. He'd imagined it starting to deaden his brother's nerves on the night in the office when George had sat slumped on the floor, spinning his ring, saying his marriage was over, missing Jill already but refusing to go and patch things up, believing she was better off without him. Fred had pictured the coma starting to lock down George's muscles on the nights just after his cancer diagnosis, his mobility reduced to the twitches of his fingers on the keyboard as he played one computer game after another. How anyone who'd just received such news could kill his possibly scant remaining time in this manner was beyond Fred's comprehension.

Fred stuck around those nights, researching lymphoma treatments, keeping an eye on him. George played each game for a few hours, then chucked the disc in the trash. It took Fred a while to understand that George was making a diagnosis of his own, of the industry to which he'd pledged his existence. On the night George finally ran out of games, he walked to the couch, lay down, and with a light, if listless, touch, delivered his findings. The first-person shooters were visions of the end state of civilization, a perfect nihilism wherein every last object was there to be weaponized. The massively multiplayer roleplaying games were a form of mass psychosis, individualism gone berserk—thousands of players, all running around following the exact same storyline in parallel, each pretending to be the chosen one, the sole savior of the world. The metaverses, the virtual worlds that had beaten Urth to market, were the reification of the hypermaterialist in the postmaterial, platforms for the endless manipulation, accrual, possession, and maintenance of a whole new world of virtual objects—designer clothes and sports cars and hairstyles and fizzy, rainbow-colored cocktails one couldn't even taste. The runaway real estate boom had spread to unreal estate, George noted, people speculating on choice virtual acreage, buying up virtual islands and beachfront parcels. He should have guessed this was what would happen, he said with a dry laugh. Should have known that all people would want was to be make-believe playboy moguls. Going to make-believe raves full of make-believe beautiful people. Meanwhile, in meatspace, sitting in their undershirts, drinking a Schlitz.

"When you get down to it," George said, sleepily, even his lips barely moving, "it's all military entertainment."

And so, mu. The thought of mu. The thought of the sound of mu. The action of thinking of the sound of mu. Meaning no. Not even no. Negation. Not even negation. Just mu. Not even mu. . . .

Boring into the syllable, Fred's mouth begins to smile of its own accord; tears—from going so long without blinking—begin running down his cheeks. The openness, the possibility returning. The feeling of being on the verge of discovery. Keep pressing. The mu like a sustained frequency. The funny thing is, the more he doubts, the more present George feels to him, as if George were pressing back from the other side of everything existent, believing the falsity of this cosmos between the two of them as Fred doubts its truth. It can all break right open, shatter like crystal. *I can do it,* Fred thinks. Can get real, really real, realer than real. Can doubt death into life eternal. Can doubt doubt right into faith. A faith without ignorance. Without flaw or vulnerability of any kind. A faith so complete even doubt is included. . . .

Or something like that. . . .

But where did it go, that openness . . . ?

Mu but the dumb and ordinary night. . . .

Mu but the tent flap in the breeze. . . .

Mu but the mocking cell phone, urine jug, LED glow 12:34. . . .

He has the answer, or almost, anyway. He's merely a player in some vast computer game made real, or almost real, the name of the game writ on the glass storefronts, in the silvery letters of some alien script whose meaning he can somehow understand—something like *Enlusionment,* or *Delightenment,* a word that's neither of these but has the same sickening inversions. Grafted to his back, poking through his white tuxedo jacket: a pair of giant wire-and-taffeta wings. Bolted to the back of his bald scalp: a brass halo. He's looking for George in the maze of too-narrow streets, looking for him behind those storefront windows, amid the displays of mannequins, some missing limbs, others half melted. Headless mannequins. Naked mannequins in piles. It goes on like this, street after twilit street. He loses count and cognizance, remembers nothing but a blur of faceless, egg-shaped heads, until, rounding a corner, stepping over mannequins spilled out onto the street, male and female forms in suits and skirtsuits, their ceramic watches and tinfoil earrings glinting in the low light, the street maze ends in a narrow ledge, beyond which lies a cloudy vortex, spiraling below.

He sees something crest then dip back into the churning clouds, fin-like, possibly the edge of a white wing. Maybe it's George. Or maybe it's a trap—how could these fake wings possibly keep Fred aloft if he follows? A ragged edge of cloud sweeps past, engulfing him, airy-white for a whimsical moment, but soon gray-black, the opposite of space—a choking sandstorm.

Gasping himself awake—

Dawn over Brooklyn—

Teetering in midair—

Sidewalk three stories down.

Fred was lying on his front, his hands formed into a pillow, his cheek resting on his knuckles, and all of him so close to the roof's front edge that one elbow draped into the air.

He froze, eyeing the front steps thirty feet beneath, the spikes of the iron fences, the colored lozenges of cars.

Then inched away.

Clips and poles bobbled in his shaking hands as he struck the tent with everything still inside it and hauled it all back down to the apartment. Clearly, he couldn't stay on the roof. Next time he might sleepwalk from the tent right off the roof. How many sleep disorders could one man accumulate? Nor could he stand another night in the apartment, with the nightmares and the walls of that bedroom closing in and the suspicion that his hapless presence was growing burdensome to his parents, that they would prefer for now not to be reminded of either George or himself. Moving quietly so as not to wake them, he broke down the tent in his bedroom. The lid of the urine jug hadn't been screwed on right—it had leaked onto the sleeping bag, which he stuffed anyway into George's camping backpack, along with George's canteen, socks and underwear, and some bread, cheese, and apples he found in the refrigerator. Into his briefcase he put his laptop, the last helmet-study check, and, after a moment's hesitation, a couple of his mother's self-help books. He scribbled a note to his parents and left.

His plan was to try to stay in Sam's Lower East Side apartment until it was sold. Sam wouldn't be there, at least not after tomorrow. As favors went, it wasn't a very big one; still, it would kill Fred to have to ask, after what Sam had done to him.

With his credit card maxed, his account overdrawn, and four dollars on his transit card, even given the new fifty-dollar helmet-study infusion, subway fare seemed too great an extravagance. So he hiked it, from Cobble Hill through Brooklyn Heights and up the narrow stone passageway to the bridge. He caught himself checking for swirling clouds as he climbed the steps, for that alien dream-script graffitied on the walls, some sign it was all a malevolent computer game.

Holonoia, he thought.

Dimly, he sensed somewhere Inner George's approval of the word.

The city, as he emerged onto the walkway, was at any rate perfect, and utterly benign: arches, webwork cables, river breeze. Glass fronts of downtown lighting up at the cresting sun. Wooden slats beneath his feet, water flashing in the gaps. He knew what that dream meant, more or less: the mangled mannequins were his guilt over militarizing George's virtual world; that cloudy vortex was just a vicious feedback loop of dreams, from Holly's to Fred's own. Sprinkle in a few choice images from the cyberstalking campaign being waged against him and bake until done. All so straightforward he was embarrassed at his simplemindedness. And yet, again, that nerve-tingling notion: *What if it wasn't his dream at all? But George's?*

Trapped in that Pretaloka. That world between worlds, where nothing was quite right.

Looking for a way back home. *Looking for me*, thought Fred.

What would George want, now? For Fred to help him die? But why had he held on so long? What if he was still looking for something? What if he just wasn't finished?

Maybe that last thing George wanted was to do Fred in, Fred thought. Or, more to the point, maybe it was what Fred himself wanted. Why else would he have crept out to the edge of the roof?

It was that damned mu.

No self, no problem.

The self was the self, he told himself. No great discovery beneath. The world was the world was the world, he was thinking, was the world was the world was the world, as, halfway across the bridge, an Indian kid proffered him a camera, then ran back to his family. Boys with side-parted, glossy dark hair. Girls with saris and bindis. Parents in back. A half-dozen toothy smiles against the gap-toothed downtown skyline.

The digital image shimmered in the viewscreen. The city around the camera shimmered as well. Fred depressed the button, feeling no click, but hearing the sampled sounds of a shutter and winding reels.

Another Monday morning was underway as Fred reached the other shore. From a park bench outside City Hall, a homeless guy with a baseball cap on top of another baseball cap held Fred's gaze as he brought an asthma inhaler to his mouth and took seven quick pumps, following that up two seconds later with another seven pumps, then holding the dense, white, curling cloud of fourteen times the recommended dosage in his open mouth like cigarette smoke before sucking it down.

On Murray Street, Fred passed a public library just as a security guard was unlocking the door. He probably had some time to kill, and wasn't relishing the possibility of having to wait for Sam in that light-deprived office. So he went in, and waited as the guard shoved an arm into George's backpack, eyeing Fred in an unfriendly way while feeling up Fred's books, cheese, apple, underwear, then freezing, no doubt having encountered the wet spot on the sleeping bag, his upper lip recoiling as he pulled free his blue-jacketed arm. The place was a low-ceilinged box, with a pale green linoleum floor and long rows of stark fluorescent lighting; it reminded Fred of the police station where he'd been held after stealing the tweezers. He found a table and took out his laptop.

He could have checked the want ads online, or brushed up on his Java. Instead, thinking of the vortex dream, and that Indian family on the bridge, he read more about Hindu cosmology, how the gods of the pantheon were energies, which, when worshipped as individuals in opposition to each other and not as components of the greater whole, would exploit the ignorant worshippers like cattle to further their particular ends.

He switched to complexity theory: How new sets of desires and aversions emerged at each new stratum of complexity, from enzymes to cells, from organisms to organizations—cities, religions, corporations, military-politico-economic complexes. How the larger systems harvested competition as well as cooperation among their parts—white blood cells competing for prey, factions of neurons warring for the electrical impulses that allowed for their particular brand of thoughts, employees fighting for positions, companies for market share, ideologies for adherents.

And back to Eastern religion: *Mahamaya*, the power of illusion, ignorance seen not as a mere absence of knowledge but a force in its own right, a veil obscuring the self-illumined immensity. *Lila*, the concept of existence as a divine, all-encompassing game. *Samsara*, existence as a theme park of delusion. Which, according to a comment ascribed to the Dalai Lama, America had perfected.

The morning sun had baked into Fred's eyes, making the office seem darker than usual.

Fred's cantaloupe box was still sitting by the door where he'd left it. A shadowy pile of obsolesced computer parts slouched against the opposite wall, looking like a fat man who'd been trying to jog and was now bent over and struggling to catch his breath. An undulating light from a monitor played on the pile, giving it the illusion of breathing. The light came from Sam's station around the corner.

"Sam?"

No answer.

There remained the microwave, the mini-fridge, a stack of cans where the metal cabinet had been, the red couch, Fred's own messy desk, and the still humming supercomputer. Otherwise, the office was bare. His coworkers' desks, chairs, and hardware were gone. The shelves were gone, too, leaving long-forgotten expanses of drywall and floorboards to flicker uniformly in the monitor's glow. He couldn't step into the room at first. It felt like his bones had been shipped off with the rest.

Around the corner, he found a folding table where Sam's desk had been, and a folding chair where Sam's Aeron had been. Sam himself was sitting where he always had, as if the furniture had been switched out from under him. A laptop took the place of Sam's computer stack and dual monitor display. On the screen, Fred saw as he approached, was what appeared to be the interior of a computer-animated church— the angle from the pews, over the backs of avatar heads. An animated preacher stood at the pulpit, his poorly animated mouth opening and closing. As the preacher spoke, with a barely audible jabber in Sam's headphones, the little church transformed into the grassy shore of a lake. The avatars in the pews were now dressed in peasant clothes. The pastor had morphed into Jesus, standing in a small, triangular boat moored to a dock, a shower of gold pouring onto him from above. From an upper quadrant, Jesus' story expanded to transform the scene again—a farmer sowing seeds; a closeup on the luminous kernels flung from his hand in slow motion; one falling on a path and being gulped by a bird; another falling amid stones, sprouting only to wither; another amid thorns, which wrapped about the seedling in sinister fashion; the last dropping on a rich bed of earth and shooting into a tall plant. Cutaway to a vast, healthy crop, gleaming under the sun; transforming back into Jesus by the shore; then back to the pastor in the virtual church, holding a stalk of wheat, over which the word PARABLE appeared in an arch of bright, gothic letters.

"Sam," Fred said again.

Sam leapt in his seat. With his silver lamp shipped off, he had no warning system. He brought the headphones down from his ears.

"So what's that?"

Already, Sam's face was recomposed, a picture of indifference. "New thing on the Christworld site. Virtual ministry. Just . . . checking out the graphics."

On the screen, a virtual collection bucket began floating down the aisle, with a cross and the words CLICK TO DONATE painted on the side.

"What's with the pack?" Sam said. "Joining the Boy Scouts?"

"I need to stay at your place. Until you sell it."

Sam hunched forward.

"I could keep things neat," Fred said through his teeth. "I could get out of the way when it has to be shown. I could help with anything you—"

"It's sold."

The service was over. Nothing left for Sam to stare at but the Christworld home page.

"It is?" Fred said. "Already?"

A desk fan on the table swept slowly back and forth.

"How long till the new owners move in?" Fred pressed. "If I could—"

"They're in."

Sam's eyes, still not meeting Fred's, were hard, but a little frightened, too.

"How could that be? Where are *you* staying?"

For a couple seconds Sam didn't respond. Then he inclined his head a centimeter toward the couch.

"But where's all your stuff?"

Sam pointed to a Rubbermaid bin by his table. If Fred had seen it before, he'd thought nothing of it.

"I'm starting fresh," Sam said. "The move-in date's Wednesday. That's when I go."

"Why not just stay in a hotel down there? Or with Rad or Jess?"

"No. No hotels. No staying with Conrad or Jesse. It's a clean transition." He seemed to consider whether or not to say more. Then he turned to his computer, his voice still monotone but his movements eager. "I fly out first thing. Arrive late morning. A day off work. Leisurely. Setting up the home front. Furniture comes in the afternoon." He clicked open photos—a modish white sofa, a matching armchair, a paisely-shaped coffee table, a couple of bright area rugs, bedroom and dining room and deck furniture, barstools. The stuff had a *Jetsons* vibe. It wouldn't have looked out of place in a cutaway *Sims* house, Fred thought, or a *Second Life* bachelor pad.

"First grocery delivery arrives at three PM. And by the end of the day. . ." With a flourish, Sam opened a photo of a glossy, black convertible. ". . . my new car gets delivered."

Sam allowed him to appreciate the sports car in silence. Fred could barely believe Sam had the gall to show it to him, what with all the money Fred had been spending to keep George alive.

"I'll tool around in it awhile . . ." Sam mousepadded his cursor in lazy figure eights. ". . . get some dinner downtown. . . ."

Incapacitated with jealousy, Fred imagined him swinging past the realtor's office, waving to Christine.

"Then the rest of the week, I'll nine-to-five it"—Sam stretched his arms—"maybe nine-to-four, tying up the last loose ends for the demo. It's all set for next Monday."

Next Monday, Fred thought. He wondered if their parents had told Sam about the plans to let George go. He was willing to bet they had, that the news hadn't affected Sam at all.

"Nothing left to deal with but those object-effect bugs," Sam went on. "Thought we'd wiped them out three times already. But yesterday, Little Len put on his air mask and dropped dead. Turned out the gas file data got corrupted and he was inhaling mustard gas from the Iraq sims."

Fred had a feeling the sabotage was only beginning. To Sam, though, it seemed barely worth thinking about. He clicked all the windows closed. They gazed at the backlit palm trees and beach on the desktop.

"New York?" Sam brought a finger to his open lips, feigning befuddlement. "What's that? Never heard of it. Oh, yeah. It's that virtual emergency response environment that'll make me rich."

Fred looked around the office, not ready to believe that Sam's New York apartment was already gone. If the new owners were already there, as he'd claimed, he must have been living here for at least a couple weeks.

"I guess that couch is comfortable enough," Fred said.

"It serves."

"You've got your fridge here, your microwave."

"Yep."

On the table next to the laptop, Lara Croft gazed up smolderingly from the August issue of *Game Developer* magazine, beside which lay a few unopened credit card offers.

"You've already been getting most of your mail delivered here, anyway, I suppose."

"More efficient that way."

A stack of neatly folded black T-shirts peeked through the open zipper of a duffle bag on the floor.

"You get your laundry picked up and delivered here, too?"

"They even fold my underwear."

"I guess you can brush your teeth and shave in the bathroom down the hall?"

"Can and do."

"So what about showering? Do you have a gym membership or something?"

A sneaky hint of a smile appeared at the corner of Sam's mouth. He reached under the table into a cardboard box and brought out a coiled length of yellow hose, ending in a rubber showerhead. He held it up, his smirk half nervous, half proud.

An uncertain laugh stalled in Fred's throat. "You . . . but where . . . ?" He thought for a moment. "That big slop sink in the janitor's closet, out in the hall?"

Sam touched a fingertip to his nose.

"That filthy sink with the mop in it all the time?"

"It's not filthy," Sam snapped. "I keep it clean."

The answer disturbed Fred. At first he didn't know why. Then he realized it was the tense Sam was using. The permanent present.

"You . . . *keep* it clean."

"It's not hard," Sam said, defensive. "Some disinfectant now and then."

"Sam." Fred felt that queasy, dreamlike undertow pulling at him again. "How long have you been living here?"

Sam began slowly turning away. "A while."

"How long is 'a while?'" Fred pivoted to keep Sam's face in view. "Three weeks?"

That little smile stretched.

"A month?"

And stretched some more.

"Two? *More?*"

Fixedly, Sam stared at the posterboard over the window. "I've been here a while, all right?" he said through his unmoving, upturned lips.

"But . . . *why?*"

"Why not? Why are you making such a big deal out of it?"

"*Why not?*"

Sam eyed the ceiling. "I miscalculated slightly. I thought the Urth consolidation would happen faster. The real estate market was at a certain place. There was no reason to wait. Who knows what could have happened between then and now. Some new attack, and it wouldn't have been worth a thing." He turned to Fred, with a frenetic gleam. "You wouldn't believe how much I got for it. People are nuts. I read an article the other day. They're still building *skyscrapers.* There's a *boom* in skyscraper building, in cities all over the world. They're building them even higher. It's like a race, who can spend the most money to live in the most doomed places on the planet."

He couldn't meet Fred's eyes for long. He faced those palm trees again, working the tensed muscles of his jaw loose with side-to-side motions. "Anyway," he said, "it's more convenient, staying here."

Fred pictured his little brother walking out into the hall, naked, late at night when no one was around, clambering into the sink in the janitor's closet, and holding that yellow hose up over his head.

"This is more convenient?" Fred grabbed the hose and shook it. "This is more convenient than just going home for the night?'"

"Sure."

Fred was actually beginning to pity him when he caught himself. It probably *was* more convenient for Sam. What did he care? He had his nest egg, his condo, his sports car, his fake little town to go settle in when all the dealing got done. His whole life in New York was dead to him anyway.

"You're a homeless person," Fred said. "I should report you to the building manager."

"Speak for yourself, *Freddo.*" Sam drew out the name. "I'm just in transition."

"—is that east or west—"
"—I'm for pizza—"
"—Mommy, is he craaaazy—"
"—look it ze hahnd people—"
Fred arrived just as they began. Through the plate glass of the defunct concession area, he saw *Guy*/Strider at the southeast corner of the observation deck, going into action, forming himself slowly into a stark human Y, like some deadly serious Bauhaus version of a cheerleader, his pompomless palms angled out toward Brooklyn. Then, to the southwest, his wife, the elf, looked around with an excited, self-humoring grimace, as though she were about to do something crazy and wonderful like take a bounding backflip to the tip of the spire. She turned to face the far towers of Newark, and in one quick motion closed her eyes, raised her arms straight up, tilted back her head, and stuck out her chest like a triumphant gymnast. Fred headed down the ramp, breasted the picture-snapping crowd counterclockwise around the deck, and spotted, facing the fulgurant plasm of Times Square, the one he called the dwarf, though in physiological terms, she was tall as well as broad, her fuzzed, gray head cresting above the tourists, her arms in a stylized U shape, like a caryatid or bearer of some outsized Grecian urn. In the last corner, Queensward, was posted the pink-faced wizard, elbows forward and palms flat up, as though straining against a lowering trash compactor. Fred's mother, as he had expected, wasn't here.

He slid past Gandalf, walked halfway to Strider's corner, and slipped through the tourists to face, through the wrought-iron barrier, the gorgeous pop-up cityscape—like the toothed, sparkling cavity of one of Holly's energy crystals. He located first the sunset mirror of the UN, then a few degrees rightward, the smaller slab of the Medical Center. He breathed, using the air in his lungs to keep down his stomach.

Before coming here, he'd been at the hospital all afternoon. George's pallor, his waxen softness, his overall smallness, had stunned Fred anew. A slowly deflating balloon, George had seemed, kept from flattening out entirely only by the ventilator's continuous huffing into his lungs. Fred had massaged the stringy, mushy remnants of George's muscles, swabbed his papery nostrils and ears and the parched cavern of his mouth, fighting the feeling it wasn't George at all but only some spare suit of flesh grown from a vat down in the subbasements; and the still stranger feeling that even he—Fred himself—wasn't quite there in the room.

All the usual things he might have said to George had gone into hiding. With the vague idea of finding something uplifting or otherwise appropriate to read aloud, Fred sat there paging through the self-help books he'd taken from their mother's shelf: Deepak Chopra, Eckhart Tolle—newer titles than the others, but aging fast, even *The Power of Now* looking yellowed and worn. At some point in its recent history, the whole cultural project of self-help seemed to have hit a wall, after which had come the tacit acknowledgment that this selfsame self everyone had been scrambling to pump up with self-worth and self-esteem was itself the problem, that one's efforts were better spent paring it down, pruning it away. He wondered if this represented a slow-motion rebellion in the commerce-laden New Age temples; or an evolution, carrying the movement into a deeper phase; or if, in the end, it would just be incorporated as one more layer in the pyramid scheme of controlling everything with one's crazy thoughts. Either way, part of him approved of the message, or of part of the message, of the call to let some air out of everyone's ballooning egos, if for no reason other than as a general health and safety measure. But the rest of him didn't get the rest of it at all. Why grow selves to begin with, if only to eradicate them? Wasn't this world, this universe, one's own biology doing a good enough job of it anyhow?

In the end, he read none of this no-self stuff aloud, not wanting to give the bag of desiccating tissue on the bed any more of an excuse not to be George; though, what with the all-important CT scan coming any minute now, he was actually finding it preferable to think of George's body as being absent of selfhood, at least for the moment. Maybe, Fred speculated with too much hope, it was all the meditation that allowed for this newfound distance. Maybe neither George nor he himself had to be here in anything but the flesh. The only way he could conceptualize the phrase "no self" was to think *not here*, to think it just possibly meant the real Fred was somewhere else, the real George too. He returned to the mu, joining his own attenuated outbreaths to the ventilator's hush, doubting for the both of them, doubting hospital sounds, hospital smells, hospital bills, hospital rooms, until two doubtable orderlies arrived with a doubtable gurney, and gathered in their muscled arms the various bags and tubes and rolling machines and the featherweight bundle of George, and they were all wheeling off down the hall. On impulse, Fred began pushing the gurney faster and faster. The two orderlies looked at each other, then at Fred, then at each other—one's greased, longish hair flipping about, the other's gold tooth sparking in the fluorescence—and they decided what the hell and joined in, racing their doubtable freight at a speed which Fred knew the real George—picture him whipping along above, a balloon on a string—would enjoy.

The unintended upshot was that they reached their destination all the sooner. The orderlies pointed Fred toward one door and wheeled the gurney through another. Fred entered a darkened control room; through its window, he could see the attendants lifting the sagging body onto the scanner platform, and a nurse unhooking George's ventilator. The nurse and the attendants then bugged out of the room as the nurse gave the go signal to a woman sitting with her back to Fred at the controls. The woman's black hair flowed through a ponytail clip to brush the collar of her lab coat. Her sheer-stockinged legs recrossed at the ankles as she leaned forward. Her ringed fingers toggled the platform into motion. The scene was so oddly familiar that he had to resist the giddy urge to fully sync the synchronicity by stepping up and resting his arm around her shoulders, as they watched through the window their test subject's head vanishing into the giant, laser-lit scanner ring. *None of this is real,* Fred averred. And if it wasn't real, how could it even touch them? He wasn't here, George wasn't there in that cyclone of X-rays. On the computer screen, cross-sectional slices began to appear, and so what? A pea. An avocado. Expanding tranches of cauliflower. Nothing but produce. Of no consequence, he told himself, but all the same, the scan was getting too real, too vivid and totalizing. His brother's skull complexifying like some kind of arthropod; tapering into the tubework of windpipe and tongue muscle and spine; then going supernova—dark hollows, flame gusts, bright, misshapen blobulations—as the Asian woman who was in no way Mira turned to Fred to ask if he was OK. He, Fred, was emitting a kind of hissing, gurgling noise, it seemed, his throat having sealed so tight there might as well have been no such thing as air at all.

After locking himself in that same bathroom for another extended freak-out on the tiled floor, Fred washed his unsteady hands with Bacti-Stat and left the hospital. He started walking, of all places, to the Empire State Building. He made up reasons on the way. He told himself his mother might have changed her mind since blowing off Dot's phone call yesterday. He asked himself if her group knew yet about George's condition, and about the plans to let him die a week from today. He told himself they deserved to know, that they'd at least meant well all this time, at least had been trying to help George all these months. He considered the possibility, in the likely event his mother hadn't shown, of asking them to look in on her. A few weeks ago, he would have been relieved to find her giving up this particular set of friends. But he worried, now, that she was worse off without them.

The stretch of 34th Street just before the entrance was empty of fire trucks, and full of scaffolding and smoke-belching buses, but was still enough like the virtual version to make him feel claustrophobic, as if the third dimension had been removed and all of this was trapped in a thin sheet of pixel light. Absurdly, before going in, he looked up for the window through which he'd jumped.

"—are those brown ones slums—"
"—some great shopping down by—"
"—I wanna pretzel—"
"—signaling the mother ship—"
Standing here atop the city, Fred was still thinking about the playtest, about following that chemotherapy angel out into the all-too-accommodating blue. That fucking angel, of course, was why he was here. Not a reasonable reason. Just the will to connect the stars of his life into some meaningful or at least recognizable shape. Just the hope that it would look so right he could tell himself it was meant to be.

Perhaps it was that virtual plunge, or that ensuing dream of the swirling vortex, or, more likely, the waking on the edge of the roof in Brooklyn that was making him so uneasy he couldn't look down at the hairline streets, couldn't even look up at the clouds, had to shut his eyes, wanting to leave, wanting never to have come. But his eyes were now shut. His hands were already above him, clutching the bars. Nothing to do but let go, uncurl his fingers.

"—there goes another—"

"—peh-foh-mance aht—"

"—repent, you seen-ers, heh heh—"

"Reiki Reiki Reiki," Fred whispered, feeling like an idiot.

Some time later, a light hand on his shoulder brought him back to the thousand reflected suns, deeper and redder now, on the East Side cityscape. The hand, Fred found, belonged to Gandalf. The others were there too, their faces peaceful and amused.

"Didn't think he'd come out of that one," Gandalf joked to the others, lifting his wide-set, manicured gray brows.

"Glad you could make it!" said the elf, with a winsome smile and two bashful blinks of her thyroidal green eyes.

Strider steered Fred and the rest of them with his nose, turning and leading the way up the ramp and inside. The wizard guided Fred by the elbow and the dwarf took up the rear. They made their way around a barricaded area where insulation foam and foil vents draped like guts from the open ceiling, a hopeful sign on the wall saying *We're Renovating! Excuse Our Mess!* The group was comparing notes about how wild the energy was up here today, how you could just feel it lashing around, how almost scary it had been at first. Gandalf asked Fred if he'd felt it, and Fred nodded, feeling, this time, that he was only half lying, those first moments after he'd shut his eyes beginning to replay—the voices, the buffeting wind, the superfluous daylight flash of a camera that may or may not have been aimed at him, the stomach-lifting sense that he was walking a plank, blindfolded over a sea storm. All the scuttled things he'd wanted to say to George had suddenly sprung back to mind, and they were nothing but questions, angry and wounded. Who were George's friends, his coconspirators? Who was spying on Fred, sending him these messages, sabotaging Urth? And why, what was in it for them? And what did they want from him? And what had George wanted from him, back when he'd helped plan whatever it was his coconspirators were doing now? Had he wanted blood? Revenge for Fred's selling out the company? Hadn't he understood Fred had been trying to save it? Hadn't he seen everything Fred had been doing for him after he'd gotten sick, battling the health care system, dragging him to the hospital, cleaning up his vomit and bloody phlegm? Couldn't he see everything Fred was still doing for him? Couldn't he? The questions kept floating past, though softer, and ever less rational—was George in that failing body? out there in the aether? and what did he want now? and what could Fred do?—until at last, Fred was down so deep that the only question left was one of such oozing, squid-like dimensions he couldn't catch hold of it, couldn't fit thought or words to it. Just a brooding, pulsing question mark in the dark.

"But the energy got smoother," the dwarf was saying.

"It sure did," said the wizard. "It felt so calm and warm toward the end."

Fred couldn't entirely dispute this, either. At least he himself had grown calmer. Too tired to fight anymore, warmed and cooled by turns as the air around him stirred and stilled, blood draining from his hands with an electric tingle, he'd drifted slowly into a lethargy verging on bliss, that state of doubting even his doubts, no up, no down, just sheer possibility . . .

"Imagine having it be stable," said the elf. "So it could be that healing all the time."

. . . during which, he'd begun to feel a warmth on his palms . . . as if George's own were pressed against them, through the mesh of that other world . . .

"It will be stable," Strider assured them all, with an authority he wore as easily as his white tunic shirt and wooden-beaded necklace, "once we can tune it to the frequency of the planet."

What, Fred thought, *in the hell am I doing here?*

They merged with a stream of tourists headed down a cramped stair-well wormy with pipes and dangling wires along the low ceilings of the landings. Another of those dazed, meaningless moments of déjà vu, this time recalling the endless stream of computer-controlled evacuees. Fred sniffed the air for smoke. At least the lights were on.

"How's your mom?" the buzzcut woman asked him.

He wondered again if they'd heard yet about George. It didn't seem they had.

"Not so well," he began, then hesitated, it occurring to him that his mother probably didn't want them to know. He went on anyhow. "Her tremors are giving her some trouble."

A sober nod from Rudolf. "She's giving so much of herself."

"She really is," said Dot, "to George, to all those patients in the hos-pital."

"To the whole city," the buzzcut woman declared.

"I hope she's getting some rest and recharging," Rudolf said.

Recharging, Fred thought. Like a Reiki battery. He told them she was. He probably shouldn't have been surprised that the return of her tremors hadn't the least bit shaken their faith, either in her Reiki powers or in Reiki power generally. The next thing to do was tell them about George, but he kept quiet as they wound their way through the souvenir gauntlet and from there down a too-small elevator slathered with bumpy gray paint. Perhaps it was true that a renovation was underway. He wanted to believe it. Though even aflame, the virtual version had seemed sturdier.

In the dim lobby, they passed the building's Art Deco self-portrait over the marble tiles, where, in the simulation, Little Sam and Little Len had tended to the roasting soon-to-be corpse. Fred's present meatspace companions, he saw when he looked up, were headed somewhere it took his eyes a moment to register—through a glass door, into a coffee shop. The place hadn't been there at all in the simulation, for which reason the group's passage into it seemed almost magical, as if they were traversing a mirror into some bright little wonderland.

"Come have a cuppa," said the wizard, from the doorway. Fred had already spent half his last fifty bucks from the helmet study, after the 10 percent cut to the check-cashing place, and the twenty-dollar admission fee to the observation deck. He was about to beg off, when, with a twirling wave of the hand, the little man added the magic words: "My treat!"

Fred didn't fully trust his ability to socialize with them, but followed anyway, grateful for the opportunity to sit, still feeling obligated to tell them about George, and on some level still hoping he might find that pattern in the stars, some reason to believe he'd been led here for a reason.

Cups in hand, they sat around a little white table by an orange wall, the only customers.

"So do you think the energy's still clear up there?" Gandalf asked. "Or have all those morons gone and messed it up already?"

They laughed.

"It's true," said the dwarf. "I walk by a place I balanced the day before and it's all barmy and out of whack again."

"We need more Reiki people!" said Dot. "We need reinforcements!"

"They're coming," *Guy* said calmly, gazing down the length of his nose at his tea.

"They are?" Fred couldn't quite keep the incredulity out of his voice.

"You're here," he observed, "are you not?"

More than the words, it was the droll look *Guy* gave him, like Fred was nothing more than some imp *Guy* had summoned from the mist to do his bidding, that made Fred want to tell him what he thought of his argument. But *Guy's* wife was already elaborating:

"People come up and ask me what I'm doing all the time. Some of them give me email addresses so we can let them know where we're meeting."

"Not all of them like it," Gandalf said with a chuckle. "This muscle-head up there shook me around. When I opened my eyes, he said, 'Keep those Devil rays to yourself!'"

"For heaven's sake," said Dot.

"Spirituality is a key," *Guy* said. "You can use it to lock yourself *in*, too, if that's what you want."

The others nodded for a hallowed moment at this supposed wisdom.

"It raises an interesting question, though," said Gandalf, swirling his frozen coffee slush. "What if someone doesn't want your help? What if they don't want to be healed? Do we have the right to send them energy?"

"It can only do good," huffed the dwarf. "That's a fundamental principle."

"But what if people don't want good?" said Gandalf.

"The energy only goes where it's needed," the dwarf insisted.

"But we direct it." Gandalf balled his little pink hands on the table. "That's our role, isn't it? If the energy only goes where it's needed to begin with, what's the point in channeling it?"

Fred perked up. Wasn't this that squid-like question of his, the one he hadn't been able to haul up? Wasn't this at least a piece of it?

"What good are we?" Fred blurted, overloud. "What are we *for*?"

The group fell silent, eyes gravitating to *Guy*. *Guy* was the go-to guy, apparently, for these sorts of conundrums. Despite himself, Fred, too, was frozen, breathless for this globe-trotting, nominal-Frenchman dilettante-shaman to dispatch the age-old chestnut once and for all.

"*Someone* needs to drink these hot beverages," *Guy* said.

The others laughed, of course.

"But if you don't know what you're really doing," Fred persisted, "doesn't it just boil down to all of you holding your hands up at the top of the Empire State Building for no purpose at all?"

Guy hoisted his cup, gazed into the billowing caldera at close range.

"That would be the ultimate." He nodded, blew. "That would be faith itself."

They *oohed.* They *aahed.* Fred simmered with rage, jealousy, stupefaction.

"So what's the frequency?" he asked, unwilling to give *Guy* the last word.

"Eh?" *Guy's* nostrils thinned, as if to filter Fred's hopeless juju.

"What's the frequency of the planet?"

Guy gave a little downward shrug of his lips. "Eight cycles per second. Why?"

He's bluffing, Fred thought. Yet the man's face remained as unperturbed as a plate of pâté.

"Just wondering," Fred mumbled.

Back in the office that night, Fred skimmed a scientific study finding evidence that Reiki normalized the heart rates of stressed-out rats, another that registered increased electromagnetic fields around the hands of healers. Other studies found no measurable effects. Others linked electromagnetic fields to cancer, though most seemed to suggest they were safe. Some websites mentioned mood changes and electromagnetic therapy, treatments for depression using electromagnetic "wands."

Straying to a site with a sky-blue background, he read that when all one's millions and millions of heart cells pulsate away in unison, they produce an electromagnetic field strong enough to be detected by an electrocardiogram from over three feet away. The field is toroidal in shape, arcing outward, downward, upward, curving back on itself, encompassing the body from the pelvis to the head, and with it, the far weaker EM field of the brain.

Another site, with all the words in boldface, said that electromagnetic tori consist of recursive frequency patterns, and are therefore holographic in structure, each part containing the overall pattern the way every fragment of a holographic slide houses an angle on the whole object. This site went on to claim that all energy systems in the universe are toroidal and holographic, that the universe itself might be one giant holographic toroid, in which versions of the whole pattern are contained in the smallest part; and that, therefore, each person, cocooned in his or her personal energy field, could contain, access, be influenced by, and in some way influence in turn the whole of the universe.

A link from this site led to another, wallpapered with astral man- and woman-shaped constellations, which claimed that pineal glands were oscillators, lungs were batteries, hearts and cellular mitochondria were electromagnetic energy coils, DNA strands were antennae—that, in short, people were machines built for transcendence and nothing else. *So what* if you were merely your body and nothing more, the thinking seemed to go, maybe your body was more than you gave it credit for, maybe materialism itself was the very realm of the spirit you'd been searching for all this time. *Hey, Paradise.* His mind teetered for a moment, something sad and plumbless opening at the memory of Margaritaville, before hurdling on. Sure. And all you had to do to activate this powerful transcendence technology was to allow the quantum potential of your visualized intention to synchronize with your pineal oscillations, exciting in turn the cerebral spinal fluid and transmitting the intention to your major heart scalar center, while electron-rich oxygen charged your lung-batteries, powering up your scalar waves to correct the noncoherent patterns of fear and ignorance of your true power, thereby resetting your quantum energy matrix; after which, it would be child's play for the primary Mobius coil of the heart to transmit its purified wave structure to the microscopic mitochondrial Mobius coils within each of your hundred trillion cells, tuning the antennae of your DNA molecules to receive life-giving biophotons from the solar system and universe.

And if that didn't work, you could always sign up for a holographic therapy session, which, terminology aside, seemed to involve the waving of colored crystals and the ringing of bells.

The humming and heat and other emanations from the great blue wall at Fred's back probably weren't giving him cancer, at least according to the current consensus. The Prayerizer's EM torus probably wasn't responsible for the baseline wooziness he was still feeling either, after the long day that had begun with him poised three stories over Brooklyn and ended with him holding his hands up over Manhattan, with a panic attack sandwiched in between. Even so, why take the chance? Why was he still putting this poor silicon stegosaurus through its paces? In its heyday, it had been a powerhouse of computation. Now, thanks to him, it was pointlessly REM cycling in machine meditation, an endless, mechanized mu. Soon enough, he'd have to put the thing out of its misery entirely. Sam was leaving for Florida in less than two days, and the office lease was up two days after that, the hedge fund next door set for another expansion. Fred told himself he should be looking into selling it for scrap. Maybe he could get fifty bucks for it and tide himself over for another week. Or if not, maybe he could at least find someone who wouldn't charge him for carting it off.

He couldn't bring himself to kill the power without checking on the stats one last time. Opening his laptop, he hooked the machine in.

Two hundred eighty-one trillion-odd prayerizations for God to DO something. He allowed himself to be impressed.

He pulled up the prayer buffer. And laughed.

"What?" Sam called out from his folding table.

"It's got thirty-five prayers running," Fred shouted, suddenly buoyant.

"Aha." Sam sounded not in the least impressed.

"That's a thirty-five hundred percent rise!"

An infinite rise, actually, if one didn't count the business he himself had given it. Nowhere near the tens or hundreds of thousands of users he'd need to sell any significant amount of advertising, even assuming he had an office to house it, an outlet to plug it into. Nevertheless, he'd had so few victories lately he felt like getting up and dancing. Thirty-four fellow humans out there, in the space of days, had received more prayers on their behalf than any and every human in human history, the living, the dead, combined, by several multiples. It didn't seem entirely like nothing, when put like that.

Way to spam the Lord, dude, said Inner George with a laugh.

"Not too late for you to buy a piece of the action," Fred shouted. "Get in on the ground floor."

"Action's all yours."

Sam was probably still fiddling with the arrangement of his furnishings in a 3D home design program, as he'd been when Fred had come in.

Curious, Fred put the prayers themselves onscreen:

```
/* DO something */
/* Dear God, please let Ken Hwang be accepted to M.I.T. */
/* Dear God, please let Savannah get assigned a seat near
Ken Hwang in homeroom. */
/* Dear God, please reward Ken Hwang's friends and smite
his enemies */
/* MAY THE MAKER OF THIS OFFENSE TO G-D CONTRAPTION DIE
PAINFULLY AND SOON AMEN */
```

The remaining thirty, Fred found, when several minutes later he summoned the strength to read them, were from Ken Hwang, or someone very, very interested in Ken Hwang's prospects.

Deflated once more, he reached under the desk, wrapped his hand around the power cord. And froze, awed by his inability to pull it.

Pull this plug, Inner George quipped, *and the terrorists win.*

Fred smiled, miserable and proud, and let the cord go. Then he got up and walked, putting some distance between him and the monster he'd created, meaning merely to pace around in circles, though in the end, loneliness brought him to Sam's station. Sam's headphones were off; he knew Fred was coming over, but made no move this time to hide what he was gazing at—a photo of a youngish woman with a pretty, broad face, a reddish nose, and blond curls. From the layout, it looked to be a dating site profile. The larger font along the heading bar bore the name of the service: FISHYSINGLES.COM. The logo, two smooching fish against a pink cross, pulsed and shimmered in the upper left corner.

"Aspiring homemaker," Sam said, his chin nested in his palm, the top half of his head moving muppet-like. "Believes in traditional gender roles." His fingers scrabbled over the mousepad. "We've got a date Friday night. I'll pick her up in my convertible. Got to remember to buy one of those dashboard Jesuses."

Maybe Fred had been wrong to worry about the sabotage, he thought. Sam and his team must have gotten everything working again, if this was how he was choosing to spend his time. Maybe the threat hadn't been so great after all, just a bit of hacker hijinks.

Sam clicked open another profile: another blonde, this one with very tanned skin, in a pouf-shouldered dress.

"Lunch with her, Saturday," he said.

"*Christian* dating, Sam?"

"I'm going to have a life there," Sam declared. "A real life. In a real place. With a real woman."

"You actually put up a profile on this site?"

"I didn't lie. I said I haven't been baptized yet. I think they think it's hot. They want to save me."

"But . . . could you believe in that fundamentalist stuff? Creationism? Heaven for Christians, hell for the rest?"

Sam picked up a squeeze ball and mashed it in his fingers. "You know what I believe in?"

The desk fan swiveled jerkily back and forth.

"Community," Sam answered himself. "And they've got that. They'll find you a house. They'll come fix your fence, your car. They'll fix you up with their daughter, their sister. They'll take you *in*. Help you build a *bunker*." His face shone with something akin to hope. "They'll get your back. When push comes to shove." Without looking her way, he'd been pointing, with the squeeze ball hand, repeatedly at the blonde on the screen, at first between her eyes, by the end between her breasts. "They'll see you through it."

"Through what? The apocalypse?"

"Well, *that* I have no trouble believing in. No trouble at all."

"Literally, though? The horsemen? The Beast?"

Sam shrugged, like the question had no relevance.

"Sam," Fred said, his voice softer, "do you have anything in common with those women at all? How do you talk to them?"

Sam studied the squeeze ball. Then glanced up. "Smiley-face emoticons, primarily."

He cracked a crooked grin. They both laughed a little. In that moment, Sam looked as bewildered as Fred felt.

"Speaking of which," Sam said, turning back to the screen. "I've got to write this one back. I've been making her wait for ten minutes. She's probably jealous."

Fred took a step away toward his own station, but couldn't help asking: "So you got those bugs all ironed out?"

"No. They're worse."

Fred stopped.

"Every fix we try just backfires. More and more behaviors are getting unreliable. Today, we had a rocket-launching firehose." Sam rubbed the raw-looking skin above his eyelids. "But I just can't focus on it. I've been working for months straight, day and night. And I'm so close. I just want my new life to start."

Why should I care? Fred thought. *Doesn't the little shit have it coming?*

Eyes downcast to George's checkered shoes, Fred was reminded of something he'd been thinking about lately. "Did George ever say anything to you about some dot-com burnouts he met on that trip to Europe?"

"No. Why?"

"Nothing. I just remember him mentioning we could get cheap labor in Eastern Europe if we'd started that new company."

"Sure. Hire a few Bulgarians. You'll be a praying computer mogul in no time." Sam looked up at the posterboarded window. "I'll have to smile in person when I go on those dates. I've been practicing in the mirror. This fucking city. I never learned to smile."

"What are you talking about? You smile. Once a year, maybe."

"Not for real. Not all the way, like other people. You have to learn that. But I've taught myself. I can do it now."

He shot an eye Fred's way, daring him to challenge the assertion.

"Oh?" Fred said, giving in.

Sam's lips parted overwide. His teeth looked like they were wired shut. His eyes, meanwhile, remained discomfitingly uncrinkled. "*Hi,*" he said, proffering his hand. "*Sam Brounian. Nice to meet you.*"

His voice was unnatural, too. He was aiming for something mellifluous, probably, but his jawbone was backed so far into his trachea that Fred's own throat began to ache.

"You weren't totally wrong with that Freddo idea," Sam said. "People can adapt." He made that strangulated grimace again, this time greeting the screen, shaking hands with the Christian girl hovering in the palm-tree backdrop.

"*Sam Brounian,*" Sam croaked, and the ache in Fred's throat redoubled, now from sorrow.

"*Nice to meet you.*"

"Sam," Fred said.

Sam turned, his teeth still clenched.

"'*es?*" he said through them.

"About those troubles on Urth . . ."

Fred brought his laptop and chair over and showed Sam the emails and the IM exchange about the Pretaloka and the angels who didn't believe they were angels. He described the chemotherapy angel's apparition in the playtest, and produced from his pocket the Swiss Army knife and from his briefcase the packing slip that had come with it. The websites he'd been sent to were no longer up, but he related what had transpired on them—the hints at a conspiracy, the seeming effort to get him involved. In the process of explaining how he was being spied on, he had to make an extended detour into the helmet study, and Mira, meeting the main road again with those angel statues in her apartment. Finally, he took out his cell phone and showed Sam the two texts.

In the early stages of his narrative, Fred felt, more than anything, a sickening guilt, like he was stamping out the last remaining ember of George's trust. He'd taken away George's company, uselessly prolonged his suffering, and now was tattling on his conspiracy, his revenge, the one thing he'd wanted to leave behind. But Fred just couldn't see George taking pleasure in this. Maybe in the planning stages, shut away in his emptying apartment, in his dying body, exchanging clandestine emails with whoever else it was who had a grudge against Armation or something to gain from the sabotage, while George himself was losing everything there was to lose. But whoever was carrying this out wasn't George; and to picture a George who could be happy with the way things were shaking out was to picture someone Fred didn't know. He could see no possible good resulting from the sabotage, for Sam or anyone.

And Sam's reaction, at least initially, reassured him he was making the right choice. No sooner had Sam gotten the broad outlines than he was scribbling notes, looking up website registries. Sam even seemed a little happy, grateful for the information, fired up by the prospect of uncovering the plot. Fred was a little happy, too, not to be alone any longer with this mystery. But when he started getting into the part about the card that had come with the angels, and how George himself must have been a part of the scheme, something changed for Sam, changed in a way Fred hadn't anticipated. He began shaking his head, the amplitude so slight it looked more like a slow palsy than disagreement. Thinking Sam simply didn't see his rationale, Fred kept going, revisiting the hints, the overall whimsy that seemed so much like George, the game-like elements, the fantastical narrative tying the whole thing together.

Sam saw it as clearly as he did, Fred could tell. But he just sat there, shaking his head.

"He wouldn't do it," Sam said, with that toneless emotionality.

"I'm sure it's nothing personal, Sam. It's Armation he hated. Not you."

Sam just kept shaking his head, eyes locked on nothing.

They spent the next few hours multiplying and dividing, converting the phone numbers to binary, to hexadecimal, comparing them with lines in the Urth code. Sam went on working fervidly, long after Fred's brain lost its ability to number-crunch. Exhausted but still wanting to help, and unable to sleep anyway with Sam pacing around, scrawling notes and numbers across the blank white walls of his alcove, Fred went online. Several pages into the search results, he finally found a full version of the Kalki Purana, which he downloaded and read from start to finish. The mayhem began—or would begin, the thing was a prophecy—about halfway through, with Kalki the Avatara and his holy horde inclining to stop and decimate various secondary people, places, and things, including an entire city of Buddhists (worshippers of Vishnu's previous incarnation, Fred noted, if he was keeping the story straight), for their lack of Hindu orthodoxy, before continuing on to butcher the demon Kali and the army he'd ride in on. Oddly, Kali himself would go down like a lightweight; the only real fight would be put up by his twin demon generals, Koka and Vikoka (cousins of Gog and Magog, perhaps), whose skulls, in a kind of gruesome prefiguration to the Three Stooges, Kalki would at last smash together. The twin demons was a curious detail, but for the most part Fred couldn't fathom what had drawn George to the blood-drenched material—a military entertainment *par excellence*, it seemed to Fred. It was like a children's book, only even more simpleminded, he thought, a children's book written by a child, in the backward childhood of humanity.

Sam was still up. Fred could hear the hurled squeeze ball thudding against the wall. Monday night, he thought, or Tuesday morning, rather. Week Four of the study, going on without him. He was too exhausted even to be properly tired. There were too many questions, and no solutions in sight. He missed Mira. He missed her voice in his ear. He had no new visualization exercise to listen to, no new bedtime story to lull him to sleep. Pulling his laptop down off the desk and into the sleeping bag, he found the Christworld site, and set it to play the virtual Sermon on the Mount he'd seen Sam watching earlier. Once more, Fred watched the little seeds falling on the path, the stones, the thorns, the rich earth. After that wheat stalk labeled PARABLE, the action returned to Jesus, the crowd now dwindled to a handful of robed disciples. Then a closeup on one of them, his animated lips opening and closing. Fred had the sound off, but the disciple's words appeared at the bottom of the screen:

Why do you speak to them in parables?

Back to the animated Jesus:

Because it has been given to you to know the mysteries of the kingdom of heaven. But to them it has not been given.

Why parables, Fred wondered, the screen's brightness in the bedroll's dark making his eyes tear. What was it about them? Was the capacity for parables itself at the center of it? Was literalism, then, one of those rootless seeds?

For a weightless, drifting moment, the venting heat from the Prayerizer was a parable. The glowing screen, the watching of it, the ache in his eyes, a parable. The blurry, virtual Jesus a parable. Jesus himself a parable—self-made, God-made, world-made, word-made.

But a parable meaning what? And what about the figurative impulse, for that matter—this urge to fill it all up with personal meaning, remake the world in our image, God in our image? Where did this rolling seed wind up?

It was all he could do to briefly blink the screen back into focus:

Lest they should see with their eyes and hear with their ears . . .

Animated eyes popping open. A closeup on a wiggling ear.

Lest they should understand with their hearts and turn . . .

A hand on a heart. Jesus radiating light, arms outstretched.

So that I should heal them.

Not literalism. Not figuration.

It was all a wavering wash of color, then simply light, thrumming on his lids. Then he was floating off into glowing, spiraling blue clouds, the laptop's electromagnetic torus, the tori of his beating heart and questing brain, both getting swept up into the larger torus of the Prayerizer, and onward into ever greater tori after that. He was looking for George, as always. But afloat in the widening spiral's central black, he found only a little, blocky, pixel man, waving his lo-res arms, kicking side to side with his nubby legs, with every spastic motion whipping up more and more whirlwinds of useless light. Looking up at Fred and seeing himself discovered, the pixel man threw up his nub-hands and skittered away, taking the light show with him, leaving in his wake something as surprising as it was pleasurable: an expanse of total stillness and peace.

Fred didn't wake up until close to noon. Too late, with the building now populated, to take a shower in the slop sink, but then he hadn't been especially looking forward to that bleak initiation anyhow. Sam was on the couch, having fallen asleep half sitting up, one foot still on the floor. Fred ate a bowl of Sam's cereal, washed his underarms in the bathroom, and a few minutes later was outside, wincing in the daylight, wielding the mu like a machete through the urban phantasm. Doubting the celebrity tourists on West Broadway. Doubting the Neural Science Building, which he couldn't help passing by. Doubting he'd see Mira but looking for her anyway. Dreading the day ahead—the prospect of having to face George, having to sit and watch him be slowly converted into cancer cells, having nothing to offer him but small talk—and doubting the dreading, doubting the despair, doubting even the moments of meditative openness, and the fresh smell of the dyed flowers outside the deli, and the pleasure in the sunlight, and the legions of zestfully slouching kids on the steps of Union Square, and the hope for new beginnings despite it all.

Cutting east and passing the Zeckendorf, he was startled and unnerved by the actual sight of Mel on the opposite sidewalk. Her sun-gold hair was longer and more curled than it used to be. Her compact little body, with its tanned limbs and abundant curves, was on display in a T-shirt and short denim skirt, a little cloth purse on a strap gently spanking her ass with each step she took. She hadn't been on his mind at all lately, he realized. Nevertheless, and though it would have been disastrous, he probably would have gone up to her in these checkered shoes and slept-in clothes, and either begged for a second chance, or barring that, begged her just to let him pretend with her for a minute that they were still dating, that the millennium was still new. But before he could unstick himself from the pavement, she reached back and intertwined her fingers with those of the guy walking beside and slightly behind her, a tallish, thinnish, dark-haired guy who, had Fred not been demonstrably over here alone and not over there clasping her hand, he might have mistaken for himself, might have wondered where he'd gotten the money to buy those groovy sandals and guayabera shirt and two-tone shades. Mel and the guy who wasn't Fred said hello to Fred's nemesis, the security guard outside the supermarket, everyone all smiles, and kept floating along, neither they nor the guard looking Fred's way.

And Fred continued east, feeling like a ghost, observing his hazed reflections in the store windows, the suit-sale hawker with the sandwich-board wings, the black woman with the blond, ring-braided halo, wondering if the one trapped in the Pretaloka wasn't George, but him.

Stepping into the room, Fred was stopped by the sight of Mira. Sitting in one of the molded chairs against the wall. Her back erect, her hands in her lap. Her gaze on George, unblinking.

"My bad," she said, her voice as stiff as the rest of her.

"No biggie," Fred mumbled, after a moment.

She was the professional version of herself today, blouse and skirt and fastened ponytail, except her eyeliner was a bit thicker, the way she kept it when she bartended. Perhaps an attempt to distract from the darkness beneath her eyes. It seemed she hadn't been sleeping much, either.

"You *were* stalking me, though." Her words came out forcefully. Then her lips set again and she was as still as before.

"Somewhat," he said. "But I didn't know about your husband."

She turned and scanned his face. After ten seconds or so, her shoulders relaxed a bit He sat beside her. They watched George, amid the tubes, the wires, the LED lights, the breathing machine. It was just about time for George's shave. His hair was getting shaggy, too. That or his face was shrinking.

"You never should have been in the study in the first place," she said without looking Fred's way. "I was only supposed to pick people who weren't in crisis. Mild depression at most. Moderately to highly functioning. No one too vulnerable, too at risk of instability. That's the only way we could get funding."

They sat. Two laughing attendants wheeled a gurney and rattling IV pole by in the hall.

"But your application, when I read it, I just thought . . . it would be good to have one person like you. Someone it could really make a difference for. Someone really going through something. A spiritual emergency." She looked down at her hands. "I thought that way I could prove what the helmet could do."

The breathing machine breathed. The sound of rubber soles and rubber wheels passed by the doorway. *A spiritual emergency.* The term seemed to suggest both crisis and metamorphosis, the emergence of some bright new state of being.

"My father went through the cases last week," she said. "We had an argument about you. Not that those statues you sent me wouldn't have disqualified you anyway."

That whole night with her made that much more sense to Fred, now. How she'd known she'd have to kick him out of the study one way or another. How she'd allowed herself, thanks to this and to her loneliness, to get drunk with him and take him home with her.

"So I suppose I owe you an apology," she went on, looking uncomfortable, her eyes starting to wander the room, "even though . . . what the hell is that?"

She'd locked on the spot, high up on the wall opposite the foot of George's bed, where now hung, upside down, the framed photograph of the leering Dan Gretta and the Bush brothers. Fred had mounted it yesterday, with some borrowed tacks from the cafeteria bulletin board.

"Plunder," he said.

It took her a while to peel her eyes from the three suited men hanging there like vampire bats, as if worried so doing might allow them to launch from the frame and sink their gleaming incisors into her throat.

"I don't regret having been in your study, Mira. It's changed me. It's changing me still. For better or worse, I can't say yet. I'm only sorry I can't finish it."

He saw gratitude in her look. Then, a spark of mischief.

"I can't get you back in—officially. But if you want, I can sneak you in for the last session."

A laugh caught in his throat. "Really? You'd really do that for me?"

"It's not a favor," she said, suddenly stern. "You've been warned. You're basically my guinea pig."

"But you could never write me up."

"No, I couldn't."

"So thank you, then."

He wanted to reach for her hand, but stopped himself, vexingly unable to gauge their closeness or distance. He'd slept with her, but she'd never really slept with him. As if sensing the stifled impulse, that hand of hers rose from her lap to brush some loose hair behind her ear. He forced himself to look away. Even so, the faint whiff of her hair alone, in these sterile conditions, was a sensory overload, like stumbling upon a fog-filled orchard on the surface of Mars.

"There's a symposium happening on campus," she said. "I've convinced my dad to go tonight. Part of my campaign to get him respectable again."

"Tonight it is."

"Eight o'clock. Meet me at the Washington Square Arch."

Getting up, she grabbed her briefcase, then lingered, eyeing Fred's in the next chair over.

"Pure coincidence," he assured her.

She nodded slowly, taking it in. "Not much of one, really," she said, still uncertain.

"No," he agreed, "not much of one."

Fred couldn't stay in the room with George any longer. He didn't want Dr. Chia to find him there and start delivering the official scan results. He didn't want to hear about that now. He wanted to be happy, to feel like his luck was turning. In part it was precisely because he was happy that he couldn't stay in the room with George, with those fat, corrugated hoses snaking from George's neck, and that long, bony face of his, into which, more and more, Fred found himself reading reproach. Something was about to change for Fred, Fred felt, to change for the good. He'd get to have that last helmet session after all, and who was to say he wasn't destined to have it? And he'd get to see Mira again. And she'd get to know him, get to like him. It wasn't impossible, was it? Maybe she'd want to sleep with him for real.

He went down to the cafeteria. It wasn't going to be easy to make the day go by. In search of something vaguely faith-inducing to ready him for the session, he navigated to Manfred's website, a bare-bones affair, Manny's simultaneous promise and disclaimer flashing near the top of the screen: GUARANTEED TO BRING ABOUT ENLIGHTENMENT (IF YOU'RE READY)! Fred clicked on one of the digital shorts. It was called "The Pie-ning" and turned out to be a jumble of relentlessly intercut scenes involving two glassy-eyed Disney employees on their off-hours, a young couple in headless Goofy and Daisy Duck costumes. In one scene, they pantomimed dog-and-duck sex in some dingy motel room. In another, the Goofy guy sat in a diner, rapidly spooning an entire blueberry pie into his mouth. In a third, the Daisy girl ran, or at least quickly waddled, down a residential street, turning every so often to look behind her with wide eyes and a strange pout that seemed intended to denote fear of some offscreen pursuer. Mixed into all this were a bunch of shaky shots from the window of Manny's van—of strip malls, phone lines, the sky, the thighs and inched-up shorts of female drivers moving in parallel below. Fred might as well have been watching it through a kaleidoscope, for all the comprehension, let alone enlightenment, he was attaining. A back-and-forth montage of the man's face covered with blueberry filling and the woman lewdly presenting her feathered hindquarters was underway when a beeping made Fred jump in his seat.

He found his cell phone. Nothing. At the next table, a resident sitting over two hot dogs and a pile of steaming sauerkraut flipped his phone open. Fred looked over those two "CALL GEORGE" texts on his own phone once more. Atlanta. Central Ohio. He ran a few Web searches, looking for tech companies—some rival to Armation, perhaps—based in both places. Coming up with nothing, he thought again about George's mention of hooking up with programmers while in Europe after his divorce in 2004. Fred wished he had George's cell phone, so he could look up his brother's contacts, but George had disposed of it along with most of his other possessions. On the laptop, Fred spent a while looking over the handful of emails George had tossed off from Internet cafés over the course of that trip—hasty replies to Fred's anxious queries, five lines tops, most less—which Fred, at his desk in the gloom of their office, had read again and again, trying to fill in the gaps of a life becoming more and more opaque to him. The dot-com burnouts were mentioned only in passing; George had spent most of that email relating the strange logic of a Finnish woman he'd met in a Budapest nightclub who he'd said looked like Jill, and who had told George she would have slept with him if he weren't American, because American men were prudes and didn't respect women who slept with men on the first night.

Back on the phone, Fred looked once more at the picture of George in that checkered outfit on some cobbled street; George had gotten whoever had taken it to text it to Fred; and Fred now wondered if perhaps the sender had been one of his traveling companions, one of those programmers, maybe. Fred didn't get many texts. Only a handful over the last couple of years. In fact, scrolling back through the record, he still had that blank message to which the picture had been attached. He dialed the number it had come from, readying himself for a confrontation with the cyberthug. But after a brief, awkward introduction, he ascertained that it was only an aging woman in Scotland, who dimly recalled being charmed enough by a rustic peasant on her continental holiday to snap a picture, after which she'd discovered he was an American and had offered to send along the image.

Maybe he was wrong, Fred thought. Maybe George hadn't been involved in these messages to him, or in this whole assault on Armation at all. Maybe that note with the angels was just an odd coincidence, like Mira's husband's old briefcase; maybe not even much of one—maybe Fred had misremembered what that musclebound nurse had said while driving the shunts into George's veins. Or maybe someone else had been listening in on them. Or maybe George had repeated the phrase to someone at some point. Fred thought about how adamant Sam had been that George couldn't have been a part of it. Sam's insistence had been so unexpected, especially given the strain between him and George in recent years, that it made Fred feel guilty for jumping to the conclusion himself. Maybe it really was just a setup like he'd first thought.

He started poking around the Web again, and discovered that there weren't too many statuary stores listed in the metropolitan area. The angels could have been shipped from a distance, but he hadn't seen any stamps or plastic sleeves with delivery slips on those boxes in Mira's apartment. She might have thrown them out, or he might have been simply too drunk to find them. But it seemed worth a shot to start calling around.

It didn't take him long to find a place in Jersey City that could order the two statues he described. It didn't take much further digging, when the proprietor mentioned how odd it was that the same two had been ordered by someone last winter, to get the man to regale him with the story of this someone: A guy with dark circles under his eyes and a small oxygen tank. Who had come in and plunked down a wad of cash. Paying extra for the sculptures to be held for seven months and then delivered anonymously to an address that would come by fax. Which had in fact happened, at last, just a few days back.

The more he knew, Fred felt, the less he understood. Every explanation just compounded his ignorance.

Who are you, George? he thought. *Who were you?*

It was getting harder and harder to hear Inner George. Some mental barrier was thickening, ever more soundproof. Though it seemed to be getting more and more conductive in other ways. He could still feel George out there, pressing against some membrane of the universe. Less a knowable person than a force of yearning, a desire so large it was almost by this point without an object.

He was about to call Sam and break the news of George's trip to the statuary store, when his phone rang in his hand.

It was Vartan.

"How's George?" he asked.

"Still on the machine. Still breathing." Fred felt a twinge of guilt that he wasn't up there in the room with him. "You and Mom coming in today?"

"No."

The answer was brusque, ominously final. A mechanical whine came from the background. Some kind of tool. Maybe an electric screwdriver.

"I booked one last birthday party," Vartan said. "It's tomorrow."

This, too, had a disturbing ring of finality. Though on the other hand, maybe it was good news. Wasn't it about time his father stopped doing magic shows? He must still be off the weed, Fred thought. Fred was pretty sure he could hear this in Vartan's voice—a low-level agitation, like he'd been scrubbing in the shower with sandpaper.

"OK," Fred said.

"You'll do it?"

"Sure. I don't mind." To Fred's surprise, he actually didn't. He needed the money. And he thought it would do Vartan good, get him out of the house, give him some closure.

"The solo act's not too different," Vartan said. "The tricks are mostly the same. Just a different story."

The noise had started up again. Vartan's voice sounded crimped, probably from wedging the receiver between his shoulder and head.

"The solo act?"

"You can come get the van any time," Vartan said, and hung up.

The park, that late-summer evening, was like a bright little solar system: the younger, hotter bodies by the central fountain, boys flipping skateboards, girls flipping hair; the dimmer, middling ones—the addicts, the aging guitar players—held in perpetually hopeful orbit slightly farther out; the stray comets of tourists passing through on their straight paths from end to end; and lurking in the outer ring, the cold gas giants, the bored old gods—eternal chess players, and pushers, like Robert the dealer, on his bench-back perch a few yards off, perusing a ruffled copy of the *Post* and pulling out a promotional Spider-Man comic book insert. When at last Fred gave in and turned to check the Arch, he found Mira standing beneath it, in dark jeans and her black nylon jacket, loose braids blown by the breeze. The answer to his first prayerization, if fifteen days delayed. She kept looking every way but his as he approached, eyes fretful and sharp. He was almost next to her when she finally saw him.

"There you are," she said, as if he were late, though they both were early. Her jacket was unfastened. Beneath it, on a white T-shirt, in red letters:

BU*LL*SH*IT*

"How many of those shirts do you have?" he asked.

"As many as it takes."

She turned, and they began walking, not fast. She'd seemed impatient when looking around for him, but was now almost dawdling, as was Fred. They were almost like any other couple, he thought, out walking on a warm night. As much as he wanted this session, he was tempted to suggest to her they skip it and just go see a movie.

"You look nice," he said.

She snorted. "I haven't even showered today."

"Don't worry. I think I've got you beat on that score."

She eyed the sidewalk. "It always gets tougher, this time of year."

For a moment, he didn't know what to say. He asked if she'd gotten her father to the symposium. She said she'd walked him there and pushed him through the door. He wasn't speaking tonight, but everyone wanted to hear the direction of his new research.

"Which," she added dryly, "he's not entirely happy to be talking about."

"He must appreciate what you've done for him, though."

"Right. The other day, he was talking about developing the technology for the entertainment industry."

Fred laughed, uncomfortably. All too easy to picture.

"So when you came back from the tunnel in the near-death session," she said, reassuming her clinician's tone, "was it like the out-of-body one before? Being in your body again, did you feel . . . 'squashed like a bug?'"

He recalled how suddenly ill she'd looked that day when he'd described this for her, smacking down one hand on the other. With an upwelling of sadness, he said, "Not nearly so much."

"Good," she said, sounding relieved. "We'll see if we can recalibrate some of that."

"Mira, why didn't you take Lionel's last name?"

After a few steps, she shrugged. "I didn't like it."

"It was worse than Egghart?"

She pursed her lips, then banked a shoulder into him, knocking him off course. The gesture felt to him as intimate as those kisses the other night, made him feel almost as light.

They were almost to the door of the Neural Science Building.

"So what is it with you and Bush, anyway?" Fred asked. "I mean, aside from what it is with everyone and Bush?"

"I don't know." Mira slid her hands into her pockets. "I did meet him, though."

"You did?"

"There were a lot of functions we widows got invited to. I mostly hung out in the bathrooms. I was looking for one when Lionel's boss's widow took me over and introduced me."

"What did you say?"

"Me? Nothing. 'Pleased to meet you.' Something stupid like that. What do you say to a president?"

"And what did *he* say?"

She turned to face him, her black-lined eyes more narrowed than usual, her lips in a leer. "*We're gonna git 'em for ya.*" Then she winked.

"Really?" Fred laughed. "He winked?"

Mira was walking again. "I don't know. It could have been a blink. He's so squinty."

She was squinting as she said it, not Bush-like, but Mira-like. Fred let the comparison go unmade. "So what did you say to that?"

"I said, 'Thank you, Mr. President.'" With deliberation, but without force, she kicked a paper coffee cup to the curb. "And I meant it."

They stopped at the entrance.

"So that was it?" he asked.

"That was it." She smiled. "The emperor of the world went on glad-handing. I finally found that bathroom, and threw up in a toilet."

Mira led the way in, presenting her ID to the droop-faced security guard, who, in the manner of all security guards these days, eyed Fred with suspicion. In the elevator, Fred watched her watch the numbered lights change, wondering if there was any combination of words and actions which might result in the two of them kissing before the doors slid open.

The doors slid open.

She unlocked the office suite, switching on lights as she led him down the narrow corridor. At the doorway to the little control room, Fred stopped.

"Can I have a peek behind the wizard's curtain?" he asked.

"Very well." She ushered him in ahead of her. He sat down in her father's chair, she sat in hers, peeling off her jacket. Through the window in front of them, the recliner's black vinyl and the helmet's sparkly finish shone in the dim light coming through from their side.

"So why haven't you ever tried it?" Fred asked.

"I told you. Scientific objectivity."

"But what's the real reason?"

She folded her arms, that third hand, the ghostly blue one, right between the other two.

"I suppose you think I'm chicken?" she said.

"No. I think you're a control freak."

Mira rotated her chair away from him. "Who cares what you think? Do *you* have a neuropsychology degree?"

"Do you?"

"I'm working on it." She woke up her computer. "The helmet software's on yours, by the way."

"So what's on yours? Or do you just surf the Internet in here?"

"I could, if you'd prefer." With a doubleclick, she called up a window with a few rows of graph lines. "Or I could monitor your vitals and make sure you're alive."

"Aha."

Fred woke Craig Egghart's machine. Mira wheeled over and pointed to a folder on his screen:

luminarium

Fred opened it. Aside from the application itself, there were a few subfolders. He clicked open the first, *consilia*, and opened up a few of its files—scanned-in sketches and electrical diagrams for the various hardware components.

"Just his plans," she said.

Fred closed it, moved on to the next subfolder, *effusio*. Five filenames appeared:

delectatio.cwv

excrucio.cwv

timor.cwv

ira.cwv

voluptas.cwv

"Older stuff," she said. "Basic emotions."

"Do they work?"

"Sure. Those are a snap."

"*Excrucio*," he muttered. "That can't feel good."

"You had a bit of that as part of the last one."

He put it together: that moment of reaching out for the jar of gel. "Right. How could I forget my own electrocution?" He pointed at the second-to-last file. "*Voluptas.* Is that what I think it is?"

They were sitting close to another, now, their shoulders almost touching.

"If you think it's arousal," she said, her voice a bit thick.

He thought of that bee-strung bow and lotus-tipped arrow.

346 • Alex Shakar

"I've got to build me one of these things."

She eyed him through slit lids. Then shoved him, sending their chairs rolling apart.

He opened the next subfolder, *recuso*.

"Reject pile," she said.

It had only one file:

vacuus

"What's that?"

"It means 'void.'"

"Void?"

It sounded like a reject indeed, Fred thought. The very name made his insides shiver.

"My dad tried to test it on himself and had to abort after less than a minute. He said he thought it was going to eat his soul." She smirked. "I'd never heard him say 'soul' before."

There was one subfolder left: *spiritus*. Fred opened it:

complexo.cwv
subterlabor.cwv
ianus.cwv
aperio.cwv

"Are these them?"

"Yep," she whispered.

Here it was, then, he thought. His spiritual odyssey, encoded as easily as a few songs on an iPod.

"Which one am I getting today?"

Mira's finger moved down to the last.

"What's it do?" he asked.

"You want the explanation now?" she said. "Beforehand?"

"I'd rather know what I'm in for, this time."

She paused. "I suppose we've pretty much demolished the protocol anyway, at this point. All right." She swiveled to face him. "This one puts the others together, kind of. And adds a few things."

She pointed at a spot an inch above her hairline.

"Cingulate cortex. It tags information—your thoughts, imaginings, sensations, all your experience—as being either real or unreal. We'll play around with this, so that by the end, you'll feel yourself to be perceiving a deeply important truth."

She aimed her index fingers toward each other, just in front of her ears.

"Amygdala—your fight-or-flight response. Hypothalamus—your pleasure center. The two systems usually don't go on at the same time, for obvious reasons. But sometimes, rarely, they can overlap, firing in quick succession, like in a crisis that gets suddenly resolved. The result is a hyperaroused emotional complex. Some call it rapture. Let's see. What else?"

She looked right, left, at her hands, still to either side of her head.

"Oh. You had a tiny bit of this in the last one, but way more now." She lowered one hand, with the other bringing a ragged fingernail to bear on the point between her eyebrows. "Corpus callosum. The only point connecting your brain's hemispheres."

Her fingertip remained there, bisecting her eyes.

"Parallel processors, to use your computer terminology. Your right parietal lobe specializing in sensory-based thought. Your left in critical and linguistic thought. Normally, they operate almost independently, your left perceiving your right as nothing more than a thin stream of data passing through this one narrow conduit."

She tapped the spot. He remembered the Hindu women on the bridge, their painted red bindis.

"*Except* when a micro-seizure happens. It's like a little storm, creating wider electrical connections. Giving your left a glimpse of that entire other sentience. Like another presence is suddenly in there with you. Familiar and strange at the same time."

"Another presence," Fred repeated, feeling a chill.

"Which, in a state of rapture . . ." Her finger drifted to the side, then pointed at the ceiling, as her lips bent into a sort of sad-clown smile. ". . . can appear divine."

Between him and the spiral galaxy, Mira leaned, two slick fingertips rubbing circles over his heart.

"That's good," he said. "A little lower, please."

"Nice try." She slapped the electrode onto his chest, reached for the helmet, and pushed it onto his head. "Oh, damn."

"What?"

"I got some gel on these little copper wires. Hold on a sec." Feeling under the trolley's main level, she grabbed a tissue from the lower shelf, then, coming in close, tilted her face this way and that, squinting at a spot inches above his head.

"You sure it's OK?" Fred asked, wishing, at some point in their association, it had behooved him to bring up her need of new contact lenses.

"It's fine." She kept peering, blinking, dabbing with the tissue. "If it blows, we've got a spare."

"If it blows?"

"Relax." She flashed a grin. "You're in good hands."

"Mira," he said, just as she was turning to go.

She stopped. "Yes?"

"Kiss me for luck."

Her smile faded. He wasn't smiling either. He'd said it like a command, in part just to overcome his own nerves.

"Fred." She began shaking her head.

"Just this once," he said, to preempt whatever speech she was about to give him. "Then send me off to God."

After an uncertain moment, she leaned down slowly. She merely pecked his lips, at first. Then, impulsively, she came in again for a longer kiss. Her lips were stiffer than they'd been the other night, and didn't seem to quite know what to do. His own lips struggled in turn, now trying too hard, now not hard enough. Perhaps the wire-frizzed helmet and the odd angle they were at contributed to the awkwardness. Just at the moment he thought they were starting to find their fit, she pulled away.

She didn't look at him as she left the room, or as, behind the window, she reached up with a flash of belly and hips and brought down the shade.

Red bulb popping on.

Gray shelves.

Gleaming cart.

He told himself it was progress, their first real kiss, the start of something. He couldn't escape, though, the misgiving that the kiss had been too strange for her, too foreign. Something she wouldn't allow herself to repeat.

Blacked-out glass.

Ceiling grid.

That high-pitched whir, intimate as a dentist's drill.

A pinching at his thigh. Reaching into his pocket. Feeling the five little round elevator buttons.

Clutching them, as a spot of ticklish heat widens at the top of his head, as a slow drip from the spot splashes down onto his brain stem.

As the drip becomes a stream, the stream a torrent.

As the room clouds with static, with strobes, the colors of blood and light and heat.

As every nerve in his neck and scalp lights up.

As a pinhole of darkness appears in the center of the unraveling galaxy.

And widens. It must be an optical illusion, the effect of continued staring, but he stays fixed on that swiveling-open black, half afraid if he looks away it won't stop, half afraid it will. In the periphery, the red bulb brightens and looms, a blossoming sun. The shelves and table flatten out, recede into some lesser dimension. The ceiling tiles breathe, exhaling into the room, charging and warming the air. The room itself expands, walls swinging wide.

He yanks his eyes away.

Hot chair.

Cramped helmet.

Bulb small and dim.

All the same. And not at all the same.

He palpates the chair arm, squeezes the trolley leg. Solid as ever. Though for some reason he feels like he should be able to crumple it all in his fists. The room is no more real than a stage set, a painted backdrop.

A ticklish, milky current flows up and down his spine.

Big deal, he thinks, to quell his fear. Another special effect.

He stares up at the flat poster. The spiral has twisted shut again, like the mouth of a bag, cinching him into this place that's no kind of place at all.

Big deal, he thinks again, and laughs.

Then jumps in his chair, as something bigger than the universe laughs with him.

"Fred?" Mira whispered, leaning in.

He wasn't sure how long he'd been staring at that poster before the red light had gone off and the fluorescents had come on. As she lifted the helmet and began peeling away the electrodes, he looked around, the walls oddly closer, the room smaller than he'd remembered. She pulled the lever and guided the chair back upright, then was in front of him, offering her hand, and he hesitated, some haywire spatial processing module of his brain fearing that, in standing, he might put his head through the ceiling. It didn't happen, but he almost felt as if it had, following her down the too-small corridor. Almost as if the ceiling had been lifted off, as if he were a mouse that had clambered up atop the walls of its maze-world, blinking in the blurred light of the astronomically larger laboratory beyond.

A lab, he thought, passing the little control room, peering within as he would the chamber of a dollhouse. *Inside a lab.*

With the phrase came an echo of that cosmic laugh, not a physical sound so much as a psychic force. He couldn't pursue the thought, couldn't follow where it went.

He sat in the blue recliner. Mira sat opposite, and put a hand on his knee.

"Tell me about it?" she said in a small voice, leaning forward, peeking up into his eyes.

She's a mouse, too, he thought, *a mouse in a lab coat.*

Instead of laughter or that mute force, the Presence, still with him, now communicated by other means, flashing images into Fred's awareness, images from his own life: Mira from above the bar, braids slightly flapping as she reached for his glass / the cartoonish cap of the trolley driver in Celebration.

Meanwhile, in front of him, Mira's mouse-like eyes went wide. A door had opened in the lobby.

"Mira?" her father called out.

"Oh God. I'll never hear the end of this. Be quiet."

She rushed out, shutting the light and slamming the door. Fred heard her strained laughter, overloud, her blurted question: "What are you doing here?" Followed by the sound of another door, murmurs from an adjacent room. The fat little baseboard star glowed.

Five-pointed, he thought. And instantly, the Presence flashed more images to mind: the five fingers of his mother's hand, trembling above his head / his own hand, holding the Swiss Army knife, prying those five elevator buttons from the panel.

Mira slid back in, flipped the light on, leaned close.

"He doesn't know you're here. I convinced him to go have dinner with me. Put everything back the way you found it. I still want to debrief you on your session. Meet me tomorrow night, same time and place."

She killed the light again and was gone. A minute later, Fred heard the main door close. He still wasn't alone. He felt as if the giant hand of the Presence, rather than the chair, were cradling him. The hand didn't seem inclined to crush him. It held him gently, protectively. And he felt inclined, more and more, to nuzzle against its warmth.

Losing some of his fear, he left her office and wandered back down the hall. Stepping into the helmet room again, he traced the cylinders rising from the holes in the sparkly sphere, the bright copper strands rising out of those and into blue and red sheathes going every which way, before coalescing into a single twist-tied bundle. He wasn't alone here, either. The Presence was still with him, looking over his shoulder, as fascinated by the device as he was. More than just fascinated. There was affection flowing from it, like a sun-warmed stream, through Fred and onto the machine, which, as if it had been washed, began to shine all the more in the dim light through the doorway. The affection wasn't just for the helmet, Fred now began to feel, with a deepening sense of awe and gratitude, but for him, too. As if, for the moment, they were the Presence's two favorite children, the helmet and he. Or its favorite toys. Beloved inventions that had presumed to transcend their clownish materials.

With fellow feeling, Fred continued tracing those wires, which ran along the jointed metal arm, then down the back of the chair, and finally into a thin steel box on the floor, about the size of a stereo component. An orange switch on the box was lit in the on position. From the doorway, not without a thrum of *voluptas*, he'd watched Mira bending at the hip to flip it on. So he now knelt and switched it off. The box was otherwise featureless, aside from a power cord and a data cord, which snaked from the back of it through a hole beneath the observation window—connecting to Egghart's computer, no doubt. As Fred glanced up at the poster on the dark ceiling, the Presence gave him another image, one that felt like a loving gift: he found himself, for a long-lost moment, sitting with George on his top bunk, the two of them in their pajamas, charting new constellations among the brand-new star and moon stickers, brightly aglow. Not so big a coincidence, the stickers and this poster, Fred thought, but even so, his life felt suddenly smaller and self-contained, a tabletop puzzle whose pieces could be snapped into a single design.

Back in the control room, about to shut down the computers, he noticed Egghart's sketchpad in a shelving bin beneath the table. It was almost too much for Fred, paging through the helmeted faces Egghart had drawn: An older man with a complicated wrinkle of concentration on his brow. A woman with dark-shaded skin, a nose stud, and dreamy, parted lips. A man with frown lines etched all the way down to his jaw. All with closed eyes, the kind of closed eyes that looked to be focused beneath the lids, lifted slightly in their sockets, like Fred's mother's while doing Reiki. His fellow adventurers, he thought. And he felt that love from the Presence streaming down onto them, making them shine like heroes. Blinking back tears, he turned the page and found a drawing of Mira, her profile, looking off, probably through the control room window. Her father, Fred thought, had managed to capture both her analytical intelligence and childlike wonderment. His throat was aching. The love from beyond was now mixed, and enriched, he actually felt, with a kind of sorrow, a sorrow for Mira's sorrow, for everyone's. For his. His throat started to clutch itself and he was bawling, a hollow knocking sound, like a rock skipping down the walls of a bottomless crevasse. He wanted nothing more, no other objective, than to love this way himself. So sorry he was for this lifetime of doubt. So grateful at the possibility of everything being different now, different and so much easier.

He turned one more page and saw what he should have by now expected, but he'd been so full of these other things he wasn't prepared at all.

It was himself. His jaw slack, his eyes all but shut, small and boyish under that sci-fi headgear. Of course, this must have been the page Mira had grilled him about, following the out-of-body session, the page he'd told her was blank.

Blank.

That's what he'd seen, and it wasn't what had been there. He'd gotten it wrong. Because he hadn't been up in the air, looking down on her and her father; he'd been right there in the chair, right where the man had drawn him.

Mira had explained it all that day, every component, every nuance of the illusion. Just as she had today, in advance, no less. Explained that this Presence was just the other half of his brain. Just these two little lobes in here, clasping and cupping, warming each other in the cold. How soon, he wondered, before the inner lightning stopped, before the other lobe went dark again, and this phantasmal higher self folded back into nothing?

Not quite yet, it seemed, for the little ripples of sadness he'd sent out were coming back a tidal wave, like God's own sorrow for Fred, a teary ocean, in which all Fred could do was tumble.

He tossed the sketchpad on the table, left the computers on, and wandered back down the corridor, letting himself into the suite's little bathroom, the velvety sound of his piss on the water making his skin tingle, the toilet flush flashing to mind the smoky vortex / Pincurls bobbing up Broadway / the homeless man sucking down a cloud of inhaler mist. Pieces of the great puzzle, or just an overexcited, overexposed right-brain image dump.

Then, turning to the sink, with a jolt, he saw George—in tears, stunned at the sight of Fred in turn—through the window of an adjoining bathroom. George blinked in confusion, recognizing himself to be but a reflection, trapped in some other universe even less real than Fred's. It was a dirty trick, Fred thought, played on both lobes alike by that fried spatial processor. Regardless, he couldn't help lingering in the magic, reading the wish in George's eyes, the wish to be here, here with this unreal Presence for which he'd searched so diligently for so many years but never seemed to find. No doubt George would be making better use of it, Fred thought, than he was.

Back out in the reception area, feeling no particular compunction to leave, he eyed the last door he hadn't been through. Egghart's office, he assumed. He opened the door. Why not? He was a mouse with the keys to the maze. Switching on the light, he saw metal shelves stacked with books and manuals, and a worktable covered with screws, wires, silicon chips, and electrical diagrams. The unreal Presence was still beckoning with images: Vartan in the lamplight, drilling into metal / George taking the first blockish avatar for a run across the undeveloped green Urth. What would mankind's busy building look like from a divine perspective, Fred wondered. Would all these objects of ours, too, someday snap together into a single, all-purpose Thing?

Stepping in, he was surprised by the office's size and layout. It was bigger than Mira's, and had the only windows in the suite, a northerly view, which should have been familiar but wasn't, or wasn't quite: Buildings of every height and width and era jostling and angling for the night air. Stonework of every description, cornices and balustrades and decorative patterns of amphoras and laurel leaves and seashells, half erased by weather or shoddy repairs or air-conditioner installations. Walls and roofs bristling with pigeon baffles, pipework, grillwork, vents and ducts, tottering old water towers. High-rises hived to bursting with their million-dollar niches, flatscreens and canned lighting, overbright, as if in the midst of a power surge. A system sumptuously on the edge. Fred reminded himself it was the other half of his brain—fearful, impressionable, overwhelmed—that was showing things to him this way. Though he couldn't help imagining the view, too, as a kind of divine warning, or alternately, boast—the utter implausibility of the city's moment-by-moment continuation as the Presence's very point of pride.

In the distance, the Empire State Building strained above the tectonic shards of Midtown, its bygone citadel peak now floodlit, unevenly, thanks to a missing light, in memorial red, white, and blue. The Presence, more insistent than ever, kept riffing, flashing to Fred's mind the virtual Empire State Building coming down / the bricks and glass and pulverized pavement wafting up into the night / the fractal explosion of color on the CT scan / the clouds of dust as his golf club smashed into the replicas / the little pixel man throwing off light / a tiny, broken rainbow over that moronically burbling fountain, the one he'd seen from the Armation terrace after tossing the space helmet over the balustrade, in that sun-dazed, shellshocked hiatus in time.

Then, it had been but a Military-Entertainment Complex he'd been lost in. Now it was a cosmos. From that empty suit, Gretta, behind his empty desk, to this empty Presence, Fred thought, in this bankrupt study. And it was almost tempting to try to combine the two emptinesses to make a whole, to lash two bullshits into a truth. After all, what other kind of faith was possible in this infinite pinwheel of bullshit wrapped in truth wrapped in bullshit, hopelessness wrapped in hope, vileness wrapped in beauty, lunacy wrapped in logic, loathing wrapped in empty, empty love . . . .

He turned to go, that Presence—that self-deluded Presence, he thought—trailing him like a lovebird on a leash. His hand on the light switch, taking one last look around Egghart's neurotheological work-shop, Fred noticed in the corner a double-doored metal cabinet, like the one that used to be in his office, which Sam had put to use as a pantry. Barely a coincidence at all. But excuse enough to stride boldly over and swing wide the doors. Nuts and bolts. Spools of wire. Voltmeters and ammeters and magnetometers. And at the very bottom, beneath a couple of stuffed manila folders, swathed in bubble wrap, the edge of a metal box, and a coil of red and blue wires.

Fred smiled. He saw the pattern—if of no grand design, he thought, then simply of his own. Even the Presence seemed grudgingly impressed, reaching into its trick pockets and showering him with a few more choice images: an animated lightning bolt zapping an animated Adam into being / the tiara-wearing birthday girl gleefully bonking him with his wand / his hand reaching into his parents' refrigerator, fingers closing around a sparkling, plastic-wrapped wedge of cheese.

Fred waited on the Broadway-Lafayette subway platform, the Presence still sharing his headspace, though it seemed less that he was of two minds than the world itself was of two realities: that of the late-leaving office workers and assorted teenagers, of thumbs a-prance on the glass of smartphones, of clean, pink ears hung with Bluetooth headsets and plugged with pearlescent plastic buds; and that of the corroding pillars, the urine stench, the greased-looking rat slipping under the third rail, the gum-blackened platform over which all those spotless, sporty, patent-leather, sneaker-shoe amalgams seemed to hover on sole-shaped beds of air.

An old behemoth of a train showed its bulldog face, rocking on the tracks as it braked. In the lab, Fred had first sensed the Presence as something like an experimenter, but here on the train, it was more like a conductor, shuttling him through the present, this frenzied tunnel of noise and light, toward his appointed destiny.

Do not lean on doors, it instructed him.

Do not hold doors open.

Whole self-help careers could be spun from these paired maxims. On the opposite bench, a Hasidic Jew snapped open the *Daily News*:

NO PAIN, NO GAIN

Fred was inclined to take this too as a personal message, a promise of divine accounting, a just reward for his ordeals in the offing. It seemed too life-affirming a phrase to be nothing but the day's decree from their president, eyes like buttons, defending tough tactics at secret prisons.

As the train pulled into his station, the Hasid folded over to the special series that week:

9/11
The
forgotten
victims

. . . and a picture of a fireman sitting slumped, hands glued to his knees, helmet weighing down his head. Fred's throat went dry, as it did in his paralyzed dreams.

But then the doors opened, no need to lean or hold, and he followed the commuters, their cheekbones lit by joggling phone screens as they climbed to the street. On the opposite corner, kids from the projects, children of the children who had jumped and fistfought him and George on that very spot, loitered outside what was now an organic market, out past the edge of their dwindling turf. It had become the very neighborhood he and George, as children, had always dreamt of growing up in, full of kids with first names like Jackson and Erikson, whose parents called out to them from book-filled parlors and leathery car interiors. Fred and George had imagined buying their parents an apartment, maybe a whole building, in a neighborhood like this, with an extra apartment that Fred and George and Sam could stay in whenever they needed to, whenever they needed a rest from the jet-setting, globetrotting lives they'd surely lead. That neighborhood of their dreams had turned out to be this very place, except that it was their parents who were the out-evolved underclass, the gentrificational missing link, clinging to their rent-controlled apartment with their hirsute fingers and prehensile toes.

Fred stood in the cramped kitchen, with its cracked and grease-spotted ceiling and the torn up linoleum floor that Holly had sponged daubs of red and green and yellow paint onto a few years back. Fred could barely believe the place still existed, that it hadn't been consumed in some nuclear firestorm, or at the very least been bejeweled and digitized and taken over by some feckless trillionaire. The sight of it was somehow overwhelming, as though he'd been away a thousand years, as though it were not an actual place anymore but a museum, not even an actual museum but a kind of museum in thoughtspace, or possibly a shrine. The memory flashes had for the most part dissipated, but in the ensuing calm, the Presence was, if anything, more present than before,

358 • Alex Shakar

helping him see just slightly further into things, a fraction of a milli-meter deeper into their surfaces, bringing out a strange new vibrancy.

Two days or more of dishes in the sink, the mess sorrowfully beautiful in the Presence's light. He resolved to do them before he left.

Carefully, he set his briefcase on the dining table. Over in the living room, half a dozen cardboard boxes sat stacked on the rug. Closer by, against the brick wall on the far side of the dining room, Vartan sat at his desk under the hanging lamp, beard and hair afloat on his blanched and luminous head.

"So what's going on?" Vartan said. It sounded like an accusation.

Fred approached, awed by the sight of his father. The lamp could have been a halo. Vartan's face an etching made of light. There was nothing exactly supernatural about the illumination; the lamp explained it all. But there seemed to be another kind of radiance as well, something coming from within Vartan, something that shone through him, that made the dry furrows of his brow all the more skin-like, those dark eyes behind his glasses all the more gelatinous, improbably material. Fred didn't know whether he was seeing in his father an angel, or, in fact, a human, for the very first time.

Fred might not have been able to stop staring, had his eyes not been diverted by the box in front of Vartan on the desk. It was white, slightly larger than a shoebox, sealed in what looked like shrinkwrap. On the side, in black ink, the word "MagicCo" was printed in stylized letters, with the two *c*'s forming a kind of hypnotic whirlwind.

"Are you going to tell me about it?" Vartan said. His tone was somber. Fred had been too busy staring at Vartan to realize Vartan been staring right back.

"About what?"

"Why are the cops after you, Fred?"

"What?"

Vartan flipped a business card from the desk edge, caught it, and handed it to him between two fingers. *Detective Bruce Nelson*, it read. There was a phone number, a city seal, no other information.

"Plainclothes guy. Came by asking where you were."

Fred looked around, as though the detective might still be lurking in a corner. His eyes stopped on his briefcase on the table.

"When?" he asked.

"Hour ago."

No, Fred thought. It couldn't be that, then. And odds were it wasn't about his antics at the Armation headquarters, either. Sam had told them they'd be getting their helmet back. Which seemed to leave two possibilities: It was about Fred's drunken, all-but-blacked-out rampage on that miniature golf course. Or it was about the conspiracy and the sabotage of Urth.

"You aren't part of a whole shoplifting ring, are you?"

"Oh, shit," Fred said, suddenly remembering. "My arraignment was yesterday. I totally forgot."

"You think I'm an idiot?" Vartan said, without raising his voice. "Detectives don't come around about tweezer thefts."

"No, I know. It's just . . . look, I don't know what it's about. But I'm not in any trouble, Dad. Really."

He wasn't sure whether his father believed him or not. But Vartan let it pass. He placed both hands on the box, and pushed it forward.

"At the start of the act, you open it up," he said. "There's a big, high-tech wand inside."

"You built it?" Fred said. "That wand George drew?"

"There's a cassette in the box, too. You pop it in the boombox. You'll hear a friendly guide"—Vartan's mustache ticked with pride just a bit—"who will talk you through the whole act, demonstrating everything the wand can do. Except the wand keeps malfunctioning. So all the tricks go wrong. It's a funny act. Here's a list of the tricks." He slid a sheet of scrap paper forward, with his penciled handwriting. "You know them all already. It's just a different sequence."

Amid the pile of tools and tins of screws and scraps of metal and plastic on the desk, Fred noticed cannibalized pieces of Vartan's electric hookah—a section of the rubber hose, the empty light socket affixed to the wooden board, a melted section of the glass jar.

"You don't want to do the show yourself?" he asked.

Thoughtful, Vartan took off his glasses, rubbed the bridge of his nose.

"You know," he said, "when I was working on that Shakespeare play last year, one day I thought I understood it. And the next, it just seemed like bullshit."

He stared through the lenses in his hand.

"The guy able to raise his kid like that on that island," he went on. "Control everything. Concoct this whole fantasy that everyone gets tricked into learning from. This scheme that makes everything right."

Vartan tapped the box between the two of them, which shone in its plastic wrap under the lamplight. It looked pretty professionally done, could have passed for an actual product one would buy in a store.

"I don't know what gets fixed with this, kiddo," he said, shrugging a thumb. "But it's all the magic I got."

His mustache and the hair on his cheek shifted to the side. Not quite a smile, but at least an effort in that direction, and suddenly that love from the other side of existence, from the other side of Fred's brain, or of Fred's heart, was welling over the dam.

A heavy thud of something falling or being dropped came from Fred's bedroom.

"All the show stuff's in the van," Vartan was saying, ignoring the noise, placing the keys on the desk in front of Fred. "Your tux, too."

"I need to borrow your drill, and some other tools." Fred was more sure of his plan now than when he'd first conceived it.

"Why? Gonna crack a safe?"

"I'm helping fix up Sam's condo for the new buyers."

There were so many facets to this lie that it was almost a world of its own, a parallel Fred branching off in some alternate universe.

"He found buyers?" Vartan brightened a bit. "Bet he made some money."

"No doubt," said Fred.

"I told the cop you were staying over there. I gave him the address." Vartan studied him again. "That's all right, isn't it?"

Fred summoned a weak smile. "Sure."

Another thud from the bedroom.

"What's Mom doing in there?" he asked.

Vartan's head sank on his shoulders as he turned and regarded the boxes in the living room.

"Redecorating," he said.

Walking to the living room, Fred lifted a flap and peeked into one of the boxes. Topping the stacks of books was one with exercises to increase one's optimism, another with exercises to increase one's luck, another on channeling spirit guides.

From his bedroom came a sudden clatter. He peered around the doorway.

"Mom?"

Holly was standing in the far corner, wearing her white down robe and, over it, the black motorcycle jacket Manny had given Fred, bundled up in the stuffy room on this summer night like it was the middle of winter. She turned to face him holding an open shoebox. Behind her, the little corner altar shelf was clear of everything but dust.

"I was hoping to have this done before you came back." She edged around the futon, on which sat another box of books.

"Aren't you too hot in that jacket?" Fred said.

"It tricks the tremors a little, even though they're not from the cold." Holly regarded her hands. "They're dumb that way."

Stopping a few feet from him at the nightstand, she picked up the vortex rock and dropped it in a box with the crystals and jade Buddha and a little polished stone with one of those Reiki symbols etched into it—a lightning bolt shooting sideways into a spiral.

"The room's all yours, now," she said, with an attempt at breeziness. She wouldn't look Fred's way. For his part, Fred couldn't look away from her. The Presence wouldn't have let him if he tried. More even than with Vartan, there was something shining through her, shining through the dull mud color of her eyes and the puffy, tired-looking skin surrounding them, those whorls of muscular habit that hitched one lid slightly higher than the other. Shining through every color-treated hair on her head and pore of her skin and each of the small, worn fingers of her quavering hands. Fred wished she could have seen herself like he was seeing her now. And he wasn't just seeing. With Holly, the luminance was something Fred could even feel. It flowed from her in silken waves. It made Fred's every cell tingle. *Is this the energy she's been speaking to me of all this time?* he wondered. *Is this what it feels like?*

He wanted to tell her what he was seeing, what he was feeling. But then he remembered the helmet, the explanations, the cingulate cortex, the amygdala, the hypothalamus, the corpus callosum. And he lost the resolve to speak.

His mother had stopped near him only momentarily, and was leaving with the box. He reached into it and pulled out the vortex rock, feeling a cloudy charge rise up his arm. She studied it in his hand, her face utterly impassive.

"Maybe you can use it as a paperweight."

She left. The shelves were empty, save for a few of George's and his old books. The chakra and Reiki symbol charts had been stripped from the closet door. The room wasn't radiating that shabby brilliance like the others in the apartment. No longer hers, no longer George's, or Fred's. Just a room. A box of nothing.

The Presence, to Fred's surprise, was aching, as lonely there as him.

He piloted the old magic van to Manhattan, still not alone, though the Presence was stepping back a bit, becoming more of a kind of background radiation, shimmering everywhere just out of view. Finding a parking spot good until 7 AM, Fred disembarked, tool bag and drill case in one hand and briefcase in the other. A white SUV idled with its high beams lit a few doors down from his office building, and he froze, wondering if it was the police, and if he'd already been spotted. He was prepared to call the number on the card and meet the consequences, whatever they were, after tomorrow morning, but not before. The vehicle had chrome wheels, didn't look like anything a detective would inhabit. He crossed in front of the lights, slipped through the lobby, and into the elevator.

The hallway was empty. From the office, he could hear the pulse of a bass line. Cracking the door, he saw only darkness, then Sam, who lay sprawled on the floor in a mottled splay of laptop light, wearing nothing but black surfer shorts. An MP3 mix of Tampa Jook music, which Jesse and Conrad had gotten the office hooked on a few weeks ago, raunched and ranted from the laptop's speakers. By Sam's bare feet was a Fresh-Direct box, empty and knocked on its side, and another, smaller box, its cover obscured by a same-day courier slip. A bag of kettle chips sat by his head, along with the champagne bottle which for months had been sitting among the soup cans, and a six-pack of St. Pauli Girl, in which five bottles remained, though all five had been de-capped, and presumably, drained. The sixth, half full, stood on the floor off to his side, loosely cradled in his outstretched hand.

"Fredoooooooo," he said, with a tilt of his head Fred's way.

"Sam?"

"Like my tan, babe?" he said to the serving wench on the label.

Now that he mentioned it, in the light from the hallway, Fred noticed Sam's wiry torso was glowing an odd, burnt shade of orange. Fred had assumed, at first, it was just some new helmet effect he was seeing.

"Is that fake?" Fred asked.

"Straight from the source." He set the last of the beer glugging down his throat, then let the bottle roll away. "If the source is a small plastic tube."

"So . . . is this you celebrating your last night here?"

"Celebrating," Sam repeated tonelessly. "Here, take a look. Celebrate away."

He spun the laptop to face Fred. On it was a 2-D Manhattan map, over which, in slow motion, a mushroom cloud unfurled. The animation was near photorealistic, except that as Fred watched, the cloud began behaving strangely, reticulating and bifurcating into more and more crooking, branching arms.

"What the hell is that?"

"The latest little wrinkle," Sam said. "All the object functionalities are getting mixed and randomized."

The cloud/tree then started folding up like an umbrella. There was something fanciful, and yet at the same time, deeply malignant, about the transformations. A seasick feeling overtook Fred, along with that bleeding nightmare unreality he'd felt in the playtest, as if those instabilities might somehow leak out of the screen and into the room.

"You should see Little Baghdad," Sam said. "Tanks flying around like Frisbees. Helicopters flopping like fish. The chaos is overwhelming the servers. Whole place is barely moving."

Fred could barely feel the Presence anymore, he realized, as if it had withdrawn at the sight. Inwardly, he kept scanning for it, feeling abandoned. On the screen, the column of smoke and fire shortened, contracting at the bottom, then bounding up and landing a little off to the right.

"I forgot we programmed in pogo sticks," Fred said, as the cloud hopped out of view.

"Sales force in Jakarta's probably going ballistic right about now." Sam rolled on his stomach. His back—orange where he'd reached, white where he hadn't, and coated with floor dust—looked like a hoarfrosted Creamsicle. "There'll be fireworks in the morning down at HQ. And a good old Soviet-style purge, no doubt. They'll probably call the Feds in. And of course my demo on Monday is toast."

The detective's card put on weight in Fred's pocket. "You could reschedule," he suggested.

Sam got to his feet, wound back an unsteady leg, and kicked one of the empty cardboard boxes to the wall. Fred just then noticed that the pile of computer parts had been scattered—hurled, it appeared—from their former position, across the whole right side of the room.

"Monday was the day," Sam said. "The *perfect* day. All those officials lined up. Awareness heightened up the wazoo." He punted the second box, then walked slowly back and picked up the champagne bottle. "When I get to Florida tomorrow? I'm not even going to show my face at Armation. I'll just put my car and condo on the market, and see if Manny can get me a job in an amusement park."

"Come on, Sam. You can't give up now. You can fix this."

Sam just stared at him, with a sudden look of such hurt and helplessness Fred was stunned to silence. A moment later, veiled in indifference again, Sam's eyes wandered down to the items still retained in Fred's hands.

"What's with Dad's hardware?"

"Just . . . a little project." It seemed the wrong time to explain. In any event, Sam didn't pursue the subject.

"You bring a hammer?" he asked instead.

"I don't think so."

"Big screwdriver?"

"Maybe."

Fred set his cargo down. Sam walked up, smelling of synthetic coconut, and offered him the champagne. There didn't look to be much left.

"Was saving it for the big sale," Sam said. "Cheers."

Fred took the bottle, fearing if he didn't, Sam might chuck that too across the room. Sam fished the desired screwdriver from the toolbag and pulled a penlight from his pocket, then started wending his way around the scattered parts toward the back of the room.

"I figured out those phone numbers you got," he said. So nonchalantly Fred wasn't sure he'd heard him right.

"What? You did?"

Standing in place, Sam began scanning the light methodically around the floor, walls, ceiling. "I was fielding emails about the video recording we were gearing up to do for the Times Square simulation. Lining up some military-grade GPS handhelds and a panoramic car-cam for the job. Then it hit me. They're not phone numbers you got sent." He was digging in his pocket again, pulling out a small handheld device of some kind. "They're longitude and latitude numbers."

"Sam." Fred laughed. "You're a genius. So . . . where?"

Sam peered into a display on the device.

"Here," he said around the penlight, now in his teeth, as he knelt and began prying with the screwdriver at a buckled floorboard.

"Here . . ." Fred processed. "This office?"

"Here, where I'm fucking standing." Spittle flew around the light. "Where his fucking desk used to be."

Sam wrenched out the floorboard. It looked like he'd been trying to do so before Fred had arrived, with a bent metal bookend nearby.

"So . . . what do you think that means?" Fred asked.

"Somewhat difficult to say, without his fucking desk."

Kneeling close, Sam shone the light into the hole. Then cursed, and flung the floorboard away.

"You think he left something here?"

"Hard drive totally wiped. Just like at his apartment," Sam muttered, on his haunches now, face in his hands, the penlight pressed to his cheek. "I cleaned his desk out myself. It was practically empty. A few paperclips. All I can think is that there could have been something hidden somewhere in it, or marked on it."

"So where is it now?"

"In desk heaven."

Fred wondered if it was just the booze, if Sam wasn't thinking clearly. "Who took the desks off our hands? Can't we call them?"

As Fred's voice rose, Sam's grew faint. "They were particleboard pieces of shit, and we were pressed for time. We broke them down and left them in the trash room. The waste management company says the scraps have been incinerated by now."

Sam was walking again, scanning the back wall. Reaching the *Matrix* poster, already all but peeled and hanging at a diagonal, he scanned its front, then peered behind it, at its reverse side, then at the wall, all of which Fred had the sense Sam had done before. Then Sam drew back, seemingly pensive. Then he tore the poster from the wall and ripped it to pieces, then kicked the wall, stabbed it with the screwdriver, rammed his head against it, and half slumped, half fell to the floor, where he sat absolutely still, the beam from the penlight, which had rolled off amid the bits of paper, illuminating him from the side.

"Sam." Fred stepped toward him. "You don't need the desk. Who knows what that wild-goose chase was about. It doesn't matter. Just go down there and stop the sabotage. Tell them what's happening. Just get Urth up and running again."

Sam looked up at him, that same awful, wounded look on his face. It wasn't even about saving his job, at this point.

"He told me to stay with the company," Sam said.

Fred was standing over him. "George? He told you that?"

Reaching out, Sam grabbed Fred's wrist. "*Sam,*" said Sam, "*stay with the company. Stay with the company, Sam.*" His eyes were quizzical, bright. "The last words out of his mouth."

Sam couldn't mean what he was saying. He hadn't even been speaking to George toward the end. "When did this happen?"

Sam's face hardened, fearful, determined.

"When he tried to kill himself."

"I was here. Working late. He called and asked me to come over. When I got to his place, he showed me a bottle of sleeping pills. He just let me look at it until I understood. He told me he needed me there with him."

They were sitting side by side against the wall, in the shadows. A creeping paralysis was taking Fred over. His mind was fuzzed with dread. The Presence had either stepped far back into the darkness or vanished altogether. He couldn't force his mind ahead where the story was leading. It was all he could do to follow, word by word.

"Why you?"

"Think about it," Sam said, his voice soggy with drink. "Would you have stood for it? Anyway, he didn't want to saddle you with that."

"So he saddled you?"

Sam stared into his fingers, as if he had too many of them to count. "No. With me, it was like a sign of trust. Before that night, I thought he didn't trust me at all. I thought he hated me, after all the shit with the company. I still told him no, no way, but then he said he'd have to die alone otherwise. He looked so sick. What else could I do?"

Sam risked a look at Fred, just as quickly looking away.

"We had a long talk," Sam went on. "We were sitting in his living room, on the floor, against the wall. Just like this." His head lolled around. "That room was almost as empty as this one. Mostly it was me talking. I didn't think I'd be able to say anything, but then I started and I couldn't shut up. I told him my whole side of things. I told him how he'd saved me. How

368 • Alex Shakar

our company had saved me. How the company was all I had. I told him how, like, that day at the diner, when he asked me to choose between the company and him—because that's what the choice was, we would have lost everything we'd done—how it was like he was taking a hatchet and chopping me down the middle."

As if it were that hatchet, Sam had snatched the screwdriver from the floor. He now turned it in a dusty slice of light.

"He just kind of smiled, like he'd known we were going to have this conversation. He said he understood. That he wanted me to stay with the company. That it would be better if I was there. Then he went into the bathroom. Then he came out and handed me the pill bottle. Empty. And told me to throw it out and not tell anyone. Then he got into bed. He started getting sleepy. He told me he could handle it from here, and that I should go. And that I should stay with company."

His grip tightened on the screwdriver.

"Why would he have told me to stay, if he was in on some plot like this? Just for revenge on me?"

He was looking at Fred again. Fred couldn't say anything. Fred didn't know either. A minute later, Sam continued:

"It was the middle of the night. I went home. I couldn't lie down. I couldn't stay there at all. I packed some things and came here."

"And I found him comatose the next morning?" Fred asked.

Sam nodded.

Fred had gone over there early. He'd had a strange premonition something was wrong.

"You and Dad both called me, and I didn't know what to do," Sam said. "I wanted to tell you to stop trying to save him, but I'd promised him not to say anything about the pills. Anyway, once I got there, I was sure there was no way I could change your mind."

Sam looked to him for confirmation, and Fred had to nod. Even had he known, Fred wouldn't have stopped trying to save George. He'd only have felt guiltier about doing so. And the last few months would have been even harder to bear.

"Maybe if I'd told the doctors about the pills," Sam said, tears gathering, "they could have given him a different treatment and brought him back."

Fred could see that this possibility, and Sam's dread of Fred's reaction to all this, had been eating at Sam all this time. Maybe it was true. Maybe they'd done all the wrong tests, given all the wrong treatments.

Or maybe there was nothing that could have been done at that point anyhow.

"It doesn't matter, Sam. They said his sodium levels were low. He might have slipped into a coma before much longer even without the pills."

Sam closed his eyes. Just as Sam's guilt appeared to be ebbing, Fred's began to swell. He'd foiled George's graceful exit. He'd fucked things up even more than he'd thought.

"It's not your fault either, Fred," Sam said, his eyes still closed.

There was a current, it seemed, that just kept carrying Fred down and down, one waterfall after the next. There might be no end to it, he thought. It might be time to give in, let himself be bounced and bashed from rock to rock with no further struggle. Though no sooner had he felt himself surrendering than the impossible Presence was back, catching him in its illusory, cloud-soft embrace and winging him upward, so that he felt himself falling and rising at once.

He crossed the room, grabbed an abandoned lamp from the corner, and plugged it in. Then he opened his briefcase and took out his laptop and the flat metal amplifier box with the coiled wires and solenoids.

Sam approached. "What the hell's that?"

"Luminarium," Fred said. He clicked open the folder he'd copied, then the *consilia* subfolder, then a file within:

Transcranial Complex Waveform Magnetic Stimulator

"From that study?"

The words ran above an elaborate diagram, filled with measurements, of a helmet with a dozen holes.

"They gave that thing to you?" Sam asked.

"I borrowed it."

"You . . ." Sam leaned around, trying to get a better view of Fred's face. "What for?"

"For George."

Sam's face just hung there.

"He's going to see God before he dies," Fred said. "Or a stand-in, at least."

A slow, lopsided, incredulous smile overtook Sam. He shook his head. Then he looked from Fred to the plans on the screen.

"So you just stick those cylinders into a helmet?"

Fred nodded.

"What are you going to use for . . ."

Sam followed Fred's glance, to the cantaloupe box. And laughed, sort of, a soundless little huff.

"You're not even joking," he said.

"Listen, Sam," Fred said. "I don't want to give you even more trouble. If you think they'll blame you for this . . ."

"Fred, it's not *my* head they'll want on a pike."

"He'd want that helmet to be the one, though," Fred said. "Don't you think?"

Sam's mouth flattened under pressure. Like he didn't know whether to frown or smile.

"I think you're both fucking nuts."

As Sam painstakingly measured out and marked points on the space helmet, Fred laid out the tools, thinking about one of the first pieces he'd read to George in the hospital, the speculative writings of a quantum physicist. How two correlated particles affecting each other at a distance might actually be just two different three-dimensional projections of the same six-dimensional particle, like two videotapes of the same fish shot from the front and side of its tank. How what you perceive as movement might just be the unfolding of patterned information in this higher dimension. How from a still higher perspective, not only all inanimate matter but all the patternings of life might be thoroughly intertwined, unfolding from it and refolding back into it continually: plants forming from seeds-sun-water-soil-air; systems marrying systems giving birth to systems; brain enfolding mind and mind in turn enfolding brain / body / the entire material universe, in a meta-system whose ultimate ground is neither mind nor matter but an actuality beyond both, a single totality, all of it and all beings changing as they are changed, enfolding one another in a creative and generative embrace.

Tightening the router bit on the end of the drill, he wondered how things might look from a higher order in which faith and doubt were reconciled, in which God and no God, even, were one in the same. In which it wouldn't be any kind of contradiction whatsoever that the only true place for God to be was nowhere—to all outward appearances false, by all objective measurements absent, real only to the extent one could, through some arduous test, some ingenious stratagem, stretch a portal to that nowhere and see Him eye to eye. Now George would get a glimpse through that doorway before he jumped. And if in the end, Fred thought, there was no door, was not even a nowhere, then at least, for George's sake, this flat old world would have striven to appear better than it was.

On the floor between Fred and Sam, the helmet's white dome shone in the lamplight, the lines and the dozen spots Sam had drawn on it giving it the look of a ladybug's shell.

"Careful about the angle," Sam said, his eyes a scalded red from the drink, the confession, the work on the helmet, the effort to sober up. "Stop every centimeter or so and let me check it."

The helmet was pretty well hardened, even against Vartan's diamond-tipped bit, but once through the outer layer, the rest was easy. Working slowly, the two of them checking and double-checking, the drilling took an hour. Fred could have borrowed his father's glue gun as well, but he didn't want to scuff up the solenoids—he'd done his best to conceal the device's absence, placing a thick book from Egghart's shelf in the bubblewrap under the folders at the bottom of the locker; he thought there was a pretty good chance he could return it tomorrow night, when he met Mira again, without her or her father knowing it had been gone. Anyway, the fit was snug enough that securing them wasn't much of a problem, even in the three holes he and Sam had made in the faceplate. Some tape and a bit of wedged toilet paper was all it took. They set the amplifier next to Fred's laptop on the cantaloupe box, and the helmet on Sam's folding chair. They plugged the cable from the back of the device into the laptop, and the power cord into a strip. Fred switched the power on and brought up the software.

"You want to try it?" he asked Sam.

"Fuck no," Sam said, and staggered off to the couch.

The thing had to be tested by someone. Fred picked up the helmet, sat down, and fit it over his head. Could this be the first time? He supposed he'd had other things on his mind. Still, it seemed funny he'd never had the impulse to try it on. Indeed, he found it comfortably padded, so well fitting as to feel completely natural and familiar, like it had been made to order. His breath fogged the faceplate. He decided to try Week One. It was the least cognitively disruptive, and he wanted to be functional in the morning. He navigated to the first file in the *spiritus* folder: *complexo.* He assumed the files were in order, but to be sure, tried *complexo* in an online Latin-English dictionary, which returned: "encompass." That had to be it.

Running it was easy as opening a spreadsheet.

A high-pitched sound.

A post-rainstorm smell.

A hot, shearing saw.

And he was out, things becoming a part of him—the chair, the helmet itself—no less strongly than the first time.

And yet, after all he'd been through since, something was lacking in the repetition; somehow it seemed like child's play, a game of make-believe. He was thinking about that earliest memory that had surfaced during the near-death session, that infant's-eye view on the world, flying with George above the stairs in their father's arms and all of it a part of Fred. That's what it was like, this experience—infantile. Freeing, joyous, but also regressive, narcissistic, less about opening himself than opening everything else to him. He wondered if the urge to return to this state of innocent containment of everything was the very root of his and every-one's problems, of the lifelong compulsion to consume and append and incorporate and be all and end all in a world ever more maddeningly beyond one's grasp. Each subsequent session had been a little less self-centered—stepping totally outside of his body in the second; outside the stream of his life in the third; and with the Presence, being given just a glimpse of a perspective outside the smallness of his own mind.

The Presence, which had been coming in and out since he'd gotten to the office, was back again, expanding with him. In the same way he was absorbing the office, he began letting himself be absorbed in the Pres-ence, dissolving as he grew, surrendering as he conquered, a whole new thrill as, together, he and it absorbed the room. They encompassed the Prayerizer, sharing the exhilaration of all that racing energy within it, like they'd just enveloped a star. What would the Prayerizer's higher self be, Fred wondered. He could almost picture it, the Big IT—crunching heroic quantities of data to preserve, amid all life's proliferations and complexifications, an order, a divine, meaning-filled, infinite supersym-metry, making sure, if not that everyone's prayers were answered, then that every deepest need was ultimately served.

And farther still they went, Fred and the Presence, encompassing now Fred's desk, now the microwave, now the red plush couch on which Sam lay curled on his side under the Army blanket, peeping out from beneath it with those raw, red eyes. A towering wave of utter terror swept over

Fred without actually making him afraid. The fear wasn't his. It was Sam's. Fred didn't know how he knew this, didn't understand the level of emotional intelligence he'd been lent, which took in all at once Sam's expression, his tensed form beneath the blanket, each little cue Fred had been processing in some less than conscious way. The farther the expansion went—the walls becoming another skin, the posterboarded window a single closed eyelid—the smaller Sam seemed, curling into himself ever more tightly, now an armadillo, now a snail. The beer bottles smooth as fingernails. The courier slip, the food delivery box crisp and sylphic as a newborn thought:

"Sam," Fred called out from deep within his bubble, the helmet braying his voice back into his ears. "When's the last time you went outside?"

And knew the answer even as the smile, diffident yet proud, spread on Sam's face.

"I stayed with the company."

Sam turned and yanked his blanket overhead.

Drifting off, now. Forgetting why his sleeping bag feels part of him, a chrysalis, the half-shed skin of a snake. All that was a dream, a dream from which he awakens in a small, white, cuboid room. Behind a control room window stands a being of light, in a pristine, white lab coat. It's the Presence. Its face pure brightness. Like a sun that doesn't hurt the eyes. Like that light at the tunnel's end.

The Presence escorts him through bright white corridors, into an elevator with a panel of buttons arranged in a spiral. With a finger of light, it presses the outermost. Fred can feel the compartment arcing around as well as pressing upward, in a vast spiral. Meanwhile, the Presence conveys it to him: an important mission is underway, a mission in which Fred has a role.

The doors open onto an observation deck. Below lies a circular, shadowy maze of a city. The roofs are all off to reveal the interiors, some of which he recognizes. He spots the dim loft room of his former office. He spots his parents' apartment, with its colorful kitchen floor and ancient living room rug. He spots a miniature golf course, glowing an unnatural shade of green. Surrounding these interiors are endless twisting corridors and drab institutional rooms. And at the center of the city lies a central darkness, a gaping hole in which a funnel of gray clouds churn. And the city is ever so slowly spiraling into it, the inner-most parts crumbling and plummeting over the rim.

The Presence tugs on Fred's white satin cape, and with that glowing finger, directs his attention upward.

The black dome above is filled with icons: A golf club. A shot glass. A lightning bolt. And many more.

The dome is not yet bright enough, the Presence telepathizes, to accomplish the mission.

Fred asks what the mission is.

He's led to understand: *to awaken a dreamer.*

Fred asks who the dreamer is. The Presence gestures to a mounted scenic viewer by the railing, through which Fred then peers: Down into the city maze. Into the innermost curl of the spiral, at a point mere yards away from where it tumbles into the vortex. Into a room edging inexo-rably, inch by inch, toward the brink. A hospital room, wherein, in bed on his back, head turned to one side, lies the little figure of George.

Fred turns to the icons. Some are luminous. Most are dim.

He asks the Presence if the mission is doomed.

The Presence hesitates. There is one icon, it suggests, that might spark them all at once.

Fred thinks: *The Presence is grasping at straws.* Which one, he asks. The Presence produces a calculator, punches keys, tilts its star-stuff head. Then shrugs and points skyward, but Fred can't see the icon through the glare of the Presence's effulgent finger. Whichever it is, though, he's got a sick, sick feeling about it.

"Please," he says. "Let's think about this."

But that too-bright finger is tapping the air—once, and once again.

Fred awoke with the heat of the Prayerizer's vented air at his back. It was the first time he'd dreamt of George since the coma. If nothing else, that felt auspicious.

Sam was already up, wrapped in a towel, an overlooked, foamy shampoo slug hanging from his ear. He handed Fred another towel and the yellow hose, and Fred went into the hall and clambered into the waist-high, mold- and disinfectant-smelling slop sink in the janitor's closet. The soap kept slipping from his hands in the darkness, forcing him to bend and reach down blindly, his knees hitting the sink's lip, his ass hitting the clammy wall on the recoil. Even so, it felt good to get clean.

He sent out emails to the Reiki group and to Manfred, urging them to be there on Monday for George's farewell, since he wasn't sure that he himself wouldn't be behind bars by then. A reply from Manfred came back immediately, saying he was planning on it, and urging Fred to check out his new digital short in the Zen Danish style, which he promised would enlighten the shit out of Fred.

In the slices of dawnlight from between the cardboard scales covering the window, Fred and Sam sat on the floor eating bowls of cereal. The modded Apollo helmet, with its solenoids and wires, watched them like a Medusa head from the folding chair. After breakfast, with extreme care, Fred put the amplifier, his laptop, and the helmet in George's camping pack, lining them all with George's sleeping bag. He slung the pack and Sam's duffel over his back and picked up Vartan's tools. Sam juggled a satchel and his plastic bin of personal effects. In the lobby, when Fred opened the front door, Sam froze, eyes going watery in the brightness. For a minute it looked as if he might faint. But at Fred's urging, his brother took a step, then another, then they were walking to the van.

They drove most of the way to the airport in silence. It was one of those strange days with mottled clouds in every direction but clear skies directly above. Sam sat forward in his seat, vacuuming in the city, and for that matter, the world, which he hadn't seen in months. Fred doubted the Presence, feeling it encouraging him to do so now, encouraging him to use its unreality as a focusing lens to doubt everything else all the more earnestly. He doubted the sad, sunlit Brooklyn/Queens hinterlands stretching off from the expressway, that vast, dilapidated, analog circuit-board of brick faces, car washes, billboards, tar roofs, lots streaked with effluent, street after street of it, a proliferation no one could have ever mentally budgeted for or planned on. He doubted the airport loop, the lane-changing cabs, the missing panes high up in the ancient hangars. The doubt was so strong, so assured, this morning that every sight was a thing of solid light and nothing more.

Parked outside the dreamlike terminal, his brother turned to face him, as dreamlike as the rest, yet sharper, too, deeper, all the more real.

"Sorry I won't be there, Monday." A dreamlike knot on Sam's dream-like brow. "Sorry I wasn't there for the last seven months."

"You were just being loyal." Fred's dream hand on Sam's dream shoulder. "Good luck saving Urth."

"Good luck with . . . that," Sam said, with a look back at the camping pack.

As Fred watched the peculiar, one-of-a-kind shape of Sam heading into the terminal, it struck him that a life would be too painful if it were real, that the pain would overwhelm it, would overwhelm everything. But since it wasn't—since, if not in some cosmic way, then just in the ordinary way, every last reality was ever-transmogrifying and fading away—maybe it could be borne; maybe in that sense, it didn't weigh a thing.

Back in the city, Fred parked the van in the hospital lot, and carried the box through the entrance. Not only could he glimpse the other side of that coin, he thought, he could take it and flip it once and for all. And live here perpetually, on the flip side of the universe, a place where there was a thing called a brain, a clump of noodles busy with things called chemistry and electricity, matter and energy, where there was a thing called science, which—if not untrue, if not inconsistent, if not even fallible—was irrelevant. Here on the flip side, the material universe was but an epiphenomenon, the manifestation of an altogether different order. How thickheaded it had been of him, all these months, to try to lock down God with scientific lingo. It was like trying to terrace-farm Space Mountain. Like flicking a Zippo inside the sun.

Passing through the ultramodern lobby to the antiquated interior, boarding the rattletrap elevator, he allowed himself the hope he'd be granted a sign—that George had gotten what he needed. George wouldn't have to wake up, the feat Holly had dreamt of, the feat Fred himself had just dreamt that the Presence, and maybe all the angels in creation, were working to achieve. George wouldn't have to come back to life. One faint squeeze of Fred's finger would suffice at this point, would be the last little nudge Fred felt he himself needed to take up residence here on the flip side, to end the wandering and build his city walls, to know that all this strife had been for a purpose, bringing him, as it had, to the helmet, the helmet to George, them both to the Presence, which, in this new land, would be every bit as present as they.

Coming through the door to George's room, Fred stopped. There was something on George's head already. It looked like a blue shower cap, but was acrawl with wires and brightly colored electrodes. By his bedside, in front of a cart with a monitor, sat a technician with a wan, ruddy face and a long chin. The man looked from George to the colored dots on the screen, from the screen to Fred, from Fred to George and back.

"What are you doing?" Fred asked.

"The doctor wanted a test."

"And?"

"You should talk to Dr. Papan."

"Tell me."

The technician sucked in his lips, as if to hide them. "I turned this brain upside down and shook it for twenty minutes."

A twitch of a smile, then another, as if in apology for the first.

"I'm very sorry. The body's alive. But up here . . . all gone."

It was something about wasps, and figs, but there were other creatures involved as well: bats, green pigeons, monkeys, and elephants. And the fig tree itself. The wasp eggs hatched in the figs. The tree protected the wasp eggs in a kind of sap. The wasps grew up in the figs, mated, burrowed out, spread the tree's pollen. The other creatures spread the tree's seeds. It was vastly more complicated than that—there were microscopic flowers, parasitical wasps that ate the fig wasps, ants that ate the parasitical wasps, seed bugs swarming beneath the tree, microscopic roundworms eating the wasps alive from within. It was important, Fred felt, that he cognize the narrative in its entirety. Because it was nature, the truth of things. And because it was also, somehow, in a way he maddeningly couldn't quite put his finger on, about him, Fred himself, or was at least being shown to him for a reason—how could it not have been, for here he was witnessing it. But he couldn't keep it all straight. He was diverted again and again by the insistent fact of his own watching of it. The fact of his existence, demanding explanation. Sitting in something called a booth, in something called a cafeteria, watching something called a television.

It wasn't quite habit that had brought him down here. He'd intended to leave the building, but, like some tethered ghost, found himself unable. Reaching his usual table, he'd opened his laptop—again, not automatically, but because he assumed he was about to cry and figured he could use the thing to hide behind. But so far he hadn't cried. He'd just sat, watching the nature documentary on the mounted TV, the sound too low to really hear.

A new old man sat in the previous old man's spot, this one in a wide-collared plaid blazer, making his rheumy-eyed way through the *Post*:

$6 MILLION

SCRATCH N' WIN

GAME CARD

INSIDE TODAY

AIR

SICK

And a subheading saying 70 percent of the WTC recovery workers were deathly ill. The *Daily News*, abandoned on a nearby table, added its own muted outrage:

KICKOFF!

SUPER NFL PREVIEW

THE SHAME OF 9/11

NO DOUBT

NOW

On the other TV across the room, a 9/11 retrospective segment played on NY1, as if anyone could possibly need a refresher: the sequential gouts of brimstone; the first mythic giant falling for the zillionth time; the sick feeling of the future being ripped away; that awful interval before the other's collapse.

Fred looked away. There was a new tear-blasted woman here today as well, sitting in the corner with nothing but a paper-cupped cappuccino, too new to have figured out the necessity of knitting needles or a book or some other prop to hide behind. When Fred looked back at the screen, the ash cloud was rolling up Broadway, engulfing the runners in sulfur, asbestos, radionuclides, diphenylpropane, hydrocarbons, polychlorinated biphenyls and dibenzodioxins and dibenzofurans, phthalates and pesticides, leaded and unleaded paint, mineral wool and fiberglass, plastic and cellulose, rubber and silicon. Bits of phones and faxes and computers. Bits of floor and ceiling tile, carpets and cubicle walls, file cabinets and files. Bits of Mira's husband. At the office, George had shown up caked in all of it. Fred had walked him down the hall to the bathroom and George had stood before the mirror, a human plaster statue, whispering hoarsely, "Holy fuck," half coughing, half laughing in disbelief. It could have been any of those substances Fred had later spent weeks researching that had done George in. Or it could have been the smoke Fred had blown in his face. Or it could have been the office microwave, or the EM tori of a dozen office computers. Or it could have been the torus of the universe itself, whipping through him with its dark light, its X-rays and gamma rays, retuning George's DNA antennae, switching around As and Ts, Gs and Cs, and powering up his mitochondrial energy coils to churn out mutant copies and spread them through his electron-rich lung-batteries. It could have been men, could have been God, could have been both or neither.

Fred closed his eyes, just for a moment, but all he had to do was blink to be confronted afresh with the image of the EEG net snug around George's head. In one blink, Fred would see in that preemptive, wire-wigged piece of headgear divine mockery, the cruelest prank yet. In the next blink, he'd see divine love, as much need for a God helmet in the world as for a head on top of a head, the real Presence already there, already welcoming George. In still the next blink, Fred would see nothing but the snarled wires themselves, the two accounts canceling each other out, the Presence itself nowhere, not even a memory. And up on the nearer screen, the little wasp was nearing its journey's end, straining to cram itself in through a tiny doorway in the fig's surface, a slot so thin that as the wasp pushed its way through, its abdomen swelled like a balloon and popped.

Then a shot of the fig's illuminated interior, the dying wasp scrambling to plant its eggs and pollinate the fig before the roundworms finished eating it from within.

Then a shot of the dead wasp, upside down on the fig floor.

For the briefest interval, Fred stopped thinking, as though his mind, too, had swelled and popped. The world utterly complete without him.

The old man paged over to the funnies.

The teary woman shredded her empty cup.

On the far screen, the pageant rolled on—Bush straddling the rubble, bearded marines in Afghani hats, video postcards from Osama, Saddam's shoe-slapped statue, "Mission Accomplished," thumbs-up chick on the ass pyramid, exploding Humvees, lines at the airport. Fred was back with his dust-coated brother before the mirror, feeling as though two balled-up swaths of felt had been stuffed down his own lungs. George might have already been one of those sandstone angels. He'd seemed less real than that, even—a 3D avatar, a holograph wavering in the air.

Fred yanked his laptop from the backpack. He brought up an Urth window, and logged in. He appeared in his last location, more or less, not falling or frozen, but just standing on 34th Street, the reconstituted Empire State Building to one side, the flattened studio-set façade of storefronts to the other, the 2D map stretching out east and west. He was still wearing a fire helmet, still too small for his cartoon head. He scrolled around Little Fred and saw he was also still wearing the air mask. It looked uncomfortable, so he took it off, hearing the moment he did the sound—all-too-familiar from all those wargaming man-hours—of a grenade pin being pulled. Remembering the sabotage going on, Fred managed to chuck it away before it exploded, though when it did, it merely splashed, like pool water around some porcine bellyflopper. He brought up the navigation panel, took out his cell phone, typed the CALL GEORGE numbers into the longitude and latitude entry boxes, and teleported downtown. Nothing here. Just the 2D plane, the Empire State Building off in the distance. He was about to give up and close the program when he noticed a sparkling dot on the ground about thirty feet off. As he approached, it grew a few pixels, but no more, until he was practically standing atop it. Only then did its shape become clear: a key.

When Fred picked it up, around him, the street outside his office suddenly appeared. It was crudely rendered, not up to Urth's current standards—part photographic backdrop, part quick-and-dirty animation. Unlike the actual street, several of the buildings here were not quite complete, presenting exposed girders, half-laid brickwork, open holes awaiting windows, through which bare studs could be glimpsed. At work inside, wielding hammers, out on the scaffolding with trowels, and up on the beams with rivet guns were a score of angels, wings protruding from flannel shirts, yellow hard hats atop golden haloes. As Fred watched, a special-effects ripple spread overhead, and as it passed, the workers' tools transformed, a jackhammer blasting one angel off like a rocket, a paintbrush in another angel's hand erasing rather than coloring a wall. Fred slowly turned in place. Another wave passed, and another, turning arc welders to bubble blowers, tape measures to jump ropes, sending a streetlight sack-racing off to freedom. The waves passed every thirty seconds, and seemed to emanate from an upper floor of his office building.

He passed through the front door into a rough facsimile of his lobby, the dimensions and colors more or less right. An elevator opened as he approached. He walked in, experiencing a phantom downward pull as the lighted numbers rose, his anticipation and apprehension rising with them. In the hallway, there were no doors other than the one to his former company. He clicked it open.

He could barely make out an office in the chaos that confronted him. Neon-blue waves rolled across the ceiling, bursting into froth as they hit the wall. Out of this same wall, strange, inverted trees, with leaves suckering to the walls like roots, and roots spreading out like branches grew sideways into the air. As he cleared the maze of foliage, Fred saw that the area where his station should have been was empty, save for cobwebs, mold, and dust. Sam's alcove housed only a tumbleweed, tumbling around in some micro-weather breeze. The window wasn't papered over, and afforded a view Fred had almost forgotten, a view Sam had only wanted to forget, of sunlit buildings to the south and west. The only difference was that where first there had been the towers, and then just the empty air, two new towers stood. They weren't as high, and weren't quite identical, though both were darkish and malevolent looking, and bristling with spires. Orthanc and Barad-dûr, he recognized, from *The Lord of the Rings*. These, too, were still under construction, minute, wingèd forms hammering at the flanks.

He turned and wended his way through a curving passage of gravity-defying desks and chairs and other floating objects—the red couch, the microwave and mini-fridge, the Lego Death Star. The backs of a dozen crammed-together monitors of varying sizes blocked from view George's little area in the back corner. It wasn't until Fred was practically inside it that Angel-George himself was revealed, his back to Fred, cross-legged on a meditation cushion afloat in midair, wings draping to the floor. Above the oxygen tank that was strapped between the avatar's wings could be seen the back of a too-thin neck, and a grayish, hairless little head. An inch above that floated a halo, and atop that a very tall, very strange-looking top hat, of burnished silver, opaquely reflective, with round brims at both bottom and top.

"My Precious! You made it!" George's voice erupted from the speakers of Fred's computer, causing Fred's heart to lurch, and a nurse, passing with a tray heaped with scramble eggs, to turn and stare. As Fred dug through his briefcase for his headphones, the floating cushion spun George about. His eyes were huge now, and his face around them had shrunk, skin withered and drawn, the oxygen line cutting deep below the ridgelines of his cheekbones. Fred managed to get the headphones plugged in before George spoke again.

"I'm betting you've got some questions. Ask away."

George's voice was full of cheer. His avatar's thin lips moved, mimicking speech, then widened into a snaggletoothed smile. At the bottom of the screen, a line of text appeared. Fred's first, pre-scripted question, he gathered:

```
--So is that thing on your head your secret weapon? Or are
you just happy to see me?
```

Fred clicked the line, wondering how much of this was automated, and who, if anyone, was here with him, watching it unfold.

"On Earth it's your hair and nails that keep growing," George said. "Here it's your formal wear." He doffed the enormous hat. "I call it the Discombobjectulator."

Little George mimicked laughter, his bony shoulders hitching. George's recorded delivery was drier, his voice raspy, as it had been toward the end. Fred imagined him in that nearly empty apartment, hunched over his computer, speaking the lines into a headset mic. The clarity with which Fred could see this only thickened the surrounding fog of his incomprehension. Another question, this one more pertinent, appeared for him to ask:

--Who's working with you? What do they want?

"No one, Fred," George said, when Fred clicked the line. "*Kghhhhhh-hhhhhhhhhhhhhhhhhhrk.* It's all me."

From George's hat, one of those rippling waves emanated in all directions—this seemed to be the source. As it passed through the desk, the dozen screens, encased in a webwork of creeping ivy, flashed like lightning. The desk, Fred now noticed, was covered with George's sickroom supplies, his tissue boxes and balms and lotions and lozenges, and a hoard of translucent-orange prescription bottles, all full of pills, except for one, which lay empty, the cap off, tipped on its side.

Fred's inevitable follow-up question had appeared:

--But . . . how is that possible?

"Do I really need to spell it all out?" George snapped, when Fred clicked the line. "Figure it out yourself. Go ahead. I'll give you some time."

Little George's eyes closed, and an undulant stream of *z*s began issuing from his mouth.

It wasn't a complete surprise to Fred. He'd been thinking about all the ways George might have done at least most of this on his own. The emails, the instant messages—with some rented server space and a little coding, he could have programmed them to be sent to Fred at prearranged times. Starting with six months from the day George had taken those pills, expecting to die. For the conversations themselves, he could have constructed a database covering a range of Fred's probable responses—which, if anyone could have predicted, it was George. As for the playtest haunting, this, too, could have been programmed in advance; George could have set his avatar up to appear somewhere near Fred's, a half-hour into Fred's next Urth login, following one of those messages—its motions *had* seemed somewhat random. With a little doing, George even could have preprogrammed an online order for the Swiss Army knife, probably with some failsafe options from backup stores in case the first choice no longer panned out. Using a robocaller program to send the text messages would have been simplicity itself.

So yes, maybe George could have done all this himself. *Would* he have? That one, Fred knew. Of course he would have.

But what about the ongoing sabotage of Urth? And what about Mira?

How could his brother possibly have predicted that? Had George known her? Could they have met in the hospital at some point? But that night at her apartment, Mira hadn't even believed in George's existence. Had she been lying?

Getting overwhelmed, Fred clicked Little George, rousing him from sleep.

"So tell me, Precious," George said. "The woman's initials you gave me. Did I get her name and address right?"

Two possible responses appeared:

```
--You . . . you did!
--Not even close, Houdini.
```

Fred hesitated, then clicked the first, sensing what he was in for.

"Ha! Beautiful!"

George laughed for half a minute.

"I wish I could have seen the look on your face! Never mind! I can picture it!" He laughed again, until he was coughing uncontrollably. More than any time since George's coma began, Fred felt haunted, as if his brother were sitting right across from him, so clearly had George pictured this moment to himself, so fully had he delighted in its possibility.

"I was keystroking you, dude. I planted a keystroke monitor in your laptop, specially focused on Internet searches. I made a little program to sift through your two-word entries, pick out the ones most likely to be names, and cross-check them in various directories. Serves you right for researching all the mystery out of your crushes!"

George laughed again. Dazed, Fred was soon laughing too. George started wheezing.

"So tell me this," George said. "Did it work? Did you get the girl?"

Three responses appeared:

```
--Girl got.
--Girl not got.
--It's complicated.
```

Fred sighed, and clicked the last. George sighed as well.

"Yeah. I guess it usually is."

Another wave pulsed from his giant hat. Fred's fire helmet, along with a nearby stapler, flapped off like a pair of bats. George had really been trying to help him, Fred was thinking. He'd really wanted him to get the girl. He'd spent his last weeks setting up all those interventions in Fred's life, as a joke, yes, but not a cruel one. He'd wanted to keep Fred company. He'd wanted to be Fred's guardian angel. Fred wanted to jump up and pull the coffee-cup woman and the old man and the doctors and nurses to their feet and dance. But then he saw his next question waiting on the screen:

--So why have you brought me here?

When he clicked it, Little George's face morphed, his lips twisting into a feral curl, his nose and brow crumpling around a point between those giant eyes, which narrowed to dagger tips, bright and malign.

"For our revenge," he said.

The hat coiled, then the top of it sprung up in an arc, Slinky-like, the upper rim landing on Little Fred's head. Fred's avatar suddenly hunched, as if under the weight. Fred noticed his neck looked thinner, his ears bigger. Wheeling the view around to observe his face, he found it much like Little George's now. Another Gollum.

Meanwhile, the screens by George's desk flashed, a single phrase lit large over all of them:

OPERATION AVENGING ANGEL

And beneath, a countdown: 2:00. 1:59. 1:58.

"It will take both of us standing here to complete the op," George said. "If you leave, the program will abort. But then you won't get to hear my dying words to you."

Fred could barely breathe. If this was George's revenge, he thought, on him as well as on everyone else, he couldn't imagine a more perfect form.

George's cushion descended a bit, turned, and slotted itself and his pretzeled legs under his desk. He began making typing motions at the keyboard.

"So," he said. "Any last questions?"

Fred's only option appeared:

--I thought this was supposed to be the Kalki Purana. Why
is it all of a sudden Lord of the fucking Rings?

Yes, Fred thought. What the hell. Wasn't he at least supposed to be the demon-slaying avatara in all this? He clicked it. George proceeded to ignore it anyway.

"I've been preparing my weapon of mass discombobjectulation for millennia."

Behind George on the wall, the arms of a clock sped to a blur.

"For years, dude," he said, in a flatter tone, almost an aside, before sliding easily back into character. "Ever since we signed the pact with the Demon Lord."

Another wave shot out of the hat. The screens blinked. Beneath the ivy, lines of code began to stream.

"At first I didn't really know why," George went on. "Maybe as a joke. Maybe as a bargaining chip. An insurance policy. You know, a way to retain some control over the place. At some point, I realized I could do more than just cause some headaches. I could really bring it all down if I wanted. Not just temporarily either."

Little George was smiling again. He sounded not so much amused as amazed.

"Not long after I made this discovery, I embarked on a journey. To the Evil One's lofty lair. I wanted to strike a deal. They could go on building Hell, for all I cared. All I wanted was to spin off a little piece, for Heaven."

One minute left. The crazy, double-bottomed hat above them began to glow and fizz with particle effects.

"I thought my secret weapon would make me feel more powerful," George said. "Like a bonafide god. Not just some code monkey. Like if things weren't going my way I could just set it off. Like then they would talk to me." He sighed. The sigh turned into a cough. The sound cut out for a moment. Then his voice resumed, his tone as even as before. "But I couldn't. I just couldn't do it. Ideals or cowardice, I don't know. I went around begging for a while. Then I just left."

Another ripple. The clock flipped and flopped in the air, like a pancake off a griddle, landing on the wall again.

"Later that night," George said, "I ascended a second summit, and sat under the Pretaloka moonlight. I don't know what I was thinking while I was climbing up there. Let's say I was thinking about the Demon Lord. His dark armor. His jet-steel wings. And about the Angel Inceptor, with his champagne halo of lore. Let's say that's what I was thinking, why not. I was pretty drunk, to be honest. But I'll never forget what I saw when I got to the top."

The counter hit 0:30. Fred was given a chance to speak.

--Let me guess. A moonlit stream of your own vomit?

Snidely. Not at all the way he wanted to speak. He didn't want to be George's antagonist, or George to be his. He didn't want to be written into this kind of story at all.

"I saw everything," George said quietly. "The whole crazy design. All the way down, all the way up. Fire worlds full of angels believing they're tortured, roasting souls. Cloud worlds full of angels dumb and dangerous enough to believe they're angels."

0:10. Fred thought of Sam, Sam's upcoming demo, his condo and car and dates with suntanned believers. Fred told himself he'd jump away at the last second. George was speaking again, his voice contemplative, almost a whisper.

"But they're all Pretalokas, every last one of them. Limbos are all we ever build. So tell me, Precious, what's there even for a hero to do?"

Fred wanted his avatar to move. He wanted himself to make it move. But he couldn't move a finger.

"Sometimes," George was saying, "I think that's all this world ever wanted to say to me. . . ."

0:00. The screens began to strobe.

". . . Hey, hero. The cancer is you."

Does Fred know he's dreaming? Does he know something here isn't quite possible? Part of him might, but the rest is too happy to care. Because they're heading in again, Fred and George and Sam, just like the first time all those years ago: across the sunlit plaza, around the fountain and its segmented bronze sphere, through the revolving door, and into the mezzanine, with its circling balcony and floor-through, minaretted windows. Then down the escalator to the elevator banks, and up, and up, and up. Every bit as nervous and excited as the first time, they're ushered into the conference room where they first raised money for Urth. The same view: the other tower to the northwest, and to the north and east, almost the whole city, including, not too far off, the little brown building that houses their office. Facing them at the table sits their angel investor, with his ruddy, cherub smile, flanked by his angel attendants. No wings, no haloes, just suits and skirtsuits. But angels nonetheless, watches and earrings and glasses dancing with unearthly light.

The brothers are back here with a pitch for another company, a new serious game they think can seriously save the world, something about players racing to update the operating systems, of themselves, of the world, before both crash forever. Sam mans the projector, in a white tuxedo and white top hat. Fred and George are in their tuxes, too. And Fred is in the sparkly gold motorcycle helmet. And George is in the big, bulbous space helmet. And in their hands are laser pointers. And on the projection screen float twin diagrams of glistening clusters and strands warped into whorls. Identical to the last detail. The first labeled "me." The second: "ME."

"The mind," Fred says, pointing to the first.

"The MEC," George says, pointing to the second.

They butt helmets, to the angels' guffaws.

Fred woke up with his head on the cafeteria table, the sleeping laptop before him. With George's parting words, Urth had scrambled into a soup of color, then vanished, interface and all, only the desktop remaining. Fred's attempts to log back on had been fruitless. He tried again—still blocked. When Armation started tracking down the people online at the time of the metaverse's collapse, they'd find Fred's username. It was not unlikely, he thought, given his history with them, that they'd blame the entire assault on him. Who would believe the true culprit had been a man in a coma for the last seven months? And how would Fred explain to them, and worse, to Sam, that he'd had the chance to stop it? George, no doubt, had foreseen all this. George's secret coconspirator was none other than Fred.

Fred had slipped out of consciousness the moment he'd laid down his head, his mind simply refusing to process an emotion which, upon opening his eyes, upon cutting through the cruelly happy fog of that dream, upon examining his clenched fists, he finally understood to be hatred. He wanted to go up to his room and slap George awake, just so he could punch his tracheostomy until he gagged and died.

I hate you, he told Inner George. The evil shit didn't answer him. It was hard to remember the last time he had. He was hiding from Fred, thought Fred, along with that two-faced Presence, which had now become an Absence, a suction at the bottom of things.

Fred himself was almost gagging. The air was thick with the smell of lunch food—he must have been out cold for hours—and wafting, it seemed to him, in strange gusts. Every table was now full, white coats or haggard patients and their families. The clamor of voices and dishes went loud and faint. No one else noticed the wind in the room, even as it whistled and eddied around them. No one else was choking, or blinking with stung eyes. No one noticed themselves disappearing in its bitter billows.

Flushed and unsteady and just plain sick of the place, Fred slid his computer back into the camping pack and made his way down the hall and out into the lobby.

"Brownie-Anne," a voice rang out.

"No. Brew-nian," said another.

Fred's heart sledgehammered. The two men—one compact in an olive blazer, with a gray skullcap of hair; the other bigger in a black windbreaker, with hair the color of french fry oil—were standing at the front desk, their backs to him.

Almost had me, Fred thought, addressing not the men but George, wherever the bastard was hiding. George, to whom he'd sacrificed everything. Everything but whatever last scrap of freedom Fred could now steal for himself. There was a magic show he needed to perform. And there was his date tonight, with the woman he loved. Not exactly a date, granted—a "debriefing," she'd called it. Even so.

He slipped out the revolving door and past a parked maroon Impala with minimalist hubcaps—a car that shouted *police* so loud it couldn't justly be called unmarked. The churning cloud was out here as well, nothing Fred could see, exactly, just an acid shimmer, a slow leach of some vital substance from everyone and everything. And a physical wind to match, the sky a blustery gray. He changed in the van, paid the garage fee with most of his remaining twenty-five dollars, the attendant blinking, not from the cloud but from the brightness of Fred's tux. Fred had over an hour to kill before the show. He cut north and west, along a route designed to hit as much traffic as possible.

As he began passing through Times Square, the first raindrop struck his windshield, and the woozy gusts seemed almost like they might lift him from his seat. Hating him no less intensely, Fred was asking George if he remembered how the two of them used to get taken along on Vartan's daily rounds around the square. The first stop had typically been an audition. Fred and George would sit in a waiting room with a bunch of men dressed like Vartan—the entire city might have been composed of such men—silently moving their lips as though in prayer. Next, to Actors' Equity, where they'd sit in the lobby, in molded plastic chairs too high for their sneakers to touch the linoleum, as Vartan scanned the bulletin boards or filled out paperwork. Then it was usually off to the Actors Studio or the Ensemble Studio Theatre to pick up some script, and after that it was time for the marathon lunch session at the Edison Hotel coffee shop, the actors griping about the day's slim pickings—a role as a murdered corpse in a photograph on a detective's desk ("They told me, 'Turn to the side and look dead'"), or as a throttled stool pigeon, having to use their own hands to choke themselves while reading out the lines. The three of them would crisscross the square repeatedly in the course of these errands, giving Fred and George the chance to view it again and again from every angle as they were pulled along in their father's grip. Fred asked George if he could recall a Camel cigarette sign featuring a man in a captain's hat, whose eerily effeminate, perfectly round mouth blew steady puffs of smoke; a giant green bottle of something called Champale pouring endlessly into a waiting glass, like those trick pitchers they used in their magic shows; those red neon signs for Live Nude Girls and those vaguely sinister XXXs. Fred's primary feeling, traversing the square, had been one of knowing himself a child in a world for adults—a gritty, grimy, gladiatorial arena, where men like their dad battled for a rarefied niche up on those lighted marquees among the booze and cigarette ads, most perishing in the attempt on the canyon floor.

Usually Fred had trouble remembering things like this, but at the moment, he could see it as clearly as if it were superimposed on what was here in front of him three decades later: Toddlers squealing their delight atop the shoulders of camera-toting dads. Planet Hollywood proudly wheelchair accessible, a smiling hostess holding open the door for a woman with a bent spine in a sporty red mobility scooter, its model name—"Celebrity"—glistening in suave silver letters. Flesh aplenty but nary an X amid the dreaming screens, the megaplexes, the shopping centers, the Madame Tussauds wax museum and laser-tag arcades and Disney and World Wrestling Federation flagship stores. The existential poles had been switched, and Fred was now an adult in a land for children, and he didn't know what it meant.

What do you *think it means, George, you cockroach?*

No answer.

And somehow, in this land for children, it wasn't out of place that outside the Army recruiting center, dress-uniformed soldiers were letting passing families sight through a bipod-mounted machine gun.

Rain spattered the windshield in gobs by the time Fred was piloting the magic van through the Upper West Side. The Absence was getting stronger, the unreal wind one moment too thick to breathe, the next too thin, as he pulled into the garage of the red-brick West End Towers and hand-trucked the magic crate to the elevators. A bit like the Zeckendorf, he remarked to George, though the coward was still hiding from him. If he could only go back in time, Fred thought, and kill George as he slept in their bunkbed. Fred's stomach lifted as the elevator slowed. He was shown into a penthouse entertainment room—cream-colored walls, a cream couch and stuffed chairs, a cream throw rug, and a corner view of near-horizontal rain battering the complex's other red tower and sweeping across the city below.

The children were just now arriving from school, one or two minded by mothers but most by immigrant caretakers. The adults gathered in the open kitchen area, where the hostess, a slender blonde, late forties, with a regal Roman nose and soft blue eyes, was charting the children's food allergies on a refrigerator whiteboard as her Latina cook looked on. The little ones, meanwhile, set to playing with their handheld games and plasma-screen videogames, their trading cards and action figures and various other toys pulled from pockets and trunks and shelves; one girl with rectilinear bangs blowing balloons, another in pigtails competing with bubblegum as bright and pink as her bubble cheeks. Fred set up in the midst of them, remarking to George, nowhere to be seen, how odd a thing it was to see so much happiness in a world on the brink; then telling him to fuck off, and die more painfully next time.

Now the mother was ushering two little forms toward Fred, the cloud-wind picking up around the pair, making them hard to see at first. Fred watched the mother speaking to him. He saw her thin lips purse and then spread across her teeth, her tongue touch the roof of her mouth, her lips spread wider still. Did he hear the word or just read it in those motions?

twins

He made them out, just then. A boy and a girl. Big, rosy slabs of cheek boxing their smiles, messy brown hair, and that was about all he saw of them before the wind in his eyes was making everything blurry and he had to look away.

Sly of our old dad, eh George? Twins. For your long-lost solo act.

That snake wasn't answering. The wind was closing in, buffeting Fred from all directions. He started the show, tearing the plastic wrap from the box, and pulling out the MagicCo wand. There was barely even a handle, so pocked and nozzled and festooned it was with lenses and radar-like dishes and fan-blade protrusions. Vartan had succeeded in making it look comical. But, whether intentionally, or whether it was just Vartan being Vartan, the thing was also disturbing, monstrously elaborate, especially when Fred turned on the switch and the lights began to flash and the dishes and blades began to whirl. It could have been from these children's dystopian future, he quipped to George, wishing he'd taken the sensible precaution of umbillically throttling him in the womb. It could have been the superbeing, the one that as adults this audience of his would labor to create, the one they'd hope would be a god to save them from the collective decisions of their forebears but would only be some panoptical corporation with an ego—the Big Inc. And what was the deal with this wind, he was asking his AWOL brother, which seemed to be blowing around inside him now. *And what did you mean, what did you fucking mean, that the cancer was you?*

Fred found the cassette tape Vartan had told him would be there, the bubble-cheeked bubble children staring as he held it aloft, finding the obsolesced thing every bit as silly and baroque as the wand. The storm was all around. He wasn't sure where he himself ended and it began. In the periphery of his vision, as he turned, he could see the cloud-wind encircling the twins in the front row, their heads leaned into each other, gooey smiles on their faces; could see it levitating them an inch or two off the rug. He slotted the cassette into the boombox, worrying, at first, that the deck had finally busted—nothing but squeaks and static. Then the slide whistles kicked in, redoubling the wind and noise in his head, and the room was spinning, and his father hadn't mentioned it, hadn't thought to mention who the salesman was. But Fred should have guessed.

"Congratulations, Mmmmmmm-agician, on your purchase of the all-new, de-luxe Mmmmmmm-agicCo wand . . ."

Adenoidal, bright and hammy. Fred was rising up over the lip of the winding storm, staring down the void within.

". . . the wand that makes magic so easy you'll be wowing crowds in no time!"

His twin was gone. Not in hiding. Just gone. That voice on the tape belonged to no one at all.

"Let's get you started with a few easy card tricks."

And another voice, too, belonged to no one. Another voice in his head. Talking to an imaginary twin. Talking to phantom future listeners, even as it understood that this story would never be told. That there would be no one to tell it. That an unreal world wasn't even the beginning. Because there was no one in this white tuxedo. No one waving this ludicrous wand. No one teetering over these checkered shoes, clutching this ruffled shirt, vomiting, to the children's delight, into this bright white top hat.

Eight PM found Fred waiting under the Arch, getting rained on, the park empty, the sky already dark. Somehow, he'd gotten through the magic show without further incident. The skit George had designed twenty-three years ago had turned out to be so good that even an existential freakout couldn't ruin it. By the time it was over, the strange sensations had passed—the wind, the wooziness, that sudden, absolute conviction of his own nonexistence. Fred had then packed up the van and driven off into the rain again, and taken the small risk of parking it back in the hospital lot. Then he'd texted Vartan the van's location; left the birthday party check in a cupholder; and on the way out of the garage, to keep the police from tracing his whereabouts, dropped his phone in the trash. It wasn't until he was on the subway, spending the last two dollars on his transit card, that he took in the staring eyes around him and realized he'd forgotten to change out of the tux.

It was soaked now, the summer storm showing no signs of abating, and Mira was nowhere in sight. A police cruiser approached, headlights right on Fred as it breasted the rain down Fifth Avenue. He tried to look inconspicuous. If an APB had by now gone out for a Caucasian male in a white tuxedo, and a white cape, and checkered shoes, and a bright blue camping pack, perhaps, he thought, based on his insouciant lean against the monument, they'd decide he didn't quite fit the bill.

The lightbar popped on, grill lights flashing in tandem. The squad car banked, then headed up Washington Place.

It wasn't until 8:15 that he began to consider the possibility that Mira had stood him up. It wasn't until 8:30 that he began to admit it.

He pictured her father opening his cabinet doors, glancing at the bottom shelf. Doing a double take.

Probably they'd called the cops on him too, by now. Probably she'd forgotten all about the plan to meet him, or simply assumed there'd be no way in hell he himself would be showing up.

He had no other place to go, no other purpose left to him. He waited another ten minutes, then trudged in his too-tight jacket, soaked and slipping pants, and water-filled shoes up the block. On the off chance Mira, or her father, or even the police, might be in there, he stepped out of the rain and into the cramped lobby of the Neural Science Building. The droop-faced security guard screwed his eyes at Fred's approach. Fred wondered what he'd done to a security guard in a previous life that the lot of them should be so inclined against him.

"Mira Egghart?" the guard said, with a lift of his thin-man jowls.

He must have recognized Fred from last night. Fred's heart gave a single thump. He nodded.

"She's up there. Didn't say anything about visitors tonight."

"I have an appointment," Fred said, not quite daring to hope.

The guard looked back and forth from Fred's face to his attire a few times. "All right."

He went back to his newspaper. Fred squish-shoed to the elevator.

The reception area of the suite was dark. A light came from down the hall. Mira's office door was open a crack. The floor lamp was lit. He went over and knocked.

"Mira?"

Within, the recliner creaked for a second.

He eased the door open. She was in the recliner, not reclined, but balled up, her blue-jeaned knees drawn up against an oversized blue sweatshirt. Her head was leaned back, her eyes shut in that too-tight way. The skin beneath them was faintly purple. He was about to tell her he had the backup helmet system with him, safe and sound, but she spoke first:

"I had to cancel our appointment." Her voice was weary, her eyes still closed. "Don't you check your messages?"

He sat down in her task chair. "Misplaced my phone."

Under the lamplight, it looked like she'd been sweating. Her forehead and temples faintly glistened. But the rest of her looked dry. It occurred to Fred he'd seen the light on down the hall. Down toward the helmet room.

"Is that gel? On your head?" he asked.

Mira put her face in her hands.

"You tried it?"

She didn't answer. Probably, she was just waiting for him to go away.

"Who was monitoring your vital signs?"

"No one," she muttered, wiping at the gel with a thumb. "I just wanted a record."

Fred wanted to reprimand her, to tell her he would have helped, if she'd only asked. But she didn't seem in the mood for lectures.

"Which session did you try?" he asked. But as soon as the question was out of his mouth, he knew. "The one you asked me about yesterday? The near-death experience?"

Her silence told him he was right. She'd chosen that session over the one with the divine Presence itself. He didn't have to ask which angel she'd been hoping to see. In front of her face, her hands balled into fists. He thought she was about to scream. But then she was pressing her knuckles into her forehead, fighting her lips. They widened, unable to close. Then began to shudder. Then she was heaving.

"Mira, what happened? What did you see?"

She shook her head violently, gasping between sobs. He wheeled closer.

"Did you see . . . him?"

Her eyes opened, reddened and wild.

"I saw you! Why the *fuck* would I see you?"

She swiped the backs of her hands over her eyes, furious even at her tears. As she took deep breaths, he placed a hand on her shoulder, until she stilled, and stared at it there.

"I don't understand, Mira."

"It was just like this," she said. "Except everything was bright. You were right in front of me. Your hand on my shoulder. You said Lionel was fine. That you saw him. That he sent his love. You said I needed to go back." Her voice went high and hoarse. "I can't even hallucinate him anymore. I can't even picture his fucking face. All I can see is . . . *you.*"

Her lower lip protruded, ejecting this final word like a sip of sour milk.

"What are you looking at me like that for?" she said.

Then her eyes wandered downward.

"Jesus. What the fuck is up with that outfit? You look like God in some Hollywood feel-good movie."

"My dad . . ." He looked away, tugging off the idiotic soaked bowtie and pocketing it. "I do magic shows, sometimes."

It took her a moment to process this.

"Really?" she asked, reality stitching itself together again.

"Moving right along," he mumbled. But when he looked back at her, she was still studying him, a trace of amusement creeping onto her flushed, tear-smeared face.

"*What?*" he said.

"I used to love magic shows when I was a kid."

"I pity you."

"What's that supposed to mean?"

"I don't know. Forget it."

They sat in silence. She sniffled.

"Do a trick," she said.

"What?"

"You heard me."

"I don't have any on me."

"Oh."

Mira wiped her eyes and nose with her overlong sleeve. Fred thought of the school photo of her on that wall of pictures: a round-faced five year-old, the death of the blond boy in the next frame, and every other disappointment large and small, as yet unimagined.

"Looks like you're out of luck. No tricks. Just this thing." He took a matchbook-sized aspirin case out of his jacket pocket and gave it a shake. "Only one aspirin left, at that." He put a hand to the side of his head. "Man, those kids gave me a headache. I guess I'll have to make this one tablet last." Opening the case into his palm, he revealed an aspirin the size of a hockey puck.

"How'd you do that?"

"Do what?" He was feeling around in his pockets again, bringing out a bubble-blowing kit. "Oh well. Not a trick. But maybe it'll keep you entertained." He handed it to her, still feeling around.

Cautiously, as though expecting snakes to pop out of it, she unscrewed the top, looked in, took out the plastic loop, and, pursing her lips, blew a stream of bubbles.

He was rifling through his pockets with one hand, swatting distract-edly at the bubbles with the other, giving them to her to hold onto—balls of transparent plastic—while the search continued.

He pretended to sneeze, and produced just in time a silk handkerchief from nowhere.

He gazed forlornly at his credit card, wondering aloud if there was any credit left on it. And sighed when, as if in response, it began floating weightless over his palm.

Mira beamed.

Voicing relief, he at last produced a pack of cards. Fanning them out, he told her to pick one. She reached, but the one she was about to pluck flew from the deck and around his body.

He caught the card, thrust it back among the others.

"Oh, never mind," he mumbled, stuffing the deck away. "Sorry. Nothing's working today."

"No?" She laughed. "Not a single trick up those sleeves, then?"

Fred allowed himself to wonder if maybe they'd have time for a dinner and a movie before his arrest. If maybe she'd visit him in prison.

"Why don't you tell me about what's up *that* sleeve." He gestured at her forearm. For a while, she and Fred both regarded it.

"I didn't want to get out of bed, his last morning on Earth," she said. "I'd been sleeping late, as usual, like the sloth that I am. Before he left for work, he tried to pull me out." She lifted her arm to demonstrate, her hand locking around the air. "I tried to pull him back down. We both gave up."

She traced with her chewed fingernail a sewn-up rip in the cuff of the sweatshirt.

"For the next few weeks," she said, "I kept imagining I still felt his grip. Once, I even dreamt it. I was out on the street at night, and everything was rising up, the whole city coming apart. And there he was, pulling my arm, and I was floating too. We got up into space and then I woke up." Her smile faded. "I kept hoping the dream would continue. That I'd find out where we were going, where the city was going. It felt unfinished."

She began turning a white-gold band on her right ring finger around and around. She must have switched it to her right hand after losing Lionel, Fred thought.

"I told you something about lucid dreaming? It was something I'd read about in school. I started reading more. I taught myself how. It's not difficult, when you're driven to learn it. And then I dreamt about him all the time. I took us up to space again. We watched the city remake itself up there and fly away. Then we started going to other planets. He's a sci-fi buff. I thought he'd like that." She was smiling again. "We went to a planet with blue trees, a planet with moons on top of moons. They were so vivid. I found it was easier in the daytime. At night I couldn't control things as well. They could turn into nightmares. Things could happen to him. So I got a bartending job. And I slept in the day. I'd pretty much dropped out of school by then, anyway."

Her gaze wandered to the snow globe on the shelf, its plastic skyscrapers poking out of the murky, half-evaporated water within.

"At some point we got tired of schlepping around the galaxy, or I did, and we found the city again. It was off at the edge of the universe. It had put itself back the way it was, and built a bubble around itself. No people, no planet, just the city, everything safe and perfect. That's where we started spending our time. Walking through the streets, hanging out in bars, parks, wherever. But more and more, we just stayed in our apartment." A small, snorting laugh escaped her. "We cleaned the bathroom. We made the place so clean. And then I'd wake up to the usual wreck."

She wrapped her arms around her shins.

"Then I started to forget his face. I'd see him for a second, but the next second I'd be alone. Or I'd see a body but no face. Then I couldn't dream him at all. I don't sleep much this time of year."

Unfolding herself, Mira stretched her legs to the floor. For the first time, Fred could read the logo on her sweatshirt:

Gore ★ 2000
Lieberman

"Maybe I do need to rest, though," she decided.

"That sounds like a good idea."

She nodded. With a few languid blinks, her eyelids had drifted down. Fred watched her for a minute. There were two questions he'd been wanting to ask her all day. He was about to speak when her eyes popped open again.

"Oh," she whispered, "I get it."

"Get what?"

"What that look of yours meant. When I told you I saw you in my session."

Her own look was full of marvel. He waited, not saying anything. He wanted her to be the one to say it.

"You thought it was your brother! You thought it was George, didn't you?"

He felt his face freeze. He'd been about to break out in a smile.

A spooked little laugh escaped her. "Do you really think it could have been?"

Fred followed her gaze to the low ceiling tiles. When his eyes came down, hers were waiting. He forced that smile the rest of the way. The answer she wanted.

She smiled too, more genuinely than he did.

"Wow," she said. "*Wow.*"

For a while, she looked thoughtful. Then, soon, sleepy again. Her eyes, once more, began to flutter.

"Hey, Mira."

"Uh-huh?" she murmured.

As for his first question, regarding dinner and a movie, he didn't bother. If she couldn't tell why else she might have seen his face rather than Lionel's, Fred knew her answer already.

"That reject session. *Vacuus.*" He took the folded blanket from a shelf above the nightlight and laid it over her. "What did that one do?"

"Don't really remember." A dreamy wave of her fingers. "Whole grab bag, I think. Direct brainstem interference. Mirror neuron patterning. GABA activation. Fusiform gyrus inhibition. Mu receptor stimulation."

"What receptor?"

"Mu?" Her eyes were closed now. "Opioid receptor. It's a Greek letter."

That Absence was back, with its unreal wind, an almost audible hiss, like air from an airlock.

"Oh," he said.

"Could you turn off the light?"

She rolled to one side, turning her back to him. For now, and, he assumed, for good.

After the onset of George's coma, Fred had also read an article about how the conscious mind only becomes aware of its decisions a fraction of a second after they're made. And one about how the sensation of a thinker or doer was a peculiarly organized feedback loop. And personal accounts from mystics of every tradition of having sailed over selfhood's warped reflection like moons over moonlit puddles. On at least one issue, then, the actual investigators in the realms of spirituality and science seemed to be in lockstep agreement: the self is a conditioned reflex; a needy, greedy concatenation of impulses; a position, ultimately, of ignorance.

He shut Mira's door gently behind him, and sat at the bare metal desk in the suite's reception area. Picking them out from among the few remaining coins in his pocket, he laid out the five numbered elevator buttons from the Armation headquarters in a column, 1 at the bottom, 5 at the top. He studied them for a while, like a gypsy reading tea leaves, then opened the camping pack and regarded the solenoids and wires peeking out from the nest of the sleeping bag. In the last month, he'd gone from seeing God as a dream, to seeing the world as a dream, to glimpsing that he himself might be the dream. It seemed he'd failed as an avatara, failed to set anything right. But one battle remained, a taunt from the Vortex, an invitation to dive down its very center.

Vacuus.

Her father had said it was going to eat his soul . . . .

Maybe the plan was insanity. Maybe, as well, Fred thought, he'd never been about getting real. Maybe all his problems in life had stemmed only from an idealism even more hopeless than George's—for if it was crazy to have faith in faith, how much crazier to have faith in doubt? And maybe it was the case that he'd sacrificed everything he'd had to the ghost of George, and that he was about to sacrifice everything he was to this other ghost of Truth.

But maybe not. Maybe, from the darkness of the magic hat, Truth itself—pure, shining, unobscured by this flailing virtual self—was just waiting to be pulled into the open.

In which case, this was it. Time to get real, for real. Or at least, as Manny would say, not *not*.

Though just in case there was an easier route to enlightenment, Fred took out his laptop, plugged into a coiled Ethernet cable by the desk, and went to kenshopictures.com. A new link blazed in the center of the page:

"HOLE IN NONE"
A NEW FILM BY MANFRED KENT IN THE ZEN DANISH STYLE
WATCH IT NOW!!!

Fred put on his headphones.

The film began with Fred in the too-short motorcycle jacket and a rumpled shirt and tie, riding the brightly lit peoplemover in the Universal Studios theme park.

"Who would watch it?" Fred asked the camera, bleary eyes blinking. He vaguely remembered having said this.

An extended tit-and-ass montage ensued, ending with the synchronized jounce of zoomed-in boobs at Margaritaville.

Next, he was seeing himself staggering through a garden at night, now wearing a suit that wasn't his. It was George's suit. It was George's haircut, too, if wildly mussed.

It was George. From not too long ago. Last summer, Fred thought. George's final trip to Florida, just after his diagnosis. This must have been the night out with Manny, after George hadn't been able to go through with his blackmail plan. George stopped, swaying in place. He, too, was drunk. The camera panned through the garden toward what he was looking at: a sculpture of an angel.

Fred again. In the space helmet, in a shaky pool of portable camera light, climbing a chainlink fence. Watching this, Fred's stomach fashioned a noose from his esophagus and kicked out the diaphragm beneath. Manfred had been with him. And here was the incriminating evidence, freely downloadable to all the world.

George again. The camera was high up, almost directly above him, this time. George deliberated, then reached out and gripped the slope before him, thick with weird shrubs. He began climbing. Off to his left, as the camera swung and righted itself, a sheer stone cliff face, or maybe a wall.

Back to Fred. They were inside now, Fred brandishing the club with both hands, the pigmy city all around.

To George, halfway up the steep slope, starting to wheeze, a wild grimace on his face. His hand slipped and he almost slid back into the darkness. Offscreen, Manfred's gruff, close-miked laugh.

"Come on, kid," Manny bellowed.

"I told you I have cancer, you old fuck," George shouted, slurring the words.

To Fred, on a green. He wound up, nearly toppled from the space helmet's weight, righted himself, swung. The camera tracked the ball as it rolled up and down the arc of the Brooklyn Bridge, plunking into the hole at City Hall.

To George, nearly at the top of the slope. The camera pulled back for a long shot of the shadowy scenery behind him: a crenellated wall, a Roman temple, pale in the darkness.

To Fred. A new challenge. He swung. The ball rolled up the spiral of the Guggenheim Museum, off the roof, and plummeted to Fifth Avenue straight down an open manhole.

George, one hand over the edge. The other. Clambering up and standing. Atop the mount. The gardens and pools and walking paths of the Holy Land spread out below. Off beyond the high wall, an empty parking lot aglow under sodium lights, cars whizzing by on I-4. And George peering out at it all. Stunned by the sight, his head, his whole upper body tilting to the side.

This must have been that moment, Fred thought. The second summit. Infinite Pretalokas. No heaven to be found.

But a few seconds later, George grinned. Then he was laughing, a loud, open laugh, up at the night. It had been years since Fred had seen him so happy. What was he thinking? What was he seeing? How could seeing nothing but limbos make him happy?

Could this also be, Fred wondered, when George's plan began taking shape? The messages? The sabotage? The haunting of all of them after he was gone?

But his laugh seemed too joyous for revenge, too free.

Why was George free? Fred didn't understand. He didn't get any of this.

Now a long shot, from under the arm of the Statue of Liberty, of Fred, a bulbous-headed monster, facing the Towers down.

"Go on," Manny shouts, close by. "You're swinging nothing but aces, baby!"

The shot closes in. Fred's helmet swivels to face the ball. Swivels to the Towers again. The club goes up. Stays up. He's marching down the green.

"Oh fuck," Manny says.

Fred spins full circle, bright club wheeling. New York goes kaleidoscopic as Manny starts to run.

You can relax all on your own by now. It's gotten so easy you barely need me here, barely need me to tell you anything. All you have to hear is

five

and

the gates are open. Pretty cool, huh? All you have to hear is

four

and here

come those soothing waves of relaxation rolling through you. Go ahead. Splash. Feel them everywhere at once. Torso! Hips! Arms and legs! Neck and head! All I have to say is

three

and—splash—through your fingers

and toes, through the tips of your hair, even, your whole body sighing with the pleasure of it. All I have to say is

two

and—splash—waves

soaking your brain, like water into a sponge, your mind so relaxed that even this picture of your brain like a sponge is going soft at the edges now. Going gentle and fuzzy and dark. So that at the count of

one

you're just

floating in dark, dark space. City gone. People gone. Just the Earth and the moon, the sun and the stars, and you. Just you and the universe. Maybe you never thought you could be so alone. Yet here you are, so relaxed, and everything is fine. And now you're going to do something more amazing still. It's time to let the universe go.

Zoom. Earth going one way. Sun another. Off goes the moon. The zillion stars, like a zillion little candles. Blow them out.

Nothing to grasp. And nothing to do.

No time. No space. So where, so when, are you?

5

september 2006

S	M	T	W	T	F	S
27	28	29	30	31	1	2
3	4	5	6	7	8	9
10	11					

From Mira's lab that Wednesday night, Fred returned to his former office. The detectives weren't waiting for him, but even if they never showed up here, the hedge fund would be breaking down the walls over the weekend. He couldn't go back to his parents' apartment, or to the hospital. He'd be picked up from either sooner or later, and in any case he needed seclusion.

So he took George's pack and bedroll down to the boiler room.

Dried, orange-brown soup still streaked the floor. Not a regular stop on the janitor's rounds. It seemed possible that no one would come in all summer—maybe not even until mid-fall, to turn on the furnace. In three trips, using the freight elevator and a dolly from the trash room, he moved the mini-fridge, the microwave, the couch cushions, and the cantaloupe box, which he'd filled with Sam's remaining canned goods and the shower hose.

The only remaining task was to put the Prayerizer, still humming away in his corner of the space, out of its misery. He couldn't bear to do this without hooking it up to his laptop and checking its prayer list one last time.

There were over five hundred of them. Prayers to have the world healed and prayers to have it done away with in holy ways. Prayers for marriages to be mended, loves requited. Prayers for cancer remissions, for peaceful passings. A prayer for a perfect 1600 on the SAT of one Ken Hwang. More prayers for Fred's death. And all the way at the bottom, the very first: Fred's plea to Whomsoever might be listening to for fuck's sake DO something. All told, the supercomputer had cycled through these REM statements over 303 trillion times.

He yanked the plug, feeling—ridiculously, he knew—like he was cutting throats in church. Within its metal carapace, the internal fans slowed to a stop. He walked out, then turned. The overgrown thing seemed so forlorn in the empty office that he couldn't close the door on it.

So he took the Prayerizer with him. Using the screwdrivers in his Swiss Army knife, he spent the next hours breaking it down into its movable pieces, carting them down to the boiler room, and reassembling them. It only just fit in the cramped space, its backside pressed at an angle against the boiler, its left rear corner wedged between two water heaters, its right rear corner mashing the pipes along the cobwebbed cinderblock wall. There was no Internet connection down here, but it could keep reciting what prayers it knew.

He realized there wasn't enough floor space left for the sleeping bag. He set the microwave on the mini-fridge next to the mainframe's floor fan, used them as stairs, and unrolled the bag atop the giant computer. What with the water heaters and the fifteen billion prayers per minute, it was hot in the two feet of airspace at the top of the room, but the basement was otherwise cool, and by wedging Sam's desk fan into the pipes that ran along the ceiling directly overhead, Fred kept the air circulating well enough. For a while, he lay there on his side, testing out the berth, staring into the room's single bare bulb a few feet off. Before long, he became conscious of a slow tapping sound, and a spreading heat on his leg. Hot water was dripping from one of the insulated pipes above him. He tied Sam's towel around the leak.

At last, it was time to set up the God helmet. The circular blue tops of the two water heaters in the corner by Fred's head served as his night tables. He placed the helmet itself on a red plush end cushion atop one of the heaters, and the amplifier box and his laptop on a second cushion atop the other. The power cords from the laptop and amplifier and Sam's desk fan ran in a taut, ugly tangle to a surge protector perched on a pipe halfway down the wall, into which the fridge and microwave and floor fan were also plugged. The surge protector's own plug ran to an extension cord, which in turn snaked across the floor to the room's only socket in the corner by the door.

It was early Thursday morning by the time everything was set up. Lying on his back, Fred reached over and brought the laptop on top of him, reached over again and switched on the amplifier. Then took hold of the space helmet, and put it on.

.The dusty pipes.

The water-stained cinderblocks.

Breath clouding the faceplate.

His reflected eyes.

Straining to lift his head, making out the laptop's screen.

Cursoring to the *vacuus* file.

Taking a breath.

Double-clicking . . .

The deep-space suction is almost immediate.

Everything inside is pressed to the surface. Until there's no interior at all. Only the flesh, only the skin. Then not even that, from all body to no body. Nothing but the sight of those fearful, reflected eyes. And a horrible pressure. And, clutching the airlock door, fighting the suction and wind, a single, screaming thought: to pull the cable from the laptop and end this.

But who's here to hear the thought?

Who's here to think it?

The *vacuus* session was repeated several times that day, and several more in the three days following. In between, there was eating, and sleeping, and post-working-hours trips to the bathroom, and a lot of sitting on the floor, on a couple of staggered cushions, lotus-legged, staring at the wall. The sessions themselves shook up all the contents and popped the cap. The sitting allowed what remained to slowly fizz and dissipate.

From Freddom to Freedom. The thought bubbled up, and floated off.

The surface thoughts were the first layer to come free. They didn't disperse altogether, but increasingly, in the minutes following the sessions, they became discontinuous enough to allow for a kind of sliding beneath them, and beneath them lay the first, euphoric glimpses of clarity. Looking around, the cluttered little room could be seen anew, from the moist grime along the sides of the green metal doorframe to the orange and green half-cantaloupe printed on the cardboard box. It was all a kind of fantastic, habitable artwork, so luscious that memories of those swank Zerkendorf apartments seemed sterile in comparison. Though it seemed what mattered wasn't the environment at all, per se, so much as the depth to which it could be dwelt in, moment by moment. Concepts of failure, poverty, squalor, could be watched like gray weather until the sky cleared once more. Concepts of success, security, luxury— these, too, were pale ghosts compared to the specific, brimming spoon- fuls of minestrone soup; the playful burble of pissing into a two-liter Coke bottle salvaged from the trash room; even the vivid aches and shooting pains of folded legs in meditation.

Once the euphoria passed, as it did on the second day, what came up was the missing of it, the desire to get it back. This desire alone was all it took for Freddom to start reclaiming its ground. Within minutes, there Fred was again, in that selfhood built of lack. Wanting happiness. Wanting clarity. Wanting to disappear.

Progress, he found, wasn't made for long without a great deal of vigi- lance. There were so many heads to the Hydra of the self, and as long as any one of them remained, he began to sense, the rest would eventually come sprouting back. It was necessary to inspect every loop of all those tangled necks to discern which could be loosened in any given moment. It took a certain amount of will not to look away, particularly when it came to loosening the will itself.

Beneath thoughts, the subsurface of emotions became the focus on the third day in the basement. These too, with awareness, could be pried up, and underneath lay a purer kind of feeling, less subject to mood and circumstance. The feeling was one of spaciousness and forward freefall, whenever the attachment to experience itself could be let go. Giving up time and becoming time, the flow itself, as the radiant faces of Buddha and Shiva and Christ looked on from their vantage, taped to the main- frame's hull.

By the fourth day, the focus was other people, the desire to be respected or loved, or to simply feel of use to this world. With thoughts of others inevitably came thoughts of self, bringing him back again, in all his guilt and all his envy: his guilt over having failed George, failed Sam, failed his parents, over sitting in a basement and doing nothing while people out there were starving, ecosystems dying; his envy of everyone out there playing and winning, making money, making names for themselves, get- ting laid, getting adulated, competing for ever bigger niches; his guilty envy of a world chugging along for better and worse without him. Seven billion ghosts, himself among them, an entire simulated metaverse in this hapless skull.

The more he opened to the racing vacuum—the more he became

it—the more powerful the program's function. He could bring its fatal beam to bear on whole populations, and watch as their inner significances and connections to him burned away. He watched Gibbon, and Lipton, and Erskine, and Gretta melt and sizzle like heated frames of film. He purged friends, too—Jesse and Conrad, waving good morning from behind their desks, going translucent, giving way to a clear white screen. Mel, smiling above him as she pinioned his wrists, her hair falling around both their faces in a sunlit curtain, bright, brighter, gone.

It took half the night before the ensuing panic subsided and the annihilating light could be turned on those closest:

There went Vartan, in his white tuxedo, with his cavernous, questioning eyes, tapping Fred's chest, tapping his own.

There went Holly, in her sunglasses, launching her hands over Broadway.

There went Sam, risking a smile at the thought of black Bermuda shorts.

With each frame that caught fire, the projector itself seemed to smolder a little more. So that by the time George flashed up—college-bound, lying with his hands behind his head on the steps of a church—and was incinerated, there remained only the dim screen, the empty theater. Even the watcher was gone.

FRED BROUNIAN

Two words. Twelve 3-D silver letters, flipping and bouncing in the void of a laptop screen.

The blood pulse in these ears.

These shallow breaths.

The drip drip drip from a soaked towel onto a pantleg.

Where am I?

But the *I*, the *am*, these words had no meaning.

Floating thoughts, probing for their missing root. Severed fingers in search of a palm no longer there.

No one staring at a bare lightbulb.

No one gripping a scalp.

No one picking up the Swiss Army knife from the water heater. Pulling out the corkscrew. Snapping it back. Pulling out the bottle opener. Snapping it back.

No one thinking of a tree falling in a forest.

This was that forest.

No self, no problem, Manny had said. Yet all the problems remained. This body remained, getting hungry, having to take a dump. These thinkerless thoughts remained, bits of exploded brain pulp, twinkling in the miasma.

Too far! Gone too far! says one.

Or not far enough? says another.

But what's left? Not a single Hydra head in sight.

These feeler-less feelings, even, lone little heart cells, pulsing for no one. The state, which was no state at all, wasn't even scary—there was no one to be scared. But it was horrible, in a dry kind of way. To whom or to what it was horrible wasn't quite clear. Something must have remained. Some tenacious, biting head amid the blood.

Certain naturally occurring experiments conducted themselves. An erection was lightly fondled in the fingers. The scattered heart cells twitched with a repulsive force. The fingers withdrew. The brainbits kept firing—*think this, don't think that, try this, try that, I'm me, I'm me.* No one to receive the thoughts. So many looping REM statements in the dark.

No one even to wait for oblivion.

Hours later, it seemed to come, in the form of sleep paralysis—even that problem remained. A dream of no dream. Just darkness. Unopenable lids. Unmovable muscles. Dwindling air supply. A lump in the chest, acid in the nerves.

How would this body wake up now, with no one, inside or out, to wake it?

Coma, said a brainbit.

Ha, said another. *Ha ha.*

No one laughing.

Without being willed, the labored breathing commenced. That old technique. Huffing and puffing. Building momentum. Even this was habitual.

Eyes opening.

The pipes, two feet above.

Drip drip drip, soaking the legs of no one.

Monday morning.

Is this it? Is this nothing all there is? This bullshit?

And there it was—spotted at last. The final head, peeping up from the dark: meaning. The desire for that.

All at once, the other heads started tumoring up again, nattering in agreement. This life should mean something. All life should mean something. *George's* life should have meant something. Everything should mean. Every last thing.

Here he was, clutching the Swiss Army knife, pulling out the long blade, wanting to plunge it into his neck. Sliding out the tweezers. He could gouge his eyes with them—*that* would give them meaning, no?

He let them drop, grabbed the laptop, shoved the helmet on. He'd play the fucking program over and over, as long as it took. He double-clicked. The suction began.

Worse than any time before, like he was being pulled to pieces. He wanted meaning. He didn't want to not want it.

Meaning what?

What meaning?

Meaning what to whom?

Rage. *Whose?*

An ownerless fist, rising and pounding. The supercomputer resounding, a muffled gong.

Now the other fist pounding. Now the legs, both at once, feet still in the sleeping bag. Fists and heels slamming and rocking the machine.

A metallic groan, and a snap, and a spraying sound, from somewhere below.

A jerk of the power cords. The amplifier box slipping off its cushion, falling toward the floor. Reaching out, lunging and catching it. But then the laptop slipping from the lap. Catching that too, leaning half over the edge, fighting for balance, amplifier in one outstretched hand, laptop in the other, its screensaver bouncing and flipping this name that names nothing:

ЙАЮЛ∩⊏Ξ∃ Œ Ξ⊏F١

And below, out from beneath the supercomputer, the floor fan, the cantaloupe box, the mini-fridge, out across the week-old minestrone soup encrustations—a spreading slick of water.

The top-heavy helmet slipping from this upside-down head, yanking the cords as it falls. Then the desk fan, down from above, clipping the back of this skull on its way, crashing to the water-sheened floor, bringing down with it the surge protector from the pipe along the wall.

A buzzing sound. Smoke.

Uh-oh, says a brainbit.

The next second, everything is electric. Metal box glued to the one hand, laptop to the other, mainframe juiced to the hull. Body writhing and juddering. And falling, feet twisting in the wet sleeping bag, useless hands still welded to the shattering amplifier and laptop, useless head smacking the electric floor for a second round of spasms. Through the smoke and steam, the surge protector. A hand wrenching free from its contortions, yanking the plug from the wall.

The room goes quiet.

Smoke rises from all of it. It rises from this body, this Fredless Fred, curls out from the cuffs of its white polyester pants. It gouts from the behemothic blue hull in great, spiraling, fractal puffs that seem to pass right through the ceiling.

Too much smoke to breathe. The sodden pair of checkered shoes are grabbed from the corner, the tux jacket snatched from the door handle. A backward fall from the room into the basement hallway.

Fredless Fred's arms are a bright, mottled red. The hands and feet burn the hottest. On its palms, massive, cloudy blisters billow, one shaped like a flower, the other like a shell. Two fingers of its right hand don't move as the checkered shoes are put on. The ribs on the left side stab like broken glass as the jacket is donned over a half-wet undershirt. There's a numb softness to the skull just above the hairline, vaguely repellant to the fingertips. And, as if knocked loose, the perspective itself seems to have just slightly shifted, a view no longer quite from inside the head, but from somewhere just above and behind.

For the moment, the body is still capable of motion. And so it moves, albeit with a limp—an abused ankle sending up shooting pains—as it climbs the stairs.

In the lobby, a man with freshly trimmed, carefully mussed hair and sunglasses, recognizable from coinciding lunch runs to the deli over the years, is just now heading in to work. The guts clench. But the guy just nods as he passes, barely cognizant, noticing nothing amiss. And here it goes, this vacuumed bobblehead, mirroring the greeting. Indeed, the figure faintly reflected in the glass door looks more or less normal. The face, though unshaven, is unremarkable, the stark stare of those eyes tempered by even blinks.

The front door swings. Morning in Tribeca: a thousand suns in the windows, sidewalks washed with light. Usually, Greenwich Street is sparsely populated in the mornings, but not today—people are everywhere.

They stroll, almost dawdle. The pace is that of a Sunday, or even a holiday, though there's some business attire in the mix as well.

The checkered shoes seem to know their heading. Already, they've swiveled, pointed themselves south. As they follow the crowd, the tightness in the stomach begins to ease. More and more, the various jabs and throbs of pain are distant events. There's neither anyone to be hurt nor anyone to be pleased by the pleasurable ache in the eyes of long-unseen sunlight.

A woman struggles to maneuver two bags and a stroller out a front door. And here's a seared, white-sleeved arm and a pulsing palm extending to hold it open. A half-block later, here goes the mouth, incredibly, rattling off directions to a young couple with backpacks. The couple thanks no one at all, and moves on.

Ahead, a group of very blond people disembarks from a charter bus, handing off cameras and poring over maps. A security guard emerges from a deli with a paper cup of coffee in one hand and a *Post* in the other:

TRIBUTE

And a picture of George and Laura Bush, dusk-lit, laying a wreath.

The crowd thickens closer to the site. Cops are everywhere, standing around, sitting in squad cars. A man with a deeply etched face stands before a display of framed photographs of message walls and smoking ruins. Another vendor hawks T-shirts with images of firemen and policemen depicted as comic book superheroes, muscles bulging under spandex-like uniforms and windswept capes.

At the barricades, people are crowding to get a view through the fence behind a row of cops, who take turns ordering the rubberneckers to keep moving. Around the corner of Broadway, the crowd expands into the plaza.

A digital camera is placed into the hands of no one. And a picture is snapped of a bowl-haircutted Asian boy in an MIT shirt, with a sly smile and a possessive arm around a buxom, bucktoothed blond girl. They stand in front a photograph of a smashed fire truck mounted on the iron fence.

Others are photographing other photographs on the fence, of smoke-blackened faces, of a fallen fuselage. Nearby, a young woman clutches the fence and cries, her face red and twisted with agony. A second woman comforts her. A third photographs the first and second.

Still others fit their lenses between the chinks and photograph what lies beyond, and others personalize the fence with private meanings—photocopied photographs of loved ones, Scotch-taped poems in children's handwriting, balloons with pictures of more superheroes—Superman, The Incredible Hulk, The Thing.

Others hold up signs. One burly, mustachioed man brandishes a yellow placard bearing the words: BUSH DID IT. Another hollers that it was an inside job. Men in crisp, black INVESTIGATE 9/11 T-shirts shout that it was a conspiracy. Another two men hold between them a banner reading: WHEN THE LEFT CALLS FOR PEACE, WHAT THEY MEAN IS SURRENDER. Another placard calls for the end of the Iraq War. Another for impeachment.

Passersby get sucked into the arguments, listening and then participating. Small crowds cluster around the disputes, perpetuating interest, everyone eager to be a part of it. A black man in a bizarre military-dress uniform studded with gold-cross emblems adds his own explications—with the aid of a megaphone—to the noise in the air on the rim of the pit: "It's not about whether you're black, white, brown, red, or yellow," he shouts. "It's not about whether you're Christian, Muslim, or Hindu. It's about coming together and expressing your feelings." With that, he hands off the megaphone to his listeners: A long-haired, balding man who shouts that religion is the problem. An old woman who cries and says something incomprehensible.

Every few yards stands a man holding up a Bible. One holds his shut in the air, reciting a verse from memory, not quite loud enough to be heard. Another mutely holds his open to a certain page, as if the mere presence of that microscopic text were doing all the work necessary. For all the crowd clustered around the others, no one pays these men the slightest heed.

Meanwhile, a string quartet plays something classical and somber, and off in another gap in the crowd, a butoh dancer turns slowly, a long, white swath of muslin trailing from her hand. Across the street, in each of the second-story plate-glass windows of the Millenium Hilton, dressed-up couples lunch from starched white tablecloths, pausing every so often to stare out over the crowd below and the gaping hole beyond.

The crowd is mostly young bodies exuding sexual excitement and the pleasure of being around other bodies doing the same. Teenagers who were just children five years earlier hold hands, caress each other's backs. Children who weren't yet born five years ago sit perched on their fathers' shoulders. A dozen clean-scrubbed youths in Southern Baptist University sweatshirts take turns standing on a broad marble promontory abutting the steps to an office building across the street, snapping pictures of the iconic cross-shaped crossbeam and a giant American flag. At the top of the steps, in a loose circle, stands a smaller group, eyes closed, palms in the air.

A pulse from these free-floating heart cells. But no, it's not the Reiki group. Or rather, not *that* Reiki group. It's an altogether new one. There's a new dwarf—a thick-hewed bodybuilder, six foot four at least, his sky-bound fingers tense as talons. And a new elf, Indian or possibly American Indian, her straight black hair in a headband, her wrists gently crossed above her forehead. And a black Strider, his dangling, beaded cornrows slowly waving in time with his lifted hands, like tree limbs in a breeze.

Something new, it seems, is happening to all these inner twinklings and pulsings. It's as if they're freeing themselves into a dance all their own, not even disconnected thought or feeling anymore so much as forces in their own right, pure energy, hectic and harmonious by turns. Even the flashing pains from ankle, fingers, ribs, temple, the burning skin of the arms and legs and hands are all sparking and diffusing into it, as the Fredless body limps around the corner of the site; as it stops at a photograph, on the fence along the southern rim, of the old pair of towers, and an artist's rendition of the bright single tower to come; as it's jostled by a loping man with a luminous bald head and a pretzel back into motion, amid hundreds of other swinging legs and arms, up through an enclosed elevated walkway, and back down to the West Side Highway.

The cameras on this side of the site are bulkier, professional-grade, mounted on tripods. They're aimed at doll-like reporters, with hair sprayed to a gloss and rouged cheeks, men and women alike. Off ahead, on a raised platform in a fenced-off area at the crater's edge, the recitation of the three thousand names by surviving family members has ended, the last echoes of taps on a bugle have dissolved, and a choir has begun to sing. A few last reports are going out, while other news vans are lowering their dishes, their crews already packing up, photographers unscrewing lenses, technicians unweaving webs of bright electrical cables duct-taped to the ground. As the reporters finish, like statues magically restored to life, they stretch their necks, look around, drain bottled water into their mouths. A peppy blond reporter who looks a bit like Mel zips off her lipstick with a thumb-swipe, widens her eyes, and sighs.

There is no meaning anywhere, and the dance of energy has become a plosive, liquid radiance. It twirls with the vibrations of the choir and the satellite feeds, the rants, the prayers, the irrepressible pheromones, the sobs and guffaws and quiet chatter. Two strangely bright forms, one of a beefy old fireman, the other of an equally beefy security guard, hug by a revolving door. "Happy 9/11," says the first to the second, with hearty pats on the back.

On the grassy slope outside the Marriott Financial Center, across the street from the fenced-in ceremony area, more beings of light, dozens, are sitting and spectating. They shine like gods and goddesses one moment, shimmer like ghosts the next. A big spirit man with an elephant pin on his shirt and a broken tooth chats up a spirit woman with a swanlike neck who busies herself with a Palm Pilot. Another spirit woman, her body incandescent as a sunrise, whispers into the ear of a spirit toddler pressing lit-up, Gummi-colored buttons on a toy cell phone.

Even the Fredless body gives off a little light, though it's mostly just the glaring tuxedo jacket and strobing shoes. It ceases its limping and stands among the dazzle of the rest, to all appearances awed, though there is no one to be awed, no one to scratch an ostensibly dumbstruck head, no one to observe its fingers coming down glistening with blood. Nearby, a midriff-baring, lower-back-tattooed spirit leans into the broad chest of a spirit with a linen jacket draped wing-like over his shoulders, and points, bangles jangling on her wrist, down at the gate of the fenced-in area, from which the mourning family members are beginning to emerge, shining forms themselves, in jackets and ties and summer dresses.

From their midst comes a tallish, Roman-haired spirit, followed by a spirit with night-black hair and a glowing moon for a face. She stops in the middle of the street, lowers her sunglasses, her dark eyes locking on no one.

There's no one to be surprised, no one to be dumbfounded, when, with a coy head tilt, she smiles—*smiles*—and waves. She walks over, the tall spirit behind her looking on with a faint, approving smile of his own.

"I had a dream about you last night," she says.

Real or no, she seems happy, at ease, freed from some long spirit toil. She squints a little, even behind those shaded lenses, the brightness all around.

"We were in some spaceship together, floating back to Earth," she says. "We'd thought we'd never see it again. But we'd found our way back. And all we wanted to do was land, so we could just go on a normal date."

She grins, embarrassed, expectant.

When it came time to sunder those inner bonds to her yesterday, there'd been no one left to carry out the task. And now there's no one left to feel any obligation to do so, to sunder any piece of this from any other. And all the vibrations, all the twinklings and pulsings, within and without, are resolving into an unearthly harmony, nothing anywhere but a single, living love. It resonates, for a spell, as if to its own possibility, then slips away as the tune keeps changing. The Fredless Fred's energy is twining in a larger body, whose wheeling extremities are afire, whose brain is a heating protostar, whose heart is an as-yet-arrhythmic drumming of plasm. The body coils and flays, dancing order from or into bedlam, life from or into extinction.

Far below, now, the little moon spirit asks a question of the clownishly attired no one, but from here, all that registers is her rising intonation as things get even brighter.

Oxygen deprivation, a brainbit twinkles.

Last minute of brainlife, twinkles another.

And the moon spirit lets out a barely heard shout, as the pixel-small avatar beside her is finally down.

Darkness. A warmth. Then a light.

A flashlight to one side.

Two trembling palms to the other.

Mom and Dad, leaning in.

A steady chirp.

Smell of antiseptic.

Two shadows in the fluorescence. A woman. And an older man, arm around her, hand on the ball of her shoulder.

Ten palms.

Five towering forms in the light: goateed/buzzcut/ponytailed/translucent-eared.

Mom overhead, upside down, eyes closed.

"Hey, nurse. It's time for a sponge bath. No, not his. Mine. Wait. I'm a filmmaker. Hey. Take my card!"

Manfred cranes his head around, two fingers in his fishing vest.

Vartan hoists an eyebrow. "The third time you've woken him up, Manny."

"This guy's a famous actor," Manfred calls out, pointing to Vartan. "Did you know that?" He turns back, grin crooked. "Your dad's gonna act again."

Vartan tilts his shaggy head. A mouth hole forms in his beard. Manfred cuts him off:

"*The Tempest.* I'll be Gonzo, the old counselor. I've got a whole new take for the island."

Vartan's mouth flattens, vanishes in the surrounding hair.

"Get this." Manny's giant octopus hands, framing: "*Atlantis.*"

"It's Sam," Holly says, pressing a cell phone close.

"Hey, Freddo."

Freddo . . .

"You don't have to talk. They say you're on some massive painkillers. I can do the talking."

The sound of a sliding door.

"So let's see. I'm sitting here on my deck. My *deck.* I can hardly believe it. On a . . . what's it called? Oh yeah. A *deck chair.* One of those kinds with the reclinable backs. With an iced tea, no less. What else? Some kind of bugs are chirping. I thought the noise must have been a power station at first." The sound of clinking cubes. "Ask me how's my new office."

The sound of the drink glugging down his throat.

"Office," he answers himself, his tone a shade darker. "That's a good one. A 'corner cubicle,' the personnel guy called it."

The sound of calling birds.

"*Urrr . . .*"

"Yeah," Sam says, "I was getting to that. I fixed it. With a whole lot of help from You Know Who."

"*Whaaa?*"

"I turned on my phone when the plane landed and there was a text from George. Saying to check my email. He sent me everything, where all the malware was and how to quarantine it. I had the place up and running again in twenty minutes. They think I'm a genius now. Talk about pressure."

"Y'OK, Fred?" Holly whispers.

"Think he needs Dr. Papan?" Vartan asks, out of view.

"Demo went well today," Sam says. "We'll see. What else? Oh." His tone flattens a bit. "I put off those lunch dates. I don't know why. Maybe I just need some time."

Cicadas in the background.

"Did check out Christworld," he adds. "The flag corps and the mimes were all right . . . I guess."

He sighs.

"The smoothies taste like ass."

"*Hhheh.*"

"He went this morning," Mom says, sitting by the bedside, leaning in close. "Before any of us even got here. And then you showed up not too long after."

She looks puzzled, like she hasn't a clue what any of it means.

"Dr. Chia said it was baffling that George survived so long."

She holds out a hand, regarding it in the light like something she's never quite seen before, her fingers fairly steady.

"He asked me to do Reiki on his tennis elbow."

Two men. One silver-haired and ruddy-faced in a blazer, the other greasy blond, his face a raucous party of freckles.

"Mr. Brounian," the older one announces, "I'm Detective Nelson and this is Detective Sullivan. Your parents said we could have a word."

The same flecked green eyes. The same hammered cheekbones.

"Cousins," Nelson explains.

"We get that look a lot," Sullivan chimes in with a grin. "I bet you're sure used to that look."

"We're very sorry about your brother," says Nelson.

"Truly." Sullivan puts a hand over his heart.

"We know you're not in peak condition right now, but we just wanted to drop in and say hello."

"We're incorrigibly social," Sullivan says.

"Mr. Brounian, someone calling himself the Avenging Angel has been stalking executives at a company down in Florida I believe you've had dealings with."

Sullivan's head lists right and left: "Emails, faxes, text messages. At work, at home."

"Nothing exactly threatening," Nelson says.

"Cute stuff. Philosophical." Sullivan strokes his chin. "About the afterlife."

"Maybe no bad intentions. But can you understand how repeated mentions of the afterlife might be misinterpreted?"

They wait.

"Is that a smile?" Sullivan says.

"Did I say something funny, Mr. Brounian?"

"Maybe it was your intonation, Nelly."

"About a week ago, Mr. Brounian, they suggested you might be someone worth talking to."

Sullivan half smiles, blinks rapidly. "They said you had a little *episode* down there?"

"End of last week, their personal bank accounts started dropping," Nelson says. "Turns out this Avenging Angel posted their names, addresses, and socials on some hacker message board."

"Look at that, Nelly," Sullivan says. "His smile grew."

"I know I didn't say anything funny that time."

"I'm telling you. It's that deadpan delivery." Sullivan leans in, a hand cupping the side of his mouth. "I keep telling my partner he should do stand-up."

"To be honest," Nelson says, "we didn't have anything on you."

Sullivan slices the air. "Zilch."

"Until you nearly blew yourself up with that big-ass computer."

"Janitor happened to mention it was from your office?"

"Some twisted shit down there, in your secret hideout."

"Hey, Nelly." Sullivan rests his chin on an index finger. "What color cape you think the Avenging Angel would wear?"

"Well, Sully." Nelson folds his arms. "I'd probably go with white."

Sullivan leans in. "My partner's a real fashion bug."

"OK, Mr. Brounian. Have yourself a speedy recovery."

"Oh, and did we mention you're under arrest?"

"Missed your arraignment. That'll serve for now."

"Still smiling, eh? You're a tough cookie, Mr. Avenger."

"What did the big, bad Avenger steal?" Nelson mutters. "Pair of tweezers, was it?"

Sullivan frowns, scrunches his eyes. "I hate that. *Pair* of tweezers. Sounds like two of 'em."

"'Cause there are two of 'em," Nelson says, annoyed. "Two tweezing thingamabobs."

"But they're joined. It's a single tool. What if you only had two pant-legs and no crotch? You'd be marching in the Gay Pride Parade."

Nelson raises a finger, suddenly animated. "But what if it was all joined, and you only had one big pantleg?" He wags the finger at Sullivan. "Then you'd be marching in a skirt."

Sullivan laughs, a nasal clucking. Nelson joins in with dry, throaty barks. They stop.

"Mr. Brounian, what's with the teary eyes all the sudden?"

Sullivan, flummoxed, turns to Nelson. "And just when you made the first joke of your life."

Guy, above. Hair falling free around his shoulders. A single palm out, slowly moving, testing the air.

"Your aura has changed, my friend."

He nods, and walks off.

Manfred's sunspotted head looms into view.

"That *Guy* guy's kinda nutty, huh?"

His craggy, windswept sea cliff of a face leans in close.

"I went over to the golf course. Me and some Holy Land pals are working on the owner. Talked about a fund drive, kicked around some rebuilding ideas. Bigger than before. Spotlights. Said he might not sic the cops on us."

He looks right, looks left.

"So'd you figure out mu yet?"

Fred takes a breath, and gives his answer.

Manfred regards him, eyes aqueous and bright.

"OK. What about this one: A guy named Yunmen once asked, 'If the world is vast and wide, why do you put on your seven-piece robe at the sound of a bell?' So he's saying: Hey monk, if you're so free, why the hell do you go on sitting there, sweating it out, day after day, tied up like a human pretzel?"

"I don't know," Fred whispers. "Why do you?"

"Damn. I don't know either. Was hoping you could tell me."

Manny rubs his chin.

"I'm getting my ass back to the monastery soon. When mu cracked open, I thought I'd reached the summit, but it's just base camp, far as those monks are concerned. Last time I saw the Roshi, he beat me with a broom and called me a dust devil." He looks off, a rare moment of anxiousness. "I didn't think he knew that much English."

At Manny's side, Vartan and Holly appear. And to the other side, *Guy* and Dot.

"Visiting hours are up," Vartan says. "Let's give him a rest."

Guy, Dot, and Manny wave and say goodnight. Holly kisses Fred's cheek and goes.

Vartan leans in close. "Kiddo," he whispers. "Don't worry. Whatever drugs you've been on, we'll get you off."

Firmly, Vartan grips Fred's arm. His eyes crinkle, dauntless.

"The first few days are the toughest," he says.

"Oh." Holly steps back into view. "Something came for you, early this morning." She holds up an envelope. "It looks like a telegram."

As he lay in the dark, the lightning pulses of the cardiac monitor beside him, Fred thought back on his first moments of consciousness, when he hadn't known which of them he was. He'd been both. He'd been George, waking from a coma. He'd been Fred at the same time, wondering what he was doing there behind George's eyes. Then Dr. Papan had started asking questions, one blink for yes, two for no, and the quantum suspension had begun to abate. Then Sam had called him Freddo, and everything had come flooding back.

Even now, though, he might have been both. That's how he felt. Or he might have been neither. Both felt equally true. It didn't so much matter to him who he was or wasn't. He was aware. He was awareness itself.

Turning off the monitor, working the sensor clip off his finger, he eased himself out of bed and, in the light from under the doorway, slipped his bandaged feet and lotioned legs into his jeans and slid the tuxedo jacket over his hospital gown, smarting from the pain. One whole hand was a big, splinted bandage. The other, at least, had its fingers free. His scalp, those fingers determined, was partly shaved, and wrapped up tight enough to know its own pulse. He'd been told that the burns were mostly first and second degree. He'd sprained an ankle, broken a couple of fingers, fractured a rib, suffered a concussion. He felt like he'd been bagged up with a bee colony and booted off a cliff. Even so, it was nice, being in motion. Every stabbing inhalation, every flinching limp down the hall, felt like freedom.

His first stop was George's old room. They hadn't put someone in his brother's place yet, so he went in and sat in his usual chair. For a while he stared at the empty bed, thinking about how George had transcended his uncontrollable illness, his coma, his unstoppable death, to play Fred and everyone else like puppets from beyond his existence. Fred wondered whether it had been George's plan from the start to restore Urth to Armation in such a way that made Sam look like a hero, or whether George's heart had softened somewhere along the way. Fred wondered whether that episode with the countdown, and George and himself joined under that malevolent hat, had been designed to punish him or, conversely, to forgive him, to grant him the opportunity to stand by George's side to the very end. To prove he'd be loyal to George no matter the cost, prove it to Fred's own conscience, so that he might then forgive himself.

He opened the envelope, the telegram his mother had left with him. Nothing but coordinates, a longitude and latitude, undisguised this time. Where was George leading him now? For a few minutes, Fred's imagination roamed once more, until he was all but certain the answer was Central Florida, the Urth version thereof, where the Armation headquarters would appear before Fred's avatar like some virtual Mount Doom—a pyramid with a flaming eye at the top, the command center of the Military-Entertainment Complex. And in it, he'd battle a twenty-foot-tall demon-robot Dan Gretta. And he'd hack into the demon-Gretta's control panel with his Blade of Many Powers, short-circuit its innards of pulsing circuitry and brain tissue, then corkscrew and tweezer and screwdriver them into an upgrade that would bring about a golden age. And Little George would appear, transformed from a Gollum into an angel in earnest, hair restored, oxygen tubes gone, hospital gown swapped for flowing white robes. And before winging off into the blue, he'd leave Fred with the plans for that game he'd spoken of in the coffee shop, that game to end the games, that game of spiritual evolution, where you start out playing one way but soon discover a whole new way to play.

But Fred's guess wasn't even close. As it would turn out, logging into Urth from his mother's computer two days later, he'd find nothing in Central Florida but a flat, gray plane. The coordinates in the telegram didn't point there at all, but instead to New York, to what on Urth was just another expanse of gray, and what on a Google satellite map was a building in the Bronx Zoo, obscured by treetops and fuzzed by poor resolution.

Getting to the actual zoo took Fred a few more days. He had his tweezer arraignment and subsequent sentencing to community service to deal with. He had a long, apologetic letter to write to the miniature golf course owner. He had to be grilled by Nelson and Sullivan again, this time in a small room with peeling paint and a two-way mirror. He had job applications to send out; creditors to plead with; injuries which ceased feeling in any way like freedom, causing him to wonder whether his former clarity and perfect joy at being alive had mainly been the result of those massive painkillers.

But soon enough, he got there. And Mira did, too—their first real date, or close enough—her unfastened hair and bare-shouldered sundress catching the breeze. Using a GPS camera Sam had sent from Armation, Fred and Mira traced those coordinates to a point precisely at the south entrance to the Monkey House. They searched the walls for graffitied messages. They peered behind the potted trees, and under the trash can. They pried at the bricks of the walkway, hoping to find a loose one with some kind of clue hid beneath. Uncovering nothing whatsoever, they trekked through the exhibit, scrutinizing the shrivel-faced capuchins and tufty-eared squirrel monkeys, the fuzzy-headed pygmy marmosets and spacey-eyed Bolivian gray titis. And they walked back out, still mystified, and glanced up above the entrance, to find, gazing bemusedly down at them, a menagerie of bas-relief monkeys crouched within the granite pediment; and a proud, sculpted baboon perched atop the apex; and a single word engraved across the entablature:

MONKEYS

They stared at the word.

"That's it?" she asked. "His parting message?"

"I guess it must be," he conceded.

They kept staring, in a haze of gloom.

"What do we do now?" Fred finally said.

Mira leaned her head on his shoulder.

"I like giraffes," she offered.

"Giraffes are awesome," he agreed.

"And hippos," she said. "And birds."

"Yeah." He nodded. "Toucans."

"Toucans," she said. "Totally."

That night, Mira not quite ready to invite him into the bed she'd shared with her husband, they opted for the futon. And despite some initial fumbling around Fred's bandages and burns and their lingering, mutual shyness, they began to devise a shared dialect of fingers, lips, and hips. And after, with his hundred trillion cells attuned to the universe, and Mira lying pressed against his back, her arm without the tattoo wrapped around his chest, he gazed at those sandstone angels, faintly aglow in the streetlight through the blinds. And they merged in his thoughts with that proud baboon statue atop the Monkey House. And he remembered having come across certain references in his Hindu mythology research over the last few weeks.

He took her hand and led her to her computer in the study. Together, they read about the monkey god, Hanuman. A divine hero, known for his loyalty, bravery, fortitude, and intelligence. Some, in fact, judged him the most powerful of all the gods. He was famed for his ability to overcome any obstacle—no problem, puzzle, or predicament he couldn't work his way through. He'd soared over an ocean to fulfill one mission, uprooted and carried off a mountain to complete another. The monkey god's only vulnerability, it was said, arose from a mild curse placed upon him, whereby he kept forgetting his own miraculous powers, and was unable to recall them until someone else took the trouble to remind him.

Bounding over an ocean . . .

Shouldering a mountain . . .

Though mysteriously, in all Fred's subsequent reading, he would never come across a reference to Hanuman tucking in a city and kissing it goodnight.

But all of that lay in a future so beyond Fred's imagination and concern that it might as well have been some parallel world. Here and now, in the hospital room that was no longer George's, that, tonight, wasn't anyone's, Fred stood up and took one last look around. The picture of Gretta and the Bush brothers still hung high on the wall. He let it hang, and switched off the overhead fluorescence. In the remaining wedge of illumination from the hall, a little red trash can with a biohazard symbol shone.

Leaning into the hip of his tired-looking mother, a balding boy in the elevator eyed Fred's swathed, half-shaved head with a mixture of sympathy and fear, fingers rising to shield his own scalp. Perhaps as an excuse to stare, the boy asked what floor Fred was going to. And removing his hand from his pocket, Fred showed the boy his bandaged but otherwise empty palm, swiped it along the panel, made a fist, held it out, and rained elevator buttons into the boy's open hands.

Then the doors opened on the ground floor, and Fred headed down the corridor, through the passageway from the old building to the new. The night watchman nodded to Fred as he crossed the lobby, and Fred nodded back. He was trying to piece together the strange patches of the last few days: The boiler room sojourn. The walk to Ground Zero after that. He kept coming to the last moment he could recall before waking up in the hospital bed. Not really a moment, not really a part of time at all, but a point at which all that too-bright light had given way to an infinite, lustrous black. It wasn't right to say he'd been in it. He'd been it. Not even nothing. The dream abated. The Big Inky.

Heading out the revolving door, the lit-up city, to his eyes, seemed so suspiciously like the one he was made for, he had to stop and wonder if he'd really woken up at all, if he weren't just in some bed, dreaming some coma dream. Or if, in fact, he'd never returned from that nowhere/ nowhen/nohow at all. Or if, in truth, he'd ever issued from it to start.

Though if he hasn't left it, I'm sorry to break it to you, but reason dictates that all his ghosts and angels—all we inner voices, loving presences, and phantom listeners—haven't left it either.

So perhaps, for the sake of argument, the lot of us would do best to assume that the void can't stay void for long. That its hunger for adventure is as hopeless as ours. That its loneliness is even more so. And that thus, time and again, with a sally of doubt, the Dreamer's the Dreamer, and we're us, brushing eyebrows with it, and back we go.

Let's picture our return together, believing as we doubt, doubting as we believe:

One.
Let's bring back the stars. Scatter them into place with a single toss.
Two.
Let's bring back the Earth, the sun. Plunge our hands into the folds of spacetime and pull them out.
Three.
Let's bring back the city—if not forever, at least for now. Just whistle and here it gallops, a glittering creature of armor and lights. Just point and watch its trillion parts stream down to their spot on the globe.
Four.
Now it's our turn. Down we dive as the land rolls into sunlight.
Down we fly over the cut-crystal island.
Dodging the spear point of the Empire State Building.

Slaloming between the pyramid tops of the Zeckendorf.

Swooping over the broad steps of Union Square.

Lower still through the Broadway canyon.

Through a maze of buildings, to the sudden absence of buildings.

And a bandstand, and news trucks, and a crowd.

And Fred's kneeling, night-haired, moon-faced love.

And his own closed eyes. An inch away. A centimeter. He can make it from here.

Now let's pull back up, about a hundred stories or so, staying focused on the furor below:

The ring of memorial mourners, hawkers, gawkers, spinners.

The raw red wound around which they gyre, clockwise, counterclockwise.

The crazy whirl. The void within.

There's our mission.

Awake our twin.

ACKNOWLEDGMENTS

The author wishes to thank Bill Clegg for coming back from the dead, and for, with so much sagacity and dedication, guiding this book back, too.

And to thank Mark Doten, editor extraordinaire, whose stellar insights and subatomic attentions were more help than a writer could hope for.

And Michael Madonick, without whose quixotic championing, well, Madonick will be happy to tell you the rest; and Joseph Skibell for the faithful dialogue; and more other reader-advisors than can be named here, but for a start: Dale Barrigar, Olivia Block, Garin Cycholl, Philip Graham, Susan Golumb, David Langendoen, Cris Mazza, Blue Montakhab, Barry Pearce, Curtis Perry, Richard Powers, Aaron Roston, and Diane and Martin Shakar.

And for technical and research assistance: Andrew Ervin, Robert Gehorsam, Spencer Grey, Det. Paul Grudzinski, Sol Lorenzo, Aaron Madrigal, Damon Osgood, John Paul, Dr. Ron Pies, Greg Shakar, Ben Stephens, Mallory O. Sullivan, Esq., Harry Yu, and again, many more.

And Saul Diskin for his loving memoir, *The End of the Twins*, from which a couple of childhood dynamics were adapted herein.

And Justin Hargett, Bronwen Hruska, Ailen Lujo, and the rest of the crackerjack team at Soho Press. And Janine Agro, Kapo Ng, and Elyse Strongin for their design magic. And Ivonne Karamoy for her icons, and radiance.

And the University of Illnois Research Board, and the Mellon Faculty Foundation, for financial support.

And you, for reading. For those interested in further reading about various topics broached herein, a few suggestions can be found at alexshakar.com